A DOG
CALLED
DUCKY

Dear Reader,

If you're anything like me, pets are your favorite people. Maybe photos of pets outnumber humans ten to one on your phone. Or when you meet someone new, you remember the name of their dog, but forget theirs. It's also possible the cute animals you follow on social media outnumber the accounts of people you know in real life—and that's where the Dog Agency comes in!

Just like actors and professional athletes often work with talent managers, so do many of your favorite animals on social media. At the Dog Agency, we help all kinds of pets share their stories and spread joy to people worldwide. Usually, those stories are shared through viral videos and photos on social media, but now you'll get to know some of the Internet's most popular pets with the Dog Agency novels!

Each novel in the Dog Agency series brings you a heartwarming new adventure starring a different real-life celebrity pet. In *A Dog Called Ducky,* this feel-good novel casts Ducky from @duckytheyorkie in a fictional story about an adorable little dog who loves to make new friends, play dress up, and who inspires everyone around him.

In this novel, Ducky ends up visiting Layla, an elementary school teacher in a small Nebraska town, and helps her face the challenges of being a teacher, be it getting along with her new teacher's assistant . . . or protecting her students from bullies. The themes of self-love and antibullying in this novel are loosely inspired by Christine Hsu's—Ducky's real-life human mom's—own experiences. Readers will be charmed by the novel's universally uplifting themes of friendship, standing proud, and loving who you are.

To continue following Ducky's (real-life) journey, visit @duckythe yorkie on TikTok and Instagram and Facebook. And for news of more books from your favorite internet pets, stay tuned at KensingtonBooks.com and @TheDogAgency!

Loni Edwards-Lunau

Loni Edwards-Lunau

founder and CEO
the Dog Agency & Pet Con

The Dog Agency Series

A Dog Called Ducky
Tatum Comes Home

A DOG CALLED DUCKY

DUCKY the YORKIE
with AMANDA K. MORGAN

KENSINGTON
PUBLISHING CORP.

kensingtonbooks.com

Contents warning: childhood bullying, racism, corporate downsizing.

This book is dedicated to my soul dog, Ducky. In 2013, you came into my life, and from that moment on, I couldn't have asked for a better companion to walk by my side through life's highs and lows, especially as a girl navigating her twenties in Los Angeles. I remember the first moment I laid eyes on you, you hopped right over to me in the grass and I knew it was meant to be. Thank you for being my constant, for the comfort and joy you've brought, and for being there when I needed you the most. May everyone find their own soul dog—a companion as special and cherished as you are to me.

—Christine

For my Grandma Mahr, my small-town Nebraska hero—I will always love you.
And for Tinker, my best friend.

—Amanda

A DOG
CALLED
DUCKY

CHAPTER 1

Layla Sandberg's front door was open.

It wasn't, like, *wide* open. But it stood slightly ajar, and Layla had very specifically remembered locking it that morning, because the door had swollen a bit in the summer heat, and even though it was September, it remained stubbornly difficult to close. She'd had to give it an extra shove with her shoulder to get the lock to line up. She'd pulled on the handle, twice, to make sure the lock had finally caught.

It had.

But now—now, the door was open a few inches. She adjusted the handles on her tote, overstuffed with books and digging into her shoulder, her keys hanging rather uselessly from her thumb. She arranged them between her fingers, just in case. She remembered some self-defense advice from college, where the woman had told her to use keys as claws in case of an attack, but now, Layla felt about as threatening as a tabby cat.

Layla took a couple of timid steps toward the door, her heart pounding in her ears. Should she call the police? Was Harold, the lone police officer in the tiny town, even working, or was he, more likely, taking an afternoon nap on one of the sofas in the town's sole furniture store? This was, after all, Two Falls, Nebraska, where the most serious crime had been the previous year when Old Lady Wilkes had called the cops because she got paranoid that Marjorie Handler-Marks, from across the street, had poisoned her prize tomatoes. Never mind that Old Lady Wilkes's "prize tomatoes" were consistently underripe and rather pitiful, but the fair judges gave her a blue ribbon every year because they didn't have the heart to tell her her time was better spent . . . well, literally anywhere else.

Go inside, Layla told herself. *There's nothing there. Maybe the door just popped open from air pressure and you didn't lock it as well as you thought you did.*

She let out a steadying breath, trying to slow down her heart rate. It was nothing. It had to be nothing. Right?

Out of the corner of her eye, she saw movement behind the curtains—just a shadow shifting inside her little house. The house she'd worked so hard to put a down payment on. It wasn't easy buying a house anymore, especially as a teacher. And she wasn't going to let just *anyone* walk around inside her home. Not without permission, at least.

Feeling a touch bolder, she stepped onto her front stoop, being as quiet as possible, as if whoever was inside wouldn't have heard her noisy old Bronco pull into the driveway. And if whoever this was wasn't scared of her . . . why should she be scared of them?

Without letting herself think too much, Layla took a deep breath and pushed the thick wooden door the rest of the way open. "Hello?" she called out, her voice quavering slightly in spite of herself. She took a tentative step inside, dropping her tote bag on the floor beside the doormat. "Is someone here?"

That was when a shadow jumped out at her.

It wasn't human, that was for sure—it was small and furry and a bit round, and it came at her with its mouth wide open and its tongue lolling out.

Layla put her hands out, palms first, and screamed, shutting her eyes tight against the attack, her keys dangling uselessly.

But . . . nothing happened.

She opened one eye, then the other, and dropped her hands. Her would-be attacker sat in front of her, at her feet: a tiny, adorable Yorkie, staring up at her, completely puzzled. He tilted his head quizzically, and Layla pressed a hand to her chest, trying to slow her racing heart.

"You almost gave me a heart attack, little guy."

The sound of laughter rang out from the kitchen, and a moment later, her best friend from high school, Christine Hsu, appeared in the doorway, a pint of mint chocolate chip ice cream in her hand and a silver spoon sticking out of the top. "Did Ducky really scare you that much?"

Layla blinked at her. "In my defense, I don't normally come home to a strange dog jumping out at me."

Christine rolled her eyes. "First of all, strange dog? You've known Ducky his whole life. Secondly, you didn't expect me? Not when you sent me a picture of the exact location of your hide-a-key?"

Layla stared at her for a moment, the pieces of her mistake clicking into place in her brain. "Oh, *crap.*"

"You forgot, didn't you?" Christine licked ice cream off the spoon. "You totally forgot we were visiting. That's why you have mint chocolate chip instead of salted caramel, which you know is my favorite."

"I didn't forget," Layla protested. "I just had you marked on my calendar for next week."

"So you thought Ducky was trying to murder you?"

"Exactly." Layla dropped to the ground, closer to the dog's level, and held out her hand apologetically. "Sorry for screaming at you, Ducky. But in my defense, you did jump-scare me."

"Which would mark the first time he almost hurt anyone," Christine said.

"What about that time he tripped your husband?"

"Accident," Christine said. "Besides, Jason deserved it. He was like twenty minutes late with Ducky's supper."

Layla gasped, pressing a hand to her chest. "Poor Ducky. Thank God he survived the ordeal."

Ducky sniffed Layla, and licked her hand tentatively, and then rubbed his head against her fingers, asking for pets. She swept him up in her arms and cradled him, and he nestled in, tucking his little head under her chin. Layla was clearly forgiven.

"Good thing he doesn't hold grudges," Christine said. "He almost peed his pants when you screamed."

"He's not wearing pants."

"Not today. Luckily."

Layla laughed. Ducky did, actually, wear pants pretty often, as well as a variety of other outfits. "Well, I'd tell you to make yourself at home, but it's clear you already have."

Christine nodded. "Absolutely. I can't wait for you to show me around all of Two Falls." She sat back onto Layla's couch, tucking a leg underneath her. "I mean, if there's any part I didn't see when I drove in."

Layla sucked her teeth, pretending to think. "Mrs. Carter got a new fountain in her front lawn."

Christine nodded. "Sounds riveting."

"Biggest news of the year."

"Not even close. Didn't you hear that Ogallala got a Walmart?"

Christine put a hand over her chest, shocked. "*No.*"

They collapsed into laughter. Riffing on Nebraska was something that only Nebraska people were allowed to do—and since Christine and Layla had been best friends throughout middle and high school, they were well-versed in Nebraska jokes.

"How's the tour going?" Layla asked, changing the subject. She set Ducky down, and he started exploring the living room, becoming very interested in a potted plant sitting in the corner. He pawed at it and then sprang back when the leaf bounced. Layla grinned, watching him. Ducky wasn't just any Yorkie—he was *famous*. He had millions of followers across social media, and Christine wasn't exactly lacking in followers either, as a bona fide travel and fashion influencer. The two were making a trek across the country to meet fans, and, of course, no cross-country trip would be complete without a stop to see her best friend—even if it was a little out of the way.

"Amazing," Christine said. "I pretty much love everyone I've met. Except for one guy who I thought was going to steal Ducky. He literally grabbed my little guy and almost crushed him with his love."

"Well," Layla said. "Ducky is very squooshable. Look at him. You just want to squeeze him. It's called cuteness aggression. It's why people grit their teeth when they see adorable animals."

"Ducky is a delicate angel from heaven."

Ducky looked over at them, his pink tongue hanging out, like he knew they were talking about him.

"He's a picture of elegance and grace," Layla countered.

"I know, right?"

Layla watched as Ducky lost interest in the plant and went to sniff at her bag of books lying by the door. She settled onto the other end of the couch, kicking off her shoes.

"Do you think you can hang for a few days?" Layla asked hopefully. She'd missed her friend, and Two Falls, although a wonderful little town, didn't exactly have a thriving social scene, unless she counted bingo nights at the local senior center. She knew that Nettie Rhodes always bought cheap whiskey and drank it in the parking lot with her friend, Elaina. And, well, anyone else who wanted to have a little extra fun shouting out numbers.

Christine pretended to consider. "It depends. Will you forget I'm here?"

Layla threw a couch pillow at her friend. "I'm sorry, okay? School just started. I'm stressed. I had you down on the calendar for next week. I swear. Honest mistake."

"First of all, school started a good month ago. Second, and most important, you know I can never forgive you."

The pair dissolved into laughter again. "Will food help?" Layla offered. "I do actually have frozen pizza in the freezer, if you want."

"Frozen pizza sounds amazing. Do you have Cheetos?"

Layla nodded. In college, they had spent many late-night study sessions splitting bags of Cheetos, smearing their textbooks and homework with orange fingerprints while they worked through their schoolwork.

So Layla tossed a fresh bag of Cheetos at her friend, and set about preheating the oven and putting paper plates on the table. It wasn't long before the two were sharing a completely unhealthy and ridiculous meal, with Ducky at their feet. It almost felt like old times.

"You didn't answer my question," Layla said finally, between bites of pizza. "How long can you stay with me?"

Christine steepled her fingers. "Actually, I have a proposal."

"I'm listening."

Christine leaned forward. "So. As it turns out, I have a skating competition. I have to be in Omaha for all things ice Monday through Thursday."

Layla nodded. It was yet another *Christine Thing*, as she liked it call it. If she hadn't known Christine forever, she would have thought her friend's life was a tad bit unbelievable. A famous influencer? Who was also a professional figure skater? With a famous dog? Sometimes, Layla felt a little ordinary next to her fabulous friend. But that was also the reason she liked Christine so much—Layla never, not once, felt treated as less than by her friend. Other people in Christine's place probably wouldn't have stayed in touch with their small-town schoolteacher friend—but not Christine. When Christine called, it was like they were still in college going for midnight chicken nuggets and no time had passed at all.

"Apparently, they're asking me to judge, and they're not exactly dog-friendly. Would you mind taking care of Ducky next week? I could take him with me, but I'm afraid he'd spend the whole week alone in the hotel room. Is there a chance you could keep an eye on him?"

Layla took a sip of her Diet Coke. "Are you sure? I've never handled a celebrity."

"Well, it's very complicated. He needs weekly manicures, eats chef-prepared human-grade food, and only poops in a temperature-controlled room with Ed Sheeran playing quietly in the background."

"Wait, really?" Layla eyed Ducky, who was running in circles, chasing his tail.

Christine snorted. "You can't forget his daily baths in FIJI Water. Evian in a pinch."

Layla wrinkled her nose. "Are there people who don't take baths in FIJI Water? Gross." She paused, pretending to consider. "What's the thread count on his sheets?"

"One-thousand-thread-count Egyptian cotton, but you could get away with silk, I suppose."

"Same, Ducky." Layla reached down and petted the little guy, who had abandoned his excited circles and was sniffing around the floor hopefully for table scraps. She looked back up at her friend, suddenly serious. "Are you sure you'd trust me to take care of him?"

Layla knew what the little dog meant to her friend. Ducky was basically Christine's child. He was her heart dog—her canine soul mate. Layla didn't take the ask to care for Ducky lightly.

"I'd much rather leave him with you than anywhere else. I know you'll take care of him better than anyone else. Besides, don't you deal with little kids all day? Ducky's easy to take care of in comparison."

Layla snorted. "I've never heard of a celebrity being *easy* to take care of."

Christine reached down and swept Ducky into her lap. "Are you kidding? Ducky's, like, the nicest celebrity ever." She paused. "Seriously, he's a breeze." She stood up, passing Ducky to Layla. "You'll be best friends in no time. You guys bond. I gotta pee."

Layla watched Ducky while Christine was in the bathroom. He looked innocently at her at first, and then squirmed to get out of her hands. She let him down on the floor, watching him carefully. Maybe she could take care of him. Maybe . . . it wouldn't be so bad. Maybe she could tell Christine she'd think about it.

"You're not going to give me any trouble, right, Ducky?"

Ducky looked at her mischievously. And then he stole a Cheeto from Christine's plate, gulping it down before Layla could snatch it away.

She sighed. "I have a feeling you're not going to make this easy."

But of course it wasn't. Because, despite being a second-grade teacher, Layla hadn't really had to care for something in a long time. And she wasn't sure if she was quite ready to do that.

She had to tell Christine no. There was no way she could take care of a dog. She could barely take care of herself.

CHAPTER 2

After only a day of eating at Runza—a Nebraska restaurant that specialized in delicious bread pockets filled with cabbage and beef—a short jaunt in the park, and a dinner where the pair split almost an entire rhubarb pie at Evelyn's Roadside Diner, Christine had gotten a call: one of her fellow judges for her skating competition was in the hospital with a ruptured appendix, and they needed Christine stat—which effectively cut their plans for a girls' weekend short.

Which, conveniently, cut Layla's plans for talking her way out of keeping Ducky short. She'd felt uncomfortable about it since Christine had asked. What if she was a bad dog parent? What if Ducky decided he didn't like her? What if he got out and ran into the road and it was all her fault?

Or . . . what if Layla got attached to the little pup? That would almost be worse.

She'd thought up a complicated plan to hire a full-time dog sitter who could bring Ducky to Christine's hotel at night, and had even downloaded a dog sitting app, stopping to screenshot the five-star dog sitters who lived near Christine's hotel.

But, before Layla got the courage to show Christine the new plan, her friend had gotten the call and now Christine was in even more of a bind with Ducky. Her parents had moved to LA, and she didn't have any close relatives left in Nebraska. There was just Layla.

Suddenly, Layla's plan felt selfish. Christine really needed Layla's help—her friend couldn't exactly tote the pup along in her cute little Louis Vuitton doggy carry bag. Besides, Ducky hated being in the cold of the rink. He shivered miserably until Christine put a sweater on him, and even then he just cuddled into her arms, his head tucked between his paws.

"Are you sure he can't just . . . hang out with you? Isn't he used to large crowds of people?" Layla said, a halfhearted protest,

"Ducky won't be the center of attention," Christine explained. "He can't handle that. It might shatter his worldview."

"But I have to work!" Layla had protested. "He won't be the center of attention when I'm not here."

"He'll be fine alone for a little while," Christine assured her. "Just check in on him during the day with your cameras. I'll be back next weekend. I promise."

"Cameras? This is Nebraska, Christine. Our security systems are *nonexistent*." She shook her head. "Wow, LA has changed you." She grinned at her friend.

Christine sighed. "If you have to hire a dog sitter, I'll pay you back."

"Dog sitters? Here? I mean, if you're okay with Mr. Rogers doing it, I'm sure we can figure it out. But I'm sure there are a lot more dog sitters in Lincoln and Omaha." She lifted her phone, ready to show Christine her screenshots.

"Wait. Mr. Who?" Christine had wrinkled her brow. "We can't let just anyone take care of my handsome boy. It has to be someone you know. Not some random person we find on an app."

Layla lifted a shoulder. Mr. Rogers was legendary. It felt strange, in a way, to explain him to someone who didn't live in the town. He was *theirs*. But . . . maybe he could help, so Layla wouldn't worry about Ducky all day. Maybe she could actually handle this.

If Mr. Rogers agreed to watch Ducky, it was important that Christine was okay with it too.

"No one knows his real name for sure. I think it's Harold or something, but everyone calls him Mr. Rogers because he's basically the most wholesome guy ever. He wears cardigans unironically, and he volunteers at the school to read to the first graders. All the kids go to his house to fundraise, because he can't say no to a good cause, so he has a house full of candy bars and cookie dough that he gives away to all the neighbors. Oh, and he volunteers at the shelter. He can't walk very far, so he just sits with the dogs, and sometimes they nap on him."

Christine nodded. "Solid, I guess." She still looked skeptical though, her brows knitted slightly closer together than normal. "I mean, are you sure about him? How well do you really know him?"

"He had a dog—Lady Ruffles—until last year. Even though, Mr. Rogers is, like, a million years old, he, like, blew up an old air mattress and slept on the floor next to Lady Ruffles the whole last year of her life, when her joints hurt too much to climb up on the bed with him. I heard that even after his dog passed away, Mr. Rogers slept on the floor for an entire month just because he missed her."

"That's super sweet." Christine hesitated, her brow furrowed. "If you trust him, I do too."

"I mean, I'll ask him. I'd feel better about leaving Ducky with Mr. Rogers than leaving him at home alone. Besides, what if Ducky decides to wreck the place?"

Christine sighed heavily, rolling her eyes. "He does that a lot. Last week, he threw a rager in my place. I still can't get the beer smell out of my couch. His friends came over and chewed all my sneaker collections. His brother, Katsu, got picked up by the cops for public urination."

"See?" Layla said. "Out of control." She paused. "Wait—what about Jason? Wouldn't Ducky be happier with his dad?"

"I promised my husband I'd never leave him alone with more than two dogs. It was in our marriage vows," Christine said. Aside from Ducky, Christine and Jason also raised Katsu, an elderly Yorkie, and Barb, a sweet little snow-white Maltipoo. "Besides, Ducky loves to travel; he gets antsy if he's home for too long. Also he hates sports, which is all Jason, Katsu, and Barb will watch while I'm gone."

"I mean . . . I guess," Layla said.

"Please?" Christine begged. "I really prefer to leave Ducky with someone I trust. And you'll hardly even notice he's there. It would really, really help me out. Plus I'll be back in a week, and we can hang out just like we planned. I swear."

Which was how Layla ended up spending her Sunday—not with her best friend, Christine, but instead at home with a tiny dog, who was looking at up her, his eyes wide and hopeful. She had to admit—she enjoyed his company. The moment she had stretched out on the couch and pulled a blanket over her legs, he'd cuddled next to her, stretching out with a cute, contented little groan. Now that she had hauled herself off the couch to head to the kitchen, he'd shown her his tummy, as if he wasn't ready for her to leave him just yet.

"Belly rubs?" she asked him. "Is that what you want, little guy?"

She could swear he smiled, his happy little doggy mouth curving upward. It was contagious, and Layla dropped to the floor, sitting closer to Ducky, and began scratching his tummy. He grunted happily, stretching his back and his little legs out as far they would go. He really was adorable. She wondered, for a moment, when Christine came back to pick up Ducky, if she should get a dog too. Or maybe a cat. Cats were more independent and could deal with her being gone during the day. But, Layla reasoned, they probably weren't as snuggly as Ducky. They probably didn't have such sweet little eyes.

It had been a long time since Layla had a dog. She'd grown up with dogs; her parents were animal lovers and had always had golden retrievers roaming around the house. She'd loved them, but after she'd left the house, her last dog, Frito, had been hit by a car. He'd always dug holes, and this time, he dug out of the backyard and ran onto the street. Her parents had tried to save him, but Frito's injuries were too much, and he had to be put down. Her parents had meant to get another one; they'd even put a deposit on a puppy before . . . everything happened. And then, there were no more dogs. The breeder had asked Layla if she wanted the little golden puppy, and she'd almost said yes, but then she just . . . couldn't. Ducky was the first dog she'd spent time with since, and it made her heart twist a little bit. He wasn't anywhere close to a golden retriever, but his pure, unadulterated sweetness brought her back. She was determined to be the best dog sitter ever.

Which was how Layla found herself standing on her neighbor's front stoop, Ducky sitting happily in her arms, his pink tongue sticking out his mouth. He was light, like she was holding a doll. He didn't squirm but sat patiently, as if he were used to being carried, and settled in comfortably. It made sense—Christine took Ducky pretty much everywhere. He was a world traveler. He'd definitely been way, way more places than Layla ever had.

She pressed the doorbell and waited. It took Mr. Rogers a while to get to the door, so she stroked Ducky's head lightly, shifting from foot to foot, until finally the door opened up and an old man with two tufts of white hair sticking out from either side of his head stood in the entryway, smiling widely. He wore his trademark navy suspenders, and in traditional elderly man fashion, his pants were pulled up high enough she could see the yellow polka dots on his navy-blue socks.

"Why, Layla!" he exclaimed. "Who is this handsome fella?"

"Hi, Mr. Rogers," she said. She held up the dog, her hands under his front legs, like he was Simba in *The Lion King*, being presented to the pride. "I'd like you to meet my friend Ducky."

Mr. Rogers's face transformed just looking at the dog, his smile widening further with joy. "Well, nice to meet you, young man!"

He motioned toward Layla. "Come on in, then, and we can all get properly acquainted." He lifted his finger in the air. "And you can tell me about the kids you have this school year. I need to hear all about those Drubbins kids. People say they're nothing but trouble, but they helped me water my wife's begonias when I twisted my ankle last summer."

Layla had the Drubbins twins in her class this year. They were a little mischievous, but nice enough kids, even if she happened to know that Avery had tried to eat chalk three different times in first grade and stuck rocks in his nose that later had to be removed in the ER two towns over. (Sandberg, the closest town to Two Falls, didn't have a hospital.) She was hoping she wouldn't have to deal with that this year. Mr. Ehlemeier, his teacher the previous year, had to keep all the chalk on a shelf too high for Avery to reach after the third attempt. Apparently, cleaning weird, chalky vomit off the floor wasn't as fun as it sounded. And it didn't sound remotely fun.

Layla followed Mr. Rogers into his living room, which was a cheerful little room, to say the least. His late wife had been a fan of florals and had outfitted the room with them in excess—the couch sported a bright floral pattern; the chair had purple flowers stitched into the upholstery; photos of bright yellow daisies were hung on the walls; and big clay pots of green plants were strewn about the room. She had been a colorful person, and after her passing, Mr. Rogers had refused to change anything about the space his wife had taken such joy in putting together. He continued to tend to the giant garden out back no matter what, and it had continued to flourish.

Layla heard the faint sound of a radio playing from the kitchen; it was, predictably, tuned to the oldies station, the sad song's low, languid tones a strange juxtaposition to the cheery living room. She'd asked him, once, when she first moved in next door, why his radio was always playing. He'd told her it made his house feel a little less empty. Now that Lady Ruffles was gone, the radio was turned up a bit louder—an attempt at filling all the emptiness around him, she was sure.

She let Ducky down on the ground, and he began to sniff around the floor. He eventually settled at Mr. Rogers's feet and peered up at him, his ears perked forward curiously. Mr. Rogers leaned down, his wrinkled fingers outstretched.

Ducky sniffed him tentatively, and having decided Mr. Rogers passed the test, he hopped up on his hind legs, front legs outstretched, like he was asking for a hug. Layla could almost see Mr. Rogers melt. Ducky had charmed him completely. It made sense how he had so many social media followers.

"Can I pick him up?" Mr. Rogers asked.

Layla nodded. "You'd better."

Mr. Rogers smiled and reached down to Ducky, who was still hopping excitedly, begging for attention. The old man lifted him easily into his lap, where the pup circled for a moment before sitting and then curling up into a furry circle, where he let out a soft, contented sigh. Clearly Ducky approved of his pet sitter—that is, if Mr. Rogers agreed.

"I think he likes you," Layla said, as Mr. Rogers tentatively petted Ducky's head, his wrinkled face still creased into a grin.

"Dogs can always tell," Mr. Rogers said. "Never trust someone your dog doesn't trust." He paused. "If a dog didn't like me, well, I'd need to take a good, hard look at how I was living my life. There's no better judge in life than a dog."

It wasn't the first time Mr. Rogers had given that advice. Once, when a strange woman had come through town, trying to buy up property for the state, Lady Ruffles had growled at her—and Lady Ruffles *never* growled. Mr. Rogers immediately disapproved of the woman, and she left without a single person in the town selling her any land. No one trusted her. The town was hurting for money, but they didn't sell out to people who clearly didn't have good intentions, and there was word she wanted to buy all the area farmland for a corporate operation—effectively putting the family farmers, and most of Layla's students' parents, right out of business. Things were hard enough as it was.

"You're a good boy," Mr. Rogers told Ducky, petting him gently. His eyes, often so sad, were joyful and clear, and suddenly, he looked more . . . awake. Younger. Happier, even, in a way that Layla hadn't seen in a while . . . not since Lady Ruffles was following him from room to room on stiff legs, faithful to the very end.

"He's my friend's," Layla explained. "She got called away urgently, and she asked me to watch him until she can get back."

Mr. Rogers glanced up at her, but his attention was quickly recaptured by Ducky, who gave a sweet, happy groan. "Who's going to look after him while you're at school?" Mr. Rogers asked.

Layla hesitated. Was she asking too much? Would he dislike the obligation? But no, she decided, watching how gently he was handling the dog, the strange light that had suddenly risen in him. "I was sort of wondering if you would."

His hand paused. "You want . . . me to watch him?" He sounded surprised, his voice a note higher than usual. He glanced up at her, tearing his eyes away from Ducky.

She nodded. "I can't think of anyone better. Assuming, you know, you want to. And you're not busy."

He considered the little dog. "Do you want to spend time with me?" he asked Ducky, his voice soft.

Ducky looked up at him with soft eyes and wagged his tail.

"I wouldn't mind hanging out with little buddy during the day." He resumed petting him, and Ducky leaned into him happily, sighing with contentment. "We're good friends, aren't we, pup?"

Layla nodded. "He loves you."

"I could use the company." He hesitated again. "Can I call you if something goes wrong? Or if I have a question?"

"Of course," she said. "I always have my cell phone on me for emergencies." She stood up, grabbing a discarded, half-crumpled envelope off a TV tray, and scribbled down her number. "I'll stick this to the refrigerator, okay?"

He nodded.

"Just call me if you need anything. I'll bring over some treats and his regular food. And I'll pick him up as soon as I'm home from school."

Mr. Rogers nodded. "Does he listen pretty well?"

Layla nodded. "He's good. He'll come when you call him. He'll steal your food though."

Mr. Rogers smiled. "That's okay, little guy."

Layla related all the instructions Christine had given her: Ducky disliked cold; he loved blankets; he had to be fed a very exact amount at a very exact time. She'd written everything down on a piece of notebook paper to make it easy. "Thank you so much," she told him. "I really didn't want to leave him alone in my house all day, especially when his mom isn't around."

Mr. Rogers smiled. "I understand. Don't worry. Me and the little guy are going to have a grand old time."

As she turned to leave, gathering Ducky into her arms to head back to her little house around the corner, Layla heard him say something that melted her heart: "It's been a while since I had a little friend."

Yep, she decided. Ducky and Mr. Rogers were going to do just fine.

CHAPTER 3

"I love that you're proud of your goats, but you can't bring them in for show-and-tell."

Anita Myers-Perkins followed her into the classroom, her hands obstinately on her hips and her mouth in a typical second-grader scowl. "But, Ms. Layla," she said, "Arlene isn't just a goat. She's my best friend. Other kids in the class have best friends and they get to be at school with them every single day."

Their best friends won't poop on the floor, Layla wanted to say. Instead, she fixed a smile on her face. "Sorry, no livestock in the classroom. School rules." She shrugged and lifted her hands.

"But I get to show her at 4-H, Ms. Layla."

"Anita, does 4-H take place indoors?"

"Some of it does," Anita said stubbornly.

Layla sighed. "No goats, Anita."

And then a voice came from the other side of the room. A strange, unfamiliar voice. A low, male voice. "I don't know, I think a goat would be a nice addition to any classroom."

It was a voice that most decidedly did *not* come from a second grader. She whirled around, the braid she'd carefully plaited her brunette hair into that morning whipping around her shoulder, and Anita still following behind her, a pleading look on her face and her hands clasped together hopefully.

At her desk, a man stood confidently, as if he belonged there, as if it were *his* classroom and *his* students. There was *an entire man* standing behind her desk. And not just any man. A handsome man with a confident, easy air. One with a short, fastidiously clipped beard that accentuated his strong jawline. A man with soft blue eyes flecked with brown. A man dressed in a crisp blue button-up and khakis that looked like they were made for him. His hands were in his pockets, but he withdrew one and offered it to Layla. She shook it, and couldn't help but notice he had a nice, strong handshake. His palms were just a bit callused, which meant he was the kind of person who wasn't afraid of hard work. And, she couldn't help but notice, he wasn't wearing a wedding ring. Then again, neither was she. It was sort of hard to date in a town so small everyone knew everyone's middle name and half the people were related somehow.

"Who's that?" Anita asked loudly. "Mister, do you want to meet my goats?"

He grinned at Anita. "I'm Mr. Henderson, and I would love to meet your goats someday." He glanced toward Layla. "Garrett Henderson—your student teacher."

Layla stared, her mind spinning. She hadn't heard anything about a student teacher. But here he was—a strange man standing in front of her, announcing that he was supposed to be working with her. Did this happen? Did people just . . . show up like this? "But I'm not supposed to have a student teacher."

"Yeah, well," he said, scratching the back of his head, "I was supposed to be working under Mrs. Meadows, but apparently she broke her hip, so a sub is taking over the class—and it doesn't really work for me to be under the tutelage of a substitute, does it?'

"I . . . guess not?" Layla was still overwhelmed. She could handle pretty much anything kids threw at her—but having a student teacher screwed up her whole syllabus for the year. Especially having a handsome student teacher. One who looked . . . like he was just a touch older than Layla, who, at twenty-six, was entering her third year of teaching, when she was really and truly getting into the swing of things. She'd never had a student teacher. She turned to Anita, who was still bouncing impatiently, waiting to interject.

"Go outside with your classmates until the bell rings. We'll talk about you bringing some pictures of your goats in later," Layla told her.

The little girl's face fell slightly, but she sighed. "Okay, fine!" she said dramatically, and stomped out the door, her crimped blond hair bouncing on her shoulders with every exaggerated step. Layla swallowed a groan. Anita would probably ask again before noon. She never stopped talking about her goats. The previous week, she had brought in a handful of goat fur and scattered it around the room—including on Layla's desk—because she said she missed her pets.

"I swear I'm not some creep trying to sneak into your class-room," the man said, motioning to the badge hung around his neck on a green-and-yellow lanyard—school colors. "And I know this is last-second. I'm sorry. Mr. Crimmons said he tried to call you yesterday."

He had. But Layla had kind of fallen asleep with Ducky on the couch, watching old reruns of *Golden Girls*, and when she'd woken up, it was after nine—too late to do anything but go back to bed. It was definitely not an appropriate time to return a phone call to the principal of the school. Besides, Sunday nights were sacred—and nothing got the Sunday scaries going like surprise phone calls from the principal. It might have been a good idea for her to listen to the message he left before arriving at school—but between lugging her books to the car and dropping Ducky off for his first day with Mr. Rogers, she was running a little behind. School began at eight, and usually, twenty minutes before that, Layla was sitting at her desk with a hot cup of coffee from the break room, her lesson plans laid out neatly. She liked having a few moments of peace before beginning her day. But today—well, today was not calm or peaceful.

"I hope not," she said, eyeing him. She wasn't sure if she trusted him. He seemed entirely too at ease.

"Well, I hope I can make your life a little easier this semester," he said. "I love working with kids."

"Thanks," she said, still cautious. She wedged awkwardly past him to her desk, and she tucked her Barnes & Noble tote bag and her lunch box under her desk. "Um, I guess make yourself at home?" Not that he hadn't already, tucking himself behind her desk before she had even arrived.

She didn't know why she was so uncomfortable around him. Maybe it was because he was so good-looking. Too good-looking, really. The kind of good-looking that she suspected had made his life very easy. Or because she was uncomfortable, since she didn't really want him there; it threw off her plan. And Layla really liked having a plan.

She was debating what, exactly, to have Garrett—Mr. Henderson—do, when Mr. Crimmons, the school principal, popped his head in the door, his white hair a bit mussed.

"Oh, good!" he said, his bright red face smiling widely. "Layla, I see you've met Garrett Henderson. Garrett graduated summa cum laude from the University of Nebraska and comes highly recommended. I'm sure you'll get along swimmingly."

"Oh, yes, we just met." She smiled with a warmth she wasn't sure she felt.

"And, Garrett, you're in amazing hands with Mrs. Sandberg. She's a favorite with the kids. I'm sorry you won't be working with Mrs. Meadows, but I'm happy you get the opportunity to work with someone a little closer to your peer group."

Garrett nodded. "I appreciate it, Mr. Crimmons. Mrs. Sandberg and I were just getting to know each other."

Mr. Crimmons bobbed his head slightly. He had always reminded Layla of a balloon. He was ruddy and red and incredibly passionate and aggressively happy, all the time, and always seemed on the verge of a breakdown, like he was overfull with ideas and emotions and about to be overcome by them at any moment. The parents loved him—which, as any teacher could attest, was a miracle.

"Well, Mr. Henderson, I trust you'll let me know if you need anything."

At that moment, something seemed to catch his attention in the hallway, and he popped out the same way he popped back in—suddenly and in a flurry of movement and emotions.

"*Ms.* Sandberg," Layla told her student teacher.

"What?" Garrett asked.

"He said Mrs. I'm Ms., not Mrs." She flushed slightly, feeling the heat creeping up from her chest, wondering if she was as red as Mr. Crimmons. Her new teacher would probably think she was hitting on him, pointing out the fact she was single. She should have let it go. Or maybe let one of her students correct him—which they would have, loudly and gladly.

"My apologies," Mr. Henderson said smoothly. He paused. "Ms. Sandberg."

"Don't sweat it," she said. She glanced at the clock. She had about two minutes until the bell rang and the students came pouring in. "Listen, I didn't have any time to prepare for you, but I guess you'll probably need to observe for about a week. I don't have recess duty today, so I'll run you through my lesson plans, and we can talk about transitioning some of this to you for the semester." She rattled off the instructions as coolly as possible, trying to seem like she'd done this a million times before, when, in reality, her heart was doing a weird little *thump-thump* thing in her chest, beating an unfamiliar, uneven rhythm. She didn't understand why she felt like this—strange and fluttery and nervous.

Her new student teacher nodded at her. "Sounds good, I guess."

"Take notes, ask me questions, whatever." She paused. "It'll be a fun day. We're going shopping."

He furrowed his brow. "What?"

She reached into the top drawer of her desk and pulled up a large bread bag, full of fake coins and dollar bills. She shook it slightly, and the coins clinked against one another. "We're learning to count money. So we're setting up a shop."

He smiled, crossing his arms. "What are we buying?"

Layla reached into her desk and produced Pokémon and baseball cards.

He scratched the back of his head. "Impressive. I'd take this lesson."

"What, you can't count?" she quipped. "Wow, colleges are really just giving anyone a diploma these days."

He grinned. "No better time to learn than the present."

She smiled back. She couldn't help it.

A moment later, the bell rang, and the students started flooding in, many of them shouting, "Hi, Ms. Layla!" at a volume that almost hurt her ears. They looked curiously at Garrett, who had retreated to behind her desk, standing with his hands in his pockets, nodding hello to the kids as they came in.

"Who are you?" Penny Jacobs asked loudly, staring at Garrett unabashedly, her mouth a little open.

"I'll tell you soon," Layla said. "Sit down, Penny—we've got a big day ahead of us. We've got a few surprises in store."

"What's *in store*?" Penny cocked her head curiously.

"I have a lot of surprises ahead for you, Penny."

"Then why don't you just say it like that instead of talking about a store?"

"Because when you know more words, you can express what you want to say a little better."

Penny sighed. "Seems like a lot of work."

She smiled. Second graders were a tough crowd. It was easy to go down a completely different path through a long line of questions—and if she wasn't careful, it would easily derail the whole day. "Please take your seat, Penny," she said, kindly but firmly. She prided herself on rarely having to raise her voice to get her students to listen.

Behind her, Garrett chuckled, low and throaty. Penny gave Garrett another long look but listened, unlike Anita, who was bouncing happily behind her pigtailed friend and seemed like she was going to approach Layla again—no doubt about her goat. Layla pointed at the desk, and Anita hung her head sulkily.

Being a second-grade teacher was like having a PhD in patience. Layla had always been patient—whether it was taking the time to explain homework to her friends or sitting with her late grandmother and explaining how to use the internet, she was an expert at toeing the line between overly enduring and effective. The previous year, her students had scored incredibly high on their annual tests, thanks to her commitment to ensuring that all her kids understood the subject matter—especially math and reading. She'd hoped the high scores would have garnered her class additional funding, or perhaps a classroom grant, but she'd had no such luck. She had to make do with the same things as the year before, and whatever money she could scrimp together to order a few things off Amazon. She'd grabbed a couple of decent picture books from the dollar store a town over, just to add something to the shelves that didn't look a hundred years old.

Finally, Layla had all the kids in their seats. Some were wriggling around, and Benny Eaton-Palmer was picking his nose, but no one was up, wandering around the classroom.

In the back, Leighton Sloan raised his hand. "Can I go to the bathroom?"

"After announcements," she said.

He rocked back and forth in his seat. She kept an eye on him. She didn't want to clean up any accidents in the classroom, but she had a feeling he'd be okay.

"Good morning, class! Raise your hand if you did something fun this weekend!"

Around the room, almost every hand shot up. She couldn't help but notice a little boy in the back didn't have his hand up. Lucas. Hmmm. She'd have to keep an eye on him, maybe work a little harder at pulling him out of his shell. They were a month in, and Lucas hadn't really spoken much yet, but there were always a couple of extraordinarily shy students who needed a little extra help to express themselves.

"I'll go first," Layla said brightly. "I had a great weekend! One of my friends visited me, and I'm babysitting her little dog! We had the best time, and the dog is staying with one of my neighbors during the day. He is such a good boy!" She paused. "Today, I want you to think about the very best thing that happened to you over the weekend, and we're all going to talk about it during sharing circle, okay?"

The kids nodded. She glanced at Leighton, who had stopped rocking back and forth in his seat. He seemed okay. "And I have another important announcement. Who noticed we have a special guest in the classroom today?"

Again, almost every hand shot up. Lucas was still staring down at his desk. She tried not to frown. Was he not paying attention? Sometimes, when kids didn't get enough sleep at home, they weren't responsive in class. Maybe it wasn't just shyness with him. Ana Waters-Riley, who had rivaled him in shyness on the first day, was finally coming out of her shell, and even volunteered to read aloud—twice. But not Lucas.

She turned to Garrett. "Class, I'm super excited to introduce you to your student teacher for the semester—Mr. Henderson! Or do you prefer Mr. Garrett?"

He smiled at the class. "Mr. Garrett is fine."

Layla gave the class a big smile. "Everyone say hello to Mr. Garrett!"

"Hi, Mr. Garrett!" the class chorused, and Layla grabbed a marker and wrote *Mr. Garrett* on the board in big, bold letters. The class recited the letters with her, which they always did when they met anyone new.

"Mr. Garrett," she said, replacing the marker on the board, "would you like to introduce yourself to the kids?"

Garrett cleared his throat and joined her at the front of the room. He looked entirely comfortable, like he'd been in front of classes a million times before. He looked . . . at home. Like he belonged here.

"Hi, everyone!" he said. "Like Ms. Layla said, I'm Mr. Garrett.

Believe it or not, I used to live here, just for a little bit, before I went to college and joined the army. After that, I—"

"You were a soldier?" one of the Drubbins twins shouted. George, she was pretty sure. She was going to have to double-check the seating chart. The boys were almost impossible to tell apart, even a month in.

"I was," he confirmed, smiling.

"Did you shoot anyone?" Aiden McGee spoke up.

"How many?" Anita hollered.

He shook his head. "Sorry, I didn't shoot anyone, fortunately. I mostly flew planes. I was a pilot." He paused. "Actually, I'm starting this semester a little late because I just got back from being deployed overseas."

Aiden looked mildly disappointed, but the rest of the kids were excited.

"Can you take us on a plane ride?" Benny asked.

"Do you have your own plane?" Leighton added.

"Class," Layla reminded them. "Be sure to raise your hand before you ask Mr. Garrett questions."

All the hands in the room shot up.

Except . . . Lucas's.

She walked to the back of the classroom to watch Garrett answer questions and to keep an eye on Lucas. The small boy had chosen the back corner seat on the first day, when she'd let them choose their seating arrangement for the first part of the year. It had helped her see dynamics between kids. But Lucas kept to himself. From day one, she'd decided to keep an eye on him as the only Asian American kid in the class, to make sure he was okay, to make sure the other kids were acting from a place of kindness. She hadn't seen anyone being mean to him, though, which was good. Second graders, while usually sweet and charming, could be incredibly mean when they didn't understand something. And since most of students were Caucasian and Hispanic, Lucas probably felt a little isolated.

Meanwhile, at the front of the classroom, Garrett had set up a mini phone projector he'd packed for the day, showing pictures of him surfing in Hawaii and a shot of when he was stationed in Pakistan. He showed his backpacking trip through Machu Pic-chu, and then a ride on a boat in Venice, which started a new flurry of questions.

The kids loved him. There was no question about it. They liked him more than her already. Layla always felt she had to work hard to make connections with each student, and she prided herself on it—at the end of the year, she had a special bond to each kid. She knew what made them tick, and they trusted her completely. But Garrett, standing in front of the classroom with a mini projec-tor (why hadn't she thought of that?), had gained the trust and adoration of all her students immediately. Lucas had even lifted his head slightly, listening as Garrett explained in detail what a gondola was.

All day, the kids followed him around, glomming on to his every word. During free-expression time, almost all the kids drew pic-tures of Garrett—Garrett as the captain of a football team, Gar-rett as a soldier, Garrett and goats. By the end of the day, the tiny flash of jealousy had been fanned into a small hot flame she was trying to ignore. At recess, though originally Layla had planned to go over lesson plans with him, Garrett played soccer with the kids, and everyone wanted to be on his team. When the final bell rang, it took twice as long as usual to get everyone out of the classroom because all the kids wanted to talk to Garrett. And he hadn't even started teaching yet. He was just observing.

She couldn't decide, really, if she liked him. The kids did, that was sure. It was kind of unfair.

By the end of the day, Layla was more than ready to go home. She was exhausted and couldn't help feeling a bit defeated. Gar-rett was clearly going to be a better teacher than she was. Maybe he already was. He had that *thing*, a magical, rare quality that captured the attention of students without even trying. The *thing* that Layla tried so hard to achieve. Was she . . . in the wrong pro-fession entirely? Ever since she was little, she'd wanted to be a teacher. And she worked hard, each day, to make sure she was helping every single kid. At night, she went home and scrawled down ideas for lesson plans that would reach her students and make learning easier. And Garrett came in and on one day . . . just had it. Layla had to work to be a teacher; Garrett, on the other hand, just *was* one.

When Layla arrived home and picked up Ducky from Mr. Rogers's house around the bend in her street, she wanted to do nothing but eat ice cream in her living room. Maybe turn on an episode of *Real Housewives* and watch other people's problems.

"You like me, right?" Layla asked the tiny dog, feeling a little sorry for herself. She licked mint chocolate chip ice cream off her spoon and settled deeper into her couch. She glanced down at Ducky, who was still on the floor, looking up at her expectantly.

"Do you need something?" she asked, a touch more irritably than she meant to.

Ducky sat up on his hind legs. He whined slightly. She leaned down to pick him up, but he danced deftly out of her grasp and then whined again.

"What's wrong, buddy? Do you have to go back outside? Go to the bathroom?"

He frowned. The first thing she'd done when she got home was let him potty outside. And he had a half bowl of kibble on the floor in the kitchen (he hadn't finished it earlier in the morning), and she'd changed his water, just in case he wanted fresh stuff that hadn't been sitting inside all day.

Ducky walked toward her bedroom and then looked back at her. She stared at him, and he ran toward her and then back toward her bedroom. When she didn't do anything, he did it again, yipping at her sharply. Layla pursed her lips. Was Ducky trying to get her to . . . follow him?

Layla set the ice cream on her side table, shoving her spoon into the middle, and walked after Ducky as he pranced into the bedroom, where he trotted happily over to a bag that Christine had left—a black-checked duffel—and barked twice, looking pointedly at it and back at her. He lifted a paw and touched the bag. Clearly he wanted whatever was inside. She smiled despite her mood. Who said dogs couldn't communicate?

Layla knelt down, and Ducky immediately began prancing excitedly, his little feet tip-tapping beside her, making excited little whining noises.

"You want this, buddy?" She poked at the bag.

Layla swore he gave a tiny nod. Apparently, whatever Ducky needed was . . . well, here.

She unzipped the duffel and dumped the contents out on her floor. It was . . . clothes. Not clothes for Christine—who had quite an impressive wardrobe and was known for traveling heavy, so she had plenty of dresses and shoes for pretty much any occasion no matter where she went. They were clothes for Ducky. Evidently, Ducky took after his owner. Layla began lifting the dog outfits—a set of adorable little denim overalls, a raincoat, a mini workout sweat suit. She couldn't help but smile. Leave it to Christine to have a wardrobe for her dog. Of course, Layla had never met a dog who actually, well, *liked* wearing clothes. Usually it was the owners who liked dressing up the dogs and parading them around in handbags. And, honestly, Christine was the type of person who would have her dog looking more stylish than most celebrities. Layla was pretty sure, though, that Ducky probably only wanted to snuggle with the clothes because they smelled like Christine. He probably just missed her. Poor little fella.

As Layla sifted through the clothes, Ducky began turning excited circles. She pushed them all into a colorful mound on the carpet, expecting him to curl up on them, or at least sniff them, but he waited, impatiently, and then pawed at the clothes.

"You really want to wear this, huh?" she asked.

He yipped excitedly, and went back to doing his tippy-tappy dance, looking at the pile of outfits and up at her.

"Okay, then," Layla said. "I was going to give you a break from dressing up, but . . . if you insist, I guess."

Ducky stood by her impatiently, looking up at her, his eyes big and hopeful. She choose a cute little striped shirt and overall set, and he waited patiently while she slipped the top over his head and secured the small metal clips of the overalls under his front legs. After he was dressed, he sat proudly, his chest puffed out, looking . . . absolutely delighted. She realized, suddenly, the outfit reminded her of something . . . from a long time ago. Back when her parents were around. They'd given her a teddy bear for her ninth birthday, dressed in a pair of denim overalls, with a happy striped shirt, almost exactly like the one Ducky was wearing. Her heart did a funny lurch in her chest.

"You do look adorable," she told him, her heart melting, just a bit. She smiled at him, and her eyes teared up. She couldn't help it. There was something special about Ducky. It was like he could tell what she needed. It was like . . . he knew she needed something and he'd figured out a way to give it to her. Christine always called Ducky her heart dog, and until now, honestly, Layla didn't get it. But now . . . she did. He was pretty special.

He pawed her leg gently, and she scooped him up into her arms and gave him a soft hug. He licked her cheek, where a tear had fallen.

"I really like you, sweet puppy," she said.

He tossed his head bit and nuzzled her gently, as if to say, *I know.*

CHAPTER 4

DUCKY

Ducky missed his mom.

But he also knew his mom would never, ever leave him, and she'd be home very soon. Besides, Ducky really liked Auntie Layla. No one could ever replace Mom or Barb or Katsu, his sweet sisters, but Ducky knew Layla was trying her best, and she was really fun, especially since she started letting him wear outfits. She was getting used to playing with Ducky, and she snuck him extra treats sometimes, and then he went to Mr. Rogers's house, and he snuck Ducky extra treats too, until Ducky's tummy was so full he almost didn't want dinner (but don't worry, he still ate all his food). Ducky liked that house that Mr. Rogers lived in. It was like a big happy garden, only sometimes Mr. Rogers didn't seem so happy.

Mr. Rogers did this thing where he looked out the window. Sometimes, Ducky looked out the window with him, just in case there was a squirrel, but there was never anything there, except for one time when there was a bird, but Ducky didn't think Mr. Rogers even cared about that. Ducky thought Mr. Rogers was sad. But his face always turned happy when he looked at Ducky. Sometimes, though, Mr. Rogers sat back in a soft chair and his eyes went far away, and it looked like he wasn't even in the room. That was when Ducky usually crawled in his lap, and Mr. Rogers went back to himself, and he petted the little dog until he started to snore. Sometimes he even let Ducky crawl up onto his shoulder, and he got all tucked in under his chin. It made Mr. Rogers laugh, which was a nice sound.

Mr. Rogers loved watching *The Price Is Right*, but he was the best at *Jeopardy!* He was good at guessing the answers. Well, Ducky thought so, at least. He wasn't really sure if Mr. Rogers was right or not, but he liked sitting next to him while he hollered at the TV and slapped his leg when the man read an answer.

"I told you so!" he'd crow happily, even though he really hadn't told Ducky anything at all.

The day before, though, was kind of scary for Ducky. He didn't like being scared. He asked Mr. Rogers for a treat, and his new friend got up to get them out of the kitchen. Layla always packed a couple of yummy snacks for Ducky, and if Ducky looked at Mr. Rogers with his cute face, he'd usually go get one for him. So Ducky made his eyes really big and looked up at him, and Mr. Rogers said, "Okay, Ducky," and pushed himself out of his chair really slow, and Ducky followed him to the kitchen. The pup wagged his tail extra hard so Mr. Rogers knew Ducky was happy.

Layla had packed Ducky one of his favorite toys too. It was a squeaky flower toy, and the little pup had been playing with it. Ducky liked that it made funny sounds, and it was so satisfying to chomp on it. Sometimes Ducky shook it really hard just to show it who was boss in case the toy got any ideas. But when Ducky was finished playing, he left it on the floor, and Mr. Rogers didn't see it when he was doing his shuffle-walk to the kitchen. And he stepped on it.

It squeaked, and Mr. Rogers did this jump thing, kind of like Ducky did when the mailman knocked on the door to deliver a package and surprised him, and then Mr. Rogers stumbled and fell into the wall. Ducky barked because he didn't know what else to do and tried to tell Mr. Rogers to be careful. The old man didn't fall all the way to the floor, but he stood against the wall, breathing hard, like Ducky did after a long walk. Except Ducky's tongue usually hung out, and Mr. Rogers's tongue stayed in his mouth. The old man stayed that way for a little while, his chest doing this funny up-down thing.

Then Mr. Rogers went back to his chair and forgot he was getting Ducky a treat. Ducky moved his flower back beside the bag that Layla brought for him so Mr. Rogers wouldn't fall over it again. He dropped his head, feeling really bad that his friend almost got hurt on the toy Ducky was playing with, and he whimpered a little bit to let Mr. Rogers know he was really, really sorry. Ducky wasn't even sad about his treat. Instead, the dog spent most of the day watching the old man and making sure he seemed okay. Ducky thought he was, but he sat next to him and guarded him to be sure. Maybe, if something happened, Ducky could bark really loud to get him help. Ducky's mom said he could be noisy when he wanted, so he bet someone would come. He hoped they would.

Ducky loved Mr. Rogers. He didn't want him to get hurt. Maybe tomorrow Ducky wouldn't play with his toys. Or maybe he just would be careful where he put them. He wished his mom were there with him. She would know what to do. And she would hold Ducky and scratch his ears and tell him what a good boy he was.

By the time Layla came by to pick up Ducky, Mr. Rogers seemed okay. Ducky watched him pretty carefully. Ducky's mom always said he was good at knowing when people were feeling down and making them feel better, so Ducky thought maybe he helped Mr. Rogers feel better too.

CHAPTER 5

Christine was back in town for the weekend, and she'd brought Layla her favorite—White Rabbit candies and Pocky sticks, as a thank-you for watching Ducky. She'd tried to pay Layla too, but Layla had flatly refused. So now the two were out for dinner downtown at the George and Theo Café, one of the few restaurants in town, which served an absolute mishmash of everything, from good old Nebraskan corn on the cob to enchiladas to shaved Italian ice, depending on what you were in the mood for. Theo was always trying to invent new desserts, so eating there was often an adventure—if a bit of a gamble, if you decided to try any of his latest concoctions. His goat cheese and cranberry muffins had been an absolute hit—but his whiskey and dried raisin version had a funny aftertaste and had Layla a little nauseated. She'd pretended to take home the leftovers but had thrown them away when she was out of the sight of the restaurant so as not to hurt Theo's feelings.

Upbeat nineties music floated through the tinny speakers of the small eatery. Layla had always liked the sound. They'd probably needed to be replaced years ago, but the sound made her feel . . . comfortable, somehow. She liked the strange, echoey quality of the music, like she'd stepped through some sort of wormhole and come out on the other side when things were simpler. Easier. Ducky, who was sitting happily beside Christine in the booth, kept looking up at his owner, like he couldn't believe his luck that she was there. It made Layla smile to see how much Ducky adored his mom. When she'd arrived back, he'd pranced in delighted little circles until she picked him up and smothered him with kisses.

Actually, Ducky made *everyone* smile. The waitress, Susan Lynn Hildeburg, had about melted when Christine walked in with Ducky under her arm and immediately reached out, like she was trying to hold a baby. Christine had handed him over carefully, and Susan Lynn had taken about four selfies with Ducky, promised Christine she'd tag Ducky on Instagram, and kissed the pup on the head twice before even offering to seat them. Two other customers had come over to see Ducky too, but now the café had settled down, people only stealing occasional glances at the celebrity dog.

"So," Christine said after the food arrived. "Tell me about your student teacher."

"He's good. Like, really good." Layla sighed. "He's definitely found his calling."

"I bet Garrett's not as good as you," Christine said, spearing a piece of dressing-drenched spinach with her fork. "How could he be?"

"He's better," Layla admittedly begrudgingly. "Well, maybe not yet, but he's really, really good. Yesterday, I did my lesson plan where I tell a scary story and then the students have to summarize what I told them. So, of course, I let Garrett tell the story, right? Since I'm supposed to let him take over and coach him?"

Christine nodded. "Sure, makes sense." She grabbed a piece of edamame from the bowl in the center of the table.

"So, he sits down, and he has everyone's attention without trying. And this, he has the idea to draw the shades and turn off almost all the lights, so the room is dark, and then he uses the flashlight on his phone to read and make scary faces. The kids absolutely loved it. Every single one was paying attention. Do you know how hard that is with second graders? To make them pay attention?" Layla sighed.

"Fortunately, I don't," Christine said. "But he's still not *you*."

"You've never seen me teach."

"Um, you literally ran all your lesson plans past me in college. And they were actually interesting. I mean, I kind of didn't care, and you made me care. You're that good."

"Really?" Layla asked, not believing her. "You're not just saying that because you're my friend?"

"You're forgetting something," Christine said, raising a single finger. "A very important fact."

"Which is?" Layla spun her glass nervously on the circle of condensation it had created on the table.

"All my friends are successful and amazing. Obviously." Christine made a flapping gesture with her hand, as if to shoo away the idea that Layla could be any less than absolutely incredible.

Layla laughed. "That is true, actually." She nodded at the little dog. "Look at Ducky. Wildly successful."

"It's undeniable," Christine said. She paused. "Wait. Can I change the subject? Only a little bit, I swear."

Layla took a sip of her Diet Coke. "Um, okay. I guess."

"If I remember right, the first thing you told me about this Garrett guy was that he was hot."

Layla blushed a little, immediately regretting that she'd confided in her friend. But she was just being honest. "I mean, I guess you could say that."

"So you guys are going to date," Christine stated, as if it were an obvious and unavoidable fact. She picked a blueberry out of her salad and popped it in her mouth.

Beside her, Ducky whined slightly. She grabbed a treat out of her purse and held it between her index finger and thumb. He took it from her and wolfed it down, making happy little grunts as he did, and then looked up, happy, his pink tongue wagging out of his mouth.

"Um, no. I'm basically his boss," Layla reminded Christine. "That would be super inappropriate. I'd probably lose my job."

Christine waved her hand. "No, no. I mean *later*. He's not going to be your student teacher for long."

Layla shook her head. "Absolutely not."

"Listen," Christine said, "I have a sixth sense about this stuff. I am getting romance vibes right now. Seriously. Like, *You've Got Mail*, *My Best Friend's Wedding*, *Dirty Dancing* vibes. I know these things."

Layla put her head down on the table, her forehead resting on the cool Formica.

"I mean, unless you hate him. Do you hate him? Is he a completely terrible person?"

"No," Layla admitted without raising her head. "I kind of *like* him."

"See. I told you. *Romance*."

Layla raised herself up to her elbows and blew a piece of hair out of her face. "Not like that. I mean, he's just . . . a likable guy. Even though I'm totally jealous he's going to be an amazing teacher, I like him. He's the kind of guy you want to dislike but then you meet him and you're like . . . dang. I can't. He's a good dude."

"Sounds like the beginning of a love story to me."

"Sounds like you need to shut it." Layla picked a blueberry out of Christine's salad and threw it at her. Christine held her hands up in defense and launched a counterattack with a brown paper napkin.

"I know the title of the movie." Christine paused dramatically. "*Lust and Language Arts*."

"No."

"Okay, fine. *Amore and Algebra*."

"Absolutely not."

"No, wait. I've got it. How about *An A+ in Chemistry*."

"That's it. You're fired. Your career as a Hallmark movie writer is over."

Christine sighed. "It was fun while it lasted. You have to admit . . . I was good at it."

"You were cringe."

"I was *a legend.*"

Layla laughed. She couldn't help it. It bubbled up out of her stomach until she couldn't hold it back. Christine grinned at her.

"You're the worst." Layla finally gasped.

"Sometimes the truth is hard to hear." Christine shrugged and reached over, cutting a tiny triangle out of Layla's banana pancake and popping it in her mouth. "Mmmmm." She started to grab another bite, and then she stopped, her fork poised halfway to Layla's plate.

"What?" Layla asked.

"You're not even eating," Christine pointed out, dropping her fork back onto the own plate of salad, which was half gone. "Instead of being anxious that this guy is going to eclipse you, can you do something for me?"

Layla nodded, begrudgingly. "I guess."

"First, I'm going to need you to eat your food. It's not like you to barely touch your plate. I'm disappointed in you."

Layla stuck her tongue out at her and took a begrudging bite. "Thanks, Mom," she said sarcastically, through a mouthful of pancake. She wasn't normally a person who had to be told to eat. Any other day, she'd be the person stealing Christine's food. She couldn't figure out why this Garrett guy was tying up her stomach in weird knots. She couldn't tell if he was getting her down, or . . . something else.

Christine ignored her. "Second, I'm going to need you to take stock of your situation. I mean, you're kind of lucky. Your student teacher is hot, nice, and *good.* That makes your job easy. You have excellent scenery in your classroom. You don't have to bend over backward to turn this guy into a good teacher. You don't even have to work that hard. And, need I remind you, this isn't a competition. More than one person can be a good teacher. I mean, I would hope so."

"Fair," Layla admitted, begrudgingly.

"And third," Christine said, "I hate to ask you this, but they're asking me to fill in regularly for a couple of months at the youth skating association, and you know Ducky hates the cold. Do you think you could watch him again?" She picked him up and held him close to her face. "Pretty please, Auntie Layla? Ducky would love it so, so much. He doesn't want to go to the doggy hotel." She kissed the little dog on the forehead.

"I mean, sure," Layla said, all the sarcasm gone from her voice. In the week she'd spent with Ducky, she'd realized . . . well, she'd really miss the little guy when he was gone. He was excellent company. She didn't mind him being there at all. Actually, she liked it.

Mr. Rogers had also loved caring for Ducky. She knew how disappointed he'd been when she'd needed him to help for only a week. He'd been so happy when she'd dropped by to pick Ducky up at night. He almost looked . . . well, younger. Like having Ducky around was its own sort of magic. And if she was being honest, she was a little happier with Ducky around too. She'd even toyed—again—with getting a dog of her own. She'd found herself browsing the Lincoln Animal Shelter Facebook page, looking at all the sad dogs in cages, waiting for someone to come love them. But she was a teacher. She was a *busy* teacher. And she wasn't sure she was ready. Looking after Ducky was one thing—but being completely responsible for her own dog? She wasn't sure she was ready for that. It had been too long since she'd had a family. She wasn't sure she could handle that yet. Ducky would be a good test run before she committed to a dog of her own. And everyone knew she was bad at commitment.

"I'll definitely pay you," Christine promised. "And I brought him more outfits, so he won't get bored."

"First of all, no money. We're friends. And . . . are you completely serious about the outfits? Does he know the difference?" Layla asked. "Can't he just . . . wear the same thing? I mean, I can wash it."

"He's very into fashion," Christine said seriously. "He has to stay on top of it. Imagine if your favorite Instagrammer repeated outfits."

"Well, that would obviously be a travesty," Layla said dryly. "I wouldn't know how to go on."

"I know," Christine said. "And I'll have you take pictures of him sometimes. You know, gotta keep the Instagram content fresh." She turned to her dog. "I can't wait to see you in your new teddy bear costume!"

Ducky looked at her happily, his tongue hanging out. He was rewearing his overalls, which, as Layla had said, was probably a travesty in Christine's eyes.

"I know he's not low-maintenance," Layla said. "I've never met a dog who actually *liked* clothes."

"Well, Ducky is a special guy." Christine swept her dog up into her arms and hugged him. He lifted his head and licked Christine, just once, on the chin. She giggled and set him down in her lap, where he sat patiently, staring across the table at Layla—and her banana pancakes. A tiny spot of drool dropped off his tongue and landed on the table. Christine wiped it up with a napkin.

"By the way," Christine said, "If I can't pay you, then I'll pay for dinner."

"Absolutely not."

"Too late. I already slid my card to the waitress when I went to the bathroom earlier."

Layla fake gasped. "How could you?"

"You'll just have to find out a way to forgive me," Christine said. "Now, come on. I need to get a video of Ducky frolicking in the park before the sun goes down."

Layla pushed out of the booth just as Susan Lynn came by, her forehead creased with concern and a smear of bacon grease on the corner of her apron.

"What's wrong, sweetie?" she asked, putting her hands on her hips. "Didn't you like your pancakes? You always eat the whole plate."

"Just have stuff on my mind," Layla said. She took a closer look at Susan Lynn. At the beginning of the shift, she'd been glowing—happy to meet Ducky. Now, her liner was smudged, and her eyes were red and bloodshot. "You okay, Susan Lynn?"

Beside her, Christine looked up at the waitress, concerned. Even Ducky tilted his head. It was strange how the little dog so easily picked up on human emotions.

Susan Lynn sniffed and swiped at her eyes with the back of her hand. "Did you hear Jarvis is considering closing the plant? It's down to this one and one up in Pennsylvania."

Layla's heart sank. A handful of her students' parents worked at the plant, which manufactured combine parts that farmers used across the world to harvest crops. And she happened to know Susan Lynn's husband did too. In fact, a large part of Two Falls had jobs there. It kept Two Falls . . . well, alive. Without it, Layla wasn't sure how people would survive. They'd have to move, and Two Falls was already struggling.

"When?" Layla asked quietly.

"A couple months from now, I think. Billy said word is they're going to start letting people go in a few weeks." She pulled at the corner of her apron, using it to dab at the corners of her eyes. "I keep hoping it's just a rumor, because we haven't heard anything official, but—I just don't know how we're going to make it without the job. Mica needs braces next year, and the payments . . ." She trailed off. "I just gotta do right by my daughter, Layla."

Layla nodded, her heart hurting a little. She'd had Mica in her first ever class, and the girl was wickedly smart and loved more by her mother than any kid she'd ever had.

"Can Billy pick up some shifts at the auto shop?" She knew Susan Lynn's husband was handy and often fixed cars on the side.

"I mean sure, but . . ." Susan Lynn shook her head and seemed to remember she was at work. She touched Layla's arm gently. "I'm sorry, sweetheart. I don't mean to trouble you with all this. I'm . . . I'm sure we'll figure it out."

"You're not troubling me," Layla said softly, touching Susan Lynn's shoulder. "We're in this together."

It sounded like a platitude, but it wasn't. Because the town had been slowly falling apart for years. If jobs kept leaving and businesses kept shutting down, then it meant Layla wouldn't have any kids to teach. And Two Falls . . . it was home. She couldn't imagine going anywhere else if they leaned out the workforce at the school. She was young, which meant she was one of the newer teachers—so if there were cuts, she'd likely be among the first to go.

Susan Lynn, quite suddenly, hugged her tightly. "Just keep us in your prayers, okay? We'll figure something out." She turned to Christine. "I'm so sorry for ruining your meal like this. I swear I'm usually better."

Christine smiled gently. "Don't worry about it for a second," she said. She stood up from the table and put a gentle hand on Susan Lynn's shoulder. When Susan Lynn turned back to attend to another table, Christine quietly slipped another twenty onto the table.

When Layla and Christine were back in Layla's old Bronco, she sighed heavily, resting her forehead on the steering wheel.

"This is bad, huh?" Christine asked.

"Yeah," Layla said. "This . . . is really bad."

Chapter 6

Garrett smelled amazing.

It was a problem. It was distracting. It was the worst. Layla couldn't work in these conditions.

Even though she wanted to.

She wanted to ask Garrett what cologne he wore so she could buy it and spray it on her pillow and everything else she owned. But that, she supposed, would be a little creepy, and, she reminded herself as she saw him running his hand through his hair and wondering what kind of shampoo he used to make it look so gorgeous, was inappropriate. She was a professional, damn it, and she was not going to be swayed by a man, no matter how attractive he was.

And he was. There was no doubt. Layla had wondered, at first, if it was just her, but Mrs. Sanchez, the art teacher, had stared at him, bug-eyed, when she came in to teach finger painting, and pulled Layla aside just as the kids were just starting to filter in from recess.

"What?" Layla asked, watching her stand, frozen.

"He's beautiful," Mrs. Sanchez breathed in her ear. "I want to paint him."

"But you're teaching finger painting today."

"Exactly," Mrs. Sanchez said, smiling. "He can be the canvas."

Layla choked back a laugh, looking toward the front of the classroom, where Garrett was deep in conversation with Anita—no doubt about goats—when Mrs. Sanchez leaned in. "You'd make a cute couple," she whispered.

"Elena!" Layla said, shocked.

Mrs. Sanchez shrugged. "I'm just stating the obvious."

But before Layla could respond, Garrett came striding across the room, smiling broadly. "Mrs. Sanchez," he said. "Can I help you get set up for art time?"

Mrs. Sanchez blushed but eagerly accepted his help. The two spread sheets of plastic over the back of the classroom, where they'd lay out the finger paints and paper, and Layla heard them laughing as they worked.

Layla knew she should have been worried about the plant, thinking about her students, brainstorming ideas to help—and she was—but Garrett was distracting. The fact that he was a good teacher was undeniable, and Layla found her jealousy vanishing almost entirely, except for a little tiny corner that lit up and burned a small hot flame whenever the students looked at him just a little too adoringly or said something like what Anita had just shouted, well within Layla's earshot: "Mr. Garrett, I wish you could be our teacher forever!"

Or when Aiden told Mr. Garrett he was the best teacher he'd ever had.

Or when the Drubbins twins finger painted his likeness when Mrs. Sanchez came by with (washable) paints.

But it was hard to be jealous of someone so distracting. She found herself liking him in spite of herself, even though she was trying very, very hard not to. And not just because he was undeniably handsome, but because he was actually *nice*. He helped clean up and reorganize the classroom without even asking. He collected student homework and graded it for her without Layla even mentioning it. He constantly was asking for her feedback or looking for ways to improve. And she had to respect that.

Also, one time, when he was writing on the board, his button-up came untucked and she saw . . . well, abs. And she had to respect those too.

During the first recess break, she sat at her desk, showing Garrett how she lined up spelling tests on her desk to grade them quickly, when she heard a small, muffled sniffling noise toward the back of the classroom. She lifted her head, leaving Garrett to check over the tests, and wove her way through the maze of desks toward the back of the classroom.

Out the window, children were running back and forth on the playground, playing hopscotch and skipping rope, but in the back corner of the classroom, one little black-haired boy was sitting behind an easel, his knees drawn up to his chest and his forehead resting on his arms.

Lucas.

Layla approached him slowly, taking small, careful steps, and then sank down beside Lucas, her back against the cold wall next to him. "Hey, buddy," she said gently.

He lifted his head slowly off his forearms and looked up at her. His eyes were bloodshot and red-rimmed from crying, and his nose was running. He sniffled noisily, and Layla lifted herself up for a moment to grab a box of dollar-store tissues off the back counter above the cabinets. She'd had to pony up her own funds to have a couple of boxes in the classroom, and they were barely better than the toilet tissue Mrs. Hardison was using this year—but having a bunch of second graders in the room with no tissues in sight was a form of germ Russian roulette Layla wasn't willing to play.

"Kleenex?" Layla asked quietly, offering him the box.

He took one with a trembling hand and dabbed at his eyes and then blew his noise quietly. She gave him a moment before speaking again.

"You okay, Lucas?"

He nodded but didn't say anything; instead, he snatched a second tissue from the box and held it tight in his small fist.

"Wanna talk about it?" she asked.

He shook his head, still not saying anything. Normally, the boy was quiet. But he didn't cry. His little face was carefully blank. But today—today was different. Today, something had happened to change that.

She studied him, carefully, wondering how far to push. Lucas was still the quietest kid in class by a long shot, but she hadn't noticed him being bullied. However, she was the first to admit it was easy to miss things in a class of second graders. To make matters more complex, last year, there had been several issues when a few white boys had ganged up to bully Katy Heng, a sweet fifth grader. It didn't matter that she was as American as they were; they were cruel and had made mean jokes that left her smiling through tears in the counselor's office, trying to put on a brave face. If something like that was happening—the thought made Layla's chest tight with anger. She wouldn't put up with it. Not in her classroom.

"If you change your mind, will you let me know?" she asked him softly.

Lucas nodded but didn't meet her eyes, and she couldn't help but think he'd never tell her. She would have to watch him more closely. Maybe she'd have to rearrange seating charts so he was sitting closer to her desk. Or maybe she'd start observing Garrett from the back of the room, like a student, so she could make sure Lucas was okay.

Of course, if the other kids were picking on Lucas, they were probably smart enough to do it away from the teacher. Which meant she'd have to be extra watchful. Maybe she could ask the other teachers to keep a close eye on him at recess, make sure nothing was happening.

Usually her kids were sweet. Kind. Funny. It was why she'd chosen to teach second grade, after all. The pay was generally abysmal, and the resources were awful, but she could come to work every day knowing that she was doing something that mattered. It mattered to her, it mattered to their parents, and, she hoped, as cheesy as it was, maybe, someday down the road, it would matter to the whole world, if only a little bit.

But sometimes, especially with kids who were raised by ignorant parents, something less than kind came through. Ignorance spread fast, like wildfire, like an epidemic, infecting a whole class and burning through before she even realized it was happening, and it needed to be stopped as soon as possible. Otherwise, it took down sweet little boys like Lucas in a whirlwind of trauma. She'd seen it happen. Most people thought that in second grade, barbs and comments didn't matter, but they did. And kids—even little ones—carried that kind of thing around for a long, long time.

She sat with him for another minute, listening to his sniffles, waiting for him to talk, if he wanted to. But he didn't, and the sniffles slowly faded. Garrett appeared in front of them, holding out a chocolate milk.

"Got something for you, buddy," he said, settling down on the floor next to Lucas.

Lucas accepted the milk, his hand a little steadier. "Thanks," he said, his voice whisper soft, and took a small drink. Layla smiled. At least he'd said something.

"Having a rough day?" Garrett asked him.

Lucas shrugged, his eyes on the ground.

"What happened?" Layla asked.

Lucas said nothing. It was as if Layla hadn't even spoken. Like the more she pressed, the more he retreated into himself.

"We're here to help you. You know that, right?" Garrett smiled at him, soft and slow.

Lucas nodded and took another drink from the milk carton. A chocolate milk mustache had started at the corners of his mouth, and he wiped at it with the heel of his hand.

Garrett and Layla sat with him, in silence. Garrett popped up a moment and returned with two extra chocolate milk cartons. He opened them expertly and handed one to Layla. "I missed these," he said, reaching out to touch his carton to Lucas's and then Layla's in a toast. "This is one of the main reasons why I wanted to become a teacher."

"Definitely one of the best perks," Layla said, taking a sip of hers. The milk cooler always kept the cartons icy cold. There was nothing like having a cold chocolate milk from the cooler. She turned it around in her fingers, reading the fun facts the manufacturers always added on the back for kids.

"Tigers have striped skin, not just striped fur," she read aloud. "Huh. Who knew?"

Garrett cleared his throat, turning his milk carton around. "Avocados are fruits, not vegetables."

Lucas looked up, handing his milk carton over to Layla for her to read.

"Squids have the biggest eyes in the whole wide world." She handed it back to him.

He held it tightly, in both his hands, for a moment, and smiled, almost imperceptibly, the corners of his mouth turning up just a tiny bit.

Progress. Layla's heart tittered. She wasn't sure she'd ever actually seen him smile before.

"I think I'm going to go outside," he said finally, his voice so quiet Layla had to lean in to hear him. But at least he was talking.

Layla nodded. "Let us know if you need anything, okay?"

He nodded, pushed himself off the floor, and walked out without looking back, stopping only to drop his milk carton in the recycle bin and stuff the tissues in his pockets. That was like him; he was so quiet, so set on leaving every room as if he had never been there at all.

"I'm really worried about him," Layla said after he walked out the door. "Something's going on."

Garrett nodded. "I've never seen him talk to another kid. Not once."

Layla sighed. "Me neither. When I put him into groups, he just looks down the whole time. He never participates."

"What about when he's with a partner?"

"We have twenty-one kids. No one ever chooses him, and he's too shy to ask anyone."

"What about when you assign partners?" Garrett pressed.

Layla hesitated. "I have. But he barely talks. And when he does, it's so quiet you have to lean in to hear him. It's not really that fair to the other kids. They end up doing the bulk of the work."

"What did the teacher from last year say about him?" Garrett pressed. "Did they ever get through to him?"

Layla shook her head, her ponytail swinging. "He's new. His family just moved here. His dad is a manager at the plant." Which meant, of course, if the rumors about the plant closing were true, that he would be losing his job—which probably meant Lucas would have to move. Again. He'd be a shadow of a memory in the back of the students' minds, forgotten by the next school year. She wanted more than that for him.

"Does he have siblings?"

Layla shook her head. "He's an only child."

Garrett sighed heavily, his shoulders dropping slightly. "And his parents?"

"Do you think I should call them? Parent-teacher conferences aren't until next month."

He nodded. "Maybe just a check-in, to see what he says about school. Maybe they know what's going on."

She nodded. "It's probably not a bad idea. They're the only family I don't know on a first-name basis. I'd like them to know they can come to us with . . . anything."

Garrett scooted over close to her, lifting his milk carton to his lips. "Let me know how I can help, okay?"

Dang it. This close, she could smell the soap he used—piney and fresh—under his cologne. She felt heat creeping up from her neckline to her face. She liked him. She couldn't help it. Elena was right. He was *handsome*, in that special way where she knew he could win a fight or build a table or cook her dinner. He was a *man*. But maybe she was overthinking this. She hadn't dated since college. Maybe it was just . . . being around a single guy. Any single guy. Especially in the eligible-man drought that was Two Falls.

"I will," she said. Layla pushed herself off the floor and approached the window to look out at the kids on the playground so Garrett couldn't see the flush spreading across her cheeks. Her stupid pale skin was betraying her, and she was supposed to be in a position of power over him, not the other way around.

She couldn't help but notice, though, as she looked out the window, her face flaring with heat, that Lucas was sitting on an otherwise empty swing set, his head down, dragging his toes through the gravel. Totally and completely alone.

It made her heart ache.

CHAPTER 7

DUCKY

Ducky made like a hundred billion new friends and it was the best day of his life. He had lots of best days of his life, which was probably the bestest way to live, if anyone asked him. Ducky wagged his tail so much his booty hurt but he was so, so, so happy. He loved meeting new people.

That morning, Layla got up early to snuggle with Ducky and gave him a treat. Then she dressed Ducky as Harry Potter, which was one of his favorite outfits. He looked pretty nice because he had a black robe and everything, and it made him feel extra special when he got to wear the little black glasses. When she dropped Ducky off, Layla called him a "handsome boy" and gave him a kiss on the head before handing him over to Mr. Rogers, who gave Ducky a little hug and a nice pet and then told him he had a big surprise for him. Ducky was so excited he could barely stand it! He even barked to let Mr. Rogers know how happy he was.

Even though Ducky wanted him to hurry up and share the surprise, he waited patiently while he walked out with him to his old pickup, which was bright green, and looking at it made the dog really happy. Mr. Roger lifted Ducky into the front seat, where he'd folded a big soft blankie for the pup to lie on. It was so fluffy! Ducky nestled right in, while Mr. Rogers slowly climbed into the front seat and put it into gear. It was a lot different than Ducky's mom's and dad's cars, but that was okay. Ducky still liked it a lot.

Ducky and Mr. Rogers stopped by the town's little coffee shop, and Mr. Rogers parked in a spot with a blue sign with a little stick man and a circle on it, and then the old man got out of the car before he helped Ducky out. Then they went inside together and Ducky had the best time ever! He liked it immediately; it was full of yummy and interesting smells, and he wanted to sniff everything, and he heard lots of fun sounds, like a little bell that went *tinkle tinkle* whenever someone came in the door. Ducky's mom, Christine, took him to coffee shops sometimes in California, but this one was different. It was smaller, and there were fewer people, but everyone wanted to talk to Ducky. The little pup loved when people said hi.

Mr. Rogers carried Ducky inside and set him on his own chair at a little table near the front of the restaurant, and Ducky waited, real patiently, until the old man came back with a cup of coffee in one hand and a little pup cup.

"This is for you, little guy," he said, setting the pup cup in front of Ducky, who lapped it up eagerly. It was so yummy, and Ducky ate it so fast he got whipped cream all over his face and even a little on his chest. Mr. Rogers laughed and helped him clean up with a napkin dipped in a glass of ice water a barista brought over when he saw Ducky was all sticky from the cream. It was worth it, even if Ducky didn't really like baths, because the pup cup was so gosh darn delicious. Ducky wanted another one, but Mr. Rogers said that it might hurt his tummy, so Ducky just chewed on the lip of the cup instead, which felt nice on his teeth.

Then a lady came over wearing a big yellow shirt. Ducky thought her name was Phyllis, but he wasn't sure. She had big fluffy gray hair, and Ducky liked it a bunch, and she wore lots of pink lipstick.

"Can I hold him?" she asked Mr. Rogers.

He smiled. "If the little man will let you, sure."

Ducky knew Mr. Rogers was talking about him because he called Ducky *little man* or *little guy* a lot, so Ducky wagged his tail to let her know it was okay. She grabbed the pup in her arms and held him real close, and Ducky laid his head on her because she felt so warm and nice.

"I have a grandson," she told Mr. Rogers, "who loves Harry Potter." She sniffled slightly. "They moved, and I miss them to pieces. My son got a great job offer over in Australia, so they set up house there two years ago. I haven't seen them since, but my son sent a picture of my grandbaby in his Halloween costume . . . and he dressed up just like Harry Potter." She gave Ducky an extra tight snuggle. "I was thinking about him this morning, but this sweetheart cheered me right up." She paused, looking at Mr. Rogers. "Thank you."

"You're welcome," Mr. Rogers said. "He's a good little man." And then he winked at Ducky.

Phyllis put Ducky back on the chair, where Ducky wagged his tail again to let her know how happy he was that she gave him a big hug, and the barista came over and gave Mr. Rogers a big, fluffy cinnamon roll that smelled so good. Ducky wanted to eat it and sniffed really loudly and stuck out his tongue so Mr. Rogers would know he was feeling extra hungry about it all.

"I don't know if cinnamon would be good for you, buddy," he said, digging in with his fork, but a little later he snuck Ducky a piece of the dough that didn't have any cinnamon on it, and the dog liked it a lot.

The barista came back a minute later, grinning. He had a nice face, with lots of metal in it. Ducky liked looking at it. The barista had big holes in his ears too. He handed the pup a little crunchy bone treat, and Ducky ate it happily, and the barista didn't even get mad at the dog for leaving some crumbs on the table. He patted Ducky on the head too, and the dog loved it a lot, so he leaned in so the barista could scratch his ears.

It seemed like everyone in the restaurant came to see Ducky

and tell him how handsome he was—a guy with curly hair wearing a black outfit with a white collar; a pretty young woman who reminded Ducky a little bit of Layla, and the best person in the whole world, his mom; a man wearing a big old greasy jumpsuit that smelled like the insides of cars; and even a couple of kids who looked almost exactly alike, and smelled alike, too. One of them grabbed Ducky a touch too hard and yanked on his fur with a sticky icky hand, but Ducky understood kids did that sometimes, so he didn't even growl or whimper. Their dad pulled the boy's hands off Ducky's fur and apologized a lot, but the pup wagged his tail to let them know it was okay and he understood.

By the time it was ready to go, Ducky didn't know who was more sleepy, him or Mr. Rogers, but on the way home Ducky fell asleep on the fluffy blanket on the passenger seat, and then they went inside and Mr. Rogers fell asleep in his big recliner with flowers on it, with Ducky in his lap. And they slept almost the whole time, even though Mr. Rogers woke Ducky up a few times with his snoring. The pair stayed that way until Layla got back to pick Ducky up, and the little Yorkie was so excited because he wanted her to know everyone complimented his outfit, so he was extra happy that she let him wear it. Ducky hoped she let him wear another one soon because he always had the best time. Plus, it made Ducky think of his mom because Mom and Ducky always dressed up and went places together and had the best day ever. Ducky was pretty lucky because he *always* had the best day ever.

Ducky hoped the next day was the best day ever too.

CHAPTER 8

Christine could skate circles around Layla. Not just metaphorically, either. Christine was literally skating circles around Layla, while Layla was struggling to stay upright on the narrow blades. She'd already fallen once, and suspected she'd have a nice bruise blossoming on her knee by evening.

Three weeks had passed since Christine had first dropped by with the little dog, and she'd come back for the weekend to spend time with Layla and Ducky, since they'd never really gotten to have their girls' weekend, so Layla had taken her to the town's little indoor skating rink—a strange, whimsical little feature for such a small town. Layla was surprised it was still running, even if it had limited hours and regularly took community donations. The thing that kept it going, she surmised, was when the folks from Lincoln and Omaha came in to have holidays parties there, often paying extra for catering from local restaurants for the authentic small-town feel. They did hayrack rides through the town square and ended the evening at the local pub, where they were poured hot toddies while Mariah Carey's "All I Want for Christmas Is You" played through the old jukebox on repeat.

"Bend your knees," Christine suggested, skating backward beside her friend, while Layla shuffled stiffly on the ice, trying desperately not to topple over. "Try to keep your ankles and hips aligned with your head, but don't stick your butt out."

Layla tried to follow her friend's instructions but caught her toe on the ice. She shuffled along for a minute, her ankles bending painfully, and then sprawled out, face-first.

Christine stopped and bent down. "You all right?" she asked.

Layla pushed herself up, grunting, her cheek throbbing where she'd hit the ice. "Not hurt enough to bow out yet. Unfortunately." She grabbed the outstretched arm Christine was offering and hauled herself awkwardly to her feet, where she managed to find a wobbly balance on the two metal blades. "I don't understand how you're so good at this. Were you born on the ice?"

"Basically," Christine said, "I'm the girl from *Frozen*." She let go of Layla and did a small jump into a pirouette to prove it. "'*Let it goooo, Let it goooo!*'"

"I guess the cold never bothered you anyway," Layla grumbled, rubbing the red spot where her cheek had met the ice.

"Let's go over to the barrier. You can hang on to it, and I'll give you advice."

Layla shakily skated—if you could even call it that—over to the side of the rink, where she held on to the barrier, moving slowly. Her legs trembled with the effort of trying to stay upright.

"Loosen up a little," Christine advised. "Your feet are too close together. If you let go of the rail, you'll fall." Her tone was firm but kind, and Layla tried her best to listen.

"Okay," she said, letting her breath out slowly.

"Feet shoulder-width apart," her friend instructed. "Don't forget to relax. You don't want to lock your knees."

"There's so much to remember," Layla said, trying to keep her knees bent—but not too bent—and her feet in the right space. But it was hard—and ice was, well, slippery.

"Pretty soon you won't even have to think of it," Christine said encouragingly. "Now, small moves. Little ones. One foot forward, and then the other." She demonstrated, but it looked . . . easy. Effortless. Flawless. The exact opposite of what it really was. Christine had told her to relax, but Layla's whole body felt like one tight muscle. She couldn't help it.

Christine skated along in front of her, occasionally taking a break for a quick toe loop jump or a spin, but came back to encourage Layla, who could feel her face turning red from exertion. She really should have . . . well, tried skating before attempting to skate with her professional friend. It had been a pretty dumb move on her part. Plenty of people in town would have gladly given her a lesson so she wouldn't have completely embarrassed herself. That being said—Christine and Layla had gone through middle school, high school, and even college together. It definitely wasn't the first embarrassing thing she'd done in front of Christine. She remembered some college parties she wished she could completely erase from her memory.

"Need a break?" Christine asked.

Layla nodded, and Christine helped her off the ice. They sat down together on the bleachers, and Christine waited for Layla to catch her breath.

"Sorry I'm a crappy skating buddy," Layla said.

Christine giggled. "I'm not friends with you for your skating skills."

Layla pretended to be horrified. "What? You're not? Are we friends based on"—she paused dramatically—"actual respect, kindness, and a genuine fondness for each other?"

Christine stared at her in mock horror. "Ew. No. I'm using you for your money. Obviously."

Layla laughed. "Don't forget my dog-sitting skills."

"That too."

Christine leaned back, resting her elbows against the bleacher behind the one they were sitting on. "This is nice," she said. "Don't get me wrong—I love LA. I love California. But this"—she motioned around the rink—"there's nothing like this."

"No ice skating rinks?" Layla asked. "I mean, have you tried Google?"

Christine shoved her. "Shut up. You know what I mean. It's

like . . . everyone calls Nebraska a flyover state. Maybe it even is. I don't know. But being here—at these little places, that someone so obviously put their whole heart into—is just different."

Layla knew. It was why she'd stayed, why she'd poured her whole heart into teaching in a small town when she could have easily gotten a ten- or even fifteen-thousand dollar raise by moving to a bigger city. But the cities didn't have . . . whatever the small Nebraska towns did. Living in a small town was like being part of some kind of . . . unbreakable chain, where everyone depended on each other. Loved each other. Watched out for each other. It was cheesy, Layla knew, but she understood what Christine was saying. There was some sort of intangible difference that made it special. Maybe even better.

But she always knew not everything about small Nebraska towns was perfect. It wasn't a Hallmark movie, where the biggest problem was whether Aunt Julia had stolen her fruitcake recipe from someone at church. Small towns could have poison in them too.

"Can I ask you something?" Layla asked, hesitantly.

"Sure." Christine was reaching down, loosening the laces on her skates.

"What was it like for you?"

"What was what like?"

"Growing up here. In Nebraska."

Christine sighed. "Honestly, overall, it was great. I had so much fun. I knew, even when I was in high school, that I wasn't going to stay here forever. I knew I wanted to travel, and get into fashion, and do big, wild things that filled my life with color. But I also knew . . . I was happy. I had a great family. I had great friends and neighbors. I had people I loved spending time with who could walk into my house and grab a snack out of the cupboard and we wouldn't even blink. We stayed up late at night playing Nintendo 64. We were . . . all friends. Even when we were mad at each other."

Layla nodded. "Was it ever—*not* good?" She was hesitant. She wasn't completely sure how to ask what she wanted to ask.

Christine studied her. "What do you mean?"

Layla forced herself to look at Christine, to stop herself from fidgeting and address her friend directly. "I have a Taiwanese kid in my class. He's sweet but super quiet, and he won't interact with anyone. I'm really worried other kids might be bullying him because he's the only Asian kid in class. I—I haven't seen anything, but . . . I guess I was wondering if you had experience with anything like that." Layla's cheeks were flushed, although for an entirely different reason than they had been the day before with Garrett. She wasn't sure why it made her nervous to ask one of her best friends about the issue—probably because she was worried that Christine might think she wasn't doing enough to protect Lucas. But that was precisely why she needed to ask—to do whatever was necessary to protect him.

"Do you mean did I ever experience racism?"

Layla shifted uncomfortably. "Yeah, I guess."

"Of course I did. If you're Asian, or Black, or pretty much any minority—of course you do. People are always going to be assholes."

Layla stared at her friend. She wasn't usually so blunt. "How did you deal with it?"

Christine shrugged. "You just did. It sucks, and it's wrong, and it should never happen—but if you're lucky, you don't even have to stand up for yourself, because someone else—someone who understands what's happening—will do it for you. Sometimes, I was lucky enough to have friends who did that, but sometimes, the worst kind of people will corner you when you're alone, or they intimidate you so you panic and forget everything you would want to say to stick up for yourself. And that's the worst."

"That's what I'm worried about." Layla paused. "I think I need to watch Lucas more closely. Something's going on, and I hope it's not racism, but . . ." She trailed off.

"You said he's the only Asian kid in class?" Christine asked.

Layla nodded.

"Yep. You have to watch out for him," Christine asked. "It sucks that you have to do it, and it sucks that it's on you to make sure it's not happening . . . but think how much it sucks for Lucas."

"Way worse."

"Way, way worse. Think about someone hating you for what makes you *you*."

Layla searched for words, but she didn't know what to say. "That sucks," she said finally, knowing her words were completely and utterly inadequate.

Christine nodded. "It totally sucks." She stood up and extended her hand to her friend. "Time for round two. Back on the ice."

Layla groaned. "Why? Haven't I injured myself enough for one day?"

Christine laughed. "Get at least one more good fall in," she said, and just like that, she was gone, floating across the ice like some sort of snarky winter butterfly.

CHAPTER 9

Lucas was hiding.

He did it a lot, Layla realized. Now that Garrett had moved from teaching a few lessons to fully taking over the class with a few minor pointers here and there, she had the opportunity to watch Lucas a bit more closely. She tried to look up from her notes often, or look over a book she was reading, or do a million other little things so it didn't look like she was staring at him all day. And she found out a lot about him . . . fast. Mainly, that whatever was going on was probably worse than she'd thought.

As soon as the recess bell rang, Lucas had the same routine that he painstakingly and unfailingly followed: he very, very slowly put all his things in his desk, one by one—papers first, then pencils, then crayons, and finally, anything else that he might have out— like his big pink eraser or his ruler. All the other kids had run out the door in a wild, energetic herd, fighting over jump ropes and sidewalk chalk and rubber four-square balls, before Lucas even stood up from his desk. He'd push his chair back to stand, and then, meticulously, put it back under the desk, making sure it was perfectly centered. Then he would walk, very slowly, toward the door, sometimes stopping to pick up a bit of paper on the floor and dropping it in the trash. When he reached the doorframe, he would pause, leaning forward, looking left and right—like he was checking to see if the coast was clear, his shoulders slumped and posture defensive—before taking a few slow, tentative steps outside. Then, he lingered in the hallway until the monitor spotted him and scooted him out the big double doors with the rest of the kids.

And he went like he was walking a plank. Like he was going into battle. Like he was going to the dentist with twelve cavities and no numbing agent in sight.

He was being bullied. Kids who weren't being bullied didn't act like that. Layla hated herself for not noticing it sooner.

"It's like he's waiting for someone to jump out at him," Layla told Garrett. "He's so skittish. The poor kid is terrified."

Garrett agreed, although, with him taking charge of the class, he'd had less time to watch Lucas. "Either he hates fun or he's avoiding someone," Garrett said. "Recess is the best . . . so I'm going to go with the latter." He was cleaning off the dry-erase board with wide, strong swipes, getting it ready for the next lesson, and Layla sat at her desk, entering grades into her computer. She hated this part. It was boring, so it was nice to talk to someone to pass the time. Garrett was good company and an excellent distraction, even when the subject matter wasn't her favorite. She'd realized she actually liked having him around. He was funny and thoughtful and smart.

And attractive. Obviously.

"But which kids are mean to him?" She watched him scrub at a particularly tough spot. For some reason, red marker was especially difficult to erase, which was why she normally stuck to blacks and greens and blues. She should have warned him before he taught an entire reading lesson using a red Expo marker. "I haven't seen a single kid actually . . . do anything. They just . . . ignore him. Which is also awful. Poor kid. He must be so lonely."

Garrett paused, thinking. "I honestly haven't seen a thing. I mean, if he wasn't acting so scared . . . I'd just think the kid was quiet. Wanted to keep to himself. But as far as bullies? I mean, Teddy's the biggest kid," Garrett pointed out.

He wasn't wrong. Teddy Sullivan towered over the other kids. His dad, Phillip Sullivan, was a former Nebraska Husker who played right guard and then went on to play a half season for the Los Angeles Rams before blowing out his knee—so he came back, like lots of Nebraska kids did, to take over the farm. Phillip was a bit of a local legend and coached the high school football team even though he wasn't a teacher. They were good, too.

"You're not wrong. But Teddy's the sweetest," Layla argued. "He goes out of his way to be nice to everyone and get them things off the high shelves they can't reach. Last year, Ellie Parker got a horrible nosebleed at recess, and everyone ran away, pointing at her, but Teddy sat by her, rubbing her back, until the teacher on recess duty came over."

She reached into her desk and pulled out a bottle of cleaning fluid. "Here," she told Garrett. "Catch." She tossed the bottle over to him, and he caught it easily and sprayed it across the red splotches the marker had made on the board.

"Thanks," he said. "So not Teddy. Another boy?" He balled up paper towels and set back to scrubbing.

Layla lifted a shoulder. "Not necessarily. All genders are sort of equal about bullying at this age."

He sighed. "Can we put a body cam on the kid?"

"Might be a tad obvious," Layla said.

"But there's gotta be cameras on the playground, right?"

"Yeah," Layla said, "but you need to have a really good reason to look at them, and they're checked out really officially, like you're researching a crime or something."

"What kind of reason?"

"Well, we can't pull it to see who called who a poo-poo head, or who cheated at hopscotch. It has to be . . . heavy. Like, a reason to suspect physical violence or sexual assault."

Garrett paused. "Wait. Please tell me we don't have that."

She shook her head. "I hope not."

When Lucas came in after recess, Garrett called on him, twice, to ask him to read aloud from the class's favorite book—*The Magic Treehouse*. Her kids loved it, and Garrett had even asked Lucas to read a paragraph. The first time, Lucas just ignored his turn to read and put his head down on his desk, and the second time, his words were so quiet, Garrett had to ask him three times what he'd said. By the second time, the other kids were snickering, and Garrett finally gave up to spare him further embarrassment.

And then it happened.

Out of nowhere, Emma Richards, who had been happily waiting for her turn to read, turned around and puked, *Exorcist* style, over the row of desks behind her. It was the kind of violent, projectile-type vomit mainly reserved for horror movies. The kind that usually required a possession of some sort. The kind that was less of a spill and more of a . . . spray.

And the smell. The *smell*. It was like rotten eggs and diapers and something else so absolutely putrid that Layla couldn't quite put her finger on what it was—and honestly, she wasn't sure she wanted to. It was the kind of smell that attached to your brain and hung out in your nostrils for hours—days—years. Layla stared in horror for a snap of a moment—and then sprang into action the way only a teacher of small children could.

First, she had to refrain from puking, and had to refrain from . . . well, all the other kids puking. Five years ago, before she'd started, apparently some third graders had had such a horrible vomit chain reaction they'd had to air the classroom out for an entire week and hold class in the music room. Even when Mrs. Edison, the third-grade teacher who witnessed the event, had been allowed to move back in, the vomit smell hung in the air, like a stale reminder of the horrific event. Mrs. Edison had retired at the end of the previous school year, at age forty-nine, and there was a rumor she'd taken early retirement because she'd never fully recovered from the barfathon. Mr. Berger, who moved in to take over the third graders, still swore he occasionally got a whiff when the air-conditioning kicked on.

That *could not* happen. Layla could not spend the rest of the year in a puke room. She would not survive it.

She clapped her hands, twice. "Kids!" she shouted. "Look up here!" She grabbed the neck of her blouse and pulled it over her nose. "Pull your shirt over your nose, now, and line up at the whiteboard, facing the door."

She glanced at her student teacher.

Poor Garrett. Poor *green* Garrett. He clearly hadn't realized second graders could just puke on an absolute dime, so he'd frozen at the front of the classroom, a copy of *The Magic Treehouse* hanging loosely from his hand, his face a petrified mask of horror. She could see his Adam's apple moving in his throat as he swallowed, hard, over and over. He was about to retch. She could tell.

She'd reacted similarly in her first puke event, so she could relate.

"Garrett," she said, her voice calm and steady. "Cover." She raised her nose to her hand to demonstrate.

He slowly covered his nose with his hand, gagging behind his fingers. His eyes had begun to water from the stench that was permeating the air, and reeking its way through the fabric of Layla's shirt. She had to act fast.

Swallowing her disgust, Layla hurried over to Emma, putting a hand on her back, where she thankfully had no splatters of sick. She rushed her toward the door, stopping only to point out the kids who had been hit by the spray and pull them out of the line. "Wash off in the bathroom," she instructed to kids. "Now. Go."

They scurried out of the classroom and into the hallway, in various states of repulsion. Aiden, a short blond kid with perpetually messy hair, actually looked a little awestruck, like he might have wanted to stick around a bit longer. He loved gross things: boogers, bathroom jokes, puke. He'd tried to bring a half-squashed spider to show-and-tell once.

Beside Layla, Emma was whimpering slightly, sick clinging to her hair and dripping down her pink Care Bears T-shirt. "Come on, sweetheart," she said softly. She looked up to Garrett, who was leaning heavily on the wall.

"Take the rest of the kids out to the playground until I come get you," she instructed. She raised her voice. The kids were starting to look sick, and one of the Drubbins kids was making heaving noises in his throat. "Line up at the back of the class, kids. It's time for surprise recess. Garrett has a fun game planned for you!"

She looked pointedly at Garrett, who nodded behind his hand, looking relieved he had an excuse to exit the classroom behind the kids. "Let's go!" he shouted, his voice a touch weaker than normal, and hustled them out the door and toward the playground. He looked happier to leave the classroom than they did.

Layla helped Emma dab at her face with a paper towel she'd grabbed off the countertop near the back of the classroom and steered her through the hallways to the nurse's office. The little girl looked awful—pale and clammy and embarrassed and altogether miserable. Poor kid. Layla had noticed she hadn't looked quite like herself when she got to school that morning, but if she were to send home every kid she'd suspected of being slightly ill, she wouldn't have had a class. Second graders were a notoriously germy bunch.

They stopped outside the nurse's office, and Layla knocked and peeked through the glass in the upper half of the door.

"Thea," she called, her voice calm. "We have a little bit of an issue."

The nurse, an older woman with a soft cloud of gray hair that seemed to always be floating about her a bit ethereally, waved her in calmly and took Emma from Layla, helping her onto a paper-covered cot and bringing over a trash can, in the event Emma might be sick again. Thea smoothed Emma's mussy hair and wiped her face with a cool washcloth. "It's okay, sweetheart. We'll get you fixed right up," she said, completely unfazed.

"Can you call her mom?" Layla asked. "There was a bit of—a

mess," she said. Understatement of the year, of course. "I need to go check on the kids I sent to the bathroom to wash off and get Earl on cleanup duty."

Thea nodded. "Of course," she said, standing up to clean the washcloth. "I'll get you on your cell phone if I need anything."

Layla paused, kneeling down at Emma's beside for a moment. "Feel better soon, okay, Emma?"

Emma nodded, her face pale. "Sorry," she whispered hoarsely.

"Honey," Layla said, "Don't worry about it. It's okay. We all just want you to get better." She hoped fiercely it was true, and that Emma wouldn't be known as Pukey Pants for the rest of the school year. Or at least until another kid blew chunks and earned an even worse nickname.

Emma sniffled.

Layla smiled gently, bid her student goodbye, and then was off: her next stop was Earl's office. He was the janitor, and while he was reasonably good, he also spent a lot of time with his boots on his desk, watching Bob Barker–era reruns of *The Price Is Right*. Still, he earned his pay when cleanup duties like this one came up, Layla didn't begrudge him a single episode. In fact, she thought he deserved a few more breaks, honestly.

"Earl?" she said, leaning on the doorframe. "We've got a red alert."

Earl followed her back to start cleanup in the classroom, and Layla checked on the kids she'd sent to the bathroom, making sure they were relatively clean and dry before sending them out to play for the rest of the day while Earl worked. She made a mental note to send the janitor a gift card or some cookies. Finally, she joined Garrett on the playground, sighing heavily. She sat down on a swing.

"How's it going?" she asked him.

He swallowed hard, but he looked a little less green. "Is it . . . does that . . . does it happen a lot?"

Layla laughed. She couldn't help it. Here she was, thinking there wasn't a single thing that she could teach Garrett, that he couldn't already do well, but here she was, completely handling a situation that Garrett couldn't. She had admit . . . it made her feel kind of good.

"You mean go full *Exorcist* and spew partially digested pea soup all over the classroom?"

He sat down next to her, putting her elbows on his knees. "Yeah. That."

She laughed. "I mean, I'd say twice a year. On average."

He nodded. "That's . . . a lot."

"You okay?"

He chuckled dryly. "Just rethinking my career choices over here."

"What happened? Did you fail your projectile-vomit training in college?"

He shook his head. "I must have skipped that one."

She laughed again. "This was good practice for you. You gotta get used to it before someone actually pukes *on* you and you have to hold it together."

"That happens?"

Layla nodded. "It's just a matter of time. Stick with me, kid. You'll get it figured out."

"Is it too late for me to go work construction with my brother?"

She patted his shoulder. "It's never too late. But then we wouldn't have these moments together."

Layla had meant it as a joke. But Garrett turned his head and smiled—a nice, thousand-watt smile. One that lit him up in a way she'd never seen. And she realized she liked it, even if it wasn't the most professional. But still, she withdrew her hand quickly. She shouldn't have patted him like that. It wasn't appropriate.

But Garrett was still smiling. "I guess it's worth it, then," he said.

And, in spite of everything—the little flame of jealousy, the little voice in the back of her head telling her to *be professional, walk away*, her best intentions—she smiled back.

CHAPTER 10

DUCKY

Ducky woke up early.

Well, technically, Layla got him up early and dressed him in another of his very favorite outfits: Harry Styles. He liked it because he got to wear these little blue-flower sunglasses and an orange knit tank and it always made him feel extra handsome and pretty. Mom let him watch Harry Styles once so he knew who he was dressing up as, and he had to say, Harry Styles was very stylish. Which is probably why Mom chose to dress Ducky like that. Every day, she told Ducky how handsome and stylish he was. So it made sense she would dress Ducky up as someone super handsome.

Layla fed Ducky a few nibbles of treats, and then they sat together while she watched a yelly television show, with a lot of people on a sandy island, kissing and then yelling and then kissing other people and then yelling some more. She sat on the couch, cross-legged, and ate her cereal. Ducky wanted to drink the milk out of the bowl, but Layla said no, that it might give him a tummy ache, so Ducky pouted for a minute, but then he remembered he was wearing his Harry Styles outfit and decided to be happy again. So Ducky sat with her and kissed the tip of her nose, which made her laugh. Ducky liked when she laughed. It sounded like she was happy-barking. She laughed a lot louder than his mom, and the first time it kind of scared him, but he felt a lot better about it now that he knew she wasn't really barking at Ducky.

Then, when Layla was done watching the yelling people on the TV, she put Ducky on her couch and took pictures of him in his outfit. "We're going to send these to your mom," she said as she held up her phone. "She is going to be very proud."

Ducky did his best to pose and look handsome, and Layla called him a good boy, and he wagged his tail.

When she dropped Ducky off at Mr. Rogers's house, the pup ran inside and jumped up on the old man's leg to say hello, wagging his tail like crazy. Mr. Rogers let Ducky outside in the backyard and let him play in the flower garden. He had lots of pretty flowers in all kinds of colors, and Ducky loved running around in them. The other day, the pup rolled around and had so much fun and smelled all the smells. Mr. Rogers came out and scolded him a little bit for getting so dirty, but he was laughing while he said it, so Ducky didn't think he meant it. Then he took the pup inside, sat him on the countertop by the kitchen sink, and he ran a washcloth under warm water and wiped all the dirt off his tiny paws. Ducky closed his eyes and sighed happily because it felt so nice. Mr. Rogers whistled while he cleaned him off. Mr. Roger liked to whistle. Sometimes he even sang, but he wasn't very good at it.

When Ducky was sleeping on one of the chairs (Mr. Rogers said he couldn't stay out in the garden), there was a big loud sound—*knock knock knock*! The sound echoed through the house. Ducky jumped right up and barked as loud as he could to save Mr. Rogers from whoever was outside, probably trying to get him. The Yorkie even growled just in case it was someone scary. He wanted them to know that there was a ferocious, brave dog there to protect Mr. Rogers, because he was Ducky's friend. Mom said Ducky was too small to be a guard dog, but Ducky thought he was still a pretty good protector. Once Layla even told Ducky he had a big spirit for such a little dog. Ducky wasn't totally sure what she meant, but he liked it a lot. Then she laughed her loud happy laugh and smiled and kissed Ducky's forehead. Then she gave him lots of butt scratches. Ducky *loved* butt scratches. They were his favorite!

Ducky had a lot of favorites.

They were lucky though, because it wasn't anyone mean at the door or someone trying to steal Ducky's treats. It was just a tall man who wore a blue shirt. He came in with a happy smile that showed his teeth and gave Mr. Rogers a big hug and brought in lots of bags of groceries that looked really heavy. Ducky was so excited he went and sniffed the big paper grocery bags, but it was mostly green big leafy vegetables that tickled his nose when he smelled them, so he didn't ask for any. The man definitely didn't bring Ducky any treats, that was for sure. Maybe he forgot. Or maybe he didn't know about what a good boy Ducky was. But he patted Ducky on the head, and the dog gave his best cute face that no one could resist. Ducky bet he remembered some treats for next time. No one could resist Ducky's cute face.

"Hi, little guy," the man said, crouching down to give the Yorkie a scratch under the chin. "What's your name?"

Ducky closed his eyes, enjoying the pets. Ducky could tell immediately the man was a dog person, and he approved of him. It was weird, but most dogs could smell goodness in people, and Ducky could tell the man was good just like Mr. Rogers was good and like Layla was good too.

"This is my little buddy Ducky," Mr. Rogers said, and Ducky thought he was kind of proud. "I've been watching him for one of the neighbors. He's been keeping me company during the day." He turned to the pup. "Ducky, this is Randall."

Ducky looked up at Randall and wagged his tail, jumping up and down with excitement. Ducky loved meeting new people! And if Mr. Rogers liked this guy, Ducky thought he liked him already. The new guy looked close to Ducky's mom's age. Maybe a little older. Sometimes Ducky was bad at telling how old humans were.

"Is he a lot to handle for you?" Randall asked him, still crouched down. "I know getting around is a little tougher than it used to be, and you haven't been using the cane I bought you." Ducky recognized a note of concern in Randall's voice. It was the same tone Ducky's mom used when she asked him if he ate something he shouldn't have. Like when Ducky snuck people food after his mom told him no. Or when she asked Ducky's dad if he stole some of her favorite candy. Jason liked to take a piece, and he thought his wife wouldn't notice, but she always did.

"Eh, I'm fine," Mr. Rogers said, flapping his hand as if to wave the question away. "Plus, this little guy is great company. He's easy. We watch TV, we eat, we sleep. A few days ago, we went into town. He was dressed as a little wizard boy with glasses and the black cloak. Harry . . . Harry something . . ." He trailed off, frowning.

"Harry Potter?"

Mr. Rogers snapped his fingers. "That's it."

"You? Went into town?" Randall stared. "You don't . . . do that a lot. Unless you're visiting the shelter or volunteering."

"I wanted to get out. Walk the little guy. It's good for him to get fresh air. Plus, he wanted to show everyone his outfit." He looked at Ducky proudly, in the same way Ducky's mom and dad looked at the Yorkie every day.

Randall stood up, still looking down at Ducky. "Yeah," he chuckled. "I noticed he's dressed as—who is that? Harry Styles?"

"Harry who?" Mr. Rogers asked. He walked over to the couch and settled in heavily.

"Never mind," Randall said. "Listen, I noticed you need a refill on your metformin. Do you need me to call that in? And have you been checking your blood sugar like you should? The doctor said you need to keep an eye on it."

Mr. Rogers shook his head. "No, I think I already did."

"Check your blood sugar or call it in?"

"Call my medicine in."

"You *think* or you *know*?" Randall asked him.

"You worry too much about me, son," Mr. Rogers said. "I've been taking care of myself for years. When Cindy was sick, I took care of her too."

"I know," Randall said, suddenly a little sad. "I miss her."

"Me too," Mr. Rogers said, and Ducky could almost hear his heart breaking. He could smell sadness and pain in the same well he could smell goodness. Ducky stood up and walked over to Mr. Rogers, leaning against his leg, so he knew Ducky was there for him. Mr. Rogers reached down and put a hand on the little dog.

The two talked, and Ducky settled at Mr. Rogers feet, listening to the comforting murmur of their voices. The pup tried to stay awake, but Mr. Rogers lifted him up and set Ducky in his lap, and the Yorkie was so comfy and warm and snuggly he dozed right off. Before Ducky knew it, Mr. Rogers was shifting him off his lap and pushing himself off the couch to stand.

"Lunch break over, eh?" he was asking Randall.

"Yeah," Randall said. "Can't be late back to the new job."

"How is it?"

Randall shook his head. "It's . . . good. But different than I expected. I'll have to tell you about it soon, when I have more time." He paused. "It's good to be back, though."

"It's good to have you back," Mr. Rogers said. "Now go. Don't be late on my account.

Randall leaned in and gave Mr. Rogers a big hug. He hesitated, looking at Ducky, and then back at the old man. "You look . . . happier."

Mr. Rogers smiled down at the dog. "I am."

CHAPTER 11

"I don't know you do it," the paraeducator, Reina, said. "You must have an iron will."

"Putting up with Vomit Fest? I know, right? I've never wanted to turn in my notice more. Maybe I should be an accountant. I don't think accountants have to deal with surprise projectile vomit."

"Well," Reina considered. "Maybe at tax time. But that's not what I'm talking about." She swept her bangs—an elegant fringe that perfectly finished the look of her sharp bob—backward, out of her eyes, fixing Layla with a stare.

Layla was excited to have Reina back. She'd taken an extended vacation to Peru—she had family there—but now she was back to help out in the classroom, and Layla realized how much she'd missed her para. Reina was one of her best friends in Two Falls, and with Garrett teaching, it gave them time to stand at the back of the classroom and quietly catch up while he held the kids' attention.

"Then what are you talking about?"

She nodded toward the front of the classroom, her arms folded across her chest and a knowing half smile curving her lips. Garrett was standing up at the front of the classroom again, in the middle of a geography lesson, pointing out where Two Falls, Nebraska, was on the big map of the USA—and then pulling down the big world map to show the students where he had been deployed. She couldn't help but notice the muscles in his forearms as he held the pointer and moved it around the map.

The kids were impressed. They were always impressed with Garrett. And Layla had to admit, grudgingly, she was impressed, too, some of the time. Well, most of the time really. Almost all the time, if she was being honest.

Reina was watching her closely. "You won the student teacher lottery, you know," she whispered.

Layla flushed, realizing she'd been caught staring at him. And also realizing that Reina was going to be exactly like Mrs. Sanchez about Garrett. She bit back a smile she could feel forming on her face.

"Yeah," she said quietly. "He's quite talented. I'm lucky. I don't need to mentor him much, really."

Much beyond how to deal with a rogue puker. Emma had returned to class, the color back in her cheeks, and Garrett had showed up the next day. Best of all, Earl had done a bang-up job cleaning the classroom, and the smell was completely gone, replaced by the strong, chemical scent of cleaning supplies. She'd gotten in early to open the windows to get some air circulation in the room so none of the kids would get headaches, but it was better than all the vomit.

"I'm not talking about his teaching skills," Reina murmured.

"Reina Douglas!" Layla said, pretending to be shocked. "Need I remind you, you're married? And you have been for five years? To a *doctor*?"

Reina grinned and lifted a hand to admire her ring, which was simple and elegant. "Married, not dead, my dear Layla. Plus, if you see a beautiful piece of art, do you ignore it because you bought a painting from HomeGoods a few years ago? Or do you stop and admire the painting, even though you're perfectly happy with the one you have at home and have no intention of buying the new one and hanging it in your living room?"

Layla snorted. "Are you really comparing your husband to a painting from HomeGoods?"

"What can I say? I'm a true lover of the arts."

Layla stifled a giggle. Reina was head over heels in love with her husband. They actually lived in Brimsley, and most of Two Falls drove to the neighboring town whenever they needed to see a doctor. But Reina loved her job in Two Falls, and so while most of the town drove to see Reina's husband, she woke up three days a week and drove to Two Falls, where she spent time with the kids. She couldn't have any of her own, so she'd decided to spend as much time with students as possible. She was good at her job. Great, really. She'd helped Layla through her first couple of years of teaching, offering guidance and a listening ear . . . and a healthy dose of humor, which Layla had desperately needed.

"You have to admit he's beautiful," Reina hissed in her ear.

"He's . . . attractive," Layla said very quietly. "But he's my student teach—"

"Attractive?" Reina cut her off, her voice a little too loud for the back of the classroom. "Excuse me? He's like a lumberjack Theo James."

A couple of curious heads flicked back toward them.

"Shhhh." Layla held a finger to her lips.

Reina crossed her arms across her chest. "Whatever. I'm not wrong."

"I'm not sure I see it," Layla said, but she was lying. She could *totally* see it. But she was *at work*, in a position of power over this guy, which felt a little silly when she considered how much bigger he was than her. The day before, she'd lifted up on her tippy toes to reach a new box of markers that morning, and he'd just—reached over her and grabbed them. Feeling him behind her, close enough she could smell his aftershave, had made her feel oddly nervous, but not in a bad way. In a way that made her smile without meaning to.

Absolutely not, she'd told herself.

"You're absolutely no fun," Reina said, as if reading her friend's mind.

"You're absolutely failing the Bechdel Test."

Reina rolled her eyes. "Whatever. He doesn't work for me." She eyed him appreciatively. "But I'd like him to."

"Reina!" Layla hissed.

Reina shrugged. "What?"

She was hopeless. Layla flushed darker. "Hey, um, can we talk in the hallway for a minute? I need to ask you something."

"Am I in trouble? I'll dial it back, I swear."

Layla shook her head. She didn't believe her friend for a second, but she couldn't be mad at her. "Nah. Just need to run something past you." Also, she'd have been lying if getting Reina to shut up about Garrett hadn't also been a little bit of her intention. Knowing Reina, she'd accidentally blurt out something completely embarrassing in front of Garrett, and then Layla would be embroiled in some kind of sexual harassment lawsuit and never work or see Garrett or her classroom again. She'd have to sell her little house and move away from her little neighborhood and live in some dingy old apartment, hiding in shame.

Or maybe she was just being dramatic.

Layla nodded to Garrett at the front of the classroom and pointed at the door to let him know he was fully in charge for a few minutes. She quietly led her friend out in the hallway, and they walked together to the teachers' lounge—which was less of a lounge and more of a room of old, mismatched chairs with stuffing sticking out of random bits, a Formica table, a kitchenette, and a glowing red Coke machine where the teachers could still get a cold pop for sixty cents. The teachers' lounge was thankfully empty and quiet save for the low hum from the fridge.

"What?" Reina asked, thumping down into an orange chair and putting her feet up on a green ottoman. "Let me guess. You guys have already kissed, and you're secretly hooking up, and you want me to be the maid of honor in your wedding."

"What?" Layla asked. "No. No way. I want to talk to you about Lucas." She sat down opposite her friend, choosing a yellow chair with a spring that usually snagged her clothes. Someone, though, had thoughtfully put a piece of duct tape across the seat, saving Layla's already meager wardrobe from further destruction.

"Sure," Reina said. "What's up?"

It was impressive, Layla had to acknowledge, how quickly Reina changed. How quickly she snapped from funny, quirky woman to serious educator. She loved kids, and she cared about them a lot. She would have made a great teacher if she ever wanted to commit to being full-time.

"What's your experience been with him?"

Reina looked thoughtful. "Not a lot. He's quiet, and he tests well, so I haven't really had a reason to work with him."

Layla nodded. It made sense; the paraeducators at the school generally worked with kids with special needs. Lucas, although incredibly quiet, usually got great grades, and his work was always done meticulously for a second grader. Other second graders had wobbly handwriting that took time to decipher, but Lucas had a steady hand, and wrote wide, strong letters—the opposite of his personality. It was odd, to say the least. But Layla had learned not to praise him too much or too often in front of the other students—he became incredibly, painfully embarrassed.

"I know this is a bit out of the ordinary, but do you have the bandwidth to keep an eye on him? I'm worried about him."

"Sure. But why?"

Layla told Reina her concerns. "I'm scared for the kid," she confessed. "I don't know if it's because he's the only Asian kid in the school, or his timidity makes him an easy target, but I'm worried. I know someone's causing problems for him. I just don't know . . . who."

"Would it be better if I pulled him out of class? Worked with him one-on-one to build his confidence?"

Layla sighed. "Honestly, I don't know. I'm afraid of doing anything that draws any more attention to him. He's trying so hard to fly under the radar."

"Can I make a suggestion?" Reina asked. She plucked at some of the fluff sticking out of the arm of her chair.

"I mean, yes. That's sort of the point of the conversation."

"Shut up," Reina said, throwing a bit of stuffing at her.

Layla batted it aside, laughing. "Stop," she said. "We don't have much of these poor chairs left."

"Seriously though. Have you had Lucas talk to the counselor? To make sure nothing is going on at home?"

"Well, yeah. He has regular sessions with the counselor already, and I have check-ins with her. I really don't think it's his parents. I called them a couple of nights ago, and they were concerned but said Lucas hadn't said anything at home except that he often doesn't want to go to school—he pretends to be sick or begs to stay with his mom." Layla paused. "It's something *here* he's scared of. The way he goes out to recess—it's like he's going to war. He's terrified of someone out there. And when I talk with the counselor—well, she just says he's shy, and to work on drawing him out of his shell. But he won't really talk to her either."

"He might be triggered by something from his past," Reina pointed out. "It's not always rational."

Layla considered. Maybe Reina was right. Maybe it wasn't something happening at school after all. "I guess I could make an appointment with Mr. Bonilla?"

Reina nodded. "And do it during recess. If Lucas doesn't want to be outside anyway, it'll draw less attention than you pulling him out of the classroom."

"Good idea," Layla said. "I'll talk to Mr. Bonilla later." She paused. "Hey—I don't suppose you've heard anything about the plant closing?"

Reina sighed. "Yeah, I have. I don't know if it's true. You know these kinds of rumors pop up every few years. Maybe there'll be some cuts, but it usually stays open."

"I hope so," Layla said. "I . . . don't know what'll happen if it closes."

"Yeah. Especially since they donate so much to the school."

"They *what*?"

"The library? The free lunch program? The new playground equipment? You think the school just bought those things on their own?" Reina shook her head. "It's community donations. And trust me when I say—it's ninety-nine percent the plant and probably one percent the bake sale that the church ladies hold in the gymnasium each year."

If she was being honest, Layla hadn't really thought about it. She'd assumed the money came from the state. It wasn't that she hadn't known that money for the school was tight—they were always facing budget cuts of some sort—but she hadn't realized how much the school had depended on the community to keep the doors open.

She found herself feeling strangely sick in a way that started deep in her stomach and reached up to her throat—a heavy, choking feeling.

If the plant went—all that went away too, effectively wiping out any chance the small-town school had at survival.

The plant would die. The town would die with it. And the little life Layla had built would be swept away.

CHAPTER 12

It was Saturday.

Layla lived for Saturdays. They were her favorite. They didn't have the sad, tainted feeling of Sundays, and she had energy—unlike Friday, when all she could do was fall on to her couch, turn on the TV, and slowly decompress from her week. That was the thing about being a teacher: she always had to be *on*. Having Garrett around made things easier in some ways, sure, but being in his presence was a whole extra stressor.

First of all, every straight woman—and some of the men—in the little school were half in love with him. Teachers were literally making excuses to stop by her classroom on their breaks. He definitely had most-eligible-bachelor status, and even Mrs. Hudley, who was seventy and taught fifth grade and had been claiming to be ready for retirement for the past twenty years, had stopped, put on her thick glasses that hung from a chain on her neck, and declared Garrett "a damn fine specimen of a man."

"Okay," Layla had said. "But do you think I can use the microwave?" She'd been standing in front of Mrs. Hudley with a rapidly thawing Lean Cuisine, the corner of the thin plastic covering already peeled back.

"Oh, sure, sweetie," Mrs. Hudley had said, moving out of the way. "You just keep an eye on that young man, you hear?"

"Well, he's my student teacher, so, you know, that's . . . my job."

Mrs. Hudley had patted her shoulder. "Well, let me know if you'd like to take my fifth-grade class for a day. I wouldn't mind a change of view."

Layla had stared at Mrs. Hudley as she'd shuffled off, smiling at Garrett, who was standing awkwardly by the door of the teachers' lounge, looking frozen and completely, entirely uncomfortable, as she passed him with a knowing smile and left the teachers' lounge, humming to herself.

"Sorry," Layla had told him as they sat down to eat together. Garrett had made himself a sandwich and packed a bag of potato chips, which looked more appetizing than the sad mess of odd-shaped meat loaf in Layla's plastic tray. She pushed at it with her fork.

He'd shrugged. "I guess if I need a date this weekend, I can drop by her classroom."

Layla had stolen one of his potato chips and threw it at him. "Shut up, Garrett."

"Are you jealous?" he'd teased.

"I mean, wouldn't you be?" Layla had shot back.

"I'd be green."

Layla had laughed. Their conversation was less stilted, easier. But it wasn't like she was comfortable around him. Sure, it would have been easy if he had been anyone else's student teacher, but he was hers, and she needed to keep her boundaries very carefully drawn. She could like him professionally. She could spend time with him at work. She could banter with him, but she could *not* take it too far.

And so, on Saturday, she couldn't feel a little . . . well, sad . . . that she wasn't going to see him. She'd gotten used to his company, his steady presence, his thoughtful questions about the students and his lessons and how seriously he took his work.

Although, she had to say, she was not feeling sad about stretching out on the couch. Ducky had curled up on her stomach—a bit reluctantly, because he seemed to be a little upset with her because she'd cut him off from eating a bunch of treats that morning. He was ready to dive into the whole bag, and then he'd whined at the fridge when he'd gotten a sniff of the leftover steak sandwich inside. Garrett had picked it up for Layla when he went out on his lunch break a couple of days ago.

It had made her laugh, to see a dog dressed as a mermaid so visibly pouting. He was a character, that was for sure. She'd never met a dog like him.

"What do you want to do today, Ducky?" she asked her tiny friend. But he was still pouting over the sandwich. Normally, he'd lick her face, or at least wag his tail, but he turned, so his booty was facing her, and made an exasperated little *harrumphing* noise.

"So you don't want to hang out with me?" she asked him, reaching out to pet him.

He stood up and moved off her stomach, settling on her legs. He turned slightly to give her a look that very clearly said, *Leave me alone.*

Layla sucked in her lips to keep from laughing. Ducky was obviously offended and wasn't afraid to show it. Christine had warned her that Ducky had an attitude at times, but Layla hadn't been prepared for how much the dog would understand—and be able to communicate back to her. Ducky was a special boy, that was for sure, and she respected his strong personality—especially because his funny tantrums made her laugh.

"I gotta run some errands, little guy," she said. "Do you want to come?"

Ducky jumped down from the couch and trotted into her bedroom without looking back.

"Guess not," she sighed. She pushed herself off the couch. She hadn't had time to make herself look presentable, but that was fine—she just had to run to the grocery store. She needed a few things for herself, but the store had a very tiny pet section that had rubber-bone toys, and she'd thought that maybe she could get back into Ducky's good graces through bribery—the kind that didn't involve giving him a tummy ache with too many treats.

She got into her car—her old Bronco that made a very suspicious banging sound whenever she started it—tucked her hair into a messy bun, and backed out of her driveway. She turned off her little street and made a right toward downtown. She was almost to the store when she saw someone running on the side of the road—someone very tall and very built, and definitely someone who was not from Two Falls.

Garrett.

He stopped running, pulling his earbuds out, and waved to her. She realized, suddenly, that she'd slowed down without meaning to. She flushed, her heat beating in his chest. What was she, some kind of creepy stalker person? What kind of woman slowed down to check out a man running? Who was she, Mrs. Hudley? Reina? What kind of boss was she?

Layla felt her pulse quicken further as panic set in, making sweat pop up on her forehead. Was it rude not to say hi? Should she just pretend like she didn't see him? Was it professional to roll down her window? Did she look like she was trying to . . . pick him up?

Garrett walked over to the car, grinning. She rolled down her window, praying he couldn't tell what a complete mess she was.

"Um, hi."

"Hi," he said, his smile widening. Like he was happy to see her. Which was a professional courtesy, she was sure. There was absolutely no reason why Garrett should be happy to see her, not when he probably had a hot model girlfriend stashed away somewhere. Guys like him always did.

Not that she was thinking of him like *that*.

Except she was.

"Do you—need a ride?" she asked, and then immediately kicked herself. Of course he didn't. He was just getting some exercise in. If he'd wanted a ride, he would have . . . driven a freaking car. Obviously. She was so stupid.

"Nah," he said. "Just out for a quick jog before it gets too hot."

"Just making sure you're not stranded. You know, they say it can take a full one to two minutes to walk across this town. I don't know how people do it."

He laughed. "It's a struggle."

"One hundred and twenty seconds of solid physical activity," she deadpanned. "I'm not sure I'd survive."

"Well, you know, pray for me," he said. Garrett paused, lifting up his arm to push back the sweaty hair that had fallen in his eyes. "What are you up to today?"

He's only asking to be polite, she reminded herself. *He doesn't really care.*

Layla leaned toward him conspiratorially. "Do you really want to know? Do you think you can handle it?"

He nodded, seriously. "I think so."

"I'm . . . going to go to the grocery store. And later, if I don't fall asleep bingeing reality TV and it's not too warm, I might mow my lawn."

He stared at her.

"I know, right? Your mind is blown right now. How could my coworker have such an exciting schedule? How does she get it done? How does she balance her intense social schedule with such a demanding job?"

He nodded. "I'm still processing." He tapped his temple. "It's a lot to take in."

"I know," she said. "but it's who I am."

He lowered his voice, leaning in further, resting his arm on her door where the window was rolled down. "Can I tell you something? But you have to swear on your life to keep it completely, absolutely secret?"

She nodded. "I'm a vault."

"I love bad reality TV."

She fake gasped. "How could you? I thought you were a gentleman and a scholar!"

He shrugged, lifting his hands, palms up. "It's a facade," he said. "I spend my nights with the Real Housewives and my cat, Lola."

"No you don't."

"I do. Ask me anything." He was smiling now, like he was enjoying their exchange.

"Who's your favorite New York housewife?" she demanded. "Of all time, I mean. They don't have to be on the show anymore."

"Easy. Luanne. She's hilarious."

"Beverly Hills?" she shot back.

"Lisa Vanderpump."

"*Vanderpump Rules*?"

"Oooh, curveball—but I have to say I've always liked Katie."

She nodded. "You're correct, sir. You are no gentleman and scholar. You're . . . infinitely more impressive than I thought.'"

He grinned at her. "I do what I can." He paused. "Hey, can I take you up on that ride? If you don't mind a sweaty man in your car? I feel like I've run around this town a million times. Not sure if I need another lap."

She found herself reaching across and opening the door so he could climb in. "If you're brave enough for the Bronco."

"Another test?" he asked.

"The biggest one."

He climbed in, patting the door affectionally. "I like it."

"You better," she said. "Betty and I have been through some hard times. Like college. The 2020 presidential election. The time when the Stop 'N Shop was out of Diet Dr Pepper and I had to get Diet Coke for two full weeks."

"Those are the best types of cars," Garrett acknowledged.

"So where to?" Layla asked. "Need me to drop you at your house?"

He shook his head. "If you're good with it, I wouldn't mind tagging along to the grocery store. I was hoping to grab a few things to get me through the week."

She stared at him, surprised. What? He wanted to go to the grocery store with her? Didn't he get enough of being around her during the week? Was this acceptable student teacher behavior?

It wasn't like a date or anything, she reasoned. He probably just wanted to get his shopping done and didn't want to take the time to run home and get his own car. He was only being efficient, and it had absolutely nothing to do with the fact she was insanely, undeniably attracted to him and got a weird feeling low in her stomach whenever he got too close.

"I mean," she said, "you must have heard about the sale on frozen pizzas too."

"I did," he said. "But I'm more of a ramen noodle guy."

"Teacher staple. Respect."

He laughed. "Rite of passage."

She grinned. She liked seeing him. It was too easy to fall into easy banter with him that bordered on flirting, which made things . . . complicated. She was almost relieved after they went into the grocery store and briefly went their separate ways.

Layla found herself almost immediately in the frozen food section after she'd grabbed a twenty-four-pack of Diet Dr Pepper, a bag of baby carrots, and a bunch of arguably unhealthy snacks. It was hard to cook for one, and if she was being honest, she didn't particularly enjoy cooking either, so she tended to get a lot of take-out and frozen pizzas.

She ended her trip in the candy aisle, which she had promised herself she'd skip, and ended up with a bag of Lindor truffles. The kind with caramel inside. She couldn't resist.

She was reaching for a bag of fun-size M&M's that she would use to reward kids for good behavior when Garrett caught up to her. She looked down at his cart.

It was overflowing. And it wasn't like hers, with various packaged snacks and frozen meals and easy things—it was, well, healthy. He had ingredients, so apparently he . . . actually cooked. He had a variety of fresh fruits and vegetables, and chicken and ground beef and quinoa and spices and eggs and yogurt and even a bag of flour.

Layla was pretty sure she did not own and never had owned an actual bag of flour.

"Well," Layla said. "One of us is an adult."

"What?" he asked.

She nodded at his cart. "Cooking for the wife and kids, huh?" She looked at him smiling. She was digging. She couldn't help it.

He laughed. "I eat enough for a whole family. Hazards of being six foot five."

Huh. So he ate alone. Maybe he didn't have a girlfriend.

She scrutinized him. "You're literally not six foot five. There's no way."

He nodded. "Way." He looked at her cart, and grinned. "Going with the old college recipes, huh?"

"What can I say? I'm loyal. Also, I'm efficient and value my time."

"And, pray tell, how do you use this time when you're not in front of an oven?"

"The way any productive human spends their spare time. Expanding my mind. Learning. Growing. Expanding my knowledge of other cultures and experiences."

"So, reading?"

She snorted. "I thought we discussed this. Bad TV. Obviously."

He laughed loudly, startling an old woman pushing a cart two aisles over. "A woman of the arts, I see."

"Would you expect anything less?"

"Absolutely not," he said. "You're a gentlewoman and a scholar."

She grinned without meaning to. Damn it, she liked him. She liked him . . . well, a lot. Whenever they talked, she found herself bantering easily with him, actually enjoying his company. And, perhaps even worse, she found herself more attracted to him with every stupid smile. Every laugh.

And that was not acceptable. Not at all.

But whenever he was around, she forgot all her worries. She didn't think about the school losing money. She didn't worry about her job, or her house. And she wasn't lonely. It was hard for her to admit, because she'd built up a nice little life for herself where she was happy and content 99 percent of the time, but . . . with Garrett around, it made the last little missing puzzle piece all the more obvious. It hurt suddenly, strangely. She spent most of her life ignoring it. She had built her world around pretending that last little puzzle piece didn't exist, filling it in with other pieces that weren't quite perfect but fit well enough—a hobby here, a trip there.

Layla didn't have a family. And besides a couple of friends . . . she really didn't have anyone. She was alone . . . and she had been, for a long time. She was okay with that. She had to be okay with that. And the little piece of her heart that had opened after being closed for a very, very long time would just have to deal.

"Ready to go?" she asked, suddenly, ending their banter. It was like a dark cloud had set over her. Garrett had seemed like the answer to her problems, but he couldn't be. Even if they could be together—who was to say he was interested? He was smart and accomplished and lovable and handsome and would be moving away for another job in December, when the semester ended, and it was already early October. No one stayed in Two Falls. Why would they? The town was dying.

He nodded at her. "Yep," he said, as if he'd sensed the sudden shift in her mood. "Let's go."

CHAPTER 13

DUCKY

Ducky was a frog.

Well, he wasn't really a frog. Frogs had warts and made little ribbiting sounds, and Ducky was still a dog. Although sometimes Ducky thought maybe he was a person, but mom reassured him he was her puppy. But then his mom called him her son, and Ducky got confused. Could he be both? Maybe his mom was the one who was confused.

It was Sunday, and Ducky didn't really know what that meant except that Layla went to church and then she spent the rest of the day at home with him. Sometimes Ducky's mom, Christine, came to see them on Sunday, but she'd called the previous night on Layla's phone and talked to Ducky. The dog could see her face, but he knew she wasn't really there, because there was no way she could fit in a phone. Ducky spun in a circle to show her his frog outfit because he thought he looked super fancy. The hoodie he wore had round eyes on the top. Layla had giggled when she dressed him that morning and made frog sounds.

"Hi, sweetheart!" she said. "I love you! You are such a handsome little froggy!"

Ducky barked to let her know he loved her too. She made his heart so happy.

"I'll be back so soon, I promise! Be good to Auntie Layla!"

She blew Ducky a kiss through the phone, and Ducky licked the screen. Christine laughed.

"He's being great," Layla assured her friend. "He's super well-behaved."

Ducky looked up at Layla, wondering if she was going to tell his mom that he got into the treat bag after she said no more last night, but she winked down at him. Whew. Auntie Layla was good at keeping secrets.

"What are you guys doing today?" Mom asked Layla, who lifted the phone back up to where she could see Christine a little better.

"You know," Layla said. "The usual. Probably will have to bail Ducky out of jail again by the end of it."

"Let me know how much that is," Mom responded. "I'll Venmo you."

"Common occurrence?" Layla asked.

Mom shrugged. "Monthly. That's why Ducky has to be an influencer. To pay his bail bond bills." She paused. "Is that what they're called? Bail bond bills?"

Layla cracked up. "I'm going to buy him a little striped jailbird outfit."

Mom paused. "Wait. Have you *converted*? Did I or did I not hear you say that dressing up dogs was—what was it—absolutely ridiculous?"

Layla pretended to hear something in the distance. "Oh, I'm sorry, I think someone's at the door. I probably have to hang up—"

"Shut up," Mom said, laughing. "I just wanted to say—"

"You told me so," Layla cut in.

"I told you so."

Ducky barked. He knew Auntie Layla would come around too.

"How's skating stuff going?" Layla asked. "Your doggy would love to see you."

"I know. I'd love to see my doggy." Mom sounded sad. "I'll try to come back soon, if that's okay. I don't know exactly when, with my schedule, but soon."

"Of course," Layla said. "Any time. And you know I was kidding. I like taking care of Ducky. It's nice having someone around. He's good company." She smiled down at the pup, her eyes all soft and kind.

Ducky leaned on her leg to let her know he liked being around her too. It was like having a bonus mom. Not that anyone would ever replace Ducky's mom or his dad. But sometimes he felt sad for Layla. He never once heard her to talk about her mom or dad. She wasn't married to anyone because there was never anyone else at her house. And other than his mom, no one had ever stopped by when Ducky was there. It was almost like she didn't have any close friends, besides Christine and maybe Mr. Rogers.

It made Ducky feel scared for her. He wanted to go back home with his mom, but he also worried about what was going to happen with Layla and Mr. Rogers if Ducky wasn't there. Mom said Ducky's job was to be adorable all the time, but sometimes Ducky thought he was put in the right place in the right time to take care of people. And sometimes . . . well, sometimes he thought Auntie Layla needed him most of all.

CHAPTER 14

Layla was downtown with Ducky. He had been so excited to leave the house to go on an adventure, so she couldn't bear to leave him behind, even though the weather had a bite and he had cuddled eagerly into her arms as soon as the cold wind had whipped around them. The wind in Nebraska was like nowhere else; it blustered through town and straight to her bones. The small buildings in downtown blocked the wind a little, but they were too short and squat to do much.

Downtown in Two Falls was tiny, no more than a couple of blocks, where most of the shops were snuggled together, side by side. It looked like a street from a Hallmark movie, something that aired during the holidays, that always put Layla in the mood for hot chocolate with melty marshmallows and a peppermint stick, even though it wasn't quite time for the holidays.

Layla loved downtown. She loved the Christmas lights in winter that cast a soft glow on the white snow. She loved the crab apple trees that turned the street pink in late spring. She loved sidewalk sales in the summer, when all the shop owners pushed wares to the streets and everyone came out to shop, even if they didn't need anything, just to support local businesses.

But this day was a little . . . *different.* There was something in the cold wind that wasn't usually there. Layla couldn't quite put a finger on it, but she didn't like it. It made her uncomfortable. She was glad Ducky was with her, and she snuggled him tighter. He laid his little head against her neck, as if to remind her he was there, and she almost immediately felt warmer.

Ducky was dressed as Piglet from Winnie the Pooh. He had been making Layla snicker all morning, because he was entranced by his piggy ears, which kept flopping over in his face. He kept trying to bite them and then ran around her living room in circles, chasing after them but never quite catching up to them. She finally grabbed him and pushed the ears back, but even now, he kept flopping them forward and snapping at them. It made her smile in spite of the grimness of the day.

Even though the strange mood permeated the downtown, people smiled at Ducky when she walked with him cradled in her arms to protect him from the cold wind, her purse tucked under her shoulder. Susan Lynn, who had the day off from the café, stopped and kissed Ducky on the head, greeting him like an old friend.

"Is something going on?" Layla had asked.

Susan Lynn glanced down the street, where the plant, a large, concrete building, loomed over the town. "Yeah," she said. "Rumors about the plant closure got out. The news station is here."

"The Lincoln one?"

Susan Lynn shook her head. "Nah. Just the Brimsley one. I'm not sure if we're big enough to reach the Lincoln news."

Layla nodded. That made sense. Even a few people in Brimsley were employed by the plant. It wouldn't just hurt Two Falls. If the town was abandoned, then Brimsley lost a lot of business and a couple of jobs.

"Everyone's down there," Susan Lynn said, looking toward the plant. "People have signs and everything."

"Is it a protest?" Layla said.

Susan Lynn started walking toward the plant, which was only a few blocks off Main Street, and Layla followed, still holding

Ducky. She had a leash for him, but he took tiny steps and got tired quickly—he was, after all, a small dog.

Susan Lynn laughed in a way that suggested there was nothing funny about it. "I'd call it a small-town demonstration."

Layla hesitated. "Is it really happening?" Layla asked. "I mean, is the plant really closing down?"

Susan Lynn shrugged. "I sure hope not, but the word is still spreading like it is. And Jarvis closed its plants in Michigan already. And you know what they say."

"Where there's smoke . . . there's fire," Layla said dourly. Jarvis Incorporated owned manufacturing plants all over the Midwest, and a couple in the rural northeast.

Susan Lynn nodded seriously. "My husband's been looking at jobs up in Lincoln. He has an interview for a forklift operator." She stopped walking and looked at Layla. "I don't want to leave, but he'd get five dollars more an hour if we move up there. And the tips in Lincoln are better too."

Layla wanted to beg her to stay. If Susan Lynn was considering leaving, then there were probably a lot of others considering pulling up roots too. Every person who left the town was a loss, one more felled tree in a dying forest. But instead, she smiled, as honestly as she could, and took Susan Lynn's hand.

"You do what's best for your family."

Susan Lynn swallowed hard and nodded. "I'm trying, Layla. I don't want to leave, though. No one wants to leave."

The whole town was at the plant. Or at least it seemed that way. Theo was there, handing out hot teas, and a couple of people even held signs, made with Sharpies.

DON'T KILL OUR TOWN!
SAVE OUR JOBS!
CORPORATE GREED RUINS LIVES!

They weren't marching or yelling. There weren't enough people for that. But they were standing, quietly, behind the reporter as he recorded his bit, motioning toward the plant as he spoke. Layla couldn't quite catch all the words, but it was something about Jarvis Incorporated reporting record losses, despite the plant being reliable and a pillar of the Two Falls community.

"I wonder if the company is going to make a statement," Layla said aloud. The reporter was finishing up now and taking his microphone off his shirt.

Susan Lynn shook her head. "I highly doubt they'd give such a small news station the time of day. And they can't really say anything if they haven't told the employees, can they?"

"Corporations have done worse," Layla murmured. She glanced toward the plant. There was no sign of any spokesperson emerging, no one to acknowledge the reporter or the people gathered outside. It was quite a crowd for Two Falls.

She spotted Isla Myers-Perkin, Anita's mother, standing in the crowd. She waved at Layla, and Layla smiled and waved back. Sometimes seeing her students' parents outside of parent-teacher conferences felt strange, but then it just reminded her how much she had at stake if the town went under.

"Maybe they won't shut down," Layla said with as much hope as she could muster, but as she did, she overheard the reporter talking to the photographer, who was shaking his head, a storm cloud of an expression on his face.

"They already cut all their donations to the school," the reporter was saying, rubbing his chin. "I suppose the plant closing is the natural next step."

Layla's heart dropped into her feet and broke into a million pieces.

"What?" she demanded. She pushed forward, holding Ducky tight to her chest. "I'm sorry, what? Did you say Jarvis is no longer donating money to the school?"

The reporter looked up at her. "Yeah," he said. "They cut fifty percent of their philanthropic spending this quarter."

"But to this school? Here in Two Falls? Or to some other school?"

The reporter hesitated. "Well . . . from what I've heard . . . they've cut funding to the school here."

"What does that mean?" she asked, feeling a little desperate. "How is the school supposed to survive?"

"I'm sorry," the reporter said. "I'm afraid I don't know that much about it. That might be a question for your administrators." He hesitated again. "Do your kids go to school here?"

She shook her head. "I'm a teacher."

The reporter held her eyes for a moment, his expression kind. "I know this isn't . . . good news." He paused. "I'm sorry."

She tried to smile, but it felt tight and wrong. "Me too," she said, but her chest was caving in.

Ducky, ever sweet, licked her chin and cuddled her extra tight, like he was trying to tell her it was going to be okay.

Except it wasn't.

CHAPTER 15

"There's been talks of budget concerns for year," Layla said quietly. The kids were at lunch, and Garrett and Layla had decided to stay in her classroom to eat while grading math homework. She sat on one side of her desk, and he on the other. She'd cleared spaces for them to put their lunches among the homework, and Garrett had brought brownies for them to share. Homemade brownies, too, not the ones from the box, which were the only kind of brownies that Layla knew how to make.

"That doesn't mean it'll happen, though," Garrett said. "When I lived here before I left for college and the military, we talked about it all the time, but it never happened. The town always figured out a way to pull through."

"You're from here?" Layla asked, raising her eyebrows.

"Sort of," he said.

"How?" she asked, intrigued. "I don't know any Hendersons here. I thought I knew the whole town."

He shrugged. "It's only my granddad now, and as he's gotten older he keeps to himself more. But yeah, I went to school here and everything. I think there's still a basketball trophy in the gymnasium with my name on it." He smiled slightly. "Not that there was a lot of competition."

She stared at him. "How did I not know this?"

He didn't meet her eyes. "It's not that important."

"Do I know your parents?" she pressed. "Are they still here?"

He suddenly stood. "I—I just forgot. I have to run down to the teachers' lounge. I'll be right back." His voice was strange— not unfriendly, exactly, but intensely uncomfortable. He stood up from his chair and rushed out, leaving her alone in the classroom. She stood up with him, trying to apologize, but he was already gone.

She frowned. What had she said? Did she do something wrong? She tried to follow him out, but he wasn't in the hallway, or the teachers' lounge, like he'd said. In fact, it seemed that her student teacher had disappeared. Her heart hopped up into her throat. She should have known better. Here she was, pushing him about his background, when she had no background to speak of. Or, at least, nothing she wanted to talk about. But she was used to people who loved to talk about themselves, who spoke of moms and dads and sisters and brothers and extended family and husbands and children. She usually asked a lot of questions so they didn't have time to ask about hers.

People around Two Falls opened up easily. They were trusting. They liked sharing parts of themselves.

And up until now . . . well, she'd thought Garrett was the same way.

She should have used the time while she waited for him for lesson planning, or grading, or making notes on Garrett's lessons where he had the opportunity to improve. But she couldn't. Instead, she sat alone at her desk, staring at the empty chair on the other side of her desk, at the half-eaten sandwich he always cut down the center instead of diagonally, at the Ziploc bag he'd prepared for her with two brownies, because he told her she needed to try something besides packaged food.

Suddenly, strangely, she found herself wanting Ducky. She wanted his calming presence, his cute little barks, how he pawed at her when he wanted something. She hadn't realized how . . . comforting he was. How she'd come to rely on him so quickly. But Ducky wasn't there; only the loud ticking of the classroom clock, and one moment of static through the loudspeaker when Mrs. Andersen, the administrative office manager, had probably accidentally leaned on the button when she leaned over to get something out of her left-hand drawer. (It happened a lot.)

But he didn't return until the bell rang.

He came in with a throng of kids practically hanging off him. Benny Eaton-Palmer held his elbow tightly, both hands clasped around his arm, and Anita was trotting in front of him, chatting happily about something or other (probably her goats).

Layla smiled at him when he came in, trying to let him know she was sorry without saying anything, and he smiled back at her, but it was a bit strange and empty, like there was nothing behind it, and it crumpled her heart a little bit.

Lucas dragged in slowly just after the rest of the kids, and right before the bell rang. His eyes were, perhaps, more downcast than usual, and his thin shoulders were slumped. She sympathized. His posture reflected her mood.

It wasn't until afternoon recess when she was alone with Garrett in the classroom again.

"I'm . . . sorry," she said haltingly. She still hadn't touched the brownies, and he'd swept his lunch back into his bag while the students were working on their reading, in one quick motion while Emma Richards was stumbling through her read-aloud assignment from *Rabbit & Bear*.

"It's fine," he said. He came toward her, resting a hand on her shoulder. The light touch sent a strange shock through her body, like a lightning strike to her core. She looked up at him, into his soft eyes, with slight crinkles around the corners, and found herself strangely overwhelmed, so she dropped her head and looked away, out the window—where Lucas was sprinting, full tilt, across the playground, a crowd of kids running after him. His face was a mask of terror.

She stood up from her desk, her chair slamming in the back wall, the bookshelf next to her desk rattling, and Garrett hopped back, surprised. She was out the door before he could ask her what was going on.

She heard his footsteps running after her, but she stopped for only a moment at the doors to swing them open. Lucas was doubled over on the pavement outside the entrance, his hands on his knees, panting heavily.

The kids chasing him were nowhere in sight. She wasn't even sure who they were. She'd been focused on Lucas, on getting outside and stopping it. She cursed herself for not noticing. She would have known who was bullying him. And by the looks of it . . . it was a lot of kids.

She opened the door carefully. "Come inside, Lucas," she said, putting a hand on his back to guide him through the door.

She walked him quietly back to the classroom. He was breathing heavily, and there were big tears trembling on his eyelids, threatening to overflow.

Layla sat him down gently in Garrett's chair, and she sat next to him, grabbing the chair from her desk. His head was bent forward, and a couple of tears landed silently in his lap.

She let him sit quietly for a moment, while she stayed with him. Garrett handed him a box of Kleenex.

"I'm going to go grab him some water," Garrett volunteered, smiling gently at Lucas before leaving the room. Layla knew what he was doing. Garrett was giving Layla the space to talk to Lucas. To try to get him to open up, one-on-one. Crying with one adult around was embarrassing. Crying with two was mortifying. So Garrett—kind, sweet Garrett—was trying to make it easier on him.

"Want a brownie?" she asked. She pushed herself off the floor and grabbed the Ziploc bag Garrett had brought her that morning that she'd had no appetite for at first. He didn't answer, so she opened the bag and handed him one. She took the other.

"Brownie cheers," she said, and touched the corner of her brownie to his.

She took a bite, and he sniffled quietly and then followed suit.

"Oh, my gosh," she said, leaning her head back on the painted cement blocks of the classroom wall. "This is amazing. Isn't this amazing?"

Lucas nodded and took another small, polite bite, and then another. "It's really good," he said, finally, a chunk of brownie stuck in his teeth.

She smiled at him. "It is."

She let him eat a little longer, and then, an idea came to her. Ducky made her feel better. Would he help Lucas in the same way?

"Wanna see something?" she asked, fishing her phone out of her pocket.

He nodded, holding his brownie with both hands, his fingers sticky with it.

She opened Instagram and typed in Ducky's handle: @Ducky theYorkie. "This is my friend," she told him. "He's a very special dog named Ducky. He's a Yorkie, and his job is making people happy on the internet."

Lucas leaned over to see her phone better. She smiled at him and started scrolling through Ducky's pictures and videos—Ducky playing with his brother, Katsu; Ducky with his head tilted at the camera and his tongue lolling out of his mouth; Ducky, sleeping in Layla's bed, covers tucked up around his shoulders, with his little paws sticking out.

"Do you know him?" Lucas asked finally.

Layla almost jumped up with joy. It was literally the only question Lucas had ever asked, in all the months she'd been his teacher.

She nodded, forcing herself to respond calmly. "Mmm-hmmm. He's staying with me right now."

Lucas looked at her, incredulously. "Really?"

"See? I even took this picture." She scrolled down and showed him a photo of Ducky dressed as Harry Styles.

"Wow," Lucas breathed. "Is he . . . a nice dog?"

She nodded. "He is very nice and cuddly. He loves snuggling with people."

"Where is his mom?" he asked.

"Well, she's a professional figure skater and travels a lot for a living, so I told her I'd take care of him."

"Who takes care of him during the day?" he asked. "Does he just stay at your house?"

Layla's heart was beating with excitement. She couldn't believe it. After months of trying, she was having a real conversation with this kid. And he didn't look sad, or terrified, or blank—he looked interested. He looked . . . happy. Like a normal, well-adjusted kid.

"He stays with a sweet old man named Mr. Rogers, who takes very good care of him, and then I pick him up at night. I walk him and feed him, and then he snuggles up on my pillow and goes to sleep with me."

She handed Lucas her phone, and he scrolled through the pictures, smiling. His fingers left brownie crumbs on her iPhone screen, but she didn't care. He could ruin her phone if he kept talking to her.

"Do you want to talk about what was happening outside?" she asked.

His fingers froze on the screen of her phone. He didn't say anything for a long time, and then finally, said one short word.

"Tag."

She hesitated. "It didn't look like it was very much fun, Lucas. And it's not very fair when everyone is it and you're the only one being chased."

He shrugged. His fingers resumed scrolling, determinedly, as if he were making a strong effort to ignore her.

"Do you want to tell me who was chasing you?" she said gently.

He shook his head. "It was a game."

Layla's heart sank.

Garrett came back and handed Lucas a bottle of the store-brand water that was sometimes stocked in the teachers' lounge. It was strangely oily, and Layla really didn't like it, but as a teacher, she really didn't get much of a choice when it came to freebies. Layla had even taken some old, stale chips home to tide her over between paychecks.

"Thanks," Lucas said. Good. He was still talking. He uncapped the water and took a sip. Garrett sat down on the floor with him, and Lucas handed the phone back to Layla.

"I see someone's been eating my brownies!" he said warmly. "Lucas, do you want me to bring you more? They were my grand-ma's favorite recipe."

Were.

That meant his grandmother wasn't here anymore.

Lucas nodded. "They were really good," he said. He turned to Layla. "Thank you for sharing."

"Any time," Layla said.

"I'll tell you what," Garrett said. "I'll make more this weekend, and I'll be sure to save one for you. Sound good?"

Lucas nodded. He paused. "Do I have to go back outside?"

Garrett glanced at Layla, as if telling her not to send him back. But she wouldn't have done that, anyway. It would be like throwing the poor kid into a den of lions.

"No," she said. "It's almost time for everyone to come back, anyway. Why don't you just hang out here until we're ready to start class again?"

He looked at her gratefully. "Thanks," he said.

She smiled at him, feeling a little sad. But at least she'd gotten somewhere with him: she knew, first, the other kids weren't be-ing kind to him. And she could work on that. He'd spoken, and smiled, and actually showed interest in something.

She let out her breath and looked up at Garrett, who was look-ing at her expectantly. She gave him a little nod.

Layla and Garrett could help Lucas. She knew it. And for the first time since she'd met Lucas, he made her feel a little hope.

CHAPTER 16

DUCKY

Something was different and Ducky was so so so so excited, he couldn't even stop wagging his tail and jumping up and down. Layla called him a hoppy frog, but she didn't dress him like a frog. Not that day, at least.

At first Ducky was kind of worried. Layla got up like usual, and stretched and yawned really big, and Ducky did too. He slept with her on the pillow beside her head. He liked sleeping close to her, and he wanted Layla to know he would protect her if anything happened. Sometimes she snored just a little and woke Ducky up, but that was okay. He usually licked her so she knew he was there to take care of her, and she woke up giggling.

Anyway, she got out of bed and picked Ducky up and set him on the floor. She made her coffee in a blue mug and took the little dog outside to go potty. Ducky loved her backyard. It was so happy and bigger than all the backyards Ducky ever visited in California. It didn't have flowers like Mr. Rogers's, but it had a nice big tree that Layla said was a cottonwood and a bench under a big umbrella that she always took inside when it got too windy. They sat outside, Layla on the bench and Ducky by her feet, and then her phone rang.

Layla answered it, her face pulled down. She smelled like she was worried. Worry smelled bitter, and Ducky didn't like it. He looked up at her and put his paw on her foot to comfort her.

"Hello?" she asked. "Mr. Rogers?"

Ducky perked up. Getting to see Mr. Rogers always made him so happy!

"Hi, Layla," he said. "Listen, I'm so sorry about this, but I can't take Ducky today."

"No problem at all . . . but is everything okay?" she asked. Her voice was worried too. She leaned forward on the bench and sat her coffee down in the grass by her feet. Ducky took the opportunity to lean forward and try it, but it was funny-tasting and yucky. Layla could have the rest of it.

"I'm just feeling a little under the weather today," Mr. Rogers said, his voice hoarse. "I got sick over the weekend, and I think I'm on the upswing, but I don't think I'm up to taking care of my little buddy."

Layla glanced down at Ducky and moved her coffee cup back up on the bench. "I'm so sorry. I heard it's going around. I had five kids out last week."

Mr. Rogers coughed, and it sounded strange and tight. "Yeah, I think I picked it up when I was downtown last week. I stopped by the coffee shop a couple of times."

"Can I do anything? Do you need me to run by the pharmacy?"

"You're a good kid, Layla, but no. I'll be okay. I think I just need to rest. My grandson got me a prescription from the pharmacy on Friday. I'm already feeling a bit better, I promise."

"Are you sure?" She sounded like she didn't believe him. Her voice had doubt in it, like when Ducky's mom asked if Ducky stole extra treats. Ducky didn't know why his mom bothered to ask. He *always* tried to sneak extra treats.

"I swear. I'll be okay to take care of the little guy tomorrow," Mr. Rogers assured Layla.

"Will you call if you need anything?"

"If my grandson can't come, absolutely."

"Okay," Layla said, but her voice was uncertain. Her fingers were drumming on her leg. "If you say so."

When she hung up the phone, she looked down at Ducky. "What am I going to do with you, little buddy?"

Ducky jumped up on her leg. He wanted her to take him to wherever she went every day. He would be so good all day. He would sit quietly and be so nice and sweet and wouldn't even bark unless he sensed danger or unless someone delivered a package or if he really, really felt like he needed to. Ducky was a guard dog, after all.

She dialed a number on her phone and waited.

"Hello?" a voice on the other end said. It sounded like a nice voice.

"Hi!" Layla said, her voice brighter than she really felt. (Dogs could tell these things.) "My dog sitter fell through—I don't suppose you have any boarding availability this morning?"

"Sure," the nice voice said. "We open at noon—the vet is making farm visits today."

"Well, shoot," Layla said. "I need to be at work at seven forty."

"Is there someone who could drop your dog by at noon?"

Layla shook her head before she even answered. "No, thank you though. I appreciate your help."

Layla bit her lip as she hung up. Her forehead was creased, and she looked even more worried. She reached down and scratched Ducky on the head. "What are we going to do with you, little guy? Do you think you'd be okay at home alone?"

Ducky looked up at her with big eyes and his cutest face to tell her he wouldn't be any trouble if she would please, please, please let him go with her. Ducky knew he'd be okay if she left him at home all day, but he would be miserable and sad and lonely. And he heard somewhere that one day for humans was like seven days for dogs, which meant he'd be all alone for almost seven dog days.

That was when Layla got a text on her phone. She said a bad word.

"Looks like Garrett's out sick today too," she said. "Shoot. I was hoping I could hide you under the desk while he taught." She scrooped Ducky up and took him inside, where she set him down in the kitchen. She put food in his bowl and refilled his water and packed her lunch.

Then, Ducky noticed, she slipped dog treats into her lunch bag. His heart leaped! He couldn't believe it! Unless she was going to eat his dog treats for lunch. Ducky wouldn't even blame her. His dog treats were pretty yummy, and he was okay with sharing. Well, maybe a little.

She went into her bedroom to change out of her pajamas into a nice outfit with a pretty blue shirt. Ducky liked it. Then it was time for his outfit: a new one that his mom sent—a cute little yellow plaid skirt and jacket set. Layla told Ducky he was Cher from *Clueless*. He didn't know who that was.

"You look extra cute, Ducky."

He spun to show her how pretty he looked.

And that was when she said them. The words he'd been waiting to hear since he started staying with Layla.

"I guess you're coming with me today, Ducky."

He was so excited he almost peed on her floor.

CHAPTER 17

Dogs weren't allowed in schools. Not unless they were service animals. Everyone knew that. Layla was pretty sure it was in the rule book somewhere, and in the education agreement she signed, and even posted on a door somewhere.

And yet, there Layla was, a cute little Yorkie in her tote bag, his head sticking out and his tongue flopping from his mouth. He was so excited. She could sense his energy. She just hoped he didn't go crazy or pee on the floor. She'd probably get in trouble as it was. At least if he behaved it would be less trouble.

Of course, Ducky was almost perfectly behaved at home. Sure, sometimes he barked a little, and he was always trying to steal food, but as long as the kids kept their lunch boxes sealed and in the cubby outside the door, there wouldn't be a problem. Except that Layla had never seen Ducky in a crowd of kids. But he was famous, right? He had to have been around lots of people before. And Ducky was still a media darling. That meant he probably hadn't peed on a reporter's leg. Plus, if Layla had really thought there was even the smallest chance Ducky would bite, she would never have brought him along. He was incredibly gentle.

She slipped into her room early, breathing hard. Whew. She'd gotten away with it.

"Excuse me? What the heck is that?"

Her heart jumped into her throat. She whirled around, and Ducky made a small whine of protest at the sudden spin.

"Sorry, buddy," she whispered, and then looked up into Reina's face.

Layla put her hand on her chest. "Reina, you scared the crap out of me."

Reina waved her hand at the dog. "Um, you scared me. What is this you're bringing into the school?"

"In some languages, this is called a dog. This one is named Ducky."

Reina put her hands on her hips. "Wow, Layla. Just wow. Of all the stunts you could pull."

"What?" Layla frowned. "You're not actually mad at me, are you?"

"You were going to sneak a dog into the school without telling me? What if I hadn't come by? What if I didn't get to say hello to this bundle of squishy cuteness? What kind of friend are you?" Reina reached for Ducky and pulled him out of Layla's tote. She held him up high and then kissed him right on nose. "Are you kidding me? Is he really dressed like Cher?"

"He likes it," Layla said. "He goes and sits by the bag of costumes if I don't dress him up."

"Well, he looks beautiful. What's his name again?"

"Ducky," Layla repeated.

"And why was this mean lady trying to hide your sweet face away from me?"

Layla crinkled her nose to keep from laughing. Reina was fawning over Ducky even more than she'd drooled over Garrett. "I was going to text you. Especially if Fishy was in the hallway."

Mrs. Fisher was a notoriously crotchety hall monitor who was especially hard on the kids. One time, Layla had to save one of the fifth graders who was getting a dressing-down because, according to Mrs. Fisher, his shirt hadn't been tucked in correctly. Layla had to admit, though, she did keep the kids in line when she was on duty.

"Oh, yeah, Fishy would have made you throw the dog away."

"They totally made an exception last year for Henry Slater's hunting dog."

"That thing was a puppy. And a fluffball. And they cleared it in advance. And the way you stole in here like a bank robber, I'm assuming you didn't clear it with Principal Crimmons?"

"Seeing as how I just found out his dog sitter is sick—no." Layla swallowed a sigh.

"Ugh. Everyone's sick. My poor husband is working day and night. And the pharmacy in Brimsley is almost completely out of cough medicine. The stock price of Kleenex is skyrocketing."

"Garrett's out too. He called me right after my dog sitter."

"Well, if he needs a nurse, he can call me." Seeing Layla's shocked expression, she backpedaled. "Come on, you know I'm kidding."

"But I'm his boss, basically. I can't . . . talk about him like that."

"Fine." Reina sighed. "You might tell him about the dog, though. Crimmons, I mean." Reina was busy rocking Ducky like a baby, and he had a sleepy, happy look on his face. "He will be way less mad if you loop him in."

"You think?"

"Unless you think your second graders will keep a dog in the classroom a secret. Which they couldn't. Because he's so cute."

"Don't steal him," Layla cautioned. "I'm dog-sitting him for my friend. She would murder me."

"Well, I'm not going to steal him in front of you. That would be a horrible idea. I'll at least wait until you leave the room." She rubbed Ducky's belly, and he grunted happily. "I'm gonna hand you back this little baby and then you need to run to the office." She paused. "Act like you're letting Principal Crimmons in on a big secret and then tell him your sob story."

"You think that'll work?"

Reina dumped Ducky back in her arms. "It's the best chance you've got."

Twenty minutes later, Layla was back in her classroom with Ducky trotting ahead of her on the leash. It hadn't been easy, and at first, Principal Crimmons hadn't been happy—his red face had been solemn and disapproving—but then Ducky had walked over and pawed at his leg, and the ruddy principal had turned from stone to putty. He said Ducky could stay—but only for the day, and only because half the staff was out with the flu and he couldn't afford to be out another teacher because he was already at the bottom of the substitute list. She'd wanted to ask him about any cuts to the school budget, but she'd pushed her luck enough for the day—and didn't want to risk putting Crimmons in a bad mood.

It was a perfect storm.

But Ducky could stay. And the dog was delighted about it. He was running around the classroom excitedly, tip-tapping his little feet and smelling everything. She hadn't seen him this excited— well, ever. At one point, he ran to the front of the classroom and then got the zoomies in the reading corner, where he jumped on and off beanbag chairs.

"So you like it here, huh?" she asked him. He ran over to her and sat, panting, his tongue hanging out.

"Will you behave with the students?" she asked.

Ducky looked at her mischievously, and his little face widened into a smile.

She had promised Principal Crimmons she would keep him on a leash, so she hooked one to his collar and sat him on the desk.

"Be good," she warned him as the bell rang. He shuffled his feet, a little nervously, but stayed put. Layla glanced at her computer, where there was a blinking instant message on her computer. She clicked it, and the window opened on her screen. It was from the receptionist, Mrs. Hildebrand.

Mrs. Hildebrand: Add one more to the list—Lucas is out with the flu.

She sighed. She had been looking forward to introducing Lucas to Ducky. Based on his reaction to her videos, she'd known he would have fallen in love. But she didn't have any more time to consider her disappointment because the kids started flowing in. There were fewer than usual—only about ten, since she had about seven out sick—but the remaining kids were excited. They crowded around the desk, asking her questions.

"What's his name?" Teddy Sullivan asked, leaning over the table to get a better look.

"He's so small!" Penny squealed, jumping up and down.

"Is he wearing *clothe*s?" Benny asked, his voice high with excitement.

Avery Drubbins reached for him, but Layla held up a finger.

"One at a time," she said. "Approach slowly, and be very gentle. Penny's right—he's very small, but if you're respectful of him, he'll be respectful of you. His name is Ducky, and he's a very good boy."

She let all the kids take turns gently petting Ducky while he sat on her desk, and she told them all about Christine and Ducky's superstar status. They were entranced, but not a single one of them knew who Cher from *Clueless* was. She sighed. She should have chosen his Bluey outfit instead.

After all her students had a chance to pet Ducky, she asked them to return to their seats.

"Okay, raise your hand if you'd like Ducky to spend time with us today." She stood at the front of the classroom while Ducky sat on the desk, looking very proud and happy. He loved the attention.

Every hand in the room shot up.

"I'll make a deal with you guys," she said. "If all of you behave extra well, I'll let Ducky stay." As if she had a choice. "If you agree to be really, really good today, we get to have a dog in the room."

There were a couple of extra squeals, but mostly, the kids sat quietly and with a forced calmness that barely concealed their excitement.

"Now, we don't have a lot of people here today since we've got so many out sick—which means I don't want to assign too much so the other kids don't get too far behind. So we're going to have a few extra games today. I'll also be letting everyone take a break for silent reading, so if you're really quiet, I'll let Ducky sit with you while you read."

The Drubbins kids high-fived each other. The kids loved getting breaks to read on the beanbag chairs, but Layla had a feeling that with Ducky around, there would probably be more snuggling than reading. But with so many kids out, she was willing to let them have a little extra freedom. Plus, she didn't have Garrett's lesson plans, and he hadn't emailed them. He must have been really, really sick.

The kids were . . . well, perfect.

The sat quietly all day, except for when they found extra opportunities to get up and drink from the water fountain and took the long route back to pet Ducky. Sometimes, there were tiny giggles when Ducky licked their noses. They were quiet and polite and every single kid was extra gentle with the little dog.

Christine would have approved.

By the end of the day, Layla was trying to figure out how to bring Ducky back to her classroom every day. Was there such a thing as a classroom dog? If there wasn't—could there be?

Reina stopped by at the end of the day, scooping Ducky into her arms and covering him with kisses. "How did it go with the kids today?" she asked.

"Other than having to send Aiden home at noon because he couldn't stop coughing . . . it was perfect, actually. It was like having Ducky there was some sort of magic charm."

"There's all these studies on how having a dog around actually makes you healthier," Reina said, rocking Ducky as if he were a baby; he loved her. "Honestly, it's good for the kids. Physically and emotionally."

"I wish there was a way I could bring him back more often," Layla said. "It would be really nice to have him around. The kids are so focused on being good so they can spend more time with him."

"You think Crimmons would go for that?"

Layla lifted a shoulder. "I don't know. I hardly got away with it today."

Reina paused thoughtfully. "What if you had Ducky become a trained emotional support dog? Or maybe even a therapy dog?"

"Would he be able to visit the classroom?"

Reina nodded. "There's a therapy dog who visits all the special needs classrooms once a week up in Brimsley. He's always in the newspaper, and he's a special guest at the football games."

"Aww," she said. "That's cute. But you have to remember . . . Ducky's not mine." Layla felt a little sad as she said it.

"How long is Ducky staying with you?" Reina asked.

Layla shrugged. "Until all these ice skating competitions are over."

"And when is that?"

"Next month. Then Christine goes home to get some rest, and then she goes on an international tour, I think."

"Damn. Who is this girl? Can I have her life?"

Layla laughed. "The dog's on loan. Plus, when would I have time to train a therapy dog? I'm already too busy."

Reina scratched Ducky's ears. "Well, I think you should. If you bring him back, it'll save me the trouble of breaking into your house and stealing him."

"Stick to Garrett, please," Layla said.

Reina snickered. "If you insist."

"Oh, shut up."

"You love me," Reina said. She handed Ducky back to Layla. "Just . . . think about the therapy-dog thing, okay? It'd be good for the kids." She hesitated. "And for you."

Layla frowned. Her? Why would she need a therapy dog? She was fine. She wanted to ask Reina what she meant, but she also . . . didn't. Because there was a big part of her that was scared to know.

CHAPTER 18

The flu swept through the town, closing businesses and sending people to the drugstore in droves. It even closed down the school for a day, the district hoping to quell the swell of sickness, and then it was gone as soon as it arrived. After only a single sick day, Mr. Rogers promised he was well enough to dog-sit. "I miss my little buddy," he'd insisted, so Layla had dropped Ducky off with him each school day since, and even let Ducky stay with him a half day when the school closed. Within a week and a half, the sickness had cycled through a few more students in her classroom and they had all returned, ornery as ever.

Garrett had been sick for three days, which let Layla get back into the swing of teaching, which she realized quickly just how much she'd missed. She loved almost everything about teaching: the way her students listened when she was walking them through an important lesson; the way their eyes lit up when they finally grasped something new; the way they told her things they'd learned and shared little stories from their lives. She remembered why she loved it so much, and some of the confidence she'd lost watching Garrett control the classroom so easily—well, it came back, and then some. She realized why Principal Crimmons had chosen her to mentor Garrett instead of choosing another teacher.

But, even at the front of the classroom, something was missing. Something that maybe she hadn't really known to miss before, or maybe an open space in her heart she had ignored completely, believing it would never be filled. Whatever it was, the strange, echoing loneliness highlighted it in a way she'd never really felt.

Layla missed Garrett.

She missed him in a way she'd never missed anyone. She missed his presence in her classroom, even when they just were sitting together during a break, not speaking. She missed seeing him interact with the kids. She missed how he smelled—fresh and clean and manly—all the time. She missed asking him questions, and his honest answers, and their silly banter. She missed just about everything about him. She didn't even mind when the kids asked him to stay forever.

Well. She didn't mind *much*.

It felt strange, admitting it to herself. Layla didn't like to rely on others. She considered Reina one of her closest friends, and Layla had never even invited her to her house. She was used to being alone; it felt safe and normal, and admitting to herself that maybe she really, truly missed someone was . . . strange, and a little uncomfortable, and she wasn't sure she liked it.

And she found it difficult when he returned, too, looking refreshed—if slightly pale—in a lavender button-up, with just a little more stubble than usual. She felt strangely awkward when he entered the room, like a teenager who'd never talked to a boy before. Let alone a man. A strong, handsome, slightly pale man who could pull off a lavender button-up.

Layla hated the feeling. It wasn't *her*.

"Welcome back," she told him, a fake bright note in her tone. "How are you feeling?"

He set his messenger bag down by her desk. "Much better," he said. He grabbed a Ziploc bag from his desk and tossed it to her.

"M&M cookies?" she asked, delighted. She liked when he packed things for her. It meant he'd been thinking of her. Maybe even in the same way she was thinking of him.

But probably not.

He grinned. "Germ-free, I promise. And I got Lucas the brownies I promised him, too."

"You're too good to us."

Garrett's face turned serious. "How is he? Lucas?"

"I . . . don't know. He's been out with the flu too. Today's his first day back."

"Shoot," he said. "I hope that time away didn't set him back."

"I know." She'd missed Lucas every day. She'd been thinking of new things to show him and had bookmarked a couple of news articles about Ducky. She'd hoped she could help him read through them.

"Well," she said, "I tried to continue with your lesson plans the best I could—without knowing what they were."

He blushed slightly. "Sorry. I tried to email them but ended up puking, so I gave up and went back to bed. They probably wouldn't have made sense anyway. I was delirious. I probably would have tried to teach the kids astrophysics or something."

"You know astrophysics?"

"No," he said. "But that wouldn't have stopped me from trying."

She laughed. Already, it felt a little more natural to talk to him, even if she could feel her heart beating very strangely, and a strange warmth rising from her chest.

"What's on the docket today?" he asked. "Anything I need to finish up?"

"Art," she said. "Mrs. Sanchez is coming in with pastels first thing. I'll run you through what you missed while you were out."

While they were going through math lessons, Mrs. Sanchez came in, rolling a cart stacked with easels and supplies. She had a paintbrush stuck through her neat black bun.

"Hey, you two!" she said, her voice coy.

Layla flushed. "Good morning, Mrs. Sanchez." She stood up from the desk too quickly, banging her knee on the drawer as she hastily extricated herself from her chair. "Do you need help with anything?"

"Garrett, would you be a dear and go get the rest of the easels? Layla and I can start setting these up."

"Sure," he said. He stood up (without banging his knee on anything) and swept down the hallway. The art supplies were stored at the other end of the school, in a large storage room.

"That man—"

"Don't," Layla snapped.

"I'm just saying, you're lucky—"

Layla gave her a warning look. She wasn't sure if she could handle anyone saying anything about Garrett, not when she was already feeling . . . well . . .

"You're lucky you got such a big classroom," Mrs. Sanchez said, smoothly switching topics, as she extended the long, silver legs of an easel. "I can't fit seventeen easels in most of the other classrooms, you know. The students in the upper grades have to share or draw at their desks."

"You're lucky the school let you buy so many easels."

"Oh, honey," Mrs. Sanchez laughed. "I bought these myself. You think the school invests in the arts? We barely can keep the free-lunch program running."

Layla got a sinking feeling in her stomach whenever anyone mentioned expenses. "That had to be expensive."

Mrs. Sanchez shrugged. "What else was I gonna do?"

When the students came in, they were immediately excited to see the easels and the big white sheets of paper hung from each. They loved art time, and Layla loved having it first thing in the morning—it gave her a time to get an extra cup of coffee from the teachers' lounge. School, she'd always thought, should start at nine anyway. It just made more sense. Mornings were for sleeping in and cozy slippers, after all.

She and Garrett sat back at her desk and watched Mrs. Sanchez take over the classroom.

"Today," Mrs. Sanchez said, standing at the front of the class, "you're going to draw your favorite thing about school. We're using a new medium today—pastels! Now, I want you to pick one up and take a look at it. It looks a little like a crayon, right? There are important differences, though—pastels are much softer, so if you push too hard, you'll break it! You'll also get brighter, richer colors from pastels."

The kids were picking through boxes, exclaiming over the bright colors.

"Now," Mrs. Sanchez added, "pastels can stain, so be extra careful not to get any on your clothes. I don't need phone calls from angry parents, okay?"

Garrett leaned over to Layla. "Wanna finish this up in the teachers' lounge?"

Layla glanced at the clock. "Yeah," she whispered. "If Avery Drubbins tries to eat the pastels, I don't want to hear what Mrs. Sanchez will do to him."

Garrett muffled a snicker as he followed Layla out of the room. She slipped the baggie of cookies into her pocket for them to share while they finished going over everything he'd missed and built lesson plans for the rest of the week. Everything was better with cookies.

"Thanks for covering for me," he said after they'd packed up their notebooks and laptops.

Layla smiled. "You were sick. Besides, I had a little experience with the class."

"You know," he said, "I could give you tips. If you need any. From an older, more experienced teacher."

She shoved him playfully. "Older? Sure. More experienced? No, just behind." She giggled, and then stopped herself, horrified. She did not *touch* coworkers. Not even playful shoves. She especially did not touch handsome men whom she was clearly attracted to.

Plus, if she was being honest with herself, even their casual friendship had a timeline. Garrett didn't even live in Two Falls. He was just staying there for a semester while he finished up his student teaching, and then he was gone. The chances he would stay were nonexistent, and there she was, getting her heart all messed up over him. It was utterly stupid.

"Let's go back and see how art is going," Layla suggested.

She tossed the baggie—the cookies were long gone—and gathered up her laptop. Garrett followed suit, and she hurried back to the classroom, determined not to have any more *banter* with him.

What they came back to was—

Ducky.

On every single easel, a pastel drawing of Ducky.

Some were a bit better than others—some looked a bit like brown blobs. But there was no doubt—all seventeen kids in her class had decided that what they liked best about school was Ducky. Even Lucas, who hadn't been around to meet him in person, had decided to draw the little dog from Layla's Instagram app. And the other kids had apparently caught on from listening to the students go on and on about the pup.

Layla wandered around the room, admiring all the art, and helped the kids hang them up on the walls and sign them at the bottom like real artists. It made her heart a touch warm, and she smiled at her room, which suddenly seemed a the tiniest bit brighter than before. And that was tough, with a group of second graders. They were always bright.

"Apparently they're as obsessed with that little dog as I am," Mrs. Sanchez said, grinning around at the classroom. "You should bring him back so I can snuggle him." She turned away, instructing the kids to start cleaning up.

Meanwhile, Garrett was frowning.

"What?" Layla asked. "Not a dog guy? More of a cat person?"

Dang it. She was doing it again.

He walked around the classroom, studying the pictures with his hands behind his back. "How . . . how do they know my grandfather's dog?"

"Your grandfather's dog?" Layla asked. "That's . . . my friend

Christine's dog. His name is Ducky. Does your grandfather have a Yorkie, too?"

"No," Garrett said. He pointed at the easels. "He has—that dog. As in, a Yorkie named Ducky. The dog that they're all drawing."

"He owns that dog? That's impossible."

"Well, he's taking care of it." He shoved his hands in his pockets. "I brought him lunch the other day, and he had Ducky there. And when he had the flu and so did I, he was so worried about him."

"Wait," Layla said, stopping short behind him on their tour of their students' artwork. "Is your grandfather Mr. Rogers?"

"No," Garrett said. "He's Randall Henderson. I'm named after him."

"But your name is Garrett."

"Yeah. I know. My middle name is Randall. And it's what my grandfather always called me. And my dad. Who's this Mr. Rogers?"

"He's my neighbor. Lives just around the corner, on Sandhill Lane. He takes care of Ducky during the day when I'm at school."

"Wait. Hold on. My grandfather lives on Sandhill Lane." He paused. "Do you call my grandpa Mr. Rogers?"

"Yeah. It's how the Ellises introduced him to me. Mr. Rogers. He's an adorable old man who wears cardigans and is nice to everyone and is beloved by the whole town. What else would we call him?"

Garrett was smiling too. "His name?"

"Don't be ridiculous. He's our Mr. Rogers. It's literally the highest compliment you can pay someone in this country."

He laughed. "So, wait. You're the person he's dog-sitting for?"

Layla shrugged. "I mean, by extension. Sort of. It's a longish story." She paused. "Wait. How come I never see you there?"

"I go see him almost every night after the gym."

Of course. She just missed him. She dropped by every day right after school to pick Ducky up; Garrett arrived probably an hour or two after, depending on how much time he was spending on his abs that day. Or his biceps. Or his quads.

She stopped and shook her head, trying to clear the image. She was at school. Not in a club.

At the front of the classroom, Mrs. Sanchez was bidding good-bye to the students, kissing her palms at them like a celebrity at the end of a miraculous performance. The kids were happy and in good moods, and immensely proud of their Ducky-decorated classroom.

And then, it was time for Garrett to take over the class.

Garrett pointed at her. "This conversation isn't over. This is—the weirdest thing I've ever heard." He chuckled. "I can't believe you're the reason my grandpa is so happy."

Something inside Layla melted. It was . . . maybe the nicest thing Garrett had ever said to her. Or the nicest thing anyone had said to her, ever.

In that moment, she was sure of one thing. A tiny little bit of her heart belonged to Garrett Henderson.

CHAPTER 19

DUCKY

It was supposed to be the best day of Ducky's life, but instead, it was the scariest.

He woke up with Layla just like always. Well, he licked her forehead until she got out of bed, and then she carried him outside and fed him and snuggled him, and everything was the best. It was easy to have the best days with her. She was singing the Friday song, which was just this silly thing she sometimes sang, and she was extra happy about it, going "It's Friday; it's the best day!" over and over. Sometimes she picked Ducky up and danced with him when she sang it.

Layla dressed Ducky up as a walrus, which was a nice, snuggly costume. Ducky saw one on TV once, and he barked at it until his mom told him to stop, but he still sat down and watched it move across the screen. It didn't even have legs, and it had long whiskers and two big sharp teeth! The costume had big sharp teeth too, but they were fluffy and soft, and Ducky thought he could use them as a pillow if he got tired at Mr. Rogers's house.

Layla put her books in her car—she called it the Bronco—and then walked Ducky over to Mr. Rogers's house down the street and around the corner and rang the doorbell.

And then nothing happened.

Ducky and Layla waited and waited and waited, but there was no answer. The little dog barked to let him know he was there, and that Ducky was so so excited to see him, and that they were going to have the best day ever.

Layla opened the screen door and knocked, and Ducky waited really patiently, wagging his tail.

That's when Ducky started smelling something funny. He thought he smelled it before, when they first arrived, but he had been so excited he didn't really pay much attention. It smelled coppery and strong, and Ducky didn't like it, but he knew what it was.

Blood.

Ducky started barking a lot then, and growling, and wiggling like crazy so Layla would put him down. Mr. Rogers was in trouble, and Ducky knew it. Something was wrong in a really bad way. When the wind hit, Ducky could smell that Mr. Rogers was hurt and in pain and bleeding and it was bad.

Ducky barked more, panicked.

"Is something wrong, Ducky?" Layla asked. She was worried too. Ducky could smell it on her, and it was strong and came through right beside the minty, overwhelming smell of fear. She tried the doorknob, but it was locked.

"Mr. Rogers?" Layla called loudly. "Are you okay in there?"

Ducky heard a small groan from inside the house, like Mr. Rogers was calling for help, but Ducky didn't think Layla could hear it with her human ears. She checked under the rug. Ducky wasn't sure what she was looking for. Then, she started looking under the flower pot. Finally, she stood up on her highest tippy-toes and reached above the doorframe, way way way way above Ducky, where he could never reach in a million years.

Layla brought her hand down, her fingers covered in dust, gripping a key.

Ducky was so relieved, but Layla needed to hurry hurry hurry. He was scared too. Really scared. Layla unlocked the door and swung it open, but there was no one in the living room. But Ducky knew where he was without looking. He could smell him. Layla set Ducky down on the floor, and the little dog headed straight to the kitchen, where Mr. Rogers was lying sprawled across the floor, blood pouring out from his head and all over the tile. Mr. Rogers had his eyes partly open, but they were really sleepy looking, and he breathed really loudly, making big, scary, thick sounds. He didn't smell or sound or look like himself at all.

Ducky ran around and checked him over, and he thought it was only his head that was hurt, but it looked bad. Humans stood on their back legs, so when they fell over, they had a lot farther to go to hit the ground than dogs. Ducky thought they should walk on four legs, but when he tried to show his mom, she didn't understand. He had tried to walk on two legs before, and it wasn't very effective. But this was the kind of stuff that happened when humans didn't listen to dogs.

Meanwhile, Layla was on her phone. "Hello?" she was saying. "Can you send an ambulance to 524 Sandhill Lane, please? In Two Falls? Urgently. I'm here with Mr. Rogers—I mean, Randall Henderson. He's fallen and hit his head on something. Yes, there's a lot of blood." She pauses. "No, I haven't tried to move him. Should I?"

She rushed to the sink and grabbed a tea towel and pressed it against the gash in his head. Layla was pale, but nowhere near as pale as Mr. Rogers. He looked like a ghost. Ducky felt very scared for him.

Ducky curled up next to him so Mr. Rogers knew someone was there to take care of him. His fingers moved, just a little, to touch the little dog.

Ducky nuzzled his hand.

Layla and Ducky stayed with him until his grandson rushed in, disheveled and scared, his hair tousled. He dropped to his knees beside his grandfather and grabbed his hand. Ducky nestled close to Mr. Rogers, just in case he needed to know the pup was still there.

"Garrett!" Layla cried out. "Thank God you're here."

Hmmm. Ducky looked up at him. The dog had thought the man's name was Randall, but whatever Layla said was usually right.

"Are you okay?" he asked. "Grandpa, I'm here. Are you okay?"

Mr. Rogers groaned softly, but it was more a wisp of air than a noise.

"How long has he been like this?"

"I just found him here when I came to drop Ducky off," Layla said. "He didn't answer the door, and Ducky started going wild, so I knew something was off. I found his hide-a-key and let myself in." She was still holding the tea towel to his head, but it was red with blood.

"Has he said anything at all?" Garrett demanded.

Layla shook her head and started to respond, but she was cut off by flashing lights and big loud sounds that hurt Ducky's ears. He ducked his head between his paws, feeling a little scared even though he was trying really, really hard to be brave for his friend, so he stayed with him anyway.

Ducky stayed with him even when two scary-looking people with serious faces rushed in.

Ducky stayed with him when one of them accidentally stepped on his paw.

Ducky stayed with him when they put a black cuff on Mr. Rogers's arm even though Ducky didn't like the beeping noises it made.

And Ducky tried to stay with Mr. Rogers when they put him on a stretcher, but Layla gently lifted the little dog away. "It's okay, Ducky," she said. "We have to let him go to the hospital. He needs help."

Ducky whined and cried, but Layla held him tightly, and the dog felt a few tears drop on to his fur.

CHAPTER 20

Layla had never once dreamed that she'd be sitting in the hospital with Garrett R. Henderson, grandson of Randall Henderson. She never dreamed that she would be clasping his hand, and she'd be . . . okay with it. She never once thought she wouldn't care who saw them. But he needed her, and she was there.

Layla was there even though every tiny little fiber of her body hurt, walking back into a hospital. It hurt because she'd been there before. She wanted to beg Garrett to stop outside, to drag her feet, to run away. But Garrett didn't stop walking. He didn't hesitate. So neither did she, even though she felt like her legs were filled with lead. Even though her whole body was tingling. Even though she wasn't sure she could live through being there again. But Ducky gave a tiny whimper and snuggled his head into her chest, giving her the bit of bravery she needed to keep going.

She'd driven Garrett to the hospital in Brimsley, following as closely behind the ambulance as she could. He was pale and white-knuckling the edges of her Bronco's seat. Layla wanted to ask him if he was okay, but she knew the answer: no. So now, they sat together, in Brimsley's overcrowded hospital waiting room, and he was holding on to her like she was a lifeline, his brow pinched, and his face a strange purple-white. She'd called Principal Crim-

mons on the way, and he'd told her not to worry—he'd call a substitute, and if he couldn't find one, he'd handle her class himself.
Ducky had huddled quietly on the back seat on the way to the
hospital, his head resting between his paws. He knew something
was wrong. They hadn't thought twice about bringing the tiny dog
into the hospital waiting room with them. He was family. He was
an extension of Layla. And she really, really needed him, in a way
she never had before.

The paramedics had butterflied the head wound shut in the
ambulance to stop the bleeding, but Mr. Rogers had to go into
surgery for stitches. They told Garrett to wait, that he couldn't
come back to see him—not until they were sure he was stabilized.
A red-haired nurse came by, once, and opened her mouth, like
she was going to say something about Ducky being in the waiting
room, but she seemed to realize that he was Layla's lifeline—that
she needed him desperately, in a way she couldn't explain—so the
nurse shook her head slightly and went on about her business.

Until then, Garrett was quiet. Once, he got up, releasing her
hand, and filled a paper cup with water, and then sat back down,
holding it tightly, his eyes focused on something far away.

"Are . . . you going to drink that?" Layla asked finally. She
flexed her hand. He'd been gripping it really hard.

"He raised me," Garrett said. He still wasn't looking at her; it
was like he was seeing something else, in a far-off place. Even his
voice was different, like he was speaking from a place deep inside
himself.

"What?"

"My grandfather raised me. My parents—they traveled a lot,
and they died when I was ten."

The words piled on Layla like bricks, made her sick to her
stomach, made her nauseated with guilt. No wonder he'd left so
quickly when she'd pressured her about his family.

"I—I'm sorry."

"It happened so fast," he said. "Ice. It was like one day I was a normal kid, and then I wasn't. And so I moved in with my grandparents. My grandpa was—still is—my best friend. When my grandma died, she made me promise to take care of him. So when there was an opportunity to student teach here, to take a teaching post—I jumped at the chance. I would get to see him. I wouldn't have to rely on the phone, waiting for him to answer on the fourteenth ring because he doesn't believe in answering machines, and worrying, each time—" His voice broke.

"It's not your fault," Layla said. But she might as well have not been there at all.

"Now I'm here, and this happens anyway. He's—he's my only family, Layla."

The statement froze her blood in her veins. He was almost *her*.

"I broke my promise," he whispered. "I should have been there."

"Garrett," she said, "we both know how independent he is. You know he wouldn't have let you. He wouldn't have wanted you staying there, not when you—"

"Could be sitting in my apartment, watching *Wheel of Fortune* reruns?" His voice was dry.

"My point is that he wouldn't have wanted you to worry about him. I've lived down the street from him for quite a while now, and honestly—he's not that type. He barely accepts my help. He's a *helper*." She paused. "That's why we call him Mr. Rogers. He wants to help everyone else. And he does. He always has."

"Well, I needed to help him," Garrett said stubbornly. "It was my job. It's the reason I'm here. I could have been in Lincoln, or Omaha, or literally anywhere else."

For some reason, the comment hurt, twinging in her stomach. But he was just venting. It had nothing to do with her. Right then, he was hurting for his grandfather, and that was okay.

His only family.

The thought made a hard knot in her throat. She swallowed. She could not break. She had to be there for Garrett. He needed her. It occurred to her, strangely, in that moment, *he* didn't have anyone else. There was only her.

Ducky, who was sitting patiently on her lap, still in his ridiculous walrus costume, touched a paw to Garrett's leg, as if to tell him it was going to be okay. Garrett looked down at the pup, and a shadow of a smile touched his lips and was gone. Ducky had that effect.

It made Layla suddenly emotional, and she pressed her lips together, trying to erase her feelings from her face before she lost control.

Garrett looked at her suddenly, almost seeming surprised she was still there. "Are you okay?" he asked.

She smiled tightly at him. "Of course. I just—don't like hospitals." It was the understatement of the century. She looked desperately for the door.

"Neither do I."

"I—I don't have family," she said finally. "My parents got sick, and that's—that's the last time I was ever here. Not here *here*, but in a hospital, I mean."

"Do you need to leave?" he asked. "It's okay. You can go, you know."

She shook her head. "No," she said firmly. "I'm exactly where I need to be." And, she realized as she said the words, she meant it. No matter how badly she wanted to leave—how much it hurt her to be there—she had no intention of going anywhere. Garrett needed her, and Layla knew it. And weirdly—she knew he'd be there for her if the tables were turned.

"I didn't know," she said finally. "I'm sorry."

"I didn't know either," Garrett said. "I wish I had."

"It's not exactly—easy—to insert into conversation."

He reached over and took her hand again. Except, this time, instead of Layla comforting Garrett—he was comforting her, too. He squeezed her hand, and she squeezed back.

On her lap, Ducky's little head dropped, and he snored quietly.

They sat together in silence. Layla didn't want to talk about how her parents had gotten sick, or how they'd died. She just wanted to sit in silence with someone she'd been honest with, for the first time in a long time. Only Christine really knew about her family—and that was because they'd known each other for years. But it felt strangely freeing to be with someone she trusted enough to talk to.

Finally, a doctor came out and called Garrett's name.

He turned to her. "Do you want to come with me?"

Layla shook her head. "You go. I'll wait here with Ducky."

He looked at her for a long moment—as if deciding whether he should try to convince her to come with him—and then back at the doctor, who was waiting patiently, holding a clipboard. "I'll be back soon," he promised, and then disappeared down a hallway and through a set of swinging doors, leaving Layla and Ducky alone.

CHAPTER 21

After almost a month of being in the big city, Christine was back, and Layla had never been happier to see her. Christine gave her a long hug the moment she walked through the door. Layla handed her Ducky, who was dressed in a big comfy sweater. Ducky had been attached to Layla like a sandbur, buried in her side, sitting in her lap, waiting at her feet. He even had followed her to the bathroom, where he'd sat, patiently, until she washed and dried her hands, his eyes wide and watchful.

"Are you okay?" Christine asked as soon as she'd released her friend from the hug as she dropped her bags by the door where she always did—a duffel, a backpack, and a couple of bags that smelled suspiciously like takeout. Layla would help her move all of it into the tiny second bedroom and the kitchen later.

"Yes," Layla said automatically, without knowing if it was really true.

Meanwhile, Ducky was wriggling with happiness in Christine's arms, making happy little grunts and reaching his head up to lick Christine's face.

"And what about Mr. Rogers?" she asked. "Is he okay?"

Layla had shared only the barest details with Christine. But her friend knew that Layla was not the type of person to share her feelings. Layla was the first to listen, to be there for others, to lend a hand—but she struggled to ask for help. So when Layla had called Christine, when she'd actually confessed to her friend she was concerned, that things weren't perfect, Christine dropped everything to come back. She had to. Layla had never once uttered one word to ask for help—not real help, anyway. Not when she really needed it. And Layla hadn't exactly asked Christine to show up, or really to do anything at all, not even this time. Layla would never purposefully worry Christine. But she'd told her what had happened to Ducky's daytime caretaker—her neighbor, her friend—and Christine just knew.

Christine was good like that.

"He's still in the hospital, but from what I hear, he's okay," Layla said. "They're trying to figure out why he fell. But they ruled out some big things so far—stroke, heart attack. Nothing turned up in his CT scan, and no broken bones in his X-rays. Just a concussion and a nasty cut."

"Did he trip on something?"

Layla shook her head. "I don't think so," she said. "There wasn't anything on the floor, unless he tripped over his own feet." It was possible, of course. Layla had tripped over her own feet plenty of times, including twice in front of Garrett when she was walking around the classroom, watching over her students, stopping to help them make it through a difficult spelling word or to figure out a new math problem.

"Do they have any ideas?" Christine asked.

"They think he passed out and hit his head on the corner of the kitchen counter. That's where he split his head open. And then he was too weak from blood loss to get up when he regained consciousness—so he just lay there. For over an hour. With no one to help him." Her voice felt strained, suddenly, and she could feel tears starting in her eyes, but she swallowed and looking away, blinking. Layla wasn't a crier. Never had been.

Christine covered her mouth. "If you hadn't been there—"

"If I hadn't gone by to drop off Ducky . . ." Layla trailed off. There were so many *what-ifs* she wasn't exactly prepared to confront. She had a quick, guilty flashback of not necessarily *wanting* to take care of Ducky in the first place, of hoping that Christine's husband could handle the pup, or maybe her parents back in California, or even a random dog sitter they hadn't vetted. Layla hadn't been ready to have any sort of close relationship—even with a dog. If Christine hadn't practically begged her to take care of Ducky—and if Layla hadn't dropped by Mr. Rogers's house—

She shook her head as if to clear the images. But she knew what it meant.

There was a strong chance no one would have stopped by. Not for a long time. At least not until the end of the school day, when Garrett swung by to see his grandfather—and usually, after the gym. And by then . . . by then it would have been too late. The head wound had been too big, and he'd have lost too much blood. It made Layla sick to her stomach to think of it. She felt queasy even now, so she changed the subject quickly.

"Sit down," Layla said, shooing her friend into the living room, toward the coach, which she'd decorated with her favorite fall pillows she'd found at the thrift store in Brimsley. "I'm sure you and Ducky need some time."

Christine kissed Ducky on the head. "We do. I missed my little guy so much." She sat down on the couch, sitting her dog on the cushion next to her.

"He missed you too," Layla said. He hesitated. "He's been good company."

"He's perfect. Oh, I almost forgot," she said. She ran back to the door, where she'd dropped her belongings, and grabbed the white grocery bags—and a big brown paper sack that looked suspiciously like it held some kind of alcohol. Christine reached in and pulled out two bottles of wine, grinning.

"Interested?" she asked.

"You didn't have to do that," Layla protested.

"Oh, shut up, yes I did." She paused. "Plus, I got one red and one white. It's called balance."

"I thought it was called casual alcoholism."

Christine balled up the paper bag and threw it at her friend. "It's called support. And love. And grapes."

Layla grinned. Christine was exactly the type of friend Layla needed—the kind of friend who knew that nice things had to be forced on Layla or she wouldn't accept them.

"What else did you get?" Layla asked, eyeing the white plastic bags.

"Um, obviously, since I drove through Brimsley to get here, I stopped at Los Cinco Amigos."

"You didn't." Los Cinco Amigos was Layla's guilty pleasure. When she wanted to splurge, she drove all the way to Brimsley for it. Their queso was to *die* for, and their margaritas were strong—so she normally only had a few delicious sips so she could drive back. But during COVID-19, they'd started doing margaritas to go. It had changed her life. After a long day of trying to teach second graders via Zoom—which was basically impossible—sometimes she really, really needed a drink. And a margarita from Los Cinco Amigos always hit the spot.

"I wasn't sure what you were in the mood for," Christine was saying, pulling Styrofoam containers out of plastic bags, "so I got a bunch—their nachos looked amazing, so I got those, obviously, but then I saw their suprema burritos, so I got two of those, and then I remembered when we go out you order enchiladas, right?" She walked back to the living room and settled down on the floor, where she began to spread out dinner, giving a warning glance to Ducky when he tried to steal a tortilla chip.

Layla nodded. "That's more than enough."

"And then, of course, I had to get chips with guac. And queso. And salsa, just in case."

"Holy crap, Christine. How are we supposed to eat all of this?"

Christine sighed, exasperated. "Believe in yourself, Layla." She handed her a Styrofoam to-go box. "Come on, then. Get started."

Layla laughed for the first time in a while, opening the nachos and fishing a chip covered in melty cheese out. "I guess we can drop what we don't eat by Mr. Rogers's house. I'm assuming Garrett'll be staying there when Mr. Rogers gets out of the hospital, and he eats like an actual horse. A very healthy, attractive horse."

"Hold up. Why is *Garrett* over there?"

"Oh, wait. I guess I forgot to tell you. Turns out he's Mr. Rogers's grandson." She ate another chip. "I guess he's been visiting him every night after teaching and going to the gym, and I just never noticed since his house is just around the bend, and I never go anywhere after I get home."

Christine froze, a freshly unwrapped burrito halfway through her mouth. "Excuse me. What? Your hot student teacher is your sweet older neighbor's *grandson*?"

Layla nodded. "I guess he wanted to do his student teaching here so he could look in on him, especially since his grandmother died—well, not too long ago. Apparently Garrett knows Ducky and everything because he stops by often." Layla shook her head. "I don't know how I missed it, except that I usually just come home after work, pick up Ducky, and zone out. Meanwhile, Garrett goes to the gym."

"Please tell me you made out." Christine was still holding her burrito, totally forgotten.

"What?"

Christine made wet, slopping kissing noises.

Layla scoffed. "Christine. *No.*"

"Why?"

"First and foremost, I am *still* this guy's boss. Second of all, the hospital waiting room—where all this came to light—is not exactly a place super conducive to romance."

Christine stared. "You—you went to the hospital? With *him*?"

Christine, of all people, knew exactly how traumatic it was for Layla to set foot in a hospital. In college, Layla had been half dead from chronic bronchitis before Christine convinced her to go to urgent care—by threatening to shave Layla's head in her sleep.

It was the only way.

And that specific urgent care had been a little tiny room in a drugstore—not an actual hospital, or even a real doctor's office. Still, the moment she walked in, her legs had filled with lead, and her heartbeat had gone strange and funny, and she was hot and cold and clammy and miserable, and when the nurse practitioner had asked her questions, she'd had to concentrate hard to respond.

"You went—voluntarily? Or did he . . . ask you?" Christine asked, her voice hesitant, like she was afraid of scaring Layla off.

"I went voluntarily." Layla said it casually, but without meeting her eyes. Garrett hadn't needed to ask her. She looked down, moving nachos around in the tray, one knee drawn up to her chest. She didn't know why it felt so weird to admit it. She should have been glad she'd been able to go to a hospital after everything she'd gone through. It was a big step for her. But acknowledging that was acknowledging the issue had ever existed at all, and she wasn't ready to do that.

Christine's face went all funny, like her mind was glitching and she couldn't settle on just one expression. "Holy shit," she said finally. "You love him." She laughed a bit wildly. "You freaking *love* him."

"I do *not*," Layla said, with the air of someone who had just been accused of a terrible murder.

Christine was still staring at her, wide-eyed and a little slack-jawed, like she was seeing her friend for the first time. "Layla. Layla. *Layla*."

"What?" Layla asked irritably. She wasn't used to having so much of the spotlight on her feelings, and she did not like it.

"Are you going to tell him?" Christine demanded.

"There's nothing to tell!"

The two friends stared at each other, both frustrated with the other, when their glowering was broken by a single sound.

Knock.

Three, to be specific, three knocks, quick, strong, rapid in succession.

Layla and Christine looked at the door, and back at each other.

Ducky, of course, immediately and excitedly started barking, hopping happily around the door, which meant it was someone he knew. Ducky had two different barks for people at the door: a sharp, friendly, high-pitched yap for friends, and a lower, gruffer sound for people he was unfamiliar with.

Ducky was standing at the door, looking up, his little tail wagging like crazy. He looked back at Layla and Christine with impatience.

Christine scooped her dog off the floor and held him to her chest, even though he was wiggling around with excitement, and Layla opened the door to see—

Garrett.

Garrett, standing at the door in a T-shirt.

Garrett, with his arms crossed in a way that accentuated his arm muscles. And wrist muscles. Did normal men have wrist muscles? Because Garrett did.

Garrett . . . holding flowers.

Layla stared at him in surprise for a moment, and then stepped outside, closing the door behind her, so she didn't have to deal with Christine staring at her while she tried to make it through this conversation. Layla knew the moment she walked back into the house, Christine was going to cross-examine her. And, she knew that Christine was probably sneakily swiping the curtains aside and watching through the window.

Garrett was staring at her, and she was staring at him, and Christine was probably staring at them both.

It was only then that Layla remembered she hadn't spoken.

"Um," she said, mentally kicking herself. "Hi?"

"Hi," he said, still holding the flowers, which had been rolled in pink paper. He thrust them toward her, looking almost as uncomfortable as she felt. "These are for you."

She forced her hands to work, her arms to extend to take the blossoms, which were a collection of daisies and lilies and baby's breath and roses in a riot of colors. The paper fluttered in the wind. "Thank you," she said. "They're beautiful." She dipped her head to smell them but leaned too close and breathed in the dusty yellow pollen. She sneezed and shook her head, embarrassed.

Garrett reached forward and then drew his hand back at the last second. "You got a bit of—uh—just there." He tapped on his own nose.

Layla tried to wipe the dust off with her sleeve. "Better?" she asked.

"Not quite." He hesitated. "May I?"

She nodded.

He reached out, and his fingers slowly brushed the very tip of her nose, and then he ran them along her upper lip. Layla shivered without meaning to. She liked his touch. It was almost worth making a fool of herself for.

"All good." He smiled at her, drawing his hand away. "I just wanted to say . . . thank you. You were really there for me yesterday. You didn't need to take the day off school, or to stay with me at the hospital, or anything, really. But you did . . . and I really, really appreciate that."

"It's no problem, honestly," she said lightly as if she regularly waltzed into hospitals, and if was absolutely no big deal for her, instead of secretly facing a crushing fear while she attempted to be there for someone else.

"It was the right thing to do," she added, and then immediately felt stupid after she said it. What was she, some kind of judgy Goody Two-shoes, doling out things based on right and wrong?"

"And," he hesitated, looking at her. "I just wanted to say— thanks for talking to me."

She nodded. "Yeah." She knew what he was talking about, instantly.

His family. His parents.

Her family. *Her* parents.

Their strange, morbid commonality.

"It meant a lot. That you trusted me with that. Truly."

She nodded, suddenly strangely aware of her breathing and how much she wasn't really ready to talk about it again. She changed the subject hastily to what she really wanted to know. "How is he?" she asked. "Mr. Rogers? I mean . . . Mr. Henderson?" The name felt strange.

Garrett smiled, finally, comfortable. "Well, he's only tried to send me home from the hospital about ten times this morning. And he yelled at me for sleeping in the chair next to his bed. Said I was going to mess up my back. And a little bit ago, he told me"— he paused, grinning—"to get out of his room and go thank that pretty girl down the street before someone else does. The nurse told me he was stable enough I could leave for a little bit, so"—he motioned at himself—"here I am."

Layla's face burned hot and red. She was grateful for the cold air. She could blame it on that. "I think he might need to stay at the hospital a little longer if he's talking like that," she said finally. She shifted the flowers uncomfortably in her arms, but secretly, her whole body was singing with excitement. What did this mean? Did Garrett think she was pretty? Was he . . . *hitting* on her? No. It wasn't possible. He was probably just repeating what an old man—an old man who was probably feeling a little loopy due to pain pills—was saying.

Garrett shook his head, his smile blossoming into a full-blown grin. "Maybe, maybe not," he said. "He tried to walk out. He said he had to work in his garden this morning," he said, rolling his eyes. "He spent like ten minutes trying to tell the doctors that he needed to check his begonias."

"He didn't."

"He did," Garrett said. "He said he hadn't missed a morning in years and he wasn't about to start because I insisted on sticking around, getting in the way when I have a life to live and so does he."

Layla laughed. "Sounds like Mr. Rogers. Maybe a little grumpier than usual."

Garrett exhaled. "I'd say. Fortunately, the nurses promised not to let him escape. Plus, I promised to water for him." He jerked his thumb toward Mr. Rogers's house. "So . . . that's what I've been up to."

It occurred to Layla, suddenly, that everything felt surreal—like she were watching the interaction from somewhere outside of herself, that she was watching someone else standing on the front porch, talking to someone who had given her flowers. She hadn't invited him inside, or offered him something to drink, or really, done anything besides exist in a terrible state of awkwardness.

Meanwhile, the cold breeze was biting, and she'd just left him outside.

"Do you want"—she mentally searched the innards of her refrigerator—"water? A soda? Something? Do you want to come in? My friend Christine is here, but . . ." She trailed off, unsure of how to finish her thought.

He shook his head. "No, thanks. I don't want to leave my grandpa alone for long. He was talking about tackling some home improvement projects when I left."

"Can't let that happen."

"No," he said, and started to turn away.

But then he paused.

Turned back.

Stepped forward.

Close to her. So close she could feel his breath on her face. She looked up at him. He looked down, and he bent his head, slowly.

Kissed her cheek.

"Thank you, Layla," he said, his voice low, husky.

And then he was gone.

CHAPTER 22

DUCKY

Christine was hopping around the room and making squealing noises. She reminded Ducky of a rabbit, and he kept trying to hop around with her. He wanted to be a rabbit too. She picked the dog up and whirled him around before setting him safely back on the ground.

Meanwhile, Auntie Layla was sitting cross-legged on the floor, a perplexed, dreamy expression on her face. Ducky had sat in her lap twice, and she petted him, but she was acting like she was really far away, which might have been some kind of game. Ducky ate two tortilla chips right in front of her, and she didn't even try to stop him, so that part was nice. Ducky grabbed a third one and ran away to watch Christine and Layla from the corner, to eat his tortilla chip in peace.

"I can't believe he kissed you!" Ducky's mom was saying while she was hopping around, clapping her hands. She was smiling and she smelled happy—really happy, the kind of happy like when Ducky got an extra treat.

"He didn't *kiss-kiss* me," Layla protested. "It was a cheek kiss."

"Still a kiss."

"It's basically the kind of kiss British people give each other to say hello. It's deeply impersonal."

"No," Christine said. "That's an air-kiss. Like *mwah mwah*." She swooped Ducky up and gave him air kisses to demonstrate.

"It *was* an air-kiss!" Layla protested. "It was like a kiss you give your sister. Totally platonic."

"No. I was spying on you through your peephole. There was skin-to-skin contact. And he *lingered*."

Layla face turned this bright, blotchy red. She'd been doing that a lot lately. Ducky didn't understand what the big deal was though. He licked Layla's face all the time and gave her big kisses and she never turned red when Ducky did it. What did it matter if Garrett licked her face? He was probably just saying thank you. He was polite.

"It was nothing," Layla protested.

"It was *hot*." Christine was still buzzing with happiness. Ducky heard her tell Jason once that she was worried about Auntie Layla, that she thought that Layla was too used to being alone and didn't know how to depend on anyone. She's said something about Layla's parents dying when she was seventeen, which made Ducky sad, so he whimpered until Christine picked him up and hugged him and scratched him between his ears. But Layla depended on Ducky. The little dog knew she did. It took them a couple of days to get used to each other, but . . . Layla was Ducky's friend, and she loved the Yorkie. Ducky knew she did. The pup was a little worried though about how lonely she'd be when Christine finished her travels and her skating competition judging and took Ducky back to California. Would Layla miss Ducky too much? Ducky knew he'd miss her. Maybe Christine would just take Layla to California to become part of their family. Ducky knew, from spending time with her, that Layla wasn't like his mom and dad. She didn't spend a lot of time with others. She spent most of it by herself.

Layla sat down on the floor, next to all the food Ducky had been sneaking, and put her face in her hands. "Christine," she moaned through her fingers. "What am I going to do? What am I *doing*?"

Christine sat down next to her, and Ducky hopped in her lap. She popped a cork out of a bottle of wine and then poured Layla a glass. "First, you're going to have a drink. And then you're going to tell me why this is a problem."

"I work with him!" Layla hissed. "I'm attracted to someone I work with! And it's worse than that—I'm his boss!" She groaned. "I feel like a terrible person. I'm breaking the most basic, number one rule of work life. Don't hook up with someone at work. And especially, no matter what, don't hook up with someone who reports to you. I am the kind of person NBC makes documentaries about."

"Wait. You hooked up with him?" Christine demanded.

"Well, no." Layla lifted her head out of her hands.

"Have you done anything inappropriate?" Christine asked.

Layla looked ashamed. "I mean, no. Besides maybe a little flirting." She sighed heavily, slumping forward. "I—I have to stop myself from taking it further."

"But you do stop yourself."

"Yes."

"So . . . what's the issue again?"

"I *want* to." Layla confessed. "I want to grab his face and kiss him."

"What's wrong with that?"

Layla grabbed another chip and stress ate it. "I finally find a guy I'm attracted to . . . and I literally can't be with him, because if I do, there's a pretty strong chance I lose my job, which means losing my entire life that I've built here. Plus . . . I don't even know if he likes me. I mean, the guy is thankful because I was there for him on one of the hardest days of his life. That's not love. That's just . . . trauma bonding."

"It's not trauma bonding unless it just started. So . . . did it?"

"No," Layla admitted. "At least, I don't think so. We . . . have fun. At work, I mean."

"I fail to see the problem," Christine said. "Also, I fail to understand why you're not eating." She grabbed a to-go box of enchila-das and pushed them at her friend. "If we're doing boy talk, you need sustenance."

"Are we fourteen?" Layla griped, but she opened it and grabbed a plastic fork.

"Hey," Ducky's mom said. "Fourteen-year-olds are amazing trendsetters. Have some respect. And eat your food."

"Fine," Layla said, still a little grumpy. Ducky left the corner and sat in her lap, just so she knew he would help her eat some en-chilada if she really needed him to. She looked down at the small dog and gave him a little smile.

"See?" Christine said. "Ducky clearly approves. And if Ducky approves—you know you're doing the right thing."

Ducky barked, because his mom was right, and then Christine and Auntie Layla dissolved in laughter, and Ducky jumped on them both and covered them in kisses. The little pup was happy they were both there, and he was feeling a lot less scared than he was the day before.

Maybe everything would be all right after all.

CHAPTER 23

Garrett had texted Layla.

She felt her heart speed up as she saw his name flash across her phone's screen.

To be fair, he did text her sometimes—to ask a question about lesson planning, generally, or to ask her if she liked raisins in her cookies (the answer was no). But this text had been different. It was Sunday, a day when Layla listened to church on the radio if it was too cold to go in person and then ran errands and otherwise did as little as possible, but the one text he sent abruptly changed all her plans.

Garrett: Want to drop by the hospital in a bit? My grandpa is asking for you. Bring Ducky too.

She stood so fast Ducky whimpered, a little scared, and she gently smoothed his fur to comfort him. She fed him, sticking a few treats in the kibble, and refilled his water, leaving him to eat while she jumped in the shower, washed her greasy hair, shaved, and regretted eating her weight in Mexican food the night before . . . and the extra two glasses of wine she'd consumed that she really, really hadn't needed. Which was in addition to the two glasses of wine she had needed, of course.

Or maybe she had needed all four glasses. Her head was still spinning a little, and her stomach didn't feel quite right, so she headed to the kitchen and downed an entire glass of fizzy Alka-Seltzer, which was a remedy her mother swore by. She'd remembered the mornings in the kitchen, her mom in an old blue terry-cloth bathrobe and Layla in fuzzy slippers, her mom stirring her Alka-Seltzer and drinking it up. "It works for practically everything," she'd told her daughter.

The memory stopped Layla short. She'd kept everything—everything about her parents frozen, tucked away behind a wall, so she wouldn't have to think about it or remember. And then, all of a sudden, a memory had escaped, come back with full color and boldness, before she had a chance to tuck it away again, so swiftly and strongly she'd been entrenched in it before she'd even realized what was happening.

And . . . strangely . . . she didn't hate it.

She didn't hate it even a little bit.

The reminder was sweet and soft and lovely, just a quiet memory, something she might have at one time called her mother to tell her she was doing—*Mom, I took your advice*—or to ask more about—*How often do I take it? Does this work for hangovers?* Instead, it just had been waiting in her mind, quiet and happy, for her to take it back out, dust it off, and fit it back into the life like a piece in jigsaw puzzle. Strangely, instead of her mind collapsing in on itself, as it once had whenever she delved too deeply into the past, she was . . .

She was okay.

It was *weird* how okay she was.

Layla dressed Ducky in small mint-green scrubs and hung a tiny stethoscope around his neck and set him in the front seat of her Bronco, where he sat, proudly. As they drove to Brimsley together, Layla found the memory kept her company on the way to the hospital, like something warm she'd put in her pocket on the cold day. And while she'd still gotten heavy feet and tingling hands when she walked through the entrance of the hospital, it dissipated, slowly, one step at a time, as she headed toward the wing that held the hospital's admitted patients, into a sense of general unease. It didn't go away, necessarily, but it was bearable if she didn't think about it too much. It was like a sprained ankle of mental anguish—she'd be fine if she didn't put weight on it.

Garrett's smile when she knocked on the door threw her into a new kind of mood. Temper. Feeling. She didn't know the right word for the way her whole body turned to liquid when he was in the room. He stood at the food of the hospital bed, halfway through folding a blanket, but it was like his hands had forgotten what they were doing, so he was just standing there, the corners of the blanket still in his heads, grinning a little foolishly. She felt her heart speed up in her chest, rabbit-fast.

Mr. Rogers was sitting up in the bed, looking grouchy, his arms crossed over his chest, scowling. His face momentarily transformed, wrinkles rearranging, into a wide smile. "Layla!" he said, opening his arms. She walked in, smiling, a GET WELL balloon she'd bought on a whim bobbing along behind her.

She gave Mr. Rogers a gentle one-armed hug, taking care not to tug on the IV in his arm, or get tangled in the various other wires—the one connected to his oximeter, or the thick gray cord to his call button. Ducky was struggling in her arms to get to Mr. Rogers, but she held him tight—she was afraid he'd hit a button or something he shouldn't.

"How are you feeling?" she asked when she pulled away. She set the balloon with a mountain of other get-well gifts on the windowsill. Ducky didn't like the balloon very much at all and growled softly at the four others that Mr. Rogers had collected from his friends.

Mr. Rogers's scowl fell back into place. "How have I been feeling? I'm great, but this place? It's the worst. They're keeping me prisoner here when I'm perfectly fine."

Layla glanced uncertainly at Garrett, who grinned and shrugged. "He's actually fine. They're discharging him shortly."

He paused. "Sorry about that. We just got the news. Otherwise I'd have had you meet us at the house."

"What? That's great!" Layla said, grinning back. "So, you can go home, like . . . now?"

"They're drawing up the paperwork," Garrett said. "They said he's going to be fine."

"Taking them long enough," Mr. Rogers said grouchily. "Like they're trying to get every cent out of me while they can. Someone's supposed to come in here and get all these wires off me. Probably giving me cancer." He brightened slightly, perking up. "How's my good buddy Ducky?" He held out his hands. "Come on, give him here. This is the kind of doctor I want to see."

She looked up at Garrett, who nodded his permission. She set Ducky in Mr. Rogers's lap, and he immediately climbed up and snuggled in under Mr. Rogers's chin.

"Ducky missed you," Layla said honestly. She'd found him sitting on the top of the couch, peering toward Mr. Rogers's house after Christine had left. "I think he's really worried about you."

"Dogs are smart like that," Mr. Rogers said, and then his frown came back. "Smarter than the people trying to keep me in this hospital so long."

Layla laughed at his grouchiness, which was out of character for her—but she'd been afraid to see him, afraid he would be pale and drawn and ill, but instead—he was himself. A grumpier version of himself, but still very much Mr. Rogers.

"Apparently, they're calling it low blood sugar," Garrett said. He touched his grandfather's shoulder. "I guess we've been skipping breakfast, haven't we?"

"I forgot," Mr. Rogers said stubbornly. "I had more important things to focus on. I'm a very busy person."

She bit the inside of her cheek to keep from grinning. He looked so funny, with his angry face and a tiny dog climbing up to lick his cheek. His face quirked back into an unwilling smile.

"A very busy person who won't skip breakfast anymore?" Garrett asked gently, crossing his arms across his chest. Layla looked away, so she wouldn't get caught staring at his biceps in a T-shirt.

"Yes," Mr. Rogers grumbled. "I guess."

Layla chuckled. She couldn't help it. The only thing wrong with Mr. Rogers—usually the most cheerful, happy person in town—was that he was in a bad mood and had forgotten to eat breakfast. Layla couldn't relate. She had never once forgotten to eat. She looked forward to eating all day. It wasn't something she'd just . . . not remember.

A pleasantly round nurse bustled in, her hair in a messy ponytail at the nape of her neck, a couple of cardboard boxes in her arms. "I thought I might help you box up all your things from your admirers," she told Mr. Rogers, winking at Layla.

"I can help," Layla volunteered. "I live close to him, so I can drive some of it home now." She turned to Garrett. "I mean, if it's okay with you."

He was still smiling. "Of course," he said.

Layla set to packing up the teddy bears and chocolates and balloons and flowers, carefully tucking them in the boxes. She stuffed all the cards back into envelopes and pushed them near the backside of a particularly fluffy teddy bear holding a bright red *I love you* heart.

The flowers were the hardest—she poured out most of the water in the sink so they wouldn't tip over and spill all over the other gifts in the box. She packed the other gifts around the vases to make sure they stayed upright.

She'd finished up just as the nurse had unhooked him from his IV and was giving final discharge instructions. Mr. Rogers was sitting up now, eagerly waiting to change into his street clothes. Ducky was sitting beside him, supervising.

"I see someone smuggled in a little friend to see you!" the nurse said when she saw Ducky nestled on Mr. Rogers. "Don't you worry, I won't say a word. It looks like he's a doctor anyway, so he'll fit right in here."

Ducky sat up straighter, as if that would make him appear more doctor-like.

Layla scooped the pup back up into her arms and pointed at the cardboard boxes. "I'll, um, just bring these down to my car. You can give me a call when you get to the house, and I'll bring them over," Layla told Garrett, hoping she could get out the door before Mr. Rogers decided to stand in his gaping hospital gown and give her a show she hadn't bought tickets for.

"There's a cart in the hallway," the nurse called after her.

Garrett helped her load the boxes onto the cart so she didn't have to put Ducky back down—because the dog was struggling furiously to get back to Mr. Rogers.

"Just text me when you get back," she told Garrett. "I'll leave to save your grandfather some dignity." She grinned. "Don't let him strongarm that nurse in there."

He gave a half smile. "I should be compensated for the amount of times I've had to see his backside the past couple of days."

Layla laughed. "I'll keep you in my thoughts. Just—call me when you need me. Or text me. Whatever."

He nodded. "I—I will. I have something I want to talk to you about." He was looking down at her, his hands on the either side of the cart.

"I hate when people do that. Now I'm going to be nervous about this conversation forever. Can't you just tell me now?" She tightened her hold on Ducky, who had just tried to take a dive onto the floor to get away from her. "Come on, buddy. You'll see Mr. Rogers soon. I promise."

Garrett shook his head, a held-back smile escaping to turn up the corners of his mouth. "Sorry. This should wait. But it's not bad. At least, I think it's not bad. You might."

"You don't want to confess your undying love for me by the nurse's station in the middle of a hospital?" she asked dryly, and then wanted to clamp her hand over her mouth as soon as the words passed her lips. Why, *why* couldn't she just shut up for one minute? Why did she have to go put her foot in it? And why in the hell couldn't she stop flirting with him? His grandfather was in the hospital, and yet, here she was.

His face flushed, but he chuckled. "Something like that."

She nodded quickly. "Okay, bye!" she sang, and pushed the cart down the elevators before she could say anything else completely stupid—or before Ducky could make another daring escape attempt.

Layla rushed out, kicking herself, almost knocking over a custodian in the process. When the sun outside hit her face along with a sharp Nebraska wind, she breathed a big sigh of relief. At least if she wasn't around Garrett, nothing stupid would come out of her mouth. And if it did, well, at least he couldn't hear.

CHAPTER 24

Layla was a coward.

Garrett had texted her—*five minutes away*—and she'd driven over with the boxes, beating them home by a good two minutes. She'd left Ducky behind, even though he'd started pouting and turned his back on her when he realized he wasn't invited.

When Garrett and Mr. Rogers pulled into the driveway, she hurriedly helped Garrett take everything inside after they'd gotten Mr. Rogers settled in his favorite easy chair, a thick quilted blanket spread over his legs. Then, she set to work, carefully ignoring any offers of help from Garrett. She refilled the vases of flowers with fresh water, and placed them around the house, where Mr. Rogers could get the most enjoyment out of them. She put the stuffed animals around his bedroom and tied the balloons together in one big bundle that she left in the corner of the living room so he wouldn't trip over any of them.

And then she gave Mr. Rogers a hug—a big one, like she'd wanted to give him in the hospital. "I'm so glad you're home."

"Me too," he said. As she stood up, he gripped her arm. "Listen . . . I know what you did for me. Garrett told me."

"It was nothing," she said.

He shook his head. "Now, Layla," he said, his voice soft, "please don't do that. You know it wasn't nothing. If you hadn't been there for me, I probably wouldn't be here now. So thank you. And give that little dog a treat for me."

She nodded. "I will."

"Thank you," he said again. He gave her arm an extra squeeze—a strong one for an old man who had just spent two nights in the hospital—and released her. He nodded at her shakily, and she realized he had tears in his eyes. She felt something in her chest seize up. Suddenly, she wanted to cry, but she sucked in her cheeks and nodded instead.

"I'm glad I could help," she said finally, honestly, and wiped at her cheeks. This was too much emotion for one day, and it was absolutely exhausting. She needed to get out of there—not because she was upset at Mr. Rogers, but just because she needed a moment to herself. To center. To think. Or not to think at all. She wasn't really sure. But she knew that being alone was what she needed in the moment, and she wasn't in the place to overthink it.

She stood, slowly, smiling at her neighbor, but she was gritting her teeth and swallowing hard.

Garrett suddenly appeared beside her, brushing her elbow softly. "Hey," he said. "Can we talk?"

The three worst words in the English language. *Can we talk.*

Strange panic flooded her, and she shook her head. "I, um, have to get back to Ducky. Call me if you need anything, okay?"

He nodded at her. "Are you okay?"

"Yep." The word passed her lips quickly, because Layla didn't have another answer. She was always okay. It was part of who she was, as much part of her as her brunette hair and the scar on her elbow from the one and only time she'd tried skateboarding when she was twelve.

And then, before Garrett could ask anything else, she was gone.

She was definitely a coward.

Layla jumped back in her car and drove fifteen seconds around the corner and up the street and back to her house as quickly as she could, her pulse beating a staccato rhythm in her chest. She looked back once, but Garrett hadn't followed her out. She wasn't sure if she was glad about that—or a little disappointed.

Both, probably.

Once Layla was inside her house, she stood with her back against the door for a moment, catching her breath. Ducky appeared instantly at her feet, looking up at her with his wide, inquisitive eyes. She scooped him up and gave him a gentle hug. The little dog touched his nose to hers.

"You're a good dog, sweetheart," she said, bringing him to the kitchen, where she started preparing his food. She had started adding chicken broth to his kibble, which he absolutely loved. She sat him on the counter while she cracked open a can. A few months ago, she would never have believed she'd let a dog sit on her kitchen counter, or that she'd be carefully preparing his dinner, or that she'd be around one at all, really. Yet there she was.

It was utterly unfathomable, she thought, how being around Ducky almost immediately calmed her. Centered her. Left her feeling calm and, if not happy . . . okay.

She sat Ducky on the floor and then gave him his kibble. She took a seat on the floor beside him and watched him eat, crunching happily on his bowl of kibble. She realized, quite suddenly, she loved him. A lot. She'd known she liked him, certainly, and she'd known how much she was going to miss him when he was gone, but the little puppy had gone from a not entirely welcome guest to . . . well, one of her very best friends. He filled part of the hole in her heart.

Maybe, just maybe, she could talk to Garrett. So she decided to text him. Be brave. She typed in the words before she could lose her nerve.

Layla: Sorry I had to leave. Do you want to come talk?

Her phone pinged back almost right away.

Garrett: It's okay. I think you need a minute. Let's talk tomorrow when we get a chance.

She smiled at the phone, her heart melting a little bit. Garrett got her. And that was truly rare.

CHAPTER 25

DUCKY

Ducky couldn't believe how lucky he was. He got to go to work with Layla again.

She dressed him up in a fuzzy Cookie Monster costume. It was soft blue fur and even had little hands that held a cookie. Ducky loved it so much. He wished it were a real cookie. It wasn't though. He tried to eat it, and it didn't taste good at all.

Layla giggled as she dressed Ducky. She was in a good mood. Ducky didn't blame her. Mr. Rogers was feeling better, and Layla said in a few days Ducky could go stay with him for the day, but she was giving him a little time to finish healing. That was okay with Ducky. He wanted Mr. Rogers to feel all the way better so they could play. Ducky had been exploring his backyard a lot, and he loved all the smells. A month ago, Ducky tried to bite a bee, though, and Mr. Rogers scolded him and made him stay inside. He said it wasn't safe to bite bees. Ducky thought that was silly, though. The bee was flying right in front of Ducky's face and invading his personal space, and besides, it was really fun to chase it through the garden.

"Be good today," Layla told Ducky sternly. "Principal Crimmons doesn't know you're coming, so I'm relying on you to be extra cute and charming so he doesn't send you home."

Which was a silly thing to tell Ducky. Anyone who knew him knew he was always extra cute and charming. It was his job. But Ducky wagged his tail to assure her. He loved going to see everyone at school and getting all the extra pets! It was Ducky's favorite! Even though sometimes all the kids trying to touch Ducky at once was a little overwhelming. But that was okay, because Layla made them all go sit down and he got to sit on her desk and watch Layla teach, which was really fun.

Layla told Ducky there would be even more kids this time, because last time some stayed home because they weren't feeling well. Ducky jumped up and down to show her how excited he was. Then he rolled over on his back and asked for belly rubs, because it was always a good time for belly rubs. All dogs knew that.

"We don't have time for belly rubs, Ducky!" she said, before dropping to the ground to undo the Velcro on Ducky's Cookie Monster costume so she could give him the belly rubs she didn't have time for.

Ducky loved being right about belly rubs. It was one of the facts of dog life. All he had to do was drop to the ground and show his tummy and wiggle a little with his paws in the air and humans dropped whatever they were doing to comply. Ducky had a theory that humans enjoyed giving belly rubs even more than dogs liked them.

"Okay," Layla said finally, after giving Ducky a few minutes of very good scratches. Her voice was stern this time, but not too stern. "We have to go. Being late would not make a good impression. And you want to be a classroom dog, don't you?"

Ducky wagged his tail to show her that he would be a very excellent classroom dog.

"We'd better get going, then," she said, picking up her totes, which were always loaded down with books. She had an extra one she brought that was blue, and Ducky knew it was just for him, because she'd let him sit inside last time, with only his head poking out. It had been kind of comfy.

Ducky followed her out to the car and waited until she scooped him up onto her seat, and he sat still and straight, like a very good boy, while she backed out of her driveway. Ducky liked her car. It smelled old and nice. He could definitely smell a Cheeto she dropped between the seats many, many months ago. He tried to stick his head down to get it but couldn't quite reach it. He pushed his head down a little farther. He could get a good, strong whiff of it there. He stuck out his tongue, but it was just beyond lick reach. If only he could reach a little farther!

"What are you doing?" Ducky heard Layla ask, but she sounded far away. Probably because one of Ducky's ears was jammed up against the center console, and the other one was pushed into the side of the seat. He stretched down, just a little bit farther, but his paws slipped off the seat, and before he know what was happening, his head and shoulders were stuck and his little back feet were waving in the air. He gave his loudest *awoooooo* he could, trying not to panic—he was stuck!

Layla gave a tiny shocked scream beside Ducky and then burst into laughter. The Yorkie wiggled harder to get loose, but only felt himself slipping farther into the crack. The car swayed and came to a stop, and then, laughing even harder, Layla put both of her hands on Ducky's torso and pulled gently.

Ducky yelped. He didn't like being crammed in such a small space. He sure wanted that Cheeto, though. Even though it was probably old and stale. But that was okay. He still wanted to taste the cheese dust really, really bad.

Ducky heard a click as Layla unbuckled her seat belt and leaned over to readjust her grip on the dog. "Be brave, Ducky," he heard her say from a bazillion miles away, and then she pulled on him again, slightly harder this time.

Ducky moved upward, just a tad bit.

Layla tugged again, as gently as she could, and it hurt, but he was trying super hard to be brave, so he whimpered, but only a tiny one. Layla gave another small tug, and then a big one, and

Ducky came free, shaking his head. Layla pulled him into her lap, and Ducky whined, his ears feeling funny.

"You okay, buddy?" she asked, her voice gentle and soft as a bunny rabbit.

Oh no! Ducky looked down. He forgot the Cheeto! He jumped over to the other seat and then dove back into the crevice, and Layla burst into laughter and pulled him back out. "Oh, no you don't!" she said. "Ducky, no! Sit!"

The Yorkie ducked his head in shame. Layla didn't tell Ducky no very often. And Ducky bet she wouldn't be telling him no if she could smell the delicious Cheeto. Ducky bet she'd be stuck down there too.

Even though Ducky's pride was clearly hurt, Layla kept looking over at him during the rest of the ride and bursting into laughter. The little dog turned his back to her to show her that his feelings were upset and stayed that way when she pulled into the school parking lot.

"I'm sorry, Ducky," she said finally through bursts of laughter. "You just . . . you just make me smile."

Ducky turned back toward her, not sure if he should forgive her.

"I'll give you belly rubs when we get into my classroom," she bargained.

He tilted his head, considering her offer.

"I bet Garrett will too," she said pleadingly. "Come on, little buddy. Don't be mad at me. Please?"

He used his nose to show her the crack between the seat, hoping she'd reach down and find the Cheeto. But her smeller wasn't as good as a dog's, so she probably didn't understand. Even though Ducky was super disappointed, he let Layla scoop him up, tuck him into her tote, and bring him into the school.

Principal Crimmons greeted Ducky and Layla as soon as they walked into Layla's classroom. "Morning, Layla!" he said. He had a bright red face. It reminded Ducky of a ball he had at home in

Los Angeles. His dad threw it down the hall, and Ducky chased it and it was the best.

"Good morning, Principal Crimmons," Layla said. "Ducky's dog sitter just got out of the hospital and isn't fit to care for him just yet, so I had to bring him in."

Garrett walked in behind Principal Crimmons, a backpack slung over his shoulder. Ducky noticed things like that because his dad, Jason, always had treats in his backpack. His dad was pretty nice like that.

"Good morning, Principal Crimmons," Garrett said. He nodded at Layla and Ducky. "Hey, Layla. Hey, little guy." He gave the dog an affectionate pat as he walked by.

Layla gave him a little bit of a silly grin. "Hi, Garrett. I have notes on your lesson plans."

Principal Crimmons cleaned his throat.

"Oh, sorry. Am I interrupting something?" Garrett asked.

"No," the principal said. "I was just commenting that we have an uncredentialed dog in the school."

Ducky decided this was an excellent moment to be extra cute, so he hopped out of the tote onto a desk. The pup skip-skip-skipped across the room, jumping from one desk to the other, until he reached the one by the door, which belonged to Benny, if he remembered right. It smelled like him, at least. Ducky looked up at Principal Crimmons and opened his eyes super wide and whimpered a little.

"I'm so sorry," Layla said, "but he was so great with the kids last time. I've never had such a well-behaved classroom—they were so excited to get time with the dog." She paused. "I think we are really underestimating canine therapy as a valuable learning tool."

Principal Crimmons looked down at the Yorkie in front of him. He was trying to resist Ducky—and Ducky knew it. He lifted a paw, and touched his own ear, and Principal Crimmons melted and scratched the dog on the head. "Are you a good learning tool?" he asked Ducky.

The little dog barked once to tell him yes, and Principal Crimmons chuckled. Ducky lifted up his front paws, and the man picked him up and held him closely. He rocked the little dog, and Ducky's tongue lolled out of his mouth. Ducky gave the man a quick kiss on his red cheek for good measure.

Principal Crimmons turned his attention to Garrett and Layla. "To clarify, I agree with you. Ducky here is clearly quite a gentleman, and a great dog. I'd actually love to see him in the classroom more often."

"Really? Layla says. "Because I was thinking—"

Principal Crimmons shifted Ducky to one arm and held up a hand. "As I was saying—I would love to see him in the class more often, but not until he's a certified therapy dog."

"But that would take months!" Garrett burst in. "And he's already well-behaved!"

"From a legal perspective, we can't have random dogs roaming around our classrooms." Principal Crimmons paused and cleared his throat. "But perhaps—if he were to start training, we could figure something out." He paused to look down at Ducky with a small smile. "And I suppose—just for this week—he can stay in the classroom. What do you think?"

Layla and Garrett looked at each other. "I think that's fair," Layla said slowly.

"Good," Principal Crimmons said. "Bring me certification he's training as a therapy dog and he's welcome to come see us any time." Principal Crimmons set Ducky gently back on the desk. "He'd be a great addition to any classroom."

And with that, Principal Crimmons patted Ducky on the head. "Bye, Ducky," he said, and left the room, closing the door behind him.

"Wait," Garrett said. "Did he just . . . say goodbye to Ducky and ignore us?"

"Yup," Layla said. "He absolutely did."

And then, they both bent over laughing until they were crying. Layla had tears leaking out of the corner of her eyes. Ducky jumped down and ran to her to make sure she was okay, but she was having so much fun the dog decided to let her be.

Humans were so confusing. It was a good thing Ducky was around to take care of them. He wasn't sure what any of them would do without him.

CHAPTER 26

"Well," Garrett said, turning to Layla, "that's one way to start off your morning. Although I prefer coffee."

Layla glanced at Ducky, who was running around the room, smelling all the desks, like he was trying to remember who sat where. "I had to start my day by pulling Ducky out from where he got stuck in the seat. Apparently he was trying to get something that fell down by the seat belt."

Garrett chuckled. "Are you kidding?"

"I had to pull over and everything. He was a hazard, and his whole butt was sticking up in the air, waving around."

Ducky looked up from his desk-sniffing task, as if offended they were talking about his embarrassing moment. Layla hid her snickers behind her hand. She loved the heck out of that dog. She realized that since she's started her gig as a dog sitter, she had been smiling about a hundred times more than usual.

Of course, a little bit of that was her super attractive, super funny student teacher.

Who was looking at her right now, with a smile around his lips. "Did you have a good Sunday?" he asked.

"Yeah," she said, remembering how she'd basically run away from him. "Um, sorry about how I ditched. You probably haven't noticed this, but I'm kind of an introvert when I'm not parading around in front of second graders."

Garrett pretended to be shocked. "Never."

"Shut up."

"I thought we didn't say *shut up* in the classroom," Garrett teased, parroting a line she'd used on Aiden McGee a few weeks before after he'd told Teddy to shut his mouth about his math homework.

Layla rolled her eyes but resisted pushing him playfully. He was back in a button-up—a light, crisp yellow that complemented his olive skin. She liked it. He looked so good in a nice button-up. But honestly, he looked so good in everything. She had a flashback of seeing him in a T-shirt—twice over the weekend—but quickly brushed it away. She didn't need to think about his arms. Or the flowers. Or that he'd called her pretty, sort of, in a roundabout way.

"Do you want to go over lesson plans?" she asked him, logging in to her computer.

"Can I ask you something first?"

Her fingers froze on the keys. "Um, what?"

He leaned forward, his elbows on the desk. "First, I wanted to tell you how much I appreciated you this weekend. I know I already thanked you—but seriously, you were there for us, and you didn't need to be." He was looking at her earnestly. So earnestly, in fact, she was having trouble meeting his unwavering gaze.

Layla blushed and looked down at the desk. "Well, um, I really care about—Mr. Rogers. He's been a good neighbor, and a good friend. It was the least I could do."

"Speaking of which," Garrett said, "Do you mind if I take a slightly longer lunch than usual? I want to spend some time with him—make sure he's doing okay without me." He sighed. "I tried to convince him to let me set a camera up in the living room, but he told me in no uncertain terms he doesn't want any *spy equipment* in his house."

Layla laughed. "Yeah, your grandpa doesn't really appreciate the internet. Or technology. Or security . . . besides Ducky, of course. But yeah—of course you can go. Take as long as you need. I'll be sure to give the kids lots of candy so they're all hyped up for your return."

"Make sure you do," Garrett said, laughing. "Hey, one more thing—"

The bell rang, cutting him short. Layla grabbed Ducky off the floor, and set him on her desk, so he wouldn't accidentally get trampled by overexcited kids. "Stay," she told him. "Be a good boy."

Ducky sat up a little straighter, as if to prove to her he was going to be very, very good.

Garrett crossed the room to open the door and stand by the entrance so he could high-five every kid as they came in. He'd started doing this the week before, and the kids loved it. Even Lucas had given him a weak high five, which was a win in Layla's book. He was just as likely to walk past an outstretched hand, his head down, like he was trying to be invisible.

She'd talked to the counselor again too, but Mr. Bonilla was stumped. He'd called Lucas's parents in, who begged Lucas to talk, but he remained the same—a closed-off fortress of a little boy. It broke Layla's heart. And she was determined to help, no matter what. She didn't want him to be the class star or someone who spoke up often; she just wanted him to be happy. Like the rest of her students.

The kids came in, jazzed up from the weekend, laughing and shouting over one another. She smiled as they noticed Ducky and got even more animated—but those who were in class the last time Ducky was allowed to attend followed the rules and sat quietly, waiting for their turns with Ducky. The other kids crowded around Layla's desk, exclaiming happily over the little Yorkie in his Cookie Monster costume, but she sent them back to their seats, explaining that Ducky couldn't possibly have so many students trying to pet him at once.

Lucas hadn't approached the desk. Instead, he was sitting quietly at his desk, but she noticed his eyes were on Ducky—he was alert—and *smiling*. It was the first time she ever remembered him smiling when entering the classroom, or even raising his eyes from his desk for more than a second. She grinned. She was so excited to introduce him to Ducky.

"Class," she said, "I'm going to let Garrett do the announcements and start class, and then, one by one, you can come up and say good morning to Ducky—if and only if you pay attention, follow the rules, and act appropriately. Okay?"

"Okay!" the class chorused. They were so excited to have the little dog back. The kids wiggled and fidgeted but did their best to stay still as Garrett read through the day's lunch menu and shared important announcements—like about upcoming parent-teacher conferences, the school's canned-food drive, and a late start the coming Friday due to teacher in-service.

"Finally, the year's annual Jarvis Pizza Luncheon has been canceled."

If there was ever a moment Layla was thankful for Ducky, it was that one. Every year, Jarvis hosted a big pizza party for all the kids at Two Falls Elementary—and donated a book to every single student before releasing them to go home early. Every year, the whole school looked forward to it, even the teachers and the support staff.

But this year . . .

Garrett caught her eye from the front of the classroom. His jaw twitched. He knew exactly what she was thinking.

Was this because of the budget cuts? Because the plant was shutting down? Because this was the first part—a small, precursory wave—of something worse? Layla felt a thick, heavy feeling in the bottom of her stomach. She reached out and touched Ducky, who leaned into her hand, sensing she needed him.

Meanwhile, at the front of the room, Garrett was quizzing the kids of the state capitals, starting with Nebraska. Every week, he had been adding a new state capital to their repertoire—and this week, they'd gotten to Harrisburg, Pennsylvania.

Meanwhile, a *ping* popped up on Layla's computer.

Mrs. Sanchez: CANCELING THE JARVIS PIZZA LUNCH?? WTH??????

Layla typed back quickly.

Layla: IKR? The kids are so disappointed, I'm sure.
Mrs. Sanchez: The kids? I'm disappointed. We got to eat pizza and got half the day off!!!!!

Layla stifled a laugh.

Layla: I know, right? That's one lunch I'll have to pay for myself now.
Mrs. Sanchez: Maybe we can pool money so the kids can still have a pizza day. Or something. I don't know.
Layla: I'd put in what I can.
Mrs. Sanchez: Can I be honest?
Layla: Of course.
Mrs. Sanchez: If they're pulling something as small as the pizza lunch . . . what else are they pulling? Are they going to shut down the programs they sponsor?
Layla: Do you think the plant is really going under?
Mrs. Sanchez: I don't know. But the stuff I've heard hasn't been good.
Layla: I'm sure it will work out in the end.
Mrs. Sanchez: That makes one of us. Honestly? I'm updating my résumé, and I suggest you do the same. My husband wants to put our house on the market before the plant goes under . . . he says it will be easier to sell if we do it now. If we wait, we're going to lose all the money we put into it.

Suddenly, Layla's ears were ringing. She wanted to tell Mrs. Sanchez not to sell, to hold out, to stay, but she couldn't do that. She couldn't ask someone to risk their livelihood for her.

Layla: I'll miss you . . . but you need to do whatever is right for your family.

It felt like an echo of what she'd told Susan Lynn.

In her heart, Layla knew she should be considering the same thing. But the idea of putting her little house that she'd worked for on the market broke her heart. It was her place. It wasn't anyone else's. It had felt more like home than anything since her parents died. It wasn't perfect—she knew it needed updates in the worst way—but it was home, and it was *hers*, and she felt safe there in a way she didn't anywhere else.

If the town went under, she wouldn't be able to sell her house. And she couldn't afford to keep it if she moved, not on a teacher's salary. It would bankrupt her; rob her of every cent she'd scraped together. Her parents hadn't left her much when they passed, their money eaten up by hospital bills, and so she didn't have the safety net her peers might have.

Layla envisioned, for a moment, a big FOR SALE sign stuck in her yard, and her eyes pricked with tears. She couldn't do it.

Her computer quietly pinged again, and Layla glanced back at the screen through blurry eyes. She blinked quickly to read the text that popped up on her screen.

Mrs. Sanchez: This sucks.
Layla: I know.

Layla closed her IM and swallowed the lump that had risen up in the back of her throat. Ducky was looking at her strangely, and she tried to give him a reassuring smile. He hopped in her lap and curled up in a ball. She felt her heart swell a little. She loved Ducky. There was no question about it.

Meanwhile, she noticed, Lucas was not paying attention to the lesson. Instead, he was staring at Ducky, his eyes wide and alert. She pulled Ducky up into a standing position from her lap and used his paw to wave across the room at Lucas. Ducky's tongue hung out of his mouth happily. Layla was sure Ducky would be excited to have so many new friends—hopefully, including Lucas. Ducky wasn't used to people who didn't rush up to greet him. She hoped that the little dog would take to the shy student.

Lucas blinked in surprise, and his face broke out into a wide, happy grin. Then, slowly, tentatively, he lifted a hand and waved back at Ducky.

Layla grinned back at him. If she had been alone in the room, she would have danced around with excitement. But instead, she remained still and calm. She couldn't believe it. Lucas was making progress. Real progress.

Garrett was making progress too. Of course, he'd started better than most student teachers ended, and she hadn't really thought she'd need to teach him anything, or that he could improve—and yet, he had. Layla kept finding herself impressed—over how he interacted with the kids, how he spoke kindly and thoughtfully to each of them, how he'd bought a book on goats in for Anita Myers-Perkins, how he'd shown Teddy news articles about his dad from before Teddy was born.

The kids loved him even more.

When Garrett had finished with the geography lesson, he cleared his throat. "Would everyone like to line up at Ms. Layla's desk and say hello to Ducky? Line up—"

But before he could finish his statement, the kids had leaped out of their desks and formed a messy line that caterpillared through the room. Emma Richards, who sat nearest Layla's desk, was first, and she patted Ducky, very gently, and gave him a big kiss. Layla laughed. "No kissing!" she reminded her students. "Ducky likes to roll around outside in the dirt!"

"I don't care," Emma pronounced proudly, and blew Ducky another kiss as she flounced back to her desk, proud to have been the first one to pet the dog.

One by one, each student walked up to her desk and said hello to Ducky. At the end of the line, Lucas waited patiently, fidgeting, looking down at his feet and then up toward the front of the line, shoving his hands deep in his pockets and then taking them out to push his hair behind his ears. He was in need of a haircut, Layla noticed, when he got to the front of the line, peering out from behind the strands that fell over his eyes. Or maybe he insisted on keeping it long. It gave him something to hide behind.

"Can I—can I pet him?" Lucas asked.

"Ducky would love that," Layla said. "He loves friendly pets. Just be gentle with him. He's very small."

Lucas nodded seriously, and reached out one hand, which was trembling.

"It's okay," she said, her voice soft. "Take your time."

Lucas nodded. His eyes were fixed on the little dog, and he reached out his shaking fingers and lightly touched the dog's fur. Ducky, as if sensing the boy's hesitation, took a couple steps toward Lucas and sat down in front of him, where Lucas could easily reach him. Lucas patted him gently, and Ducky closed his eyes, enjoying it.

"See?" Layla asked. "He likes you."

Lucas's smile was radiant. "He does?"

"Look at his tail," Layla pointed out. "See how it's wagging?"

Lucas nodded.

"It's because he's happy."

Ducky leaned forward and licked Lucas's hand. The boy giggled. It was a wonderful sound, high and cute and clear as a bell.

"He must think you taste good too," Layla said.

Lucas giggled more.

At the front of the classroom, Garrett was setting up a science experiment—it was volcano day, which the kids were very, very excited about. Second-grade volcano day was a very big deal, and Garrett had brought baking powder and lemon juice for the occasion.

But Lucas was still petting Ducky, looking adoringly at him, his face full of the kind of blissful happiness Layla had never seen in him before.

Finally, she stopped him. "Looks like Mr. Garrett is starting the next lesson, Lucas. Will you come back to say hi to Ducky a little later?"

Lucas nodded. "Okay. Thank you."

Layla wasn't sure if he was talking to her or the dog, but she didn't care. Lucas walked back to his desk, his shoulders held just a little higher than usual, and he cast a long, happy look over his shoulder at Ducky, who was still sitting proudly on Layla's desk.

"Good dog," she whispered to Ducky. "You just made that boy's whole month."

Ducky's chest puffed out just a bit farther.

At the front of the classroom, Garrett was showing the bottle of lemon juice and the baking soda and had unveiled the giant volcano he'd constructed from papier-mâché just for this lesson. *That* was the kind of teacher he was—he spent hours and hours of his own time planning a perfect lesson for kids.

"Did you know," he asked the class, "that mountains have names?"

The kids shook their heads.

"It's true. What kind of names do you think mountains should have?"

Leighton Sloan raised his hand, and Garrett pointed at him. "Eric," he said seriously.

Garrett swallowed a smile. "That's a very good name. So, we are going to call this Mount Eric. Who can name other famous mountains?"

Avery Drubbins raised his hand. "Mount Doom."

"That's a name from a book," Garrett said. "Very good, Avery. Has anyone heard of Mount Everest?"

No hands raised.

"Mount Everest is the highest mountain in the whole world!"

"Have you been there?" Teddy asked.

Garrett shook his head. "Nope. It's right on the border of China and Nepal, so it's very, very far from Nebraska."

"I bet I could beat you in a race to the top." Aiden told Teddy.

"Bet I would beat you," Teddy challenged back. Layla smiled a little. Being in Nebraska, most of the kids hadn't spent much time around actual mountains. They probably thought of them as big hills.

"It's much too cold—and way too far—to race to the top," Garrett said. "And it takes a really long time."

"Like an hour?" Anita asked.

"Like months," Garrett told her. "It's very dangerous. But guess what, Anita?"

"What?" she asked.

"Goats live there."

Garrett might as well have told her they were taking a field trip to the moon. Her eyes shone with a bright, surreal happiness. "Wow," she whispered.

"I know," Garrett agreed.

Meanwhile, on Layla's desk, something else had started to happen. Ducky, who had, until that point, been sitting proudly on her desk, behaving well, had leaped into Layla's lap—which wasn't entirely strange in itself as he spent a lot of time curled in in laps.

But instead of lying down and falling asleep, the little dog in his Cookie Monster costume rebalanced and hopped on the floor.

"Ducky!" Layla hissed. "Come back!" She hadn't leashed him, since he was always good. Except for now.

Normally, Ducky would have trotted back to Layla happily, but he ignored her, as if she hadn't spoken. Layla frowned. What the heck was this dog up to?

The children giggled as Ducky weaved his way through the desks, the volcano at the front of the classroom forgotten, peering down at him as he made his way to the very back of the classroom.

He passed the Drubbins twins, who both made greedy grabs at the pup, but Ducky skillfully dodged them. He paused, for a moment, by Emma, and looked up at her with a big doggy smile on his face, and then continued on—past Benny and Teddy and Anita and Aiden, until he finally stopped and looked up, tongue hanging out, at the feet of one very specific kid.

Lucas.

At the front of the classroom, Garrett had stopped talking, a bottle of lemon juice in his hand, posed over the volcano, a pair of science goggles on his face, looking, if Layla admitted it, adorable in a very nerdy way. His mouth had been just a little open, and then it widened into a smile.

Ducky stood on his back legs, his paws up.

He wanted Lucas to lift him.

Lucas looked down at the little dog uncertainly for a long moment, and then reached down to pick Ducky up and sit him in his lap, where Ducky perched happily. Then the dog looked up at Garrett, as if to say, *Well, aren't you going to continue the lesson?*

Garrett shrugged. "Well, now that our class pet is comfortable, do you think I should make this volcano erupt?"

The kids giggled. And Lucas? Well, Lucas was having the happiest day he'd ever had since Layla met him.

He was enthralled with the dog. He always had at least one hand touching Ducky, no matter what, and Layla knew he probably wasn't paying as close attention as she would like—but she let him be. He was happy—no, not happy. Overjoyed. Elated.

And the kids—they were smiling in Lucas's direction all day. It was, without a doubt, the most positive attention he'd received from the other kids. And the first time he'd been okay with it.

Throughout the day, Ducky insisted on staying with Lucas. During morning recess, Layla took Ducky off Lucas's lap so he could go outside and play—but Ducky let out a high-pitched, sad bark, and wriggled out of Layla's hands to run back to Lucas and sit by his feet.

"Can I stay in and play with Ducky?" Lucas asked, his soft voice a little stronger than usual.

Layla glanced at Garrett, who shrugged. He was headed out for recess duty, so it really was up to Layla. But after one look at Lucas's hopeful face and Ducky's wagging tail, the decision was made. "Just this once," she found herself saying. She reached into her purse. "Would you like to give him a treat?"

Lucas nodded excitedly. "Yes, please."

She grabbed a baggie of chicken and waffle treats out of her tote and handed him one. "Break it up into small pieces," she told him. "Ducky's a small dog, so we don't want to feed him too much and give him a tummy ache."

Ducky, who was sitting impatiently on the floor next to her, gave her an annoyed look, as if to say *Don't ruin this for me.* Layla stifled a laugh.

Lucas carefully broke the treat up and held out a piece to Ducky, who grabbed it greedily from Lucas's fingers and gulped it down.

Lucas giggled. "He's hungry."

"He's always hungry. If I let him, he'd eat everything in my house. I wouldn't have anything left."

Lucas giggled again. Layla loved the sound—it was pure happiness. Looking at him with Ducky, it was hard to believe he'd been the kid who wouldn't even look up or speak. She felt like the Grinch, like her heart was growing three sizes just watching him.

Lucas offered Ducky another piece of the treat, a little more confidently. Ducky took it and gobbled it up hungrily.

After Lucas had finished feeding Ducky, the dog inspected the boy's hands to make sure there wasn't any more treat hiding between his fingers, and then climbed onto Lucas's lap to give him a great big lick on the face.

"He's saying thank you," Layla said.

Ducky jumped and licked Lucas again, and then, in a moment straight out of movie, pressed his little black nose to the tip of Lucas's nose.

Lucas stared back at Ducky intently, until laughter overtook him once again and he lay back on the floor, wriggling around as Ducky tried to lick his face. The two romped and played and snuggled until the bell rang, when Lucas returned to his desk.

Ducky ran over to Layla, as if to check on her, and looked up at her, wagging his tail.

"What do you want, little guy?" she asked.

Ducky barked once and then weaved his way through the desks and back to Lucas, who scooped him up. Ducky hopped onto his desk and sat down, like he was just another member of the class, ready to learn.

The rest of the students rushed in, and for the first time, they all gathered around Lucas's desk—to talk to him, and to pet Ducky. Layla couldn't help but feel a little proud. This was the most positive attention Lucas had received from the other students—and the first time he hadn't shrunk away from it.

Garrett came in and smiled at the crowd of students around Lucas's desk. "You know," he said, sitting down on Layla's desk, arms crossed over his chest, "I think we just might need to make Ducky an official classroom dog."

"How are we doing to do that?" Layla asked. "Besides, I can't take him away from Mr. Rogers to get him trained." She ignored the fact that eventually, Ducky would be taken away from all of them—probably sooner rather than later.

Garrett's mouth curved into a mischievous half-smile. "I've got an idea."

Layla waited, but Garrett didn't say anything. "Are you going to . . . I don't know . . . tell me what it is?"

Garrett shook his head. "Nope. Not yet."

CHAPTER 27

"And so," Garrett said, smiling, "that's why my grandfather should train Ducky as a therapy dog."

"I don't know," Layla said, a little doubtfully.

"What's the problem? Garrett demanded. "I think it's a great idea. The doctor says he needs to stay busy and that he needs to exercise his body—and his mind. This is perfect."

Layla had dropped by Mr. Rogers's house with Ducky after school so the little dog could say hi to the friend he missed so much. Garrett, of course, was already there, and after greeting Layla and offering her Crystal Light lemonade, Mr. Rogers had pushed them out the door.

"Don't let this day go to waste," he'd cautioned them. "It's going to get really cold soon, so you've got to take advantage. It's one of the last nice days." And then he walked toward them, scooting them out the door, and telling them to take Ducky out with them. And he was right. It was already November. The days were getting shorter, and the sun was already setting.

"Promise you're not going to do anything you shouldn't while we're gone?" Garrett asked his grandfather.

Mr. Rogers snorted. "I've been doing whatever I want for years, son."

And before Garrett and Layla could change his mind, they were standing on his stoop with Ducky, the door closed behind them—so they walked, as Mr. Rogers had asked.

"What if it's too much for him? After everything that's happened?" Layla asked. She paused next to a big rosebush that was growing a bit out of control at the end of the block. Ducky sniffed it, sneezed, and then trotted along happily until they got the next mailbox, which belonged to the Wellsleys and had a big white goose wearing a hat painted on the side.

"Honestly?" Garrett paused. "I think it would be the best thing for him. Besides this health scare—this is the happiest I've seen him in a long, long time."

Layla looked down at Ducky, who had decided to roll around in the grass, squirming joyously.

"You think he'd be up for it?" Layla asked, a little doubtfully.

Garrett nodded. "He could do the basics. And, you know, we could help him with the hard stuff. The long walks. Stuff like that."

Layla tilted her head, considering. She'd been worried that Mr. Rogers wouldn't be well enough to continue to dog sit for Ducky during the day, and now Garrett was proposing that Mr. Rogers take on *more* responsibility.

"He needs something to do," Garrett explained, as if he could read the hesitation on her face. "It'll be good for him. Trust me."

That was the thing. Layla really did trust Garrett. More than she probably should have trusted him, or anyone.

"Has he . . . trained dogs before?"

Ducky tugged on his leash, eager to visit yet another mailbox. She picked up her pace to match his.

Garrett shrugged. "I mean, not therapy dogs. But he trained every hunting dog he ever had."

"So you're saying he has more experience than me."

"And me," Garrett said. "The dog I had when I was young? I don't even think he knew his name."

"The dog when I had when I was a kid—Norman—he could sit and shake. But he also would poop right on the doorstep on the back patio whenever he was mad at us."

Garrett snicked. "So he was a revenge pooper?"

Layla nodded. "He was."

"I can assure you," Garrett said, "that Mr. Rogers trained all his dogs not to revenge poop. I'm not trying to oversell him, but . . ."

Layla nodded. "I think he's hired. I just need to talk to Christine before we sign Ducky up for anything."

Garrett pumped his arm in victory. "This is perfect. He's been bugging me for something to do. I think being home on glorified bedrest is driving him nuts. It's not like he was super social before, but now that he knows he's been banned from doing anything, he's incredibly ambitious. He wanted to redo his flooring yesterday now that it's too cold to work in the garden."

"But his flooring is fine. It's super nice, in fact. Perfectly preserved."

Garrett sighed heavily, his big shoulders dropping. "I know. If we don't give him a project, he's going to tear up the house. Except for the flowers." He smiled, a little sadly. "He'll never change the flowers."

"Well, at least for now, he can continue to watch Ducky. And . . . I'll let you know what Christine says, I guess." She tried not to feel doubtful about it. Garrett knew what was good for his grandfather better than she did, right?

And maybe she didn't even need to worry about it. Layla wasn't sure what Christine would actually say. On one hand, she couldn't see Christine having any objection to it. In fact, she was pretty sure her friend would agree Ducky would make an excellent therapy dog. On the other hand . . . it was a big decision. One that Christine would need to be the one to make—and, likely, to walk Ducky through. If anyone was going to train him to be a therapy dog, it made sense that it would be Christine.

"Also," Garrett said, "I have a question for you." He stopped walking and faced her. She stopped a couple steps later, uncertain, and Ducky trotted back to them to see what the holdup was. He waited inquisitively at their feet, his soft brown eyes sharpening with curiosity as he looked back and forth between Garrett and Layla.

"You know that movie at the theater?" he asked.

"*Meeting Blindly.* The one that's been on Netflix for two years and we just now got it here in Two Falls?"

Garrett snickered. Layla was exaggerating, but not too much.

"That's the one," he said. "I've heard it's good."

"Wait," Layla said. "You haven't seen it? I thought the whole world had seen it. It has a whopping 2.7 out of five stars on Rotten Tomatoes."

"So you've seen it?" Garrett challenged, his mouth tight with a held-back smile.

"Well, not exactly."

Garrett laughed. "So, let's go."

Layla shook her head. "It's PG-13. It's not exactly kid-friendly. We need to wait until, like, the next Disney movie comes to town. And somehow convince the movie theater to let the class see it for free, because it is definitely not in the budget."

Garrett shook his head, his blue eyes oddly bright. "We don't have to bring the kids."

Layla felt her heart beating strangely. He couldn't mean—no. He wouldn't.

"Does your grandpa want to see it?" Layla asked, a note of panic starting in her stomach. She felt oddly queasy, like the ground was moving beneath her feet.

"What if it were just the two of us?"

"Garrett Henderson! Are you asking me on a date?" The words spilled out of her mouth before she could stop them.

"I guess I am." He met her eyes solidly. A muscle in his jaw ticked slightly as he waited for her answer.

"Yes," Layla said. "I mean, no. No, I can't."

"Wait. Yes or no?"

Layla wanted to say yes.

She wanted to kiss him. She stared at his lips, which were slightly parted in anticipation. They looked soft and nice, like he was waiting for her to lean in, tilt her face up. It would be so easy to close her eyes, to lean in, to let her kiss be the answer. To run her hand over the sharp line of his jaw. To forget the should-dos and lean into what she really wanted.

"Garrett," she said. "I'm basically your boss."

"Well, not quite."

"Okay, I'm more like your teacher. Which is *literally worse.* Teachers get fired for dating students. They go to jail."

"We're both consenting adults, aren't we? Assuming you consent, I mean."

"Yes, we are. I mean, no. I literally can't date you. Imagine I show up with you at the theater tonight. Imagine we go on a date, or we even kiss. Imagine people *see* that."

Garrett shrugged. "I'm not embarrassed to be seen with you, Layla."

"I'm not embarrassed to be seen with you, either. I'm worried about it. Honestly, we shouldn't even be walking together right now. We're talking about my *job*, Garrett."

"Then why are you standing here with me, right now?" Garrett asked. "Why are you risking it?"

"Because Mr. Rogers is important to me." She was telling only half the truth, but she couldn't chance being honest. His face dropped, and it hurt her to the core, a deep, strange pain, like she could feel what he was feeling.

"My job is all I have here," she said. "I would lose everything without it."

"Listen," Garrett said. "I respect your decision. I understand. It's not a good look. But . . . just let me know if you change your mind. Because—"

"Garrett," she whispered. Her pulse was in her ears.

He held up a hand. "Let me get this out. I want you to let me know if you change your mind, because I think you're smart and funny and gorgeous, and I feel better when you're around—when you're in the room, when I see you smile, when I watch you helping the kids. You're the person everyone's told me to look for, my whole life. And I couldn't live with myself if I didn't say it—if I didn't tell you."

Layla swallowed hard, the words stripping her defenses away until she had nothing left. "I—I have to go," she sputtered finally, the words half-caught in her throat, She turned away and started walking, feeling tears trembling on her eyelids. She blinked them away and swallowed the lump in the bottom of her throat. His eyes were deep and dark and she wanted to drown in them and forget everything.

But she couldn't.

When they parted, he paused, and looked back at her over her should. "Layla," he said. "I'm not going to push it. I swear I'm not. But I think you like me."

She looked back. She couldn't help it. "It doesn't matter how I feel," she said, because she couldn't deny it.

"Your job doesn't have to be everything, Layla," he called after her. "There can be more."

But she kept walking, Ducky trailing after her. He kept looking back at Garrett, whimpering slightly.

And still, Layla kept walking.

Sometimes the circumstances just didn't match up.

And sometimes, people just weren't meant for soul mates. Not ever, not in any circumstance, or any lifetime. Layla had always told herself that she fit into that box, and it was okay, because she'd never really wanted to get married or have children or any of that stuff. She hadn't dreamed of being a heroine in romance books.

But as she walked away, her back to Garrett, she started thinking maybe it wasn't okay at all.

CHAPTER 28

DUCKY

Ducky's mom was on the phone! Her whole face was looking at Ducky, and she had a big, happy smile. She looked so beautiful with her long black hair. She was an Instagram model. Ducky wasn't sure what that was, but he knew she was really pretty and that had something to do it with it. Ducky wished she were here at Layla's because he would snuggle with her so much. Mom was the best snuggler. Of course, Layla was really good, and so was Mr. Rogers, but no one cuddled like Ducky's mom.

Layla was sitting in front of Ducky right now, still in her pajamas, her hair looking like a big fluffy cloud of dark brown curls. She was holding the phone so Ducky could see that his mom was talking to him.

"Hey, Ducky!" she said. "I miss you so much!"

Ducky barked excitedly at her and ran in circles. Sometimes he got so overwhelmed with happiness he had to run to get all his happy out.

"Guess what, buddy? I have some news for you! You get to come to Omaha with me this weekend!"

Ducky did happy tippy taps. He couldn't wait to spend the weekend with his mom. He loved car rides and traveling and train rides and airplane rides. He liked seeing new places with his mom.

"What's going on in Omaha?" Layla asked. "Skating competitions done?"

"Nah," Christine said. "We're actually headlining a charity fashion show!"

Christine dressed up in all different kind of outfits, and sometimes people even paid her to do it. It made sense that she was going to be in a fashion show. Ducky was just excited he got to go with her. They always had just the best time ever, no matter what they did. Unless his mom took him to get his nails done. He didn't like that very much.

"Will you have time to watch Ducky?" Layla asked. Ducky couldn't help but think she was going to miss him, and she seemed really sad. The Yorkie was a little bit worried about what would happen to her if he wasn't there.

"That's the best part," Christine said. "It's a dog fashion show! I'll be dressing in matching clothes with Ducky. We're doing it to raise money for the Nebraska Humane Society We're just doing a walk-through this weekend—the actual show isn't for a month—but they want Ducky there to understand the whole experience!"

"Oh my gosh," Layla said. "That's so incredible!"

"I know, right? We are going to raise so much money! In fact, we're partnering with Siesta Clothing—which has already donated two thousand dollars to the event, and a few other local businesses are pitching in to donate clothes and cover costs. All profits from the clothing are actually going straight to the humane society. We're going to help cover the costs of spays and neuters for the next year, and get this: all dogs who walk in the show are adoptable. I mean, except Ducky."

"That's really, really incredible, Christine."

Christine squealed with excitement, covering her mouth. "I'm so excited to spend a weekend with you, Ducky! I've just missed you so much, sweetie!"

Ducky made happy little excited sounds so his mom knew he was ready to go be in a fashion show with her. It had all Ducky's favorite things—his mom! Dressing up! And probably treats! Lots of treats. When he went to big events, usually people always had yummy snacks for him.

Ducky looked at Layla, who was still holding the phone. Her face was a little sad, the corners of her mouth downturned. "Isn't that great, Ducky?" she asked, but the high-pitched tone in her voice was a little off-pitch or something. She sounded funny.

"Anyway," Christine was saying, "I have to go. But I'll be there again Friday to pick Ducky up, so just pack up his bag. We can grab dinner or something, but I'll have to swing through quickly so I can get back to Omaha in time for the preshow reception. Does that work?"

"Oh, sure," Layla said. "We can go to the café."

"Yes, and you can dish all about your hot student teacher again. Okay?"

"Okay," Layla said, but her face got even sadder. It was a good thing the camera was still on Ducky.

"Okay, love you guys. Bye! Bye sweet Ducky! See you soon!"

Christine blew Ducky kisses through the phone, and he licked the screen. She giggled, and then her face was gone.

Layla set the phone on the floor, looking lost, like when Ducky could smell food but wasn't totally sure where it was. She lay down on the floor and sighed heavily, so Ducky jumped on top of her and sat on her stomach, looking down at her to make sure she was okay.

Layla giggled a little, which was a good sign. Ducky snuggled into her so she knew he cared, and her hands came up to run over his fur.

"Thanks, Ducky," she whispered. "You're the best dog."

Ducky gave her his biggest doggy smile, because he already knew that. Of course he was the best dog.

"Shoot," Layla said, after his mom was gone. "I forgot to ask her about Garrett's therapy-dog idea. But we can ask her Friday, right?"

Ducky barked to let her know he thought that was probably okay. He couldn't wait until Friday.

CHAPTER 29

Garrett brought Layla homemade chocolate chip cookies. He arrived early and left a fresh Ziploc bag of them on her desk. She smiled, but she felt a sudden, deep pang in her chest. Why was he so perfect?

Ducky had rushed over to Garrett the moment they'd arrived in the classroom, bouncing at his feet, sitting up on his back legs and stretching his little paws up toward her student teacher, who swept him up into his arms and kissed him on the head. Mr. Crimmons had told Garrett and Layla, a bit begrudgingly, Ducky could stay a few extra days due to the extenuating circumstances. Their principal was kind of a big ol' softie.

"Hey, little guy," he said, smiling. He looked up at Layla and met her eyes, the soft blue almost electric. She tried to smile back at him.

Garrett crossed the room to stand in front of her, Ducky still in his arms. It was like Ducky was telling her what a big mistake she'd made. "Listen," Garrett said, glancing at the door. "I just— I wanted to apologize to you."

Her eyebrows raised. "Why? There's really no need—"

"There is, though. I put you in a really uncomfortable position I had no right to put you in. I misread signals and I thought I saw something there that wasn't. You were just being kind. And I appreciate that more than I can say. I'm really sorry I crossed a professional line, and I hope you can forgive me."

Layla felt something inside of her crack. She hated that he thought she didn't want him. She hated he regretted asking her. She hated that she couldn't throw herself into his arms and tell him he was right, completely right, and there had been something there, and she didn't care at all about professional boundaries. "There's—nothing to forgive," Layla said instead. "If circumstances were different . . ." She trailed off, words stuck somewhere in her throat. She couldn't say what she wanted to. She looked away, unable to keep eye contact.

"Regardless, I shouldn't have done it. I apologize."

Layla nodded. "Thank you, but it's really not necessary." She hated how professional she sounded. How dry. It wasn't her. She already missed their witty banter, their jokes, the electric feeling that went through her whenever he brushed her arm or her hand or—well, anywhere, really.

"I made you some cookies," he said. "As an apology." He smiled wryly. "It was my mom's recipe. My grandmother saved it for me when—yeah."

"Thank you," she said. "I, um, have to go." She turned and walked out of the classroom as quickly as she could, leaving Garrett and Ducky alone. She needed a minute, just a minute to collect herself.

She stood in the staff bathroom, staring in the mirror, her hands gripping both sides of the sink. It was okay that she'd said no. She had to. She literally didn't have a choice, especially when saying yes meant likely sacrificing the little life she'd built, brick by brick. Why did she keep having to remind herself why it was the wrong decision? This was her life, after all.

A life that maybe, just maybe, she wouldn't mind sharing. A life that she'd started envisioning Garrett in, just a bit. Like how he'd look standing at her refrigerator, looking for a snack. Or how he'd look baking things in her oven. Or pushing her lawn mower in the backyard. It was strangely easy to see how he'd fit into her life, but it had never seemed like a real possibility.

Until now.

Until she'd had to say no.

And she'd done all the wrong things that were supposed to be the right things.

Her feelings twisted up in her chest, and she took a few long, slow breaths to calm down, to quiet the pounding in her head. She didn't feel well at all. She wasn't used to all of these . . . emotions. She'd always been so good at keeping them at bay, at arm's length, at skirting around them, and now that she'd cracked open the door to her heart, just a little bit, they'd all come crowding in, all at once, overwhelming and strange and wonderful and awful and—

The bell rang. She shook her head and hurried back down the hallway, where kids were already flooding into the classroom. Garrett was standing at the door, high-fiving the students as they walked in. She paused, looking at him.

He lifted his palm for a high five.

She grabbed his hand instead and held it tightly before she could think better of it. "It's okay," she whispered. "Everything's okay."

She was a liar.

But then she pulled away like nothing had happened, leaving him to high-five the rest of the kids. She walked around the classroom, greeting the students brightly. They were excited to see Ducky again, and the little dog was flitting around the classroom, wagging his tail so hard he was apt to take flight at any moment, whirring around the room powered only by his adorable, overwhelming excitement.

He really would be the perfect therapy dog.

And then Lucas walked in.

Layla's heart, which had sunk somewhere into between her

ankles and the soles of her feet over the past few days, made a sudden, eager leap. Ducky swiftly went from excited to wildly, impossibly happy. He beelined to Lucas, ducking under desks and hopping over Benny's backpack—which was supposed to be hanging in the hallway—and right into Lucas's arms.

Lucas grinned widely, a gap showing in his mouth where he'd lost a tooth since the day before. Ducky licked his face and nuzzled him, wriggling with the kind of pure happiness that can only be had between a kid and a dog.

Layla usually celebrated when her students lost teeth. At the beginning of the year, each student would guess how many teeth the class would lose collectively and put their guesses in a big jar she stored on the edge of her desk. They'd get to go put a shiny pearly tooth sticker on a big chart at the back on the room, and every month, they counted the number of teeth lost—and then, at the end of the year, they had a big party, where Layla handed out awards and the local dentist, Dr. Micklebee, provided toothbrushes in all the colors of the rainbow, and little fun-sized toothpastes that had cartoon characters on them. Whoever guessed the closest to the total number of teeth lost got two movie tickets to the theater in Brimsley, since the local theater rarely showed movies for kids—maybe twice a year, if they were lucky.

But it struck her—because Lucas never talked, and until recently, never smiled, she'd never noticed if he was losing teeth. He certainly wasn't going to speak up on his own behalf.

Still, she knew that even with Ducky, he wasn't the type to want unnecessary attention—so while she normally would have announced a lost tooth to the class, and asked everyone to clap, she quietly handed him a sticker with his name written across it in Sharpie.

"Would you like to put this on the poster?" she asked.

He nodded, bouncing up and down a little with excitement.

"Here, Lucas. Let me hold Ducky, and you can go put this up."

Lucas took the sticker and pranced over to the back, where he very carefully and proudly placed it in the lower left-hand corner of the tooth chart—away from the rest of the stickers plastered around the top and the middle of the poster.

"Good job," she told him when he returned to his desk. "Say, the other kids want a turn with Ducky today, but if you'd like, you can spend some of morning recess in here, petting him."

It was as if she'd told Lucas he'd won a million dollars. "Really?"

She sat Ducky on his desk. The pup panted happily. "Absolutely."

Layla returned to her desk and tried to focus on Lucas, not Garrett. Not Garrett, who despite looking a little extra tired, looked extra handsome.

Garrett, who . . . had feelings for her.

So it hadn't all been in her head. It hadn't all been a silly fantasy.

It was real.

And it was impossible.

If she were being honest with herself, she was a little flattered. No, *really* flattered. That a man like Garrett Henderson would be remotely interested in a small-town nobody like herself.

Not that it mattered.

She put her head in her hands for a moment while Garrett was reading through the announcements, feeling dizzy from the sudden swing of emotions, but when she felt eyes on her, she cleared her throat and straightened up. "Sorry," she muttered, generally, in case someone was listening. "Headache."

And she managed to hold it together through the day. Well, more or less. Sometimes sort of less.

But what really got her was when the kids went to lunch, and Garrett left to check on Mr. Rogers—and had taken Ducky along with him, to say hi, upon Mr. Rogers's specific request. Layla, with a rare moment of private time, took a stroll around the class, stopping to admire the tooth chart, which finally had a Lucas tooth— and was filling up quickly with pearly stickers.

Except the sticker Lucas had so proudly placed on the poster earlier in the day.

Someone, unbeknownst to Layla, had pried off the sticker. Except they hadn't gotten the whole sticker off, so there was a sticky white residence still left on the poster board. And not only that, but a big black X had been scrawled onto the poster where the sticker had been, as if someone had been absolutely determined to erase everything about Lucas from the class.

Before she knew it, she had tears running down her cheeks. Why were people so awful? These were *kids*. Who was teaching them to hate so much? Lucas had never done anything to them. Lucas had never done anything to anyone, except keep to himself.

"Hey, are you okay?"

She jerked her head up. Reina had walked in without her noticing. She put her hand on Layla's shoulder.

Layla wiped her eyes with the back of her hands, leaving long, black streaks of mascara. Crap. She'd need to go touch up in the bathroom before the students came back.

"They're just being . . . awful. To Lucas. Someone took his sticker off the tooth chart today." She pointed at the big X on the poster, sniffling. "I'm sorry, I never cry. I don't know what's wrong with me. I'm just an emotional wreck lately."

Reina waved off her apology. "Has Lucas noticed it's gone yet?"

Layla shook her head. "I don't think so. Ducky's in class today, and he's been too involved to notice. But he was so excited to finally get to add a sticker of his own. He's been too shy, all year, and when I asked him if he wanted to add a sticker . . ." She trailed off. "It's weird. When Ducky's around, the kids all seem to get along. But when he's not . . ." She shook her head. She sniffled and cleared her throat.

Reina brought her a Kleenex, a black Sharpie, and a fresh sticker. "Write Lucas's name on this," she instructed, "and put it back where it was."

Layla blew her nose and did as instructed. To cover the big X, Reina started drawing little stars all over the board, behind many of the students' names. She colored in a big star behind Lucas's name, too.

"See?" Reina said, capping the marker when she was finished. He'll never even know someone did anything to it."

"Unless they do it again." Layla crossed her eyes, blinking her eyes quickly. "I'm so frustrated! Why can't I catch them? I was here all day. I thought I was keeping a good eye on him—but I was watching Lucas, not one of the other kids. But it seems like the only time he has a good day is when Ducky is around. Garret left to take him to see Mr. Rogers, and . . ."

"Do the other kids bother him when Ducky is around?"

Layla blinked. "Well, no. I think they waited until Ducky was gone with Garrett. I walked by right before recess, and I didn't notice anything. They must have done it when I left for a minute to go to the bathroom."

"There might be something there."

"What do you mean?" Layla studied the chart to make sure the X wasn't noticeable. It just looked like she had done some extra decorating, and Lucas got an extra big star. Usually, she was careful to make sure all the kids got equal treatment, but she had a hard time caring. He deserved a big star. And those kids needed to leave him alone.

"I mean Ducky. The dog. He sort of . . . protects the kid, right? Maybe there's value in keeping him around."

"Ducky isn't even an officially recognized as a therapy dog," Layla protested. "And without his mom's approval, he may never be. Besides, the day after tomorrow he's going back to Mr. Rogers's place, so he won't be in the classroom as much. I was hoping to keep him here all week, but Garrett said Mr. Rogers really wants to see him." She smiled a little. "He's like his own personal therapy dog."

"Still."

"I don't even know who the bullies are, Reina."

"Hey," Reina said. "Listen. Between you, me, and Garrett, we will figure it out. Is the counselor still zero help?"

Layla sniffled. "Um, okay. And yeah. He's no help. We're splitting him between our school and Brimsley, so he isn't here a lot. He barely knows Lucas's name."

"Okay. So the good news is we know what we're dealing with. Tell me, Layla. Have you ever failed a kid?" Reina asked.

Layla shook her head. "I mean, I hope not."

"Well, neither have I. And Lucas isn't going to be the first."

Layla nodded, and Reina turned her toward the door of the classroom. "Now," she said, "let's go to the bathroom and fix your makeup. If those kids see your mascara trails, they're really going to be scared, and you're going to have a whole different set of issues. You look like Marilyn Manson right now."

Layla choked on a surprised laugh but followed her friend down the hallway. And somewhere, deep beneath her embarrassment, was a lot of gratefulness for her friend.

"Thanks," she told Reina when they were in the bathroom together, Layla applying concealer under her eyes with her ring finger.

"Please," Reina said. "Don't mention it. Just consider it payback for the time when I had a meltdown when Jade at the salon turned my hair orange. Or the other meltdown I had when the neighbor kid started my yard on fire when he lit firecrackers under a bale of hay. Remember that?"

Layla remembered. There had even been a newspaper article about the second instance because it had burned Reina's mailbox down. Of course, pretty much everything made the news around here—prize cucumbers, a new neighborhood sign, a litter of kittens.

"Okay," Layla said uncertainly. "But this is one meltdown. I think you've had, like, fourteen in the time we know each other. So we're not even yet. I might need to call in additional favors."

Reina tossed her long hair over her shoulder. "Don't worry, grasshopper. You have a way to go, but I'll help you explore your true emotional range and express yourself. If you want to experience true trauma, I'll give you the number of my old hairdresser. I hear she's still working. Somehow."

Layla giggled. Letting people in was awful, but sometimes, it was also kind of great. "I'll pass for now, but I'll let you know if I change my mind."

Reina linked her arm through Layla's. "Okay, let's go. I'm helping in your classroom the rest of the afternoon, and I don't want to miss a minute of Garrett. I literally want to sign up for second grade again if he's teaching."

Layla wanted to roll her eyes, tell her friend not to talk about her student teacher that way. But then again . . . Layla hadn't exactly been the picture of a professional either. She supposed she could let the comment slide, just this once.

CHAPTER 30

Layla had volunteered for recess duty.

She and Garrett were already taking extra shifts, but when Mrs. Sanchez had needed someone to step in, Layla had been quick to volunteer for a few reasons: first and foremost, Mrs. Sanchez almost always covered for Layla whenever she needed it, but it also gave her time to watch Lucas—time when the kids wouldn't expect her there. And while Layla adored Mrs. Sanchez, she also knew she spent a large portion of her recess-duty time on her phone. Last of all, she wouldn't have to be in the room alone with Garrett. Things were still awkward, and Layla didn't trust herself to say the right things. Or to resist him.

So Layla woke Ducky up from his long nap (he'd been sleeping on the reading beanbag all morning after he almost fell off her desk), hooked a leash to Ducky's collar, and headed outside, where the kids were playing—chasing each around in games of tag, swinging on the swing set, pumping their legs back and forth—and a group of rough-and-tumble students were playing soccer on the football field. Normally, they begged Garrett to come play with them, but he'd declined. "I have to grade your spelling tests," he told them. "Ask me next time."

So Layla walked up and down the football field, Ducky trotting along happily. It was cold, and since she hadn't planned on recess duty, she didn't bring the thick parka she normally did, or her gloves. Instead, she'd grabbed a mug of coffee, hoping it would keep her fingers from stinging from the harsh Nebraska wind. Her hands got cracked and dry during the winter.

That was the thing about Nebraska. It got cold, sure. But it was the wind that was truly miserable at times and was known to take already frigid temps far below zero. It whipped around her like an icy blanket, and before she'd finished one walk around the playground, Ducky was shivering miserably in his little old-timey detective costume. She should have left him inside with Garrett. She swept him up and tucked him in her too-thin coat, where he cuddled up to her. Only his head was sticking out, which made the red-cheeked kids smile.

She decided to stand near a protruding wall next to one of the fourth- and fifth-grade entrances to the school that blocked a little of the wind. Out on the playground, a group of third-grade girls were hiding under the tornado slide, doing the same.

Out of nowhere, Ducky started barking frantically, in a way she'd never heard him, high-pitched and terrified. He wriggled wildly, as if he was trying to jump out of her jacket, so she put her hands on him, trying to get him to stop before he leapt out and hurt himself. "What is it, Ducky?" she asked.

And that was when she saw it.

A bunch of kids, gathered around the jungle gym, kicking gravel toward the center, and, carried over by the wind, the low, sad sound of someone crying.

Layla rushed over, one hand holding Ducky tight to her chest so she didn't slip down farther in Layla's coat. She arrived, panting, and the kids scattered as she did, but not before she saw their faces—the Drubbins twins, Aiden, Benny, and even Emma Richards.

In the middle, under the jungle gym, his knees drawn up to chest and his head tucked under his arms, was Lucas. Lucas, uttering soft, quiet cries. Lucas, covered in dust and bits of gravel the kids had been kicking at him.

Layla touched his shoulder gently and helped him to his feet, her hand on his back. "Come with me, Lucas," she said, her voice strong and confident, even though she felt anything but. She waved to Mr. Phelps, the other playground monitor, signaling she was taking Lucas inside. Mr. Phelps, who had been completely unaware of the jungle gym activity, gave her a two-finger salute, totally oblivious, and went back to monitoring a heated four-square match.

Lucas followed her into the classroom, where Garrett looked up in surprise, looking back and forth between Layla and Lucas before springing into action. He knelt down by Lucas, who still had tears streaming down his cheeks and was taking deep, gasping breaths between sobs.

"What happened, buddy?"

Lucas only cried harder, his chest heaving with sobs. Layla let Ducky out of her jacket, and he hopped down, licking Lucas's tears and circling the little boy, his soft eyes filled with concern.

"Will you watch him?" Layla asked Garrett brusquely, but it was more of an order than a question. "Take him down to the nurse's office to get checked over? Make sure he wasn't hurt? I have some kids to address on the playground."

Layla marched back outside, no longer feeling the bite of the icy wind. The five offending kids were huddled near the monkey bars, whispering together. They looked at her, a little ashamed, when she approached—and they already knew she was angry.

"My classroom. Now."

The kids followed her as she marched in, not bothering to look back to see if they were behind her. She wasn't just angry. She was livid. These were kids she *cared* about. Kids she protected. Kids who she believed would never, ever hurt a fly, let alone Lucas. His tormentors had been under her nose, and she'd missed it.

But not anymore.

Avery Drubbins was already crying and snotty, which normally would have softened her a little. But in this instance, she didn't feel anything. Instead, she marched them all into her classroom and had them sit in the desks at the front of the room while she stood over them, her arms crossed.

"What happened out there?" she asked. Her voice wasn't cold, exactly, but she meant business, and she made sure they knew it.

All five heads were down. A few tears landed on a desk, so Layla grabbed her Kleenexes off her desk and set them in front of Avery—a little harder than she normally would have set a box of tissues down, sure, but she wasn't in the mood for niceties.

"Why were you kicking gravel on Lucas?"

Emma lifted her head. "He punched me."

"I will be giving you more detention if you lie, Emma," Layla said sternly.

Emma's head dropped again, her red hair falling in front of her face.

"I need real answers," Layla said. "And if I don't get them, we'll be adding however long this takes to however long I decide you need to stay after school. I'm not afraid to make detention a week long. Two weeks if needed. Teachers have to stay after school anyway."

Aiden lifted his head. "He's weird."

"Excuse me?"

"He's weird. His eyes are different and his hair is too shiny and my parents said his parents are stealing our jobs and probably aren't even legal."

Layla's mouth dropped open. She stared at Aiden, blinking for a long moment, and then took a sharp breath in, feeling like she'd just been kicked in the chest. Was her second-grade student really just . . . spouting such casual racism? There was no doubt he'd heard it at home. No doubt the hate had been brewing in his family for a long time. She'd been ready to hear that they didn't like Lucas, or they thought he was a loser, but she hadn't been ready . . . for *this*.

"And you?" she asked Avery Drubbins.

His twin, George, spoke instead. "Aiden said he needed our help. And Aiden is our best friend. We have to help him."

Emma nodded in agreement. "Best friends," she echoed.

"And you really thought that hurting someone was a good idea? Because your friend told you to do it?"

The twins shifted uncomfortably, looking properly ashamed.

"Has anyone ever told all of you," she said, very quietly, "that hating someone because they look different or because they're from somewhere else, or because they come from a different background is very, very wrong?"

Aiden kept his head up but didn't quite meet her eyes.

"What if you moved somewhere—say, Switzerland—and everyone was mean to you because you were American? What if they tore your stickers off posters and kicked gravel at you and made you sit alone, every single day?"

"My mom says we'll never leave America," Aiden mumbled. "She says every other country is trash."

Layla's breath caught at the base of her throat, almost choking her.

"Aiden, your mom is *wrong*. And things happen in life we don't expect. And I'll tell you that if you ever, *ever* exhibit this type of behavior again, you'll be looking at an expulsion on your permanent record. As it is, I am going to recommend—"

The bell rang, interrupting her speech.

She cleared her throat. "As it is, you'll each be spending thirty minutes with me after school for the rest of the week, not counting today—because we're sending you to see Principal Crimmons now and you're heading home after. You'll be in in-school suspension until your parents come to pick you up. While you're waiting, I also expect each of you to write apology notes to Lucas."

Now all the kids were crying, but not Aiden. He still looked like he was sure he was right and she was wrong. It made her sick to her stomach, to see such hate in such a young kid—a kid she had thought was kind, if a little ornery. Then she walked them to the principal's office, her stomach still feeling a little wobbly, wondering if she had gotten through to them at all. She had barely been able to speak when Principal Crimmons had asked her for details and she'd had to repeat what Aiden had told her. She felt sick and angry and confused and terrible, and she was sure none of it even was close to what Lucas was feeling—had probably been feeling since the first day of school.

For the first time, she felt really and truly shaken in her confidence as a teacher. It wasn't the mild bout of jealousy she'd felt when she met Garrett, or second-guessing herself occasionally when a lesson plan didn't go the way she'd pictured it in her mind. This was something else entirely, and she wasn't sure she hadn't just messed it up completely.

Even when she'd entertained it as a possibility, enough to ask Christine—she hadn't necessarily believed it was a reality. Lucas was too sweet. She needed to figure out how to get it all to stop, immediately, before it spread further, before it grew roots and became invasive and took over her classroom and the little town.

After a few minutes, Garrett returned with Lucas. Physically, the nurse had said he was fine but recommended sessions with the counselor. For all the good that would do. Happy, smiling Lucas was gone. Instead, he had retreated further into himself. His small shoulders were slumped, his head dipping so far down all she could see was a mop of black hair. He wasn't crying, but his red sweater had tear stairs from where he'd used it to wipe his eyes. Lucas was defeated.

Miserable.

And no wonder. He'd been a target for months, and Layla was just not catching it. She knew Reina had told her she wouldn't fail Lucas, but she felt like she already had.

She quietly brought Ducky to him during a reading break, but Lucas barely lifted his head. One hand snaked out to touch the dog once, gently, but then retreated. Still, Ducky stayed by Lucas's side. And when Ducky was there, the kids didn't bother him. That, at least, she was thankful for.

CHAPTER 31

DUCKY

Ducky's mom was back, just for a few hours, to have dinner and pick up Ducky. Layla seemed happy-sad, so Ducky was happy because maybe Christine would cheer her up. Layla always smiled more around her best friend, and they talked a lot.

"Wait," Ducky's mom, Christine, was saying. Layla, Christine, and Ducky were sitting at an Italian restaurant in Brimsley with fake, flickering candlesticks and red-and-white-checked tablecloths. Christine convinced the waitress to get Ducky his very own child booster seat so he could sit high up with them, which made him feel very important. He was sitting quietly but feeling very jealous because no one had offered him any bread. His mom said garlic was bad for dogs but Ducky was pretty sure she was thinking of vampires. And now, instead of offering the little dog bread, she was leaning forward across the table, a fork gripped in her hand. "You really said no to Garrett? After he confessed his undying love for you? Layla!"

"He didn't confess his undying love, Christine. He asked me to a movie." Layla was fiddling with her napkin.

"Same thing. And you said no?"

"Um, I'm still his boss." Layla twisted her fork in her spaghetti. Ducky whimpered slightly and gave her a cute look, hoping she would notice how hungry he was. Dogs could eat spaghetti, Ducky thought. At least they did on *Lady and the Tramp.*

"You won't be forever. You have, what? A month as a half and then you're not his boss?"

Layla, for some reason, looked a little sad. "A month and a half and he moves away. Forever."

"Says who?"

"Says anyone who ever student teaches here. Says anyone who visits Two Falls. As far as I know, we don't have any openings. Besides, who wants to stay with rumors of school budget cuts?"

"Have there been any?"

"Yeah," Layla said. "The annual pizza day."

Christine hesitated. "Is that . . . it?" She finally grabbed a piece of her baked ziti and held it out to Ducky with two fingers. He gobbled it down quickly, before she could change her mind, and then licked a little spot of sauce off the table before she noticed. Ducky didn't know why his mom did that. He was very good at cleaning and he always offered to lick the plates but his mom used the dishwasher, which he thought was very silly and wasteful when Ducky had a hungry tummy just waiting for more food.

"The pizza luncheon is something everyone looks forward to all year. It's a huge morale killer that it's gone. And I think the scariest part is that it's paid for by Jarvis—which apparently donates a huge amount of money to the school for *multiple* programs. If they shut down—and there are rumors they will—a lot more programs are going to be cut, and half my students' parents will be out of jobs. There isn't exactly an abundance of jobs here. People come here to work at the plant. That's why they're here. The place has— *had*—great benefits, and the pay wasn't terrible, either, especially not for people who valued living in such a small town."

"What about farmers?" Christine questioned. "I mean, Nebraska has no shortage of farmers. Every time I go back to Los Angeles, I think about all the steak and the corn and wheat."

"Don't forget the sunflowers. And the soybeans." Layla paused, shrugging. "Those are the other half, sure. And it would be really tough for them to commute to Brimsley. But you have to understand—people are already thinking of putting their homes up for sale, pulling up roots. They're even thinking of leaving Brimsley. And the farmers aren't enough to keep the community going. Not by themselves. I don't think the businesses will have enough traffic to stay alive."

"So people are leaving even though nothing has happened yet?" Christine asked. "That makes no sense."

"Home prices drop if the plant goes," Layla points out. "It's the only way they can get their money back—selling now, while jobs still exist."

"So what you're saying," Christine said, "is people need faith in the market."

"Faith isn't going to do them much good if the plant closes, Christine."

"If they move early, then they're giving up on the town." Christine's voice went up a note.

"And saving their families. They're making the choices so they don't end up bankrupt with worthless land in a ghost town. I want to be mad about it, but I can't fault them for that."

Christine's shoulders slumped. "Layla," she said. "Why didn't you tell me you were struggling this much?"

Layla lifted a shoulder. "I mean, I'm fine."

Christine raised her eyebrows, like she was considering challenging Layla but decided to let it go.

"Literally nothing you have told me today says fine to me." Christine raised her arm, signaling for the waiter to come over. "Can we get some wine, please?" she asked politely. "I think we really need it."

Layla opened her mouth like she was going to argue but closed it abruptly. Instead, she reached over and scratched Ducky under the chin. The dog closed his eyes, happy. He loved chin scratches. And ear scratches. And butt scratches. Well, he guessed he liked pretty much any old scratches. He was going to miss Layla over the weekend, that was for sure.

Ducky's mom thanked the waiter as he brought over the wine. She poured a glass for Layla and then for herself. "So," she asked. "Here's my big question, then."

"Okay." Layla took a sip from her wineglass.

"How can I help?"

"Oh, no. You've done enough. More than enough. You basically lent me your child as an emotional support animal. You've bought me more takeout than any person should reasonably eat in a century. You're also . . . just my friend. And trust me, that's plenty."

"So? Friends help each other."

Layla leaned over, touching Christine's hand. "You have been helping."

"Well," Christine said, a little crossly, "I'm going to figure something out." Christine was really stubborn when she wanted to be. And lots of times, she wanted to be. She was determined.

"Okay," Layla relented. "Let me know if you think of something."

"Okay, subject change," Christine said, perking up like Ducky when he heard the crumple of a food wrapper. "Ready to fail the Bechdel Test?"

"We already talked about something non-man related. So we passed."

"Good, then the runway is clear. Back to Garrett. My first priority."

Layla pursed her lips. "Sure."

"When you're done being his boss, ask him on a date. Yes, people will gossip, but you like him and he likes you. I can't tell you how rare that actually is."

"He's going to leave. You're just assuming he wants to stick around this town where he probably doesn't have a future."

The waiter returned, bringing Ducky a bowl of water. He patted the dog's head affectionately and wordlessly, and Christine thanked him.

"Did I ever tell you," Christine said dramatically, taking a sip of her wine, "that I'm a little bit psychic?"

Layla laughed. "No."

"Literally I can see a little bit into the future. It's a gift. Probably from my grandmother. And what I can tell you is this: you're the reason that man will stay."

"You're full of it."

Christine shrugged. "Maybe, maybe not. But you should know not to mess with what's meant to be."

Layla burst out laughing. "Okay, Madame Christine. I'll definitely fall in love and run away with my student teacher."

Christine winked at her. "Who said anything about running away?"

Ducky knew that he would never run away. And if anyone tried to leave, he was pretty fast. He could catch them.

CHAPTER 32

Layla missed Ducky.

She missed the sound of him scuttling around the house. She missed how he pawed her to get her attention whenever she wanted something. She missed the way he always seemed to know exactly how she was feeling and somehow knew exactly how to make her laugh, no matter how low she was. Sometimes, she regretted ever agreeing to take care of him—because if this weekend was any indication, it was going to be really, really tough to say goodbye to him. The dog had weirdly opened her world up, wider than it had been in a very long time, and while it had made her intensely uncomfortable, she didn't regret it.

Christine was bringing Ducky back Monday, which meant Layla had to last only the school day before she got to see her little friend again. Christine was spending the night until Tuesday, which she was excited about too. She was almost getting used to having a slightly more active social life. Plus, she got to see Garrett on weekdays, which she looked forward to—in spite of any awkwardness. Which was most *definitely* there.

Yet she found herself arriving earlier than usual Monday morning, pulling into an almost-empty parking lot. But her house felt too empty and quiet without Ducky, so she had gotten ready quickly and headed into school. She'd even found herself filling up his water bowl before remembering he wasn't there, which made her feel completely lonesome when he hadn't come trotting into the kitchen to take a drink.

Garrett arrived about twenty minutes after, swinging his messenger bag down beside her desk. "Ready for in-service?" he asked. She looked over her shoulder, in the middle of pinning up the new fall-themed spelling words. She took a tack from between her teeth and pushed it in the corner of the spelling word—*leaf*—and then turned to Garrett, smiling wryly.

"Get ready for the most exhilarating day of your career," she muttered. "It's what we all live for." She grabbed another handful of pins from the bowl in her top drawer. She liked to add pictures associated with spelling words. She found it helped visual learners remember the meanings and spellings a little bit better.

"That bad, huh?" Garrett was getting used to her sarcastic sense of humor. She grabbed one of the pictures—this one of a tree—and began tacking it to the wall on the opposite side of the spelling list.

"Thanks. And yeah, that bad. And then some."

"So what happens during these magical days?" He grabbed another tack.

"Well, usually Principal Crimmons talks for a while, and then we get training on new policies, so whatever extra rules and crap we have to follow. Oh, and we can't forget staff development." She used finger quotes around the last two words.

"What kind of staff development?"

"Well, we don't have a big budget, so usually we just pack into the music room and watch whatever the state has assigned via webcast that has absolutely no information or value. Usually, everyone brings snacks, and we eat our feelings to prevent being bored to death." She turned to dig into her tote, and then pulled out some trail mix she'd prepared the evening before—mostly popcorn and plain M&M'S—and tossed it on her desk.

"No nuts?" Garrett asked.

She shook her head. "Nut allergies seem like they're getting more common, so I avoid bringing them to the school altogether. We had a kid need an EpiPen last year, and he had to be transported by ambulance to the hospital. It was very scary stuff."

"Wow. Because of nuts?"

Layla nodded seriously. "Some kid decided to pass out trail mix in class. They were apparently sneaking it, so the teacher didn't realize until it was too late. And of course the kid with the trail mix had no idea. He just thought he was sharing."

"Guess I should leave the walnuts out of my brownies," Garrett commented.

"Probably not a bad idea." Layla took a beat. "If I can ask . . . where'd you learn to cook like that?"

He smiled, just a little, like he'd just visited some familiar, faraway place in his head. "My grandma. Man, she could cook anything. Or bake it. And she didn't use recipe books. She did everything based on instinct."

"Wow. I mean, I can't even use the microwave based on instinct. My food just ends up half frozen."

Garrett chuckled. "Well, lucky for you"—he knelt down, digging in his bag—"I brought us a little something too." He pulled out a bag of macaroons—all vanilla.

She gasped. "Are you kidding me? Who are you, Gordon Ramsay?"

He made a so-so gesture with his hand, tilting it back and forth. "I mean, I'm a little nicer, but sure."

"I have to say, Garrett. You're probably going to make in-service day just a tiny bit more bearable."

He grabbed a macaroon out of the Ziploc and popped it in his mouth. "Personally, I think in-service day sounds amazing. In fact, I can't believe I am so lucky I actually get to be here while our students are at home, watching cartoons and sleeping in."

Layla felt a small bit of warm happiness spreading through her body, loosening her muscles and calming her down. She also had to admit—she was a little glad that things were, quite slowly, getting back to normal, and some of the clunky awkwardness was gone. They'd banded together over the kids. Over Lucas. Over making things better. It was strange how a few minutes with Garrett could make her feel so much better.

She still hadn't told Christine about Lucas. She'd been so overjoyed with the news of the fashion show, Layla hadn't wanted to bring her down.

"The good news is," Layla said, "we usually do get out a little early, so we can finish lesson planning and grading for tomorrow. And at least I won't have to stay late after school since those kids aren't here."

Garrett nodded. He knew exactly who *those* kids were. Lucas's bullies. When she'd related the whole story, he had been quietly furious. She could tell by the way his jaw clenched, the way she could see his muscles tighten beneath his shirt, his hands flex into fists and then back out. They were committed to protecting students, to doing everything to keep them safe, and they'd just been . . . letting it happen, under their noses.

"I think Aiden's the ringleader," Layla said. "He told me he's mean to Lucas because . . . of things his parents have told him."

Garrett made a disgusted noise in his throat. He ran his hand over the back of his head, frustrated, leaving some hair sticking up in the back. Layla tamped down the desire to run her palm over it to smooth it down. She wondered, briefly, what his hair felt like. Or his beard. Was it soft? Would it scratch her face if she kissed him?

"What do we do?" Garrett asked.

Layla let out her breath, leaning back against the wall. "I mean, I talked to them. I told them their actions were wrong. I sent them home, I talked to their parents . . . I think it was mostly a game of follow the leader. But Aiden—I'm not sure he understands what he did was wrong. His parents have taught him to see Lucas as less than. And Lucas is an outlet for—something. It's tough when you're going up against their parents. And Aiden, he looks at his dad like a hero. I've just . . . got to figure out a way through that."

"Well, now that you caught them, maybe they'll chill," Garrett suggested.

"I hope so."

"What did Lucas's parents say?" Garrett pressed. "Did you get to talk to them?"

She nodded. "I asked them to stop by, but they declined, so Principal Crimmons and I just talked to them on the phone. They were quiet. Hurt, I think."

"Did they have any concerns?"

Layla nodded. "His mother made me promise to protect her son. And I promised I would . . . but, Garrett, I feel like I've done such an awful job."

"Hey," he said gently. "Hey. Listen. I know you watch me every day, but I watch you too. Because you're an amazing teacher, and you're amazing to the kids, and I have so much to learn from you. And I know you watch that kid like a hawk. I've heard you talking to other teachers about Lucas, and signing up for extra recess shifts, and going above and beyond to get that kid out of his shell." He paused. "Could you do better?"

"Yes," she said, swallowing hard.

"You're damn right you can. And that's your job, and my job. To show up for these kids every day and do better. But I know you, and I know you're not going to give up on Lucas. We're not going to let this kind of stuff fly—in our classroom, in this school, in this town. And we're in a place of power. So we can fight what Lucas can't."

Layla nodded. "Here I thought I was supposed to be teaching you."

Garrett smiled gently. "You are."

"You are so cheesy."

His face spread into a grin.

The bell rang, and Layla stretched her arms behind her back and yawned, preparing herself for the long day. "Let's go," she told Garrett. "Have a good day being hit on by all the other teachers."

He snickered. "I'll stick with you. Maybe it'll stop them."

"Oh, no," she said. "They literally have no shame." She stopped in the hallway, facing Garrett. "If it does make you uncomfortable, ever, please let me know. I've asked them to stop. I can escalate it."

He shook his head. "I'm fine, I promise. But I do appreciate it."

She nodded. "Okay. Time for the most painfully boring day ever. Let's go."

Garrett followed her to the gymnasium, where the teachers were standing, chatting in small groups, avoiding the time where they'd be forced to sit down and start their day. Finally, Principal Crimmons walked up to the front, on what appeared to be a makeshift stage that wobbled with every step, as if it was in danger of imminent collapse.

"Is that safe?" Garrett asked. "I mean, I feel like that wouldn't pass code."

"It wouldn't." Layla happened to know that the teachers had banded together to ask the school board for the funding for a new stage two years ago, but unfortunately, it had been deemed unnecessary. And, in the grand scheme of things, it probably was—especially when things like new textbooks needed to be ordered. She happened to know the fifth-grade science class was sharing three students to a book, and they took turns taking them home to complete homework.

"Welcome!" Principal Crimmons shouted from the stage. The PA system had long since died, which would have been a larger issue if, well, the school had been larger. But Principal Crimmons had a healthy set of lungs on him and was known to make entire speeches at a high volume that reached the very back corners of the largest rooms in the building.

The room gave a collective groan, and the principal gave a good-natured—if a little fake—laugh. He ran through the announcements quickly: upcoming changes to physical education; state testing requirements, and a choir concert for the kindergarteners that he "strongly encouraged everyone to attend."

Then, he cleared his throat, his typical jovial manner dropping. "I understand there was recently a racist incident at the school that occurred on the playground, when a ground of white students ganged up on an Asian student. While no one was physically hurt and the teacher addressed the issue immediately, let me be very clear: racism is not tolerated. Bullying is not tolerated. Hate is *not tolerated*." He punctuated the last remark with a stamp of his foot on the shaking stage.

A weighted silence had fallen over the room.

"While we are choosing to believe the students in question have the ability to learn and grow, we are taking this incident very seriously—and our first priority is the safety of the student who was threatened—no, not threatened. Let me call it what it was. It was an attack. As a result, each student involved in the incident was suspended for a day. Upon further reflection, we realized that it is not an appropriate punishment, so we've increased the suspension to a full week. The students will have several counseling sessions until we are sure they will not be a threat to the student in question—whether physical or mental. Their parents have been called in to discuss their behavior and appropriate corrective action. If we hear of any other incidents, we will not hesitate to suspend or even expel students. We as teachers have a responsibility to protect our students from this despicable rhetoric. *Is that clear?*"

Garrett and Layla exchanged a look. Layla was glad for Principal Crimmons's unquestioning support for Lucas. He had been horrified, immediately calling in the students' parents for an emergency conference.

Aiden's parents, of course, hadn't shown, citing other plans. But the others had shown up and gladly participated in the plan to course correct any negative behaviors—and incorrect beliefs.

Layla had spent time the last week meeting with three sets of parents alongside the school counselor, who was terribly frazzled over the incident. He had been split between not two, but three schools. He could barely keep up with the wear and tear on his car.

"Now," Principal Crimmons said. "Onto one other, less than fun issue."

Layla's heart sank a little further. There was another?

"You've no doubt heard that due to budget cuts, Jarvis was unable to fund our pizza luncheon this year."

There were grumbles throughout the room.

"I'm afraid to tell you that due to some statewide cuts—and further expense pressures at Jarvis—we are forced to immediately cancel our free- and reduced-lunch program."

"What?" Layla asked, before she could help it. But she wasn't the only one. All around the room, whispers were breaking out, and a note of panicked buzzing had risen.

"What does this mean?" Mrs. Hudley asked, standing up. "Is the plant closing?"

For once, Layla appreciated Mrs. Hudley's seventy-year-old bluntness. It was what everyone was thinking.

"How will the kids eat? Half of our kids are on that plan, and their parents are already strapped for cash!" Mr. Ehlemeier yelled out.

"Might as well shut the school down now!" Mr. Creider yelled.

Principal Crimmons held up his hands, and the room slowly quieted, their energy spent. For teachers who spent all their time reminding students to raise their hands before speaking, they weren't very good at it themselves.

Of course, Layla couldn't blame them. All the same thoughts were racing through her mind. It was everything they had all been afraid of.

"I'll answer your questions the best I can," Principal Crimmons said finally. "First and foremost, I do not have any information about the plant closing. I do know that they are trying to reduce expenses wherever possible before closing other plants, as we've expressed to Jarvis how important the plant is to our community. Not to mention, our plant, to my limited understanding of their business deals, makes them a good deal of money."

There were mumbles throughout the gymnasium, mostly of disbelief. Layla understood: it felt like more and more and more was being taken from them. Death by a thousand cuts, and no way to stop the knife.

"Secondly," Principal Crimmons said, "I'm afraid I don't have a good answer about our lunch program. I understand it's very important for the children. We're already prepared applications for additional aid from the state, but that will take some time, and is unlikely to yield results based on the recent budget cuts."

More grumbling. Mr. Ehlemeier put his head in his hands.

"And thirdly, I don't intend to give up on this school—or any of you. And I certainly hope you don't give up on me. We're in this together. So if any of you have contacts at businesses, or have fundraising that can help get us through this rough patch—please, please let us know. In the meantime, we'll be restarting the bake sale a little bit early to make the free lunches last a little bit longer."

He cleared his throat. "Now, I'd like to have you each get out your phones, where you'll find an email with some detailed policy changes. We'll go through these together."

Layla slipped her phone from her pocket, but instead of pulling up the emailed policies, she opened her text thread with Christine.

Layla: Everything's falling apart.

Christine: What? Why? Are you okay?

Layla: I'm okay. But the kids' lunch program has been cut. I don't know how much longer this community can be held together.

Christine: I'm canceling everything today. I'm driving out and I'll meet you at the house after school. We're going to fix this.

CHAPTER 33

The rest of the day was awful, and not even Garrett's homemade macaroons could make it better.

Well, that was a lie. They made it a little bit better. They were really good. But otherwise, the day had gone from reasonably good to boring to awful. Everyone was worried—and moody. Which was fair, considering everyone was scared for their students, the town . . . and their jobs. Garrett was, of course, super sweet, and kept asking her if she was okay. But she wasn't. She was barely even there. She somehow made it through the rest of the day and practically bolted to her old Bronco, telling Garrett they could go over lesson plans the following morning.

"Text me if you have any questions," she told him, throwing her tote over her shoulder and rushing out to her old vehicle, which was waiting for her in the parking lot like a refuge.

She leaped in and sped home, where Christine's car was already parked. She rushed inside, where her friend was sitting in front of the TV, Ducky beside her, dressed like Super Mario, overalls and all—and Layla's Nintendo 64 was hooked up to the TV.

Layla stopped short. "What . . . are you doing?"

"Stress relief," Christine announced. She patted the floor beside her. "Come on. I'm going to destroy you in *Mario Kart*."

"Are you serious? I just had the worst day, and you want to play . . . *Mario Kart?*"

Christine twisted around, fixing her friend with an intense glare. "Deadly serious. Get over here." She pointed at the floor. "Don't keep Ducky and me waiting."

Layla slipped her tote off the shoulder, gave Ducky a quick pat, and then settled in next to her friend, who handed her the green controller—Layla's go-to—complete with a rumble pack. The two friends had spent a lot of time in college with the retro platform, playing classics—*The Legend of Zelda: Ocarina of Time, Wave Race,* and, of course, *Mario Kart* had been in frequent rotation. They'd even won a dorm-wide tournament once, which snagged them more Natty Light than they'd ever wanted to drink. Probably more than pretty much anyone wanted to drink.

Christine chose Toad as her racer, and Layla selected Princess. She'd been Princess Peach since she was a little girl, and she'd never had the heart to switch racers, even after she'd abandoned her princess stage.

"Peach? So cliché," Christine jabbed as they started the race with Peach pulling out ahead—she had better acceleration than Toad.

"Oh, we're trash-talking? You think Princess Peach can't beat your little potato?"

"He's literally a toadstool!" Christine protested.

"Same thing."

"Literally not even close!"

"They're food."

"Well, my toadstool is going to kick your princess butt!" Christine cried. Toad zoomed ahead as Princess skidded off the track on a sharp turn. Ducky barked and hopped in front of the screen, trying to be involved. His little red hat fell off in his excitement, and he put both paws on the screen, growling at the cars as they sped along the virtual track.

Layla waited impatiently as a turtle fished her out of a pond, and then she spun out from accelerating too fast. She sped up, trying to make up for lost time, but before she could, Toad had already crossed the finish line in his third lap.

"Ha!" Christine cried, punching the air with delight. "Got you!"

"Rematch," Layla said. "You've been here for God knows how long, practicing. Meanwhile I haven't played in months. That was just my warm-up."

"The outcome's not going to change," Christine teased.

They raced five more times—with Princess winning only once, and Toad coming away as the winner a whopping four times.

"Have you been practicing?" Layla asked her friend.

Christine grinned. "My husband and I might have weekly game night. Keeps the romance alive."

"I was going to say. You're much better than you were in college." Layla was drinking a can of Diet Dr Pepper. They'd decided to have a soda night. Layla wasn't in the mood for wine. Although honestly, if someone had asked her a few hours before, she would have insisted there was absolutely no way she was in the mood for video games.

Christine shrugged. "I like to think it's raw, natural talent." Her dog crawled into her lap and curled up. "By the way—Ducky and I have a surprise for you."

"You and Ducky, huh?" Layla asked. "The last time Ducky surprised me it was with a fart. I almost died."

Christine cracked up. "You're disgusting. I love you. No, not about that. It's about the fashion show."

"Do you want me to come to Omaha and watch?" Layla asked. "I'd be honored. I'll cheer super loud from, like, the third row. I doubt they'll let me in the front row considering most of my fashion is from Old Navy. Or the thrift store."

"No need," Christine said. "We're moving the fashion show here."

"Um, excuse me? What is here? My house? My living room? The floor?"

Christine's face split into a giant grin. "Remember how you said the school lunch program wasn't being funded anymore? How Jarvis was cutting their donations and the school is hurting?"

"Yes," Layla said slowly.

"Well, I convinced my agent to call the Two Falls fairgrounds and work with the Nebraska Humane Society to move the entire show here! As in, to Two Falls! Apparently, they're trying to support underfunded shelters in small towns, too—and when they heard about the school's plight, they agreed to fundraise for the Two Falls Elementary School lunch program along with the Nebraska Humane Society, so long as dogs can be in the show!" she bounced, excitedly, as she told me, clasping her hands together in excitement.

"Are you . . . serious?" Layla felt bowled over, like someone had just handed her a check for some obscene amount of money and she wasn't sure how to react. "They're coming . . . to Two Falls?"

"Yup," Christine said proudly. "Never underestimate the power of Ducky. And, of course, adorable children from the school. Who will all be invited to come watch the show—parents permitting, of course. And guess what? Three vendors have already committed to match donations up to one thousand dollars—but I think I can get five to match, if I play my cards right. They're already matching donations to the shelter, so since we're expanding to the school, it just makes sense."

"You think . . . people are going to donate one thousand dollars? People don't have the money to spare around here. That's why so many kids are on the lunch program to start with."

"No, silly. The *Lincoln Journal Star* and the *Omaha World-Herald* are already running ads. It's going to be amazing, trust me. They're capitalizing on the small-town hipster vibes. Everyone's going to come."

"We have . . . small-town hipster vibes?" That was probably the last way Layla would've chosen to describe Two Falls.

"Now you do." Christine grinned. "Trust me, this is going to be amazing. When everyone sees how people come together for a town, maybe people won't feel so bleak. Maybe people will start to believe in it again."

Layla stared at her. "Christine?"

"Yeah?"

"You're . . . the best friend I ever had."

Christine flipped her hair back behind her shoulder. "I know."

"I'm going to owe you. Forever. You know that, right?"

Christine wrinkled her nose at her friend. "Why do you think I'm doing it? I'm going to call in such a huge favor. You have no idea."

Layla laughed. "Well . . . how can I help?"

"Two things. Get your sexy student teacher to walk in the show—he'll be a huge draw, I swear—and be my on-site liaison. I'll be driving back and forth a bunch to get all of this set up, so if you could help me—"

"Of course. And I'm sure the kids and teachers would love to. Anything. They'll do anything."

"Excellent," Christine said, steepling her fingers like a comic book villain.

Layla swept Ducky up and spun him in a circle. She cuddled him tightly against her neck. "Sweetheart," she sang, "you're going to save this little town. Just like you've saved so many other people." She kissed him lightly on the head, and he nestled into her, grunting happily.

She turned back to her friend, suddenly remembering. "Christine," she asked. "Have you ever thought of Ducky being a therapy dog? Because I have an idea."

———※———

The next week was a whirlwind.

First of all, Layla got to break the news to Mr. Rogers: Ducky was going to be a therapy dog.

"What's that?" Mr. Rogers had asked curiously.

"It's a dog who helps people," Layla explained, handing him Ducky, who happened to be dressed in a fluffy little Ewok costume. Layla had realized Ducky liked snuggly costumes when the wind was particularly cold, like it was that day. Mr. Rogers was still recovering but kept trying to overdo it, according to Garrett—so she'd made him sit back in his favorite floral chair before she handed him Ducky and made him swear not to do anything crazy.

"No fetch. No long walks. No dog dance parties," Garrett said. He was spending most of his time at Mr. Rogers's house, making sure he was eating properly and keeping his blood sugar up. He was kneeling by Mr. Rogers's chair, securing a blood pressure cuff to his arm.

"Wait," Layla said. "You have dog dance parties?"

Mr. Rogers turned a little red. "It's good exercise. And Ducky loves it."

"I'm sure he does," Garrett said, looking at the screen on the cuff before standing up. "But the doctor said you need to take it easy for a while longer. Give it a few weeks before you get back into full *Saturday Night Fever* mode."

Mr. Rogers sighed a little dramatically. "Okay, well, what's this therapy-dog thing, again?"

"Therapy dogs visit schools, hospitals, retirement homes—basically, they're specially trained dogs who provide comfort whenever and wherever they're needed."

Mr. Rogers smiled fondly at Ducky. "Well, the little guy here does that already."

"Yes," Layla explained, "but if we get him certified, then he can go wherever he needs to go to help people. Like my school, for example. And Christine can take him anywhere! Imagine Ducky being able to go to children's hospitals in cute little outfits!"

Mr. Rogers smiled. "That would be great. I can't tell you how much better he made me feel when he dropped by." He paused, considering. "How do you get the little fella certified?"

"Well," Garrett said, "That's actually where we were hoping you could help. The doctor said we should find ways to keep you active and engaged."

"I thought you said I should take it easy."

"Short-term, yes—while you're healing from a head injury. Long-term, we're signing you up for marathons."

"Garrett," Mr. Rogers said with a sigh, "has anyone ever told you that you're very frustrating?"

Garrett considered. "Yeah, once or twice. But who else is going to raise your blood pressure?"

"So," Layla said, "what do you think? Would you be interested in helping out? There's a trainer starting a course next week in Brimsley, and they still have a couple of openings. It's a long process, but we could get you started."

What she didn't mention was that if he didn't jump on it, there likely wouldn't be another course in Brimsley for at least six months. There just wasn't a big demand for trained therapy dogs in such a small town. But she didn't want to put any undue pressure on Mr. Rogers.

"I can help drive to sessions," Garrett said, firmly. He held up his hands when Mr. Rogers opened his mouth to argue. "No discussion. Layla already gave me the time off. And I want to help."

"And Christine can drive you too, sometimes," Layla added. "She'd going to be here during some of the lessons, and I know she wants to watch the training. She'll probably make videos."

Mr. Rogers, for some reason, accepted the possibility of Christine's presence much more readily than Garrett's, Layla noticed—probably because Garrett was being so protective.

She liked that about him. He was such a good person.

———◆———

To make sure students could walk in the show, Layla had to talk to Principal Crimmons—but Christine was already ahead of her. Apparently, Christine had asked Brynn Cohen, one of the leads at the Nebraska Humane Society, to contact the school before she'd even run it past Layla, and so Principal Crimmons had received a phone call after enduring in-service the day before, when

Christine had broached the idea with her partners in Lincoln and Omaha. And, of course, after the reception his announcements had received in the gymnasium, he was desperate for any kind of help. He'd clasped her hands urgently when he caught her in the hallway.

"Thank you. I can't tell you how much I appreciate this, Layla," Principal Crimmons had told her. "You and that little dog just might be our saving grace. But now we need the whole school on board. I'll add it to school announcements tomorrow, and I'd like you to work with the office staff to get some notes printed up inviting all the kids and their parents."

"Principal Crimmons," Layla had said, "did I tell you that we're getting Ducky trained as a therapy dog starting next week?"

His red face lit up even brighter. "Well, I'll tell you what. A therapy dog in training is certainly welcome in our school any day of the week. I hope to see him here very soon."

Layla almost exploded with excitement. But instead, she said a polite, "Thank you, sir," and went to make copies of event flyers and math homework like absolutely nothing super exciting had just happened. She used her planning period to hang them in the hallways and leave them on each teacher's desk. She wanted a good turnout at the event. Actually, she *needed* it—and so did everyone else.

Christine had designed the flyers the night before, and she'd asked Layla to spread the word to local businesses too—so Layla went out among the town after school, handing out flyers and introducing everyone to the star of the show—Ducky, who was dressed as none other than Dolly Parton, the patron saint of country music. The locals who hadn't already met him went crazy for the little dog, who had donned a shiny blond wig and tiny pink doggy cowboy boots.

It was as if the world was already reflecting her sudden lift in mood—the day was unseasonably warm and sunny, and she counted three bluebirds and two robins on her walk, all of them singing. It made her think of her very favorite poem by Emily Dickinson:

> *"Hope" is the thing with feathers—*
> *That perches in the soul—*
> *And sings the tune without the words—*
> *And never stops at all*

That was probably the only thing she didn't like about teaching second grade (besides the vomit, obviously). Her students, while adorable and sometimes whip-smart, weren't quite ready for Dickinson just yet. She passed out flyers, allowing herself to keep the tiny flame of hope alive, like a carefully tended fire in a snowstorm.

"Will the little dog be there?" one woman asked Layla as she looked over the flyer, which, of course, featured Ducky. She had close-cropped hair and wore horn-rimmed glasses and a big blazer with patches on the shoulder. She reminded Layla of her childhood librarian, and she immediately liked her.

"Will he be there?" Layla repeated. "Are you kidding! He'll be the star!"

The woman laughed and promised to attend.

It was strange to meet someone she didn't at least vaguely recognize around town, so Layla called after her as she walked away. "Excuse me, um—what's your name?"

The woman turned back. "Siobhan," she said. "Sorry, where are my manners? I completely forgot to introduce myself. I just moved to town—I work remotely in tech, and my husband just got the open director job at the plant."

Layla's heart leaped. "The plant is hiring?"

"I mean, I guess. We were looking for a little small town to settle down in. Raise our family."

Layla grinned. "Well, welcome. I'm Layla. I teach at the elementary school. You chose the right one. I love it here."

Layla walked away from the encounter practically skipping.

If Jarvis was hiring, maybe they weren't shutting down after all. Maybe they were just . . . executing expense reductions. While she still wasn't happy about the cuts to the school programs . . . maybe there was hope for the little town after all.

Layla walked around downtown, finishing passing out flyers, with a lighter step and a little more hope fluttering around in her chest.

Her class was probably the most excited about the fashion show. Layla and Garrett passed around permission slips for the kids to attend the show. They all, of course, wanted to walk with Ducky, but Layla had to tell them Christine would probably walk her own dog down the runway. After all, they weren't just asking Ducky to be there—Christine was a big draw in her own right. Christine and Ducky were double the star power.

"Can we dress like him?" Anita asked.

"If you want," Garrett said. "We just want you all to have fun!"

The George and Theo Café—the one business in town that was always bustling—had agreed to donate cake pops for the event— along with an extra $500. Even Mr. Ford, the barber, had kicked in an early $100 for the cause. He'd pressed a handful of bills into Layla's hand. "Let me know if you need more, and I'll see what I can spare," he told her, pulling another wrinkled five out of a pocket in his apron. "I know what you're doing, and I want to help."

Layla felt a big swell of gratitude rising up in her chest. She wrapped him into a hug. He stiffened, and then she felt his arms tighten around her. "You're a good kid, Layla," he said. "Don't forget that what you do matters."

CHAPTER 34

DUCKY

Ducky could not even believe his luck.

First and foremost, Ducky was back in Two Falls and his mom was spending a ton of time there to help get ready for the big show, which meant that he got to hang out with *so many* of his favorite people at once! It was like his tail never stopped wagging, and he never stopped making happy little grunts that made Layla giggle. He ran back and forth from his mom to Layla and then back to his mom and then back to Layla until he collapsed, panting, into a fuzzy little puddle. And then he got up and did it all again.

Then, his friend Mr. Rogers told him he had a big surprise for him, and loaded him up into his truck, where he got to sit on soft blankets. Ducky was so gosh darn happy his friend was feeling better. Ducky could see where his head had gotten hurt, but the doctors had put some stitches in so his wound didn't look too scary.

"I'm glad you're back, little guy," Mr. Rogers said, climbing into the truck. "I have to say, my house was pretty lonely without you around."

Ducky crawled over to the middle seat and cuddled up next to Mr. Rogers, so the old man knew how much Ducky had missed him. Mr. Rogers reached down to scratch his back, and then shifted the old truck into gear. The truck made a sound like it was grumbling as it pulled out of the driveway.

"Guess where we're going today?" Mr. Rogers asked Ducky. "We're going to start your therapy training, little guy. We're headed over to Brimsley for a couple hours. They're going to do temperament testing and take us through the process. Does that sound like fun?"

Ducky looked at him, his eyes big and his tongue hanging out happily. He crossed the seats and hopped up with his paws on the door to try to see where they were going, but he was still too short.

Mr. Rogers chucked. "Don't worry, little buddy. We'll be there soon. Just don't tell my grandson. He thinks he needs to drive me around, like I'm some kind of child." He scowled for a moment, and then sighed. "He's a good kid though, Ducky. I think we raised him right." Ducky panted in response. He liked Garrett, too.

When the duo pulled into the parking lot outside the outlet mall, Ducky was practically wriggling with excitement, his feet doing dancing little tippy-taps all over the seat. Mr. Rogers hooked his leash onto Ducky's collar securely and helped him out of the car, where he sat him slowly on the ground.

"All right, Ducky," he said, a bit sternly, "this is important stuff, so we need to be on our best behavior today."

Ducky wagged his tail happily. He loved meeting new people, and everyone loved him, so he wasn't very worried.

The pair shuffled, just a tad more slowly than usual, toward a place with a bright blue sign. Ducky couldn't read, so he wasn't sure what it said, but it smelled like dogs. A lot of dogs. Ducky sniffed the sidewalk, and then followed Mr. Rogers inside, where there were wood floors and a big, open space that looked perfect for zoomies. Ducky wondered if zoomies meant being on his best behavior or if he should save those for later.

"Good morning!" said a young woman with a happy face. "Welcome to Best Pals Dog Trainers!"

"Good morning," Mr. Rogers said. "I have an appointment here with my friend Ducky. We'd like to start his therapy-dog training."

"Excellent," said the woman. "Well, my name is Lilac, and I'm so excited you're here. Christine Hsu called me last week to talk through the process, and she sent over all the paperwork I need." She knelt down on the floor, reaching her hand out to Ducky, who sniffed her. She smelled like a nice person. She smelled like a lot of dogs too, which was a good sign.

"Hi, Ducky!" she said. "Are you ready to have some fun?"

Ducky smiled really big, panting, to show he was super happy— and maybe just the tiniest bit nervous. He loved Mr. Rogers a bunch, but a little part of him wished his mom were here. But she'd told Layla that morning she had to call some vendors for the show, whatever that meant, and so she'd let Mr. Rogers handle it this time.

"Okay! Let's start with a short walk, if that's okay with you?" She glanced at Mr. Rogers.

He nodded stubbornly. "The doctor said I need to get more exercise, so I guess we start today," he said. "You ready, Ducky?"

Ducky hopped with excitement. He loved walks! And he loved that Mr. Rogers felt good enough to take him on one! He had been so worried about his friend. He'd watched out the window for Mr. Rogers when he was at Layla's house, but the way the houses had been built, he couldn't see Mr. Rogers's house or driveway from Layla's sitting window, so he couldn't tell if he was coming or going.

"We'll take it slow," Lilac told Mr. Rogers. "We mainly want to see how Ducky responds to stimuli. We need to make sure he doesn't get too scared or get aggressive. The best therapy dogs are calm and don't get stirred up easily."

Ducky stopped hopping around, and walked beside Mr. Rogers back out the door. They took a stroll through the parking lot and down the street. A car honked at them, and Lilac waved, but Ducky was perfectly behaved.

Later, another family walked a dog by, who wanted very badly to lick Ducky. Ducky looked over at the other dog, politely stepped away, but didn't growl or bark or try to win the family over by stopping to beg for belly rubs in the middle of the sidewalk. The little dog was very clearly on his best behavior.

Ducky also watched Mr. Rogers carefully. The pup was very attentive to the old man, whom he loved very, very much, and had spent a lot of time worrying about, especially after he'd seen him lying on the floor. The smell of blood had scared him so terribly, but he had to be brave for Mr. Rogers. And that meant when he was walking with Mr. Rogers, Ducky had to be a perfect gentleman. He didn't pull on his leash to run after squirrels, or bite at insects on the sidewalk, and he walked in a very careful, straight line so he didn't get his leash all twisted up in Mr. Rogers's legs.

"What a good boy," Lilac commented. "He's got a steady temperament, doesn't he?"

A shiny blue sports car sped by, blaring music. Ducky wanted to bark at it, but instead he walked back into the building that smelled like dogs with Lilac and Mr. Rogers.

Mr. Rogers sat down on a bench, breathing a little hard, but otherwise he seemed fine. Ducky knew, because he checked on him four times and made sure to sniff him to confirm he was okay. Then Ducky turned back to Lilac, who swooped him off the ground quite suddenly and rubbed his back. She had long nails, which Ducky liked for scratches.

Then, she sat him down. "Keep hold of his leash tightly," she advised Mr. Rogers, and walked through a big metal door in the back.

Lilac returned only a moment later, holding the door open— and behind her, a pleasantly fat gray tabby cat with half an ear missing trotted past her into the room.

"Ducky, sweetheart, I'd like you to meet my Frances. She used to be a street cat, but one day she wandered into our little place here, and she's been with me ever since."

Ducky cocked his head to the side, watching Frances the cat walk across the floor, in the majestically unbothered way that only cats could manage. And this particularly cat outweighed Ducky by half. Compared to the pup, the feline looked like a mountain lion. She did a long, unaffected stretch, as if she were the only one in the room, and yawned, showing sharp white teeth.

"Don't be scared, now," Mr. Rogers said, in his kindest voice. "I won't let anything happen to you, good boy."

Ducky wondered what would happen if he barked. If he ran at the cat, as fast as his legs would carry him. It might be fun to make the cat run. Maybe the cat would even play with him, and that would be extra fun!

But then Ducky glanced back at Mr. Rogers, who was looking at him hopefully, his bushy white eyebrows lifted. And Ducky knew he couldn't chase Frances. He couldn't let Mr. Rogers down. What if Mr. Rogers tried to run, too, and tripped and fell again? What if he had to go back to the hospital? No, Ducky had to behave.

Ducky puffed out his chest. He *was* brave. He walked up to the cat, hesitantly, who had sort of flopped down on the floor, and was switching her fluffy tail back and forth but was otherwise unmoving, except for her keen eyes. She looked very nice and squishy though, and Ducky wondered if she would be a good snuggler.

Ducky sniffed the cat.

The cat didn't move.

Ducky sat down next to the cat, and looked over at Mr. Rogers, as if he was telling his friend the cat was okay after all and that Mr. Rogers could pet him, if he wanted, as long as he didn't like the cat better than Ducky.

"Very good, Ducky," Lilac said. She hauled Frances up in her arms, cradling her like a very well-nourished, furry baby, and walked her back into the room.

Lilac did a series of other small tests with Ducky, like clapping her hands loudly, or throwing toys in front of him (which Ducky looked at for a moment before grabbing a red ball with a squeaker it in and settling in for a nice chew) and playing various loud sounds from a stereo system.

Ducky didn't like the sounds. He mostly just wanted to play with the toy. And he didn't really understand what Lilac was doing. He liked her, but nothing she was doing made sense. He rather liked Frances and wondered if she would be like squeaky toys. She looked very tough, but also very soft, like a super cuddly, warm bed. Maybe if he were very nice, he could lay his head on her.

But instead, Mr. Rogers stood up, slapping his hands on his legs. "Welp," he said to Lilac. "What do you reckon?"

"I think our friend here is very promising!" Lilac said, smiling down at Ducky. "I'd love to welcome him into our therapy-dog program. And wonderful news—we waive our fee for any veterans bringing their dogs in."

"Well," Mr. Rogers said, "I'm afraid I must decline. I'm a veteran, but I'm only Ducky's dog sitter, even though I like to think of myself as his grandpa."

"Will you be going through the training with him?"

"Yes, and I'll be working with his owner, as you know."

"And you served our country?" she pressed.

"I did," Mr. Rogers said proudly.

"Then his training is free. We're starting a new series on Thursday at ten a.m. I'll get you the schedule. Training is twice a week from then on out."

Mr. Rogers tried to protest again, but Lilac shooed him out the door, telling him she had to get to another appointment and she did not, under any circumstances, have time to argue.

Mr. Rogers unlocked his truck and helped Ducky get settled back onto the seat on a cozy blanket.

"Good news, little guy. You're going to be a therapy dog."

Ducky wagged his tail. He was happy to be back to having more best days ever.

CHAPTER 35

The kids were buzzing about the fashion show. Mrs. Sanchez had been in first thing in the morning with fresh paper and colored pencils and instructed the students to each draw what they would wear if they got to design outfits for the show, and they loved it.

"Can one of my goats be in the show?" asked Anita, raising her hand. "I have overalls for Hector. He's a boy. My sister sewed them for her 4-H project."

"I'll talk to Christine about it," Layla said, although she doubted it would be good to let a goat take the place of an adoptable dog.

"Do you think that Hector can come to the classroom if he doesn't get to walk in the show? Ducky gets to," Anita pointed out, pouting a little.

"Is Hector potty-trained?" Layla asked.

Anita shrugged. "I dunno."

"Well, work on that, and let me know how it goes." Layla asked. "Why don't you just draw Hector in the show for now?"

Mrs. Sanchez weaved through the desks, her hands clasped behind her back, watching the students work. Layla had to admit—Mrs. Sanchez was great about getting the kids interested in art. It was fun, anyway, and often a welcome break from regular class. Layla loved it too—she liked seeing the kids happy, but sometimes, well, she just needed a break. That was the thing about being a teacher. She had to be *on* all the time, and it was hard. Sometimes, she wondered if she'd like corporate America, and envied the way businesswomen got to spend time in front of a computer instead of in front of a classroom all the time. But if Layla just sat and worked at her computer without Garrett in the room, running the show, there would be mass chaos. She knew that the Drubbins twins would figure out a way to light something on fire, and Teddy might write a naughty word on the whiteboard, and inevitably someone would try to taste the rubber cement. Her money was on Avery.

Layla and Garrett strolled around the room, watching the students work. Garrett paused by Lucas's desk, frowning. His eyes flicked up and caught Layla's—and then he jerked his head, slightly, motioning her to come over. She crossed the room slowly, pausing to look at other students' work so as not to make it obvious she was trying to reach Lucas—complimenting each student's art, giving an encouraging smile here or there, or picking up a rogue colored pencil that had rolled off a desk before it was stomped to death by a stampede of second-grade sneakers.

She stood over Garrett, who met her eyes and looked pointedly down at Lucas's paper, which had nothing but a little sad scrawl in the corner.

Quietly, slowly, she knelt down next to him, resting her arms on the desk, so she was at his level.

Lucas didn't look up, or even give any indication he knew she was there. "What are you drawing?" she asked. "Does this have something to do with the show?" she asked softly.

She felt Garrett's eyes on her. She knew he wanted to help, but she also knew he realized she'd gotten just a little further with getting Lucas to open up—so he wasn't going to push it. She was impressed with his self-awareness. So many people wanted to help so badly they ended up doing the opposite, pushing kids deeper into their shells.

Lucas rolled a black colored pencil between his fingers. He finally shrugged, lifting and dropping his shoulders heavily, like the one small movement cost him an enormous amount of effort.

"Do you want to tell me about what you're drawing?"

He shook his head, still not looking up at her.

"Well," she said, sensitive that a couple of her students' heads had started flicking toward them, "let me know if you change your mind, okay?"

He didn't move; gave no indication that he'd heard her. But then, his fingers gripped the colored pencil.

OK, he wrote on the paper.

She smiled at him and then stood up, pretending that the interaction had been totally normal, that he hadn't left a bit of worry fluttering around in her chest like a moth. At least he was communicating with her. But the sweet, happy boy who liked spending time with Ducky was gone, very far away.

She returned to her desk when Benny raised his hand.

"Do you have a question, Benny?" Mrs. Sanchez asked.

"Yes," he announced, "but it's for Ms. Layla and Mr. Garrett."

"Sure, Benny," Garrett said. "What's up?"

"My mom said there is always someone really important opening and closing the fashion show. Do you know who that will be?"

Layla knew it was probably Ducky and Christine doing both, but Garrett smiled mysteriously. "I guess you'll have to be there to see."

The kids oohed.

"I bet it's Taylor Swift!" Leighton said.

"I bet it's Tom Osborne!" Teddy countered, wiggling in his chair.

Layla hid a smile. Tom Osborne was Nebraska royalty. Other cities had pro sports teams and big shopping malls and huge airports—but Nebraska had the greatest football coach of all time—at least if someone asked any Nebraskan. He hadn't coached since the nineties but had since served in Congress in

Nebraska's third district and taken a job as the athletic director for the Huskers. And, of course, he won back-to-back national championships. So even though none of her students had actually *seen* Tom Osborne coach a game—they all admired him as fervently as if they'd watched every play.

Garrett shoved his hands in his pockets and shrugged, his face pulled into a mischievous half smile. Layla couldn't help but notice how incredibly handsome he was when he did that. He had a boyish charm that tempered his Brawny-man good looks. She wondered, for a moment, why he wasn't modeling, or working as an anchor for a TV station, or doing some other handsome-man job.

She also wondered why he was single. How was someone so wonderful not attached? She didn't get it. It was obvious, for example, why she was single. She lived in a tiny town and was emotionally unavailable. Duh.

Garrett, on the other hand? It was probably because no one was perfect enough.

He liked you, and you aren't perfect, whispered a little voice in her head, but she tamped it out, putting out the flicker of hope before it could get too bright. She was trying so, so hard not to fall into their witty banter, into their conversations that felt natural, like she was talking to a best friend. She found herself telling him things she'd never told anyone, and it felt . . . right.

"All right, class! We have five minutes left. Please finish your drawings, and we'll be coming around the classroom, collecting your colored pencils," Mrs. Sanchez said, popping open a small, scratched Rubbermaid container, which was where the colored pencils lived. She walked from desk to desk, helping students put a rubber band around each set of pencils, and paused just a second longer at Lucas's desk. Her pencils were all set neatly to the side of his desk, and his page was still lonely and stark-white, with the word *OK* and one sad dark spot off to the side.

Mrs. Sanchez stopped and caught Layla's eye, who shook her

head, telling Mrs. Sanchez not to question the boy. Mrs. Sanchez, like the rest of the faculty, had heard what happened to Lucas and was taking extra care to be kind to him.

That day, Garrett took recess duty. He slipped gloves on his hands and smiled at Layla before he went out. "Wish me luck," he said.

"Good luck," she said. "Watch the jungle gym closely."

He nodded and headed outside, into the bustling halls, filled with students. Layla sighed and thumped down at her desk, but hadn't even started working on an update for Garrett's advisor on his progress when she heard a slight rustling in the hallway.

Very, very quietly, she rose from her desk, being careful not to push her chair back—the rollers always squeaked—and moved along the side of the wall. No one should have been messing around outside her classroom door. The only thing there was all the kids' lunches, where they dropped them in a cubby each morning if they weren't going to eat the school lunches. There weren't usually many; most kids relied on the free-lunch program.

Layla took slow, small steps toward the door, keeping herself close to the far wall. Whoever was outside the door was still rustling around, and she heard the ripping sound of Velcro as it was pulled open.

Could it be the fifth graders? Last year, a couple of kids had been found sneaking food from lunches during recess. She hoped not. It had been quite an ordeal to figure out who was doing it, and why, exactly—it had been kids whose parents were too proud to sign them up for the free-lunch program, but the kids were always hungry and occasionally lunchless. Which is why they went foraging. She couldn't really blame them.

She took a couple of slow, quiet steps edging along the back wall. Then, she leaped forward and quickly swung open the door.

It was Aiden.

Aiden, his back to her, and Lucas's green lunch box in his hands. He'd opened the lunch, popped the top off the bowl inside—and was spitting in Lucas's noodles.

"Aiden!" she said. "What are you doing?"

He looked up at her, still hunched over the lunch box, and wiped the saliva collecting on his chin. His face flushed.

"Come with me. *Now.*"

She marched him toward Principal Crimmons's office, casting looks up and down the hallway to make sure he was acting alone. She didn't see or hear anyone else, just her heels click-clacking down the hallway. She heard Aiden's reluctant shuffle behind her. She felt anger build in her chest. What was happening in the world that he would go this far? Why would he think it was okay to do this? How long had it been going on? And why, *why* hadn't she caught it before? She owed this to Lucas.

"Come on," she told him crossly. She was so . . . mad. And hurt. And confused. She'd seen Aiden be so gentle with Ducky. She saw him sit and politely listen to Anita while she talked and talked and talked. He was sharp, and she'd proudly given him some of the best grades in the class, marking his papers with big green *A*s. (Sometimes, she got tired of using a red pen.) He'd sometimes tell her his parents hung his papers on the fridge.

She had stupidly hoped the playground incident would be the last of it, but Layla was being naive. Things like this weren't solved with a scolding. And Aiden wasn't born with hate in his heart. Someone had taught it to him. Fed it to him, bit by bit. And somehow, in the time she had with him, she needed to figure out how to undo it.

But she needed to create a safe environment for Lucas. It was her responsibility as a teacher. And getting rocks kicked at him on the playground and having his lunch ruined was not it.

Layla pushed through a pair of double glass doors, into the lobby where the administrative office manager sat. The principal was in his own office, off to the side, with a window that looked over the parking lot. As far as a view, it wasn't great.

Mrs. Anderson looked up, her glasses pushed far down on her nose, inspecting the scene in front of her. "What's this?" she asked. It was as if she *knew* Aiden was in trouble and wanted to be sure Aiden knew it too. Half the students in school were more scared of Mrs. Anderson than they were of the principal.

"Is Principal Crimmons busy?"

She glanced at her watch. "He's in a meeting for another fifteen. Do you want to wait?"

Aiden started to turn around, back toward the glass double doors.

"Yes," she said firmly. "We'll wait. Aiden, go ahead and sit in one of the chairs beside the office, please."

Layla sat next to the boy, her mind reeling. Should she try to talk to him? Did he feel bad for what he'd done? How could she fix this? Did Lucas know?

She was quite sure this was one of the worst parts of being a teacher.

She pulled her phone out of the back pocket of her jeans and texted Garrett.

Layla: Caught Aiden spitting in Lucas's lunch. Please toss it. Taking him to see Crimmons.

Her phone vibrated almost immediately.

Garrett: What??????

Layla: I know.

Layla glanced up at Aiden, who was pulling on a thread coming loose from his jeans while rocking back and forth at the edge of the seat. He finally looked at Layla and then quickly back down at his lap.

"Am I . . . in big trouble?"

"Yes." Layla didn't mince words. She was usually gentle with her second graders, but Aiden needed to understand what he'd done.

Garrett: I'll give Lucas my lunch. I'll pick up something when I go out to check on Grandpa. Do you want anything?

Layla: I'm good. I brought one of those frozen microwave meals you love so much.

Garrett: I'm buying something for you.

Layla: No need.

Principal Crimmons's door opened, and he stepped outside. Layla stood, but Aiden stayed seated, his cheeks still red.

Principal Crimmons nodded to Layla and then turned to Aiden. "Young man," he said, his tone firm, "do you want to come into my office and tell me why you're here?"

Layla followed Aiden in, but Principal Crimmons caught her at the door. "Layla, I'm so sorry, but I've been on calls all morning. I have to use the restroom. Are you okay waiting two minutes?" He flicked his wrist up, checking the big silver watch on his wrist.

"Of course," Layla said. She walked into his office and took a seat next to Aiden. They both stared at the big mahogany desk that Principal Crimmons sat behind. Layla supposed that once, long ago, it was a beautiful piece, but now it was scratched and filmy and in desperate need of refinishing. His degree from UNL hung on the wall, and an old trophy was displayed on a mismatched side table.

"Are you going to tell him?" Aiden asked finally, his voice high-pitched and shaky, like he was trying not to cry.

"I'd prefer you do that," Layla said. "I think if you're going to do something you know is wrong, you should own up to it, don't you?"

"I promise I won't do it again."

"Aiden," Layla said, "why did you do it in the first place?" She was tired. Desperate. Angry. Sad.

"I dunno."

"I think you do."

Aiden was silent for a long moment, and then, all at once, his shoulders deflated. "My dad seems mad all the time," he said. "And it makes me mad too."

"Do you know why your dad is angry?" she asked, a little more gently.

He shrugged. "His job went away at the plant because of Lucas's dad. Now he's mad. At me sometimes. At everyone. He says we have to move because all the new people moving here are taking his job." His shoulders dropped a little more. "My mom works at the hair salon, and she doesn't want to go."

New people. Of course. And Lucas's family were just about the only new people in town in the past year. Which made them an easy target. It would be even worse for Lucas if his father was the one responsible for Mr. McGee's firing.

"So, because your dad is angry you want to be angry?"

"Yes. And it makes me feel sad."

"Aiden," she said quietly, "How do you think it makes Lucas feel when you're mean to him for no reason?"

He shrugged, not meeting her eyes.

"Do you think it makes him sad?"

"I dunno," he said, in that precisely evasive tone kids used when they knew exactly what the answer was.

"What if you have to move and the kids at your new school are mean to you? Would you like that?"

He shook his head. "No."

"So why do you do it to Lucas?"

He dropped his head. "I dunno."

"Is there another reason you don't like him?"

Aiden kicked the heels of his sneakers on the ground. He opened his mouth and then Principal Crimmons walked in the door, drying his hands on his tie.

"Apologies for the wait," he said, closing the door behind him. "Ms. Layla. Aiden." He sat down behind and leaned forward, his elbows resting on his belly and his fingers steepled. "Why do I have the pleasure of seeing you both today?" His voice suggested the opposite.

Aiden looked out the window. When he looked back, tears had started in his eyes and were pouring down his cheeks.

"I did something bad," he said finally.

CHAPTER 36

"And then what?"

Garrett and Layla were sitting together in the classroom. They'd had a mountain of papers to grade, and it was nearly five on a Tuesday night—so they were stuck in an almost empty building, grading geography tests. They were so bleary-eyed they'd taken a break to raid the vending machines in the break room, and they'd come back to the classroom with their arms filled with chocolate bars and potato chips and M&M'S and Skittles. They'd also moved from the desk to the beanbag chairs in the corner, where the students did silent reading. Layla was exhausted, but she had to admit, she didn't necessarily hate spending time with Garrett, even if they were stuck in grading hell.

"Well," Layla said, pouring a couple of Skittles in her palm, "Aiden cried, and I ended up having to tell Principal Crimmons what he did."

"And did he go easy on him?"

"Nope. Two-week suspension with an eight-week detention when he returns. After COVID-19, spitting in food is an act of bioterrorism, and honestly, a hate crime if you consider the intent. We had to bring his parents in yesterday and tell them if it ever happened again, we'd be expelling him. And they have to drive him to Lincoln for early-intervention racism sensitivity counseling for four weekends, or else we'll expel him."

Garrett whistled. "Well, maybe that'll make the other kids think twice before they mess with Lucas again."

"We can hope." The whole situation was weighing heavily on her. She and Garrett were behind on their grading because they'd made excuses to both be on lunch and recess duty as much as possible to make sure no one was giving Lucas a hard time. And so far, no one had. But Lucas had been sitting under the tornado slide, alone, his hair falling into his eyes and his chin resting on his knees, which were pulled in tight to his chest, as if he were trying to block out the world. When Layla had offered him a rubber ball to start a game of four-square, or even a jump rope, he'd shaken his head at her without looking up.

Layla sighed, putting her face in her hands. "I just . . . hope we're doing the right thing."

Garrett leaned forward. "We are."

"It just . . . feels weird. I've never punished a kid so severely. And I'm doing it for what his parents taught him. He's a baby, and he's already learned so much . . . horribleness."

"He has to unlearn it at some point. Better now than later. Before he can spread racist behavior further. Kids like Aiden are powerful. They lead others. And if they're on the wrong path, a bunch of people go with them."

"And how long was this going on before we actually caught them, Garrett?" she asked. "Lucas has been hiding in his own little shell all year. We're getting near the end of the semester, and we're just catching it now?"

He nodded. "I know. But these young kids—they're just starting to form ideas. Opinions. And we're lucky we're in a place where we can steer them in the right direction."

"How does that help if we're the only positive influences they have in their lives?"

"We get these kids for almost seven hours a day, five days a week. That's a lot of time to make a difference."

Layla hesitated. "I have an idea," Layla said. "For a lesson plan that might help them . . . understand. Just a little."

"What is it?"

"Let me map it out a little better before I share it. I want to make sure it's tight, and then I want your opinion. And we need to wait to do it until Aiden is back."

"If you say so." Garrett looked down, making a red checkmark on a geography homework. He sighed. "Benny can never remember the capital of South Dakota. I had it on a bonus point question on this week's spelling quiz, and he remembers Wyoming every time—just not South Dakota."

"That's the second one we did," she said. "He'll get it. He's good with mnemonic devices if you can figure that one out."

"Good to know," he said. "He does repeat rhymes often."

"Yep," Layla said. "I've recommended him for the advanced readers program. Assuming that doesn't get cut too." She bit back a sigh. Advanced readers got to join a book club in the library—and got to read books the school provided. It was something Jarvis probably funded too.

"Do you think it will?" Garrett was shuffling through papers on her desk, gathering the science papers on different types of clouds. Next week, weather permitting, they were taking the kids outside to point out cumulus, nimbus, and stratus clouds.

"Well, I did meet a lady who just moved to town because her husband got some big job at the plant. Would they be hiring new people if they were planning on shutting it down?"

"Probably not. But sometimes big companies like to bring someone in to figure out where they can cut. Or how to transition the business to the plants they intend to keep running."

"Wow. Sounds like the villain in a Hallmark movie. Too bad we don't have a sexy small-town farmer who can steal his heart and convince him to stay."

"There is the small issue of him clearly being married," Layla pointed out. "Affairs aren't very Hallmark. Plus if you're only here to basically dismantle a town, wouldn't you just book a hotel for a few weeks? Why would you drag your wife along?"

"You're probably right." Garrett said it in a wistful way that made Layla think he wasn't sure if he believed it. But he wanted to—as much as she did. But they were afraid of hope. It was scary and unpredictable and fleeting.

"Maybe."

He finished stacking the papers and quickly rearranged the others littered across the desk. They were almost done. Which was good, considering the time, and the fact that the sun had sunk below the horizon.

"My granddad is gonna have a really hard time if the whole town just up and moves. He *is* this town."

"And the town is him." It was strange to think of Two Falls without Mr. Rogers—without his slightly off-key singing voice at church, with someone else living in his friendly little house around the corner, or without him attending the school bake sales, buying more sweets than he could possibly eat.

Garrett settled across from her, leaning on the beanbag chairs. He used his teeth to uncap his pen.

"You're going to break your teeth like that," Layla said.

He shrugged and flashed her a brilliant smile. "I'll risk it. I've been okay so far."

Out in the hallway, the janitor started the vacuum, and Layla stood up to close the classroom door against the noise. She was normally long gone by the time the nighttime janitor crew came in to clean.

"Will you do me a favor and grab me a highlighter?" Garrett asked, settling back onto his beanbag so he was almost lying down.

"I mean, don't get up. Can I get you a glass of wine while you're down there? Maybe I can hand-feed you grapes?" She grabbed a blue highlighter off the desk and tossed it to him. He caught it easily and uncapped it with his teeth.

She sighed. "All my writing utensils are going to have teeth marks on them, aren't they?"

"Writing utensils? What is that?" He wrinkled his nose, pausing from circling a cloud on the paper.

"What do you call them?" she asked, grabbing a yellow highlighter for herself.

"Writing . . . instruments. Writing . . . tools."

"No one calls them that. Literally no one."

"They should. And yes, they're all going to have teeth marks on them. I rarely have two free hands. I'm a multitasker."

"Gross," Layla said, laughing.

"Efficient." He tapped his temple, smiling at her from across the room in that way that he did—with one corner of his mouth slightly higher than the other, with his eyes crinkled happily, with his smile reaching every inch of his face.

She walked back across the room to join him on the beanbags when a sharp knock at the door startled her. She whirled around, her braids whipping over her shoulders, and took a step backward.

It was just the vacuum. The janitor had banged it against the door when he was sweeping up the hallway outside her classroom. She let out a relieved high-pitched giggle and turned around—but caught her foot on Garrett's sneaker, which he had stretched out to rest on the other beanbag.

Layla could feel herself teetering. She windmilled her arms, trying to regain her balance, and she could also see herself, as if her mind left her body as it happened, falling over, right onto the big pile of reading beanbags.

And right on top of Garrett.

She caught himself over him, on her elbows, but it wasn't enough—the beanbags didn't exactly make for a solid landing, but he sure did. Her elbows and knees sank into the soft beanbags, and she was lying on top of him, breathing hard, the wind knocked out of her. It took her a moment to register exactly where she was, and how she'd landed, and the surprise froze her for a moment.

He was definitely *not* soft. She could feel the hard lines of his body, his warm skin. The rise and fall of his chest as he breathed. And she could feel vibrations from his warm, throaty laugh.

"I—I'm sorry," she said, pushing herself up, but she found herself pausing, looking down at his face. A strand of hair had escaped from her braid. He reached up, tucking it behind her ear.

"You know," he said, "you're really beautiful."

She glanced down at him, at his bright, beautiful eyes, his stubble, his full lips, and he lifted his head, slightly, as if inviting her to kiss him, to forget the papers strewn around them, to stop worrying about the rules and finally, just finally, give in after all this time she had spent wanting exactly this.

She lowered her head, slightly, and brushed her lips against his.

His touch sent a shock through her. It startled her right back into herself, and she sat up, realizing, finally, that she was in a very compromising position, and if the janitor were to open the door to look inside, it would look like they were doing—well, exactly what they'd almost done.

She leaped up, her heart hammering against her rib cage.

"I'm so sorry," she said, feeling the blood rush to her cheeks. She felt dazed and electric and embarrassed and ashamed and joyful, and her pulse was doing some funny little dance in her veins, and she couldn't stay there, not after what she'd just done.

"It's okay," he said. "I promise, I don't mind at all."

She shook her head and rushed to her desk, grabbing her handbag. "I have to go," she told him without looking at him.

"Layla," he called after her. "It's okay."

But she was already rushing out the door, forgetting her tote bag underneath the desk, and Garrett was still lying among the beanbag chairs, where she'd kissed him.

And she'd liked it.

It was wrong, and she knew it, but she'd liked it.

And she wanted to do it again.

And the worst part of it all was knowing he did too.

Chapter 37

Ducky

Ducky had a very special day.

To start the day, Layla let him have a little bit of turkey out of the sandwich she had packed for lunch. It was super-duper yummy, and Ducky loved it so much. He tried to jump up on the counter to grab her whole sandwich because he wanted more, but Layla chuckled and put the sandwich into her lunch bag. Then she dressed him as a small astronaut and dropped him off at Mr. Rogers's house, who was so happy to see him that Ducky was pretty sure if the old man had a tail, he would be wagging it too. Ducky felt a little bad he didn't have one.

Then Mr. Rogers put him in his old truck, and Ducky napped on the soft blanket in the front seat while they drove and drove and drove. It might have been all day. Ducky didn't know any better because he napped. It was a good nap, and he liked curling up while Mr. Rogers took him places.

They pulled up at the same outlet mall where Ducky had been taken his tempratmint test—at least, that's what Ducky thought it was called—and he'd been going to lessons with Mr. Rogers ever since. Ducky loved it even though sometimes he thought he should be in charge. He usually knew best, after all.

"Good thing they got you in early for your intro lesson, Ducky,"

Mr. Rogers said, smiling. "It's Thursday, and you're already on your second one. You'll be a therapy dog in no time."

Ducky smiled his happy doggy smile.

He walked in that morning wagging his tail, and greeted Lilac, who walked out of the room and knelt down to gather Ducky into her arms and give him a big hug and a kiss on the nose. She sat Ducky back down on the floor.

"Who's a good boy?" she asked.

Ducky spun in a circle to show her that he was, indeed, a good boy.

Lilac looked up at Mr. Rogers and straightened to speak to him. "How is training going?"

"Been working with him every day," Mr. Rogers said proudly. "He's very good at sit and stay. He needs a little bit of work with heeling though. Sometimes he gets underfoot."

"We'll figure it out," Lilac said. "Are you ready to go through some commands?"

Mr. Rogers nodded. "We're ready, right, Ducky?"

Ducky loved doing commands. He knew that if Lilac was going to help him register to be a therapy dog, he needed to be really, really good at doing tricks and listening. His mom had helped him learn a lot of commands, so Ducky felt like he had a head start on his training.

"Okay, Ducky!" Lilac said. "Sit!"

Ducky sat, watching her.

"Ducky, stay!" she said, her voice firm. She clapped her hands, but Ducky stayed put. Then, she got out a squishy turtle toy—one with a squeaker in it—and tossed it in front of Ducky.

Ducky eyed the toy. He really, really wanted it. It would be so fun to play with. Maybe he could even sneak it home. Maybe he could get the squeaker out. He loved getting the squeaker out.

He looked up at Mr. Rogers, who was sitting behind him, on the bench next to the wall, and then Ducky looked at Lilac, who was waiting, her arms crossed.

The pup cocked his head, wondering what to do. He looked

back at the turtle, and then waited, glancing back at Lilac. Maybe this was a test, like when she brought a bunch of people in and didn't let Ducky get pets.

"Okay," Lilac said, and Ducky jumped up and grabbed the toy, sitting with it happily in his mouth. He chomped it, and it squeaked.

"Good boy!" Mr. Rogers said. "Very good boy!"

Ducky would have smiled if his mouth wasn't full of turtle. He squeaked it again, to show how happy he was.

"He's doing great," Lilac said. "I think we're ready to introduce another dog, and maybe more people—but we want to do it in a different environment. We want to see how he's going to listen with more distractions. What do you think?"

Mr. Rogers grinned. "I think that sounds great. Say—do you think I could drop by the school with him today and surprise my grandson and my neighbor?"

Lilac nodded. "As long as the school clears it, I don't see why not. It would probably be great for him to try out some commands around the kids."

Which was how Ducky ended up getting to do his super-fun lessons and visiting Layla and Garrett and all the students. He walked in very proudly, at the end of his leash, which Mr. Rogers was holding on to. Ducky always walked extra careful with Mr. Rogers and tried to remember not to get too excited and chase after a bird or anything, no matter how much he wanted to make the bird fly away. He also knew he shouldn't pull on the leash and go running off after any chipmunks.

He hoped Mr. Rogers appreciated the efforts he made to make sure the old man didn't get lost and/or stray from the sidewalk. Walking humans was hard work. Ducky's mom liked to stop so Ducky could smell things, and didn't mind if he pulled on the leash when a squirrel ran by. He would stop and roll in the grass and scratch his back. But he knew walking with Mr. Rogers was different, and he needed to be very careful.

So when Mr. Rogers went into the school, Ducky walked very

slowly and calmly toward Layla's classroom. He didn't need Mr. Rogers getting lost. When Mr. Rogers stopped to wave at the people in the office, Ducky tugged him gently forward so Mr. Rogers didn't get distracted.

When Ducky walked into the classroom, the kids almost exploded in excitement. It was like getting a million billion treats all at once. He was so excited to see them! Mr. Rogers let go of his leash, and he ran through all the desks, stopping to say hello to all the kids, who were ignoring the spelling test on their desks to reach down and pet the excited puppy.

"Well, isn't this a nice surprise!" Layla said.

Garrett crossed the room to put an arm around his grandfather. The Drubbins kids had jumped up to give Mr. Rogers hugs. Anita was hopping up and down, already inviting Mr. Rogers back to her farm—apparently, he had lunch with her parents once a month, right after church, and knew all her goats by name.

Ducky walked by all the kids, but he was looking for one particular person—someone very special, who he liked a bunch. So he said a friendly hello to Garrett and Layla, and then he ran across the room and jumped in one very special kid's lap.

Lucas.

At first, Lucas didn't even move. He just stared at the little dog, who sat down on his legs, and looked up at Lucas. Ducky kissed his nose, and Lucas smiled and laughed, the sound bubbling out of him.

Ducky wagged his tail. He loved that sound.

"Well," Layla said, "it looks like Ducky has found his seat for the day."

"If you don't mind," Mr. Rogers said, "it looks like he's very happy. I think it's best if leave him here with you and this young man. It looks like he has quite a handle on this dog."

Garrett looked at Layla, who was already nodding. "Certainly," she said. Ducky panted happily, his tongue hanging out of his mouth. He'd been wanting to spend more time with Lucas. He had smelled really sad today, and Ducky wasn't going to leave him, so matter what. Not until all the sad and scared he smelled was replaced with happy.

Of course, when it came to sadness—or strangeness—there was something going on with Garrett and Layla too. Something he didn't really like. But for now, he needed to help Lucas, and that was that. He could think about Layla and Garrett later.

Ducky always knew best.

CHAPTER 38

"Wait. Are you telling me you *kissed* him?"

Christine was back in town to help prep for the fashion show, and she and Layla were out scouting the location for the Two Falls Charity Fashion Show. Ducky was in Christine's arms, and he kept looking up at her and nuzzling the bottom of her chin, like he couldn't believe she was back again so soon. The weather was cold in a way that Layla always forgot was possible until it had arrived—cold wrapped up in wind, the kind of wind people could see moving the branches above their heads and whipping the last shriveled autumn leaves across the sidewalk. That was Nebraska though. The wind was a constant. Nebraska on an overly still day would have felt wrong; unearthly, almost, like the earth was holding its breath.

Layla, for a moment, was glad for the wind. It disguised the flush rising on her cheeks. The flush that was happening more and more often lately. She was mentally beating herself up for bringing Garrett up in the first place. Christine wouldn't leave it alone—she'd examine it closely; turn it over; put it under a microscope to inspect it.

"We'll have the event in the building back there," Layla said, pointing at the fairgrounds structure to avoid answering while she composed her thoughts. "Do you think it'll be big enough?"

Christine snapped a photo of the long sidewalk between the trees, shifting Ducky into one arm. "This location is perfect," she said. "We can do a little red-carpet entrance into the fair building," she said, pointing toward a long building squatting at the end of the sidewalk. Off to the side, a couple of semi trucks were parked. A couple of times a month, farmers from neighboring communities came in to bid on cattle that lumbered around in the attached corral, which was surrounded by a few rows of metal bleachers. It was also where the 4-H kids came to show their livestock—including, of course, Anita and her goats. Which meant it wouldn't be the end of the world if one of the dogs had an accident on the floor. The cracked concrete was pretty tough.

"It is," Layla agreed. "The fair building is pretty plain inside, but honestly, we can dress it up. People use it for wedding receptions and stuff all the time. There's even a little kitchen in there."

"Perfect," Christine said. "Wait. I'm distracted. Stop changing the subject. You kissed *Garrett*? After all your hand-wringing about, you know, it not being appropriate, and how you could never, and blah blah blah?"

"It was an accident. I fell on him." Layla kept walking up the sidewalk.

Christine jogged behind her to catch up. Layla could practically hear her rolling her eyes.

"Well, yeah. I fall on Jason all the time."

"Shut up. No, I accidentally tripped over his shoe and fell on top of him. We stayed late, and we were grading papers on the beanbags. You know, in the reading corner."

"Of course, *the reading corner*," Christine said, her voice awash with amused sarcasm. She giggled. "And then what? Your face fell on his face and your tongue landed in his mouth?"

Layla huffed. "Um, no. I fell on him and I was overwhelmed with attraction and I . . . brushed my lips against his. And then I regained my sanity. There was no *tongue*. It was purely a proximity thing mixed with temporary insanity."

Layla could tell Christine was fighting back laughter. Even

Ducky, who was tucked into her neck against the cold, looked amused. "I hate to break it to you," her friend said, "but when two people mash their mouths against each other we don't call that 'lip brushing.' We call that a *kiss*."

"I barely touched his mouth."

"So you kissed. And . . . then you regained your senses, had an emotionally mature conversation, and agreed you love each other and you're going to be together and live happily ever after?" Christine asked hopefully. She stopped to take another photo on her phone.

"Um, not exactly."

"Then what happened?"

"I ran away and have been avoiding the conversation ever since." Layla looked straight forward.

Christine stopped short. "Um, why?"

"Because it's not appropriate."

"And falling on him, kissing him, and running away . . . that is, what? Appropriate? The epitome of professionalism?"

"Obviously not," Layla said. "I shouldn't have done it."

Christine shook her head. "I can't with you sometimes."

"You definitely *can* with me. I'm amazing and hilarious. If lacking in good judgment occasionally."

"You definitely live with a healthy sense of denial," Christine said, sighing. "Hey—how's that kid in your class doing?"

The two had approached the big glass doors at the front of the building. Layla tugged on both of them, and the left one opened. Most places stayed unlocked in Two Falls. They weren't worried about anyone stealing anything, not really.

Layla tried the lights, and they slowly flickered on, a fluorescent buzz filling the large room. Christine let Ducky down on the hard floor, and he ran around delightedly, only stopping to sniff at the floor before taking off again.

"You mean Lucas?"

"Yes," Christine said. "How is he doing?"

Their voices echoed in the room, as if the whole world were listening.

Layla felt her heart drop lower in the chest, until it was sitting somewhere on top of her stomach. "I don't know," she said. "I found some kids kicking rocks at him on the playground. And then I found another kid spitting in his lunch. I've been keeping a close eye on him, and the offending kids were punished, but— I can't help thinking I'm still missing things. I just feel like—I'm not protecting him enough."

"Why are they bullying him?" Christine asked.

"Hmmm?"

"Why are the other kids bullying him?" Christine repeated. "Is it because he's Asian?" Christine stopped walking and faced her in the middle of the big empty room.

"Yes. And it doesn't help that Lucas's dad likely fired Aiden's dad from the plant."

Christine cursed, her face going pink. "So he's getting revenge through his son?"

"I think it's this one kid in particular causing the issues. He's . . . latching on to some ignorant stuff from his parents."

"Poor kid."

"I know. Lucas is really suffering." Layla dropped her head. "He's safe in the classroom, I think, but outside of it? I just— I don't know. We had an assembly, and all the other teachers are keeping an eye on him . . . but I worry. What if we miss something?"

"Poor Lucas," Christine said. "But this other kid. Have you ever thought of how incredibly screwed up his life is going to be? Lucas will have great people like you in his corner, but this other kid—he's going to either become a real racist, just like his parents, or he's going to realize that his parents are inherently bad people. Either way you slice it—he's got a rough life ahead of him."

Layla stared at Christine. "You aren't angry at them?"

"I mean, sure. I'm human, so obviously. But how much good is me being angry going to be?" Christine asked. She started walking again, snapping photos of the space. "I mean, yes, they're assholes. But they're ruining their kid's life—to the point their kid is trying to ruin other peoples' lives. And that's just . . . sad."

"I think you're too nice."

"You know," Christine said, "it's easier than being a horrible person. Less guilt to carry around."

Layla sighed. "Christine. I aspire to be you. You're like . . . the Dolly Parton of Instagram."

Christine took her arm. "Let's not get weird."

"You know what's kind of strange?" Layla asked. "When Ducky is around, the kids . . . they're . . . different to Lucas. They're nicer. It's like Ducky is his protector, or he's . . . I don't know. They like Ducky so much they forget to be hateful. Or maybe, I don't know, Lucas just feels a little braver around him." She watched the Yorkie. He was still running around on the floor, and then stopping short to slide. Layla smiled at his giddiness, at his excitement at exploring the big space, at just being included.

Layla expected Christine to laugh at her, but she didn't. Instead, she just nodded.

"Ducky's special like that. He sees people for who they are. He can see people for what they *need.* He always has."

Layla nodded. It was strange; had someone told her that without ever meeting Ducky, she wouldn't have believed it, would have passed it off as some owner being too proud of their dog. But she'd witnessed it with Ducky, time and time again.

"Come on," Christine said. "Let's go check out the kitchen. And if there's somewhere we can turn into a green room so the models can get dressed."

"You know," Layla said, "There's always the corral."

"We'll save that for my high school boyfriend if he shows up."

Layla snickered. "Are we expecting him?" she asked.

"You never know," Christine said seriously. "He slid into my DMs a couple of weeks ago. Creepers be creeping."

"Creepers be creeping? What is that—some kind of ancient proverb?"

Christine nodded. "Stick with me, kid. You'll go far." She paused. "Speaking of my wise and all-knowing ways—I have an idea on how maybe we can get through to Lucas."

"What is it?"

Christine grinned mischievously. "You're gonna have to trust me on this one."

CHAPTER 39

Three days until the fashion show.

Fourteen days since Layla had discussed anything with Garrett besides schoolwork and students.

Four minutes since Layla had checked him out.

Two minutes since Layla had caught Garrett checking *her* out.

Zero seconds since Layla had felt so awkward she wanted to melt into the floor like the witch in *The Wizard of Oz*. Zero seconds since she had lived in a perpetual, painful state of cringe. Zero seconds since she considered running out of the room, starting a homestead, and retiring from society forever with seventeen cats.

Garrett wasn't being weird, of course. Or, at least, not any weirder than Layla was. There was an awkward moment when he reached for a ruler at the same time she did. He had touched Layla's hand, just for a moment, and she got almost that same electric shock moment she had when they kissed. It hadn't been as powerful as the kiss (or *almost* kiss) but it had been undeniably *there*. They'd both pulled back.

Layla wondered if he felt it too.

But of course she'd never ask him. She couldn't.

Even though it was killing her.

Even though it kept sneaking into her thoughts, no matter how many times she'd promised herself it wouldn't. No matter how many times she tried to distract herself, her thoughts floated back to *him*. Garrett was always there. He was there every day, working with the kids. And even after everything, he still left her homemade goodies on her desk. He'd stopped handing them to her directly, but a couple snacks made it to her each week, sealed safely in Ziploc bags, tucked under homework, or slipped into her top drawer, sitting alongside her pens. Monday had been fudge; Wednesday had been cinnamon rolls, and last week, he'd even brought her a macaroon. He usually wrote on the Post-in note in a light scrawl, usually with a blue pen. *Fudge—no nuts. Macaroon—strawberry. Cinnamon rolls—extra frosting.*

It was like he was trying to tell her it was okay. And maybe, just maybe, he was trying to tell her more than that. But she couldn't let herself think about that. It was too far removed from her reality, the narrow confines from which she was committed to living her day to day. She'd peeked outside of it.

She liked to think of him in the kitchen. It was true; he was a former military man who resembled a lumberjack more than a baker, who seemed too big for such spaces, but apparently he liked it. Almost as much as he liked the gym. Which, incidentally, was the only reason Layla hadn't realized Garrett's connection with Mr. Rogers sooner—every day, after school, he went directly to the gym—did not pass go, did not collect $200. He'd told her once it was stress relief for him, a habit he'd picked up in the military.

If the gym was stress relief, by the looks of Garrett Henderson, he must have had an awful lot of stress to work away. She could tell by the way his forearms looked when he was writing something on the whiteboard, the easy flex of his muscles as he moved his wrists. By the effortless way he plucked Israel Reyes, a fourth grader, off the slide when he was planning on Superman–ing off the edge to impress his classmates. The way his shoulders moved under his button-up.

Layla shook her head, as if to clear the images. She had more important things to deal with. Like the day's lesson plans. She and Garrett had been working hard to make them absolutely perfect. They'd even stayed late the night before to run through them, but they'd stayed far, far away from the beanbags, and maintained an appropriate distance, which, Layla told herself, was the right thing, even if she didn't like it.

As if he could tell she was thinking about him, she looked up—and there he was. Looking at her right then, fidgeting slightly at the front of the classroom. They'd put together a whole presentation, and he'd pulled down the projector screen and was waiting for her expectantly. He crossed his arms over his chest and cleared his throat, raising his eyebrows.

Crap. It was her turn.

Layla nodded, standing up quickly and banging her knee on the bottom of her desk. She walked around her desk, ignoring the throbbing joint, and moving the mouse closer to the side near the front of the classroom so she could use it as a clicker to advance her slides.

This was it. It wasn't going to fix everything. It was one step. One step that might help Lucas. One step they had to take. One thing they had to try to do, to keep the world from spinning back on its axis.

It wasn't going to be enough. But maybe, just maybe, it would help.

"Today," Layla said, taking a slow, deep breath, "we're going to have a special lesson. We're going to talk about supercool inventors. Would you like that?"

"Inventors?" Benny asked. "Like who invented Nike?"

Garrett nodded. "Exactly, Benny. We're going to talk about some people who make your lives a little better because they invented some really cool things. Things that probably changed your life!"

The class was interested, leaning forward excitedly. Teddy was rocking a little in his seat, which he only did when he was very interested.

"How many of you guys watch YouTube?" Layla asked.

She hit the mouse, and YouTube filled the screen, playing a cartoon where a dog walked across the screen, stopped, farted, and then covered his face with his paw. The kids giggled, and their hands all raised. Even Lucas raised his hand tentatively, but he held it below his shoulder, as if afraid that someone might notice he was actually participating. She wished, for a moment, Ducky was in the room, to bolster his confidence, to stand guard over him.

"Awesome! Today we're gonna talk about the guy who invented YouTube! Can you imagine being the person who invented YouTube?" Garrett asked. He walked over to the bit of whiteboard not covered by the projector. "What kinds of words would you use to describe someone who was responsible for such an awesome invention?"

"*Smart?*" Anita asked.

"Good one, Anita!" Layla said. "I would say *smart* too."

Meanwhile, Garrett uncapped a blue marker with his teeth and wrote *Smart* on the board.

"*Cool?*" asked Avery.

"I'd absolutely say someone who invented YouTube is supercool!" Layla said, and Garrett added the word to the board.

"*Smart!*" Aiden repeated.

"Yup," Layla said. "You're right, Aiden, but we've already got *smart* on the board. Do you want to try another one?"

"*Nice!*" Aiden shouted.

Layla smiled. She was happy Aiden was participating. As a second grader, his line of thought wasn't nuanced yet, but it made sense a second grader would think someone who invented something good was nice.

"Very good, Aiden," she said, and Garrett added it to the board.

He added *supercool, awesome, best person ever, president,* and even *cats* to the list. Layla smiled. She loved exercises like this that showed how her students' minds worked. Most likely her students used YouTube to watch cat videos. As, Layla surmised, most people probably did.

Then, Penny yelled *potato*.

Layla smiled. "Penny, tell me more about that."

Penny shrugged.

Part of being a second-grade teacher was also about moving on. She turned back to the board, and Garrett read out their list of words. "I think we can all agree that whoever invented YouTube is probably pretty awesome, right?" Garrett asked.

Every head in the class nodded.

Layla's heart did a tiny jump. They had them. They were interested. Sometimes, it was hard to predict what would land with second graders. But they were interested. They were hanging on to their every word.

"Do you guys want to see who it is?" Layla asked.

More nods. Teddy was still bouncing with excitement, and the legs of his chair were moving back and forth on the slick carpet.

She clicked the mouse and an image of Steven Shih Chen filled the screen, smiling, He had a small silver hoop in each ear and wore thick-rimmed black glasses. He looked every bit like the Silicon Valley rock star—the kind of person who showed up to do TED Talks and left the audience awed.

And, of course, he was Taiwanese American.

"Guess who this guy is?" Garrett asked, jerking his thumb at the screen. "Only one of the coolest guys ever. The inventor of something I know you guys watch all the time. And I bet your siblings and your parents and maybe even your grandparents watch too."

"My grandma likes dance videos where the girls go like this." Emma stood up and did a dance move where she moved her back and hips up and down, like a cat trying to throw up a hairball. Layla swallowed a laugh that was rising from her belly and threatening to overwhelm her.

Garrett coughed. "Um, thank you, Emma."

Layla glanced back at Lucas, who was sitting up a little straighter than usual, his eyes wide and fixed on the screen. She smiled a little. "This is Steven Shih Chen. He's one of the guys who invited YouTube—one of the most popular sites on the internet. You guys know how many people live in Omaha? More than that visit You-Tube every day. Lots, lots more."

It was hard to describe numbers to kids in terms they understood. But most, if not all, of the kids had been to Omaha, Nebraska's largest city.

"It's way, way more people than Memorial Stadium when the Huskers play," Garrett added. "Think a big bunch of those, all added together."

"Wow," George said. "I watched YouTube yesterday. But my mom told me I had to go to bed. I watched car races. One of the cars crashed."

"Is he rich?" Anita asked.

"He's a millionaire," Layla said, crossing her arms over her chest. "He could buy more goats that you could count, Anita. And, Benny, he could buy enough Nintendo Switches to fill a mansion. He could buy the biggest house in town."

"He could buy all the houses in town," Garrett added.

Everyone was very impressed.

"Is he nice?" Lucas asked.

Layla turned, almost startled. Hearing Lucas's voice was strange, especially when it was loud enough to be heard above the other kids, who were buzzing.

"Well," Garrett said, "I haven't met him, but he donates a lot of that money to good causes. Like schools. He actually gave a million dollars to his old school. And he supports a lot of places that do good things in California."

Lucas smiled, looking almost relieved, as if the inventor had passed his test.

"Now, the really fun part," Layla said. "We're going to be learning about a lot more inventors, so we're going to hand out our famous-inventor trading cards." She grabbed a stack of cards off the desk, which she'd paid out of pocket to have printed up in

Brimsley, when she'd driven Mr. Rogers to a therapy-dog lesson with Ducky. She handed half to Garrett, and they walked pass them out to the students. Each one had a different fun fact about the inventor.

The kids exclaimed and showed each other the cards.

"Now," Layla said, "Each time we learn about a new inventor, you can earn a card!"

Garrett grinned at the kids. "But that's not all. We have a very special guest today who is actually famous too. Two special guests, but who's counting?"

"Taylor Swift?" Anita asked, perking up. She loved Taylor Swift almost as much as her goats.

Layla laughed and crossed the room. "Um, no. But it's someone else you might recognize from your parents' Instagram. She has hundreds of thousands of followers and is known for traveling all over the world and seeing awesome things while wearing super-cool outfits. She's also our friend Ducky's mom!"

As soon as she said *Ducky,* the kids were hooked. They were turning around in their seats, straining their necks, waiting to see who would walk into the classroom.

Layla swung open the door, and Christine walked in, grinning and waving. "It's Christine Hsu, who is responsible for our big fashion show happening this weekend!" Layla clapped, and the kids joined in, the excitement infectious. Avery cheered, and Teddy made whooping noises.

Christine grinned and gave a shy wave. Despite being famous, sometimes she still was a little tentative when she was the center of attention—which was why Layla had been so surprised when she came up with the idea to drop by the classroom and talk to the kids.

Layla watched Christine take a deep breath, exhale, and then, she was standing at the front of the room, waving to the class and grinning like she was born to be in front of an audience.

"Hey, guys," she said. "I'm Christine." She took the time to shake every kid's hand—even the slightly sticky ones, which were a constant in every second grade classroom—and then walked to the front of the classroom. "Who's excited for the fashion show this weekend?"

Every hand shot up. Penny was wiggling with excitement in her seat.

Layla had been worried that the kids wouldn't be interested in Christine, because she wasn't someone they saw on TV, but she was wrong. The kids were so incredibly excited to meet someone who was famous on Instagram. Layla had heard that with the younger generation the old-school celebrity rules no longer applied—sure, they loved people who appeared on their TVs or in movie theaters, but they adored the social media stars, the influencers, the people who lived in their phones and spoke to them. Although none of her second graders had their own iPhones, they all played on tablets and watched YouTube and leaned in to watch when their parents were scrolling through Instagram and TikTok.

Christine was, in no uncertain terms, a star. She was undoubtedly the most famous person anyone in her class had ever met, including the Husker tight end who had visited the school last year to talk to the kids about staying drug free. (Layla's students had been deemed too young to attend, but he'd still come by the class to give everyone high fives and fist bumps.)

The lesson ran long. Christine stayed through reading, talking with each and every student—all of whom insisted on taking pictures with her. She did funny poses with each one—big, goofy smiles, peace signs, upside-down finger glasses—anything the kids wanted. Even Aiden approached, somewhat shyly.

"Can I have a picture?" he mumbled.

Layla glanced at Garrett, worried. After how he'd treated Lucas, they were both concerned about his reaction to the lesson—but even more so about Christine. Layla had originally declined Christine's invite to visit the classroom to talk to the kids because she didn't want Christine in the line of fire—what if the kids didn't react well to her? What if they said something racist? What if Aiden acted out of pocket? She didn't want her friend exposed to any of that, even by second graders. But Christine had insisted. She wanted to do it—for Lucas. After all, she knew what it was like to be the only Asian girl in class.

But Layla seemed to have been worried for nothing. Aiden was as starry-eyed as any of the other kids. And, having just returned from his suspension, he was on his best behavior.

After the encounter, Layla watched Garrett motion him over. "Hey, Aiden," Garrett said. "Did you know that Christine is Asian American?"

Aiden had looked at Layla, tilting his head to the side, not understanding.

"Christine's family is from Taiwan. And so is Lucas's family," he told Aiden quietly. "And so is Steven, the inventor of YouTube."

Aiden looked at him in surprise. "Do they know each other? From Taiwan?"

Garrett shook his head. "I don't know. Lots and lots of people live there. Millions and millions."

Aiden nodded seriously.

"But Christine and Lucas are both from Nebraska. So you never know." Garrett winked at Aiden, and the boy looked over at Lucas curiously.

Layla's heart sped up. Would this help? Even a little? Could it be the gentle push in the right direction Aiden needed?

Then, there was another knock at the door—and Mr. Rogers strolled in with Ducky on a leash. Ducky and Mr. Rogers wore matching suspenders and brown corduroys, and the dog had donned an adorable newsboy hat that sat jauntily between his fuzzy little ears.

The room almost exploded with excitement, and Layla crossed the room to stand with Garrett while Mr. Rogers walked Ducky around the classroom to greet the students. Lucas hung back, as usual—which was perfect, because it gave Christine the opportunity to kneel down by his desk. She smiled at him, and he smiled back.

Christine had told her before, but it was lovely to see it in action—representation mattered. And here Lucas was, looking at someone who looked a little like him, who was happy and smiling and successful and just happened to be the dog mom to his favorite canine.

"Lucas," Christine said, kneeling down by his desk, "Can I ask you a question?"

Lucas looked at her for a quiet moment, filled with wonder. "You know my name?"

Layla was filled with relief. She had been worried Lucas would be overcome by emotion and slip back into shyness, behind a thick wall that took days to penetrate. But no—Lucas was looking at Christine with interest and was sitting up straight. His arms were crossed in front of himself a little protectively, but for Lucas, this was a big step. She nudged Garrett and gave a subtle head nod toward the duo, who were busy chatting.

"Of course I do," Christine was telling Lucas. "Ms. Layla told me all about you. She said you're very smart and kind."

Lucas blushed, pink coloring his cheeks, but he didn't duck his head.

"Did you know I used to go to school around here too?" she asked. "Just about an hour or so away, in Omaha, and I was the only Asian kid in my class. I loved school so much, but sometimes it was really hard."

Lucas looked at her. "Why?"

Christine rested her chin in her hand. "Well, sometimes some of my classmates were really mean to me. It made me sad, and sometimes I wanted to scream, and sometimes I wanted to cry. It was pretty tough, because it's not okay to be treated badly because your ethnicity is different. Ever."

"What did they do?" Lucas asked.

Christine sighed. "Not nice things, Lucas. One time, a kid put gum in my hair, and my mom had to take me to the hairdresser to get it all cut off. I didn't want to go back to school for a week. Does that kind of stuff ever happen to you?"

"What?" Lucas looked at her skeptically.

"Kids being mean to you? Maybe not liking you just because you're Asian?"

Lucas looked down at his lap. But then, after a long pause, he looked up and nodded solemnly. "Yeah. They kick rocks at me, and sometimes they mess up my lunch. Sometimes they chase me and one time someone put my face in the dirt. It tasted pretty bad."

Christine nodded. "That's pretty mean stuff."

He nodded. "Yeah."

"You know, Lucas, I'm going to tell you something it took me a long time to learn. First of all, you matter. Even when they make you feel like you don't. Second, what's important is not how a few mean kids feel about it. They don't understand what we understand—that how they treat us says more about them than it does about us. Does that makes sense?"

Lucas shook his head.

Christine leaned forward. "If you see someone being mean to someone, what do you think about them? Do you want to be their friend?"

Lucas shook his head. "I probably think they're not very nice."

"What about the kid who's always nice and maybe keeps to himself a little bit? Maybe he's a little quiet? Which one would you rather be friends with?"

"The quiet one," Lucas mumbled.

"Hey," Christine said. "Me too. Did you know I used to be that quiet kid too, just like you?"

Lucas shrugged. "Not really."

"And when I started being myself, I made my own friends. Good friends. We told each other jokes and went over to each other houses and played video games. And I started having fun at school. And do you know what I realized?" she asked.

He shook his head.

"What's really, truly important is that you love yourself and that you're proud of who you are and where you come from. None of these other kids come from the same culture as Steven Shih Chen, but you and me? We do. And people who don't like you just because of your race or how you look—well, Lucas, this might be hard to understand, but you don't want those kinds of people for your friends anyway. You don't want to be friends with anyone, ever, who makes you feel like less than the amazing kid you are. Okay?"

Lucas nodded.

"Now," Christine said, "if you ever need me, you just tell Ms. Layla, and I promise she'll put us in touch, and I'll listen. But I want you to know one really important thing, Lucas. You're great. You're smart and kind and thoughtful, and you have awesome things to look forward to. And being different doesn't mean bad. In fact, I'd say it means you're pretty special."

Christine grinned at him, and Lucas grinned back.

Layla realized, suddenly, that she'd been gripping Garrett's arm throughout the exchange, watching it with concern. She let him go, and he rubbed where her fingertips had probably created indentations. "Sorry," she whispered.

"Don't sweat it," he whispered back.

But Christine wasn't done with Lucas. She had a surprise for him. A really big, really important one. Layla inched a little closer, not wanting to miss a word.

"I have a question for you, Lucas. I hear my dog really, really likes you. Is that true?"

Lucas nodded solemnly. "We're friends," he told her, as confident in Ducky as Layla had ever seen him.

"Do you think you could walk Ducky down the runway during the finale of the fashion show?"

Lucas stared at her before answering, as if his brain was catching up to her question. As if he couldn't quite figure out what was happening. But then his face broke into a big, happy smile. "Yes. Yes I could."

"Okay," Christine said. "Can you give me your parents' phone number? Ms. Layla and I will call them and get their permission."

Layla's heart fluttered, and she felt . . . light and strangely happy. It was . . . a little like magic.

When the bell finally rang for lunch, Mr. Rogers had taken Ducky back to his house, and Christine had signed autographs for all seventeen and said her goodbyes, Teddy Sullivan tapped Lucas on the shoulder.

"Hey, Lucas," he said. "Do you maybe wanna play soccer with us today?"

Lucas stared at him open-mouthed, as if he couldn't actually believe one of his classmates was talking to him. Not ignoring him. Not bullying him. Just . . . talking.

Aiden stopped on his way out the door. "Yeah, come on, Lucas. Let's play soccer."

Lucas followed them outside, a little uncertainly, but without taking the time to center his chair or put away everything on his desk. Layla almost couldn't believe it. Had it worked? Was Aiden actually going to be nice to Lucas now? Were the kids going to include him? She put her hand on her chest and walked to the window, watching them walk down the sidewalk and down to the big grassy field.

Layla turned to Garrett, smiling. "Wanna go watch a soccer game?" she asked. She wanted to keep an eye on Lucas. Just in case. She knew one day wouldn't fix everything, but maybe it could help. Maybe, just maybe, they would all move together, in the right direction.

He grinned back at her. "Sure."

CHAPTER 40

DUCKY

Ducky was a proud therapy dog.

Well, almost. But he was working really hard at it. Mr. Rogers said he had to be really, really good at obedience, which Ducky was. Well, most of the time. It was really really hard not to sneak some of his mom's food when she wasn't looking. And sometimes he just wanted to leave the sidewalk and pee on stuff. He didn't understand how humans didn't want to pee on stuff on the time. How else did they leave messages for other humans?

Well, phones, probably. Or the little things they wore on their wrists. Or something. But pee worked better. He could tell a lot by that. It was like a doggy phone call.

He was trying to sniff around an old cottonwood tree outside the fairgrounds when Layla swept him up into her arms and brought him inside a big old building where there was a frantically happy hustle and bustle. A man he'd never met before threw up his arms when he saw him.

"If it isn't our little star!" he shouted. He looked over at Christine, who was setting up the last in a long line of chairs. The chairs were cold metal with big red bows looped over the back that looked kind of fun and exactly like the kind of thing Ducky would have pulled on, but his mom gave him her best *Oh no you don't* look, and so he decided not to grab one. Well, at least until after the fashion show.

Ducky liked the fairgrounds. He smelled cows. At home in California, it wasn't something he smelled a lot, but they were just about everywhere in Nebraska. They were like big stinky giants, and he wanted to meet one really bad, but whenever he pulled on his leash to get close to one, Layla or Mr. Rogers—whoever was walking him at the time—would pull him back gently.

Ducky ran around the big room happily, greeting everyone he saw, even though a lot of people were strangers. Even so, they all stopped to exclaim over him and pet him and compliment his outfit. He was dressed as Woody from *Toy Story*, which was especially appropriate because Woody was a cowboy. He probably got to hang out with real cows.

The whole town was bustling—not just the fairgrounds. When Layla had driven him over, she'd kept pointing at things excitedly. "Look, Ducky!" she'd said as they drove down Main Street. "There's a No Vacancy sign at the motel! And look at all the cars!"

Ducky had tried to look, but he was short, so he couldn't see very much. But he could hear there were more cars than usual, and that made him very excited.

"And the café is packed!" Layla said. She laughed then, high and a little nervous, and the sound made Ducky crawl across the seat to lie against her just in case she needed him.

"Thanks, little guy," she said, patting his head. "I sure hope this works. This is the busiest I've ever seen Two Falls."

Ducky hoped it did, too. He really loved the little town and the kids in Layla's class and pretty much everyone he'd met here. No one could ever replace his mom and dad and Katsu and Barb, but he was very happy having more family.

The volunteers were setting out cookies shaped like dog treats wrapped in something all around the room. Ducky wondered if they would give him one, but figured they were probably human food. He tried to hop up on a chair to see if he could reach the table, but his legs were too short. A lady name Brynn, who always smelled like a million dogs and was friends with his mom, was saying things in a loud voice and pointing. She had taken over his mom's clipboard.

Ducky sniffed, trying to smell the sugary sweetness of the cookies—when he caught a scent he hadn't expected. A familiar scent. A scent that made him happy. He looked up just as his mom was gathering a very familiar boy in a big hug. It was Lucas! And two grown-ups were with him—two people who looked like maybe they were his mom and dad! Ducky ran across the room as fast as his little legs would carry him and jumped up and down until Lucas leaned down and patted him hello.

"Hi, Ducky," he said shyly. "These are my parents. My dad works at the plant, and my mom works on the computer on secret codes."

Ducky offered them both his paw, and they each leaned down and greeted him with big, happy smiles.

"Is this the little dog we've been hearing so much about?" Lucas's mom asked.

Ducky barked and ran in a circle, and then ran back to Lucas, panting. Lucas sat down on the floor, and Ducky climbed in his lap and licked his face. Lucas giggled, which was a wonderful, beautiful sound. Ducky loved it very much.

Christine walked over and introduced herself. "I see you've all already met Ducky," she said. "He's definitely outgoing." She bent down and touched Lucas's shoulder. "Thanks for helping me out, Lucas. I think you're going to be the star of this show."

Lucas looked at Christine like she'd just told him he could have an entire jar of peanut better treats.

"I have something for you to wear tomorrow. Something special that my friend just drove down from Omaha. Do you want to see?"

"Yes, please," he said. "Can Ducky come?"

"Absolutely," Christine said. "Come on, Ducky!"

Ducky followed Lucas and Christine back to a room they kept calling the green room, which seemed silly because it wasn't even green. At least, as far as Ducky could tell. Once, Christine had told Ducky dogs saw color differently. But it looked like a plain old white room. Which was disappointing. Ducky had wanted to see a green room.

While Christine showed Lucas his outfit, Ducky spotted something on the floor—half of a broken cookie! He was starving. It had probably been almost an hour since breakfast. He darted across the floor and gobbled it up as fast as he could.

"Ducky!"

He looked up, still chewing his treat. Layla was looking down at him, her hands on her hips but an amused smile on her face. "You're so sneaky!" she said, laughing.

Christine and Lucas looked up from whatever they were doing. Ducky tried his best to look very cute and innocent, sitting straight and tilting his head in a way he knew was especially adorable.

"You have frosting on your nose, Ducky," Lucas said, giggling.

Ducky licked his nose, making Lucas laugh harder.

"Do you need me for anything?" Layla asked, poking her head in. "Oh, hey, Lucas, buddy! Good to see you!" She turned back to Christine. "I'm done setting up all the chairs, and we've put a few baskets of the cookies all over the room. Super sweet for Theo to donate them, right?"

Christine nodded. "I have your outfit. And your dog."

"Um, what?" Layla asked. "My outfit? I'm not walking."

"Yes, you are," Christine said. "I have an outfit for you that was donated by"—she stopped to check the papers on a clipboard she was holding under the elbow—"Omaha Fashion Shop. Plus, we need someone to walk Judith."

"Judith? Who's Judith?"

"A senior American bulldog who has been in the shelter for, like, four hundred days."

Ducky watched Layla fidget, biting her lip and doing something funny with her fingers, like she was pulling on each one individually. "I don't know," she said finally. She sat down on the old orange couch that was pushed up against the far wall, opposite of the giant rack of clothes Christine was pawing through. Ducky really wanted Layla to walk with him. He worried about her. Sometimes he thought if he wasn't around she'd barely leave her house.

"Please, Ms. Layla?" Lucas asked. He looked up at her with big eyes. It was a good trick, Ducky knew. He used it all the time. "I'm walking. Please do it too?"

"I guess," she said, resigned, her shoulders dropping a little. "Whatever you think."

Ducky wanted to jump for joy. He was so excited to show off his new outfit for the show—and now his auntie Layla would be part of it too, not just helping behind the scenes! He wagged his tail so Layla knew he was happy.

Christine pushed a garment bag into Layla's hands. "Just don't get it dirty, okay?" she asked. "People can purchase the clothes. Everything is donated to the dogs or the school."

Layla nodded. "Um, okay," she said, but Ducky thought she was looking like she didn't really know what she'd gotten herself into.

CHAPTER 41

Layla was nervous.

There were a lot of reasons. One was that she had to walk down a red carpet in front of everyone without tripping.

Another was that if this went badly, a lot of people were out a lot of money and the school lunch program would be permanently dead. Without it, lots of kids wouldn't eat. It would be another problem for the little school. Maybe the problem that finally made parents decide to send their kids to Brimsley, where they had a free- and reduced-price lunch program.

The other was that Christine had asked her to basically wear a red . . . something. It was not Layla's style. It was the *opposite* of Layla's style. It was silk and had a slit all the way up her thigh and was like nothing she had ever worn, or even planned on wearing. It did not scream second-grade teacher.

The garment bag Christine had given her the night before had held a sweatshirt and matching sweatpants. She could do that. She had not been expecting to wear a silk number better suited for the love interest in a James Bond film.

"They sent it in the wrong size," Christine said apologetically, holding it out to her. "I'm so sorry. Veda was set to wear it, but it doesn't fit her at all—so if we can swap you into this dress, and she can wear the hoodie set the sportswear place donated—I mean, that would be perfect."

"Can't someone else wear it?" Layla asked doubtfully. It was the kind of thing that maybe she fantasized about wearing, sure, when a rich billionaire took her out for dinner. It was not something she *ever* thought about wearing in Two Falls.

"Well, it's too big for me and too small for Garrett. You're the only one who fits into it." Christine hesitated. "I mean, if you don't want to, we can definitely just have someone sort of walk it down the runway on a hanger. I don't want to make you uncomfortable."

Layla swallowed hard and forced a smile. "Um, of course not." She took dress off the hanger, holding it up in front of her hung on her thumbs. "It'll be great!" she said out loud, trying to convince herself.

The idea of wearing the red dress in front of Garrett made her want to die. It made her want to melt into the floor. It also kind of made her want to twirl into his arms and kiss him, the skirt flaring slightly around her legs. She hoped he liked it.

That was another thing. Christine had asked Garrett to walk in the show, and of course Garrett had agreed. He was nice like that, even though Layla had never even imagined him walking a runway. But she figured he would look great.

So she locked the door to the green room and slipped into the red dress. She stared at herself in the mirror, taking slow, deep breaths. She could do this. Everyone was doing this. She happened to know the mayor was planning on wearing swim trunks donated by a business in Lincoln, and if he did a little dance at the end of the runway, they were throwing in an extra $500—$250 for the shelter, and $250 for the school lunch program.

They even offered to throw in an extra $300 if he jumped in a snowdrift at the end. Which he probably would. And there were plenty of snowdrifts around for him to choose from—including an especially muddy one in the back of the corral, which was a prime contender. It had snowed two nights ago—a big snowstorm with wild, soft flakes blown around in the wind, creating a perfect winter wonderland set up for the fashion show.

But Layla's mind wasn't on the show. There were so many numbers being thrown around she couldn't keep them straight in her head. The money—it could really help her students and their families. It was more, she was sure, than her paltry teacher's salary. More than she could ever hope to give the school. But only if this all worked. If no one showed up—if all the cars just belonged to vendors and no one showed up to donate money, to buy the clothes, or adopt the dogs—well, then she was in trouble. It had to work . . . for everyone. People had to be willing to drive to town. People had to care every bit as much as she hoped they would.

Layla slipped into the dress and straightened the silk straps on her shoulders. The mirror on the back wall reflected someone she wasn't entirely sure she knew; someone more sophisticated. Someone who didn't spend their days cleaning glitter glue out of her fingernails. Someone who'd led an entirely different life.

Layla smoothed the skirt down on her legs and held her hair up. She didn't have time for a fancy updo—she'd been working with Christine all day to get all last-second items in order—making sure everyone had their clothes, that the dogs had a waiting area while they waited to strut down the aisle—but maybe a low ponytail would work. She pulled the black elastic off her wrist and was tying it back when she heard a knock at the door.

"I'll be right out, Christine," she shouted.

"It's Garrett."

Layla's heart did this funny little leap fueled by joy and nerves. She swung the door open, and Garrett stood there, holding his own black garment bag, waving at someone outside the door.

"I just heard great news," he said. "The plant isn't closing, it's just—"

Then he looked at her, and stopped in the middle of his sentence, his eyes widening.

"Um, what? The plant isn't closing?"

He didn't say anything. He cleared his throat and blinked and then looked away, nervously.

She wanted to grab him and force him to look at her. What was wrong with him? He was being weird. Of course, she couldn't really judge, considering she had been weird every single day since . . . well, forever. Probably since the first day he'd become her student teacher.

"Garrett!" she said. "What's going on?"

"Uh," he said, and cleared his throat again. A pink flush was rising in his cheeks. "I just talked to Susan Lynn. She said the plant isn't closing. They're cutting costs, which is why the school lunch program went. But they're staying open here—at least for now. A few other plants, though—they're gone. Already. People laid off. But not ours. Not yet, at least."

Layla laughed, delight lifting her up like helium in a slowly inflating balloon. "What? You're serious? Tell me you're serious."

He nodded, breaking into a smile. "Yeah. Apparently it was just a rumor that gained steam when they closed other locations. Granted, it made sense for everyone to be nervous. And they're not out of the woods yet—apparently Jarvis's stock price is in the toilet. But they're not getting rid of our plant. Not yet."

"What?" She still couldn't believe it. "Garrett! That's amazing!" She bounced forward and wrapped him in an impulsive hug, her joy making her practically buoyant.

He paused for a moment, frozen, and then his arms lifted to hug her back. She let go, too happy to care that maybe she shouldn't be hugging her student teacher. But her town would last a little longer. They weren't gone yet. Besides, the semester was over in a few days. She could get away with an excited hug,

Pulling back, Layla smoothed her hair, tightening the ponytail she'd been working on. "Do you need to use this room?" she asked. "I'll get my purse. I think there's a little closet somewhere I can throw it in. You can get changed in here if you want. I think most people are dressing at home, but honestly, I've been here all day, and I haven't had the time . . ." She turned to grab her hand-bag, but he stopped her with a gentle touch on her shoulder.

"Your tag is flipped up," Garrett said, his voice a little husky. "May I?"

She nodded and held her ponytail out of the way. She tried not to shiver when his fingers brushed her back as he tucked the tag back inside her dress.

"There," he said, his voice startlingly low. She turned around to face him, and Garrett was still looking at her strangely. Almost hungrily.

"You can be on tag duty tonight, okay?" she asked.

He nodded. "You . . . you look beautiful," he said finally, his words stilted, as if he was trying to hold back what he really wanted to say.

She nodded and ducked her head, feeling heat creeping up from her chest until her skin probably matched the dress. "Thank you," she whispered, stepping to the side. "I'll, um, leave you to it."

She escaped the room, her pulse a steady thrum in her ears, and stood outside, breathing hard.

Nearby, Christine was straightening Mr. Rogers's bow tie, and Ducky rested next to the old man, leaning against his leg. Layla sat heavily in a folding chair next to him, letting her breath out in a big whoosh.

"Are you okay?" Christine asked, a knowing smile on her face.

Layla gave her a look that could melt iron. "I'm fine," she said sternly.

Mr. Rogers reached out and grabbed Christine's hands. "Christine, dear, I'm fine. Would you mind going to get my cane? I want to look dapper, and I can't without it."

"Of course," Christine said, smiling. "I'll go find it."

Mr. Rogers watched her leave—and Layla looked at him, surprised. He was notorious for not wanting to use his cane. So why would he send Christine after it?

"You know," Mr. Rogers said finally, when Christine was out

of earshot. "I don't particularly like flowers." His eyes were fixed on Layla.

Layla looked at him, shocked. It was like he'd just told her that he was secretly an Olympic athlete. *Of course* Mr. Rogers liked flowers. They were part of his whole personality.

"What?" Layla protested. "But they're everywhere. All over your whole house."

He nods. "They make me happy. Do you know why?"

She waited.

"Because they made my wife happy. And when I keep her floral pillows fluffed and on the couch where she left them, or water the flowers in the garden and see them big and bright out my window, I think of how much she would have liked that. And that's how they make me happy too."

He paused, leaned in close. "You know, Layla. I know that maybe you don't want to change your life. Maybe you think that life has given you a certain set of circumstances, and you're afraid to step outside of them. But maybe you should think about what makes you happy, even if you have to let something you weren't expecting in along with it. I know you like giving to others. I know you never think about yourself." He paused. "But sometimes, someone comes along who makes you a better person and makes you happy at the same time. And that doesn't happen often, and it doesn't happen for everyone. Which is why when it does, you need to hold on to it, as hard as you can."

Layla wanted to run away. She didn't want to listen. And she didn't want to believe that Mr. Rogers, of all people, had caught on to what was happening.

Of course he would. He knew Layla, and he obviously was close to Garrett. He'd seen Layla and Garrett's interactions—the way they'd avoided each other, or the looks they'd given each other when they thought no one was watching. She was stupid to think he wouldn't have noticed.

Mr. Rogers took her hand and squeezed it. "Do what makes you happy. And you might just fall in love with something you never thought you wanted. Layla . . . you might be surprised."

A lump climbed into Layla's throat, choking her. She felt tears in her eyes, and she pressed them closed. She was wearing mascara. She couldn't cry. Christine had done a quick makeup look in the green room earlier, and she wouldn't have time to reapply it if Layla cried it away.

She blinked and opened her eyes. Mr. Rogers was watching her carefully, a kind smile on his mouth, and Ducky was looking up at her with hope in his eyes, as if he were trying to tell her the same thing.

Christine came running out, a cane in her hand. She handed it to Mr. Rogers and inspected Layla carefully. "You okay?"

Layla nodded. "I'm fine."

"Good." Christine paused to check her phone. "I need to get Ducky to Lucas." She patted her thigh, whistling, and Ducky popped up to follow her. "And, Layla—it's time for you to meet Judith."

CHAPTER 42

Judith was perfect.

She was huge, for starters, as far opposite of tiny little Ducky as Layla could have imagined. She had imagined being matched with a French bulldog, barely bigger than Ducky—small, easy to manage, adorable—and she'd been intimidated for a half moment when the big, lumbering gray bulldog had entered the room. But Judith had sniffed Layla for a half minute and then leaned into her happily, grunting and rolling over so Layla could scratch her big belly.

"She's had a lot of puppies," Brynn, who was coordinating the event, advised. "We think she was used as a breeding dog and then dumped. She just needs a home where she can be taken care of. She just wants to sleep and watch TV." Brynn smiled at the canine fondly for a moment before leaving to get another dog out of the heated trucks waiting just outside the fairgrounds.

Layla's heart broke as she looked down at the big gray dog, who looked like she was smiling. A long line of drool was already forming from her mouth. She was so sweet. How could anyone abandon a dog? She tried to imagine someone being heartless enough to leave Judith and never come back. But she couldn't. Who would do that?

Judith had followed her around ever since she'd been assigned to Layla. It was like she had known that Layla was her person, at least temporarily, and lumbered after her, wherever she went, her big soft feet padding as she walked. When Layla went into the bathroom, the dog even followed her into the stall and sat against her knees, like she was trying to make sure no one was going to sneak up on her.

Layla was in love with her almost immediately. She walked her around the fairgrounds, trying to get her used to the area. The building looked amazing.

It had gone from a big, empty room with a concrete floor (that was admittedly cracked) into the closest thing to a glam event the town had ever seen. Red and green tulle hung from the exposed metal rafters—a nod to the holiday season—and rows of Edison lights were hung in big swooping arcs along the walls. There were also tiny little lights on each side of the runway, along with some large spotlights a local theater company had donated—just for the day, of course. Little images showing dogs and scannable QR codes to donate both to the school and the humane society were everywhere—on posters, on tiny little cards sitting on tables, and, as a final touch, on all the T-shirts the volunteers were wearing.

And, most importantly, the room was packed.

It was like the entire town was there and then some; Layla searched the faces—she saw Mrs. Sanchez almost right away, and her neighbor, Cassie Ellis, and Theo from the café, Pastor Decker from the Baptist church, and, naturally, Reina. But they were mixed in with strangers. More strangers than locals. Strangers carrying around plastic wineglasses and chatting and looking absolutely stunning. Strangers chatting, looking toward the stage, waiting excitedly for it all to start.

They'd come.

Layla stomach lurched nervously.

Soft music played over the loudspeakers—funny hits like "Ain't Nothing But a Hound Dog," "Old Red," and even "Who Let the Dogs Out." Layla had helped Christine compile a dog-themed playlist before the event, giggling over their choices as they added more.

Layla was watching the event unfold from a crack in the folding screens behind the runway. The green room had been too small for all the dogs and models, so they'd had to set up holding space so they all could stand in line and wait for their turns to walk down the runway.

The room was noisy. Layla hoped it wasn't too scary for the dogs. And it would probably only get louder as the show started. Christine was standing next to her, fidgeting with the ends of her long hair, shifting back and forth from one foot to the other. They'd left Mr. Rogers, Lucas, Ducky, and a sassy Chihuahua named Biggie Smalls in the green room. Ducky and Biggie Smalls were playing, and Biggie Smalls's outfit—a dapper little tuxedo—was a bit of a mess. His tie was already loose, and he kept tripping on it while he walked. Fortunately, Ducky wasn't in his outfit just yet.

"Stop fretting about us and take care of the show!" Mr. Rogers had told them, waving them away. "I'll handle these heathens." He looked at the dogs fondly.

And so Christine and Layla had left, entering the back portion of the large room behind the screens, where the models and some of the assigned dogs were waiting. Christine had immediately started lining up the dogs and humans, her trusty clipboard balanced on her hip, until a woman from the Nebraska Humane Society named Brynn had almost forcibly taken the clipboard and forced her toward the runway.

"It's time for you to start the show," she'd told Christine. "Go."

"But I want to meet the dogs," Christine said, waving at a wrinkly little sharpei with one eye who looked very much like he was smiling at her, his smile infectious.

"You can meet the dogs later," Brynn said. "We have ten minutes to get started. Go."

"But the rest of the dogs haven't even showed up!" Christine protested.

"Go," Brynn had said. "They're on their way. They'll be here."

"Is a phone set up to stream the event?" Christine asked. "Is someone going to hit play when it starts?"

Brynn sighed. "Yes, Christine, it's ready. And before you ask, I put Lucas's parents in the front row. And yes, I double-checked the internet speed. We're good to go. I promise."

And so Christine had taken her place at the front of the line, but Layla remained behind her. "You're going right after me," Christine said. "And so you can get it over with."

"Thank you," Layla said gratefully. She hadn't had to tell Christine that she was asking a lot of her; this wasn't her thing. Not her style. Not her . . . anything. Except she was willing to do just about anything to help Christine. And her school. And her town.

"Where's Garrett?" she asked Christine, suddenly feeling like she needed to see him. Christine pointed down the line, but she couldn't find him. She knew he was supposed to be walking a corgi.

They'd had thirty models volunteer from the community. Or be voluntold by Christine and Layla. All the ladies at the hair salon had signed up eagerly, as well as the town mechanic, James Mickelson, who was known for taking off his shirt and parading around whenever he'd had one too many . . . and whipping his T-shirt above his head in circles. His showmanship and his eagerness for attention made him perfect for the show.

The other models were starting to fidget too. The lights were low, but there were small lights behind the screen, so no one was tripping each other, and the dogs kept a respectable distance from each other.

"Keep them in line," Brynn instructed as she walked up and down the line, "and keep a few feet of distance in between. We don't need dog fights back here."

"It's going to be great," Christine said, more to herself than anyone else. "It's going to be great. It's going to be great."

"Are you okay?" Layla asked. "I mean, yes, it's going to be great. But are you . . . great?"

Christine fixed a perfect smile in place. "Of course. I mean, why? Do you think I'm not?"

Layla placed a comforting hand on her friend's shoulder. "Of course it's going to be great, Christine."

Christine blew a couple of strands of hair out of her face and nodded, taking a couple of jogging steps in place.

And that was when the back door opened, and the last of the dogs started coming in, one at a time. Brynn and the young man who'd been at setup began assigning dogs quickly, easily, walking them in and attaching them to a model with efficient kindness until all thirty people were standing with dogs of various shapes and sizes. Susan Lynn from the café was holding a dog with fur so thick Layla couldn't even see his eyes, but he was already licking her face. Layla had an unreasonably powerful urge to pet him.

The music started, and the lights lowered.

Judith whined, just slightly, and Layla reached down, putting a comforting hand on her neck.

"It's time," Christine whispered to her friend. "Wish me luck."

That was when Brynn brought Ducky and placed him in her arms. Ducky, who was wearing—wings. Adorable dragon wings that would span almost the width of the runway. Christine took off her robe and handed it over to Brynn. Underneath, she was wearing gold armbands and a white dress that looked like it had come straight off the set of *Game of Thrones*. She looked like a queen.

"Okay, then." Brynn clapped her hands. "I'll leave it to you to kick this off. You good?"

Christine took a deep breath and blew it out. "I'm good." She looked at Ducky. "You good, boy?"

To his credit, Ducky didn't look the slightest bit nervous.

Layla gave her friend a quick hug. "You've got this."

Christine nodded and squared her shoulders. Layla watched from the side of the stage, peeking out from behind the curtains, as her friend walked out in front of the packed house and waved, and then began walking down the runway, Duck trotting in front of her, his wings spread wide.

They were a majestic couple.

Christine looked amazing and beautiful and confident and perfect. Christine *was* perfect. She waved to the audience and plucked Ducky up, holding her little dragon high as she reached the end of the runway, where there was a microphone waiting for her.

"Good evening and welcome!" she said to the crowd, who roared in response—or as much of a roar as you could expect in Two Falls. "We're so excited to have you here at the Two Falls Charity Fashion Show, which will benefit the Nebraska Humane Society and Two Falls public schools!"

The crowd applauded, and Christine held up the tiny dog. Layla found herself wishing she could see her friend's face, but since she was watching from behind the runway, she had only a clear view of her back and the enormous crowd watching. "This is Ducky. He's my very best friend in the whole world. Ducky lives with me, and he has access to things the other dogs you'll see tonight don't have: permanent food, water, shelter, and a loving family. So I'll keep it short: the dogs you're about to see need—no, deserve—a happy home. So tonight, we're going to do a few things: as you know, we're going to have a fashion show and accept donations for the shelter. But we also wanted to let you know that every single dog walking tonight is adoptable—except for Ducky, of course."

The crowd cheered. Someone in the back whooped.

"If you're here, you also know we're raising money for another very special cause: Two Falls public school's free-lunch program. I know a lot of this kids in this community really need it, and it was a major blow when it got cut. So our goal tonight is to keep that program funded through the rest of the year. You can do that through donating or bidding on the clothes the models are wearing." She did a slow spin to show off the little skirt and blazer set. "So whether it's the dogs or the duds, we've got you covered! A special thanks to all the amazing stores for donating the looks you'll see this evening! You'll see their signs throughout tonight. Please consider shopping with them the next time you need clothes."

Layla was amazed at how easily hosting seemed to come to Christine. How naturally she spoke to the audience while holding the small, fuzzy pup. How the nervousness and fidgeting from backstage had completely vanished.

"And now," Christine said, gesturing behind her, "we have model citizens—and model pups—waiting to walk. So please turn your attention to the runway, where second-grade teacher Layla will be walking Judith, a senior American bulldog!"

Christine stepped off the runway, taking the mic with her so she could continue to announce each model and dog as they walked down. She took her place at the end of the runway, where a phone was live-streaming the event on Ducky's social media account, and then looked expectantly toward the back of the room, where Layla was supposed to be walking out.

A strange mix of fear and excitement shot through Layla's body, a hot-cold spread of nerves that started in her feet and flooded her before she knew what was happening. Judith grunted below her, putting her weight against her, as if to remind Layla she was there. Layla leaned down and put a hand on Judith's head, and the big dog leaned into her touch, panting happily.

Layla felt something crushing in her chest as Judith looked up at her lovingly, with such trust. She was such a sweet dog. She'd known the big girl all of an hour, and already, she knew the chances of this dog leaving Two Falls was low. Someone was going to adopt her. Someone had to. Layla couldn't let her go back to the shelter.

She had to do this. For Judith. She could not throw up or pass out or run away, never to return, no matter how much she really wanted to.

"Let's go, sweetheart," she whispered, and the dog stood obediently.

Layla walked out, onto the runway, a smile fixed to her face, and Judith lumbering along beside her like a very small hippopotamus.

Layla walked down the skinny runway, a small, well-lit peninsula between rows and rows of folding chairs, her eyes on the back wall, giving a small wave when she reached the end. She pointed down to Judith, who sat down heavily at the end of the runway, as if she'd had enough of walking.

The crowd giggled, but Layla took it in stride, not letting herself get distracted or overwhelmed by everyone watching them. It took two gentle tugs to get Judith back on her feet, and she followed Layla back down the runway and exited stage right, on the opposite side of all the other dogs.

And then, as quickly as it had started, it was done. That was all she had to do. A few brief seconds of walking Judith in a slinky red dress, and she was free. She knelt down and embraced the dog, her mind blank and relieved.

The dog leaned into her embrace, like she'd been waiting for years just to get a big hug, and grunted happily.

And then, just like that, Brynn was there with her assistant.

"We'll take her," Brynn said, gathering the leash from Layla. "We don't want her fighting with any of the other dogs when they come back here."

"Can I keep her a little longer?" Layla asked. "I . . . really like her. Plus, I don't think she seems like a fighter."

She didn't know how else to say she what she was feeling, but Brynn was shaking her head.

"I'm sorry," she said. "It's in and out for these dogs for their safety. If someone is interested in adopting, they can certainly request a dog can come out after, but we need to get them back into a calm environment."

"Okay," Layla said reluctantly. She squatted down and kissed Judith on the nose and gave her an extra good scratch on her hindquarters. She handed the leash over to Brynn's assistant, who led the big dog away. Layla felt a little like she'd lost a friend.

"Oh," Brynn said, checking something off her clipboard. "Christine saved you a seat by her, right behind where she's commentating if you're interested in watching the rest of the show. Come on, I'll show you—I've got to go grab Ducky for his costume change anyway."

Layla nodded and found her seat, trying to ignore the little drop of sadness that had entered the night. A few months ago she'd been hesitant to take care of perfect, sweet Ducky—and now she was immediately sad about a lazy bulldog she'd known for less than an hour. She barely recognized herself. Maybe dogs were her flowers. Something she never wanted and had grown to love.

Or maybe it was someone else too.

Layla gave Christine a thumbs up as she sat down. Christine winked at her, and Layla expected to feel a rush of relief as she watched the other models walk down the runway, showing off their outfits and their dogs. It wasn't that it didn't make her happy—it did—but then the reason for her anxiety came striding down the runway, a fluffy corgi mix trotting proudly beside him, head held high.

Garrett. Garrett was . . . what was he wearing? And then the vision came to her: he was dressed like David freaking Bowie from *Labyrinth*, with tall leather boots and a black vest over his white shirt, complete with a rock-star gray-blond wig. His dog was dressed like the baby from the movie, in a little red-and-white-striped shirt, and was striding along proudly, looking very impressed with himself.

And Garrett looked . . . amazing. Delicious. Shockingly handsome. Although Garrett did not resemble Bowie in any way . . . he pulled it off.

Whoops and whistles of appreciation rose from the audience, and Layla found herself smiling and giddy. She clapped as he neared the end of the runway, where he paused—and then scooped the dog up off the ground, did a spin, then set him back down on the runway and took a deep bow.

"Wow," Christine said. "That's a walk to remember."

Layla felt her smile stretch into a grin. She couldn't help it. Everyone was right. Garrett was handsome and perfect. And maybe even Mr. Rogers was right. Maybe she needed to welcome something into her life she was a little scared of.

She clapped again as he walked away, disappearing to the right of the runway, and she missed him as soon as he was gone.

And then, something happened that drew her attention away from Garrett—for a moment.

Christine. Her whole face changed. It was like she forgot she was holding a microphone and her eyes went super wide and her mouth dropped open. She pressed a hand to her cheek.

"Wait," Christine said, as a man walked down the runway with a sweet, goofy Yorkie and a fluffy snowball-white pup—all of whom who looked very familiar. "Is that—Katsu? And Barb? And my *husband*?"

Layla grinned up at the stage where Jason was striding down the runway, a leash in each hand, with Barb, a fluffy white dog, on one side and Katsu, an elderly Yorkie, trotting along with his tongue out, on the other. Jason reached the end of the carpet and blew Christine a kiss. He turned, as a big DONATE NOW was printed on his suit jacket, along with the QR code and #SAVETWOFALLS.

Christine's hands were over her mouth, and tears were in her eyes. She turned to Layla. "Are you kidding me? Did you know he was going to do this?"

Layla shrugged, smiling mischievously. "I can neither confirm nor deny."

Christine met Jason at the end of the runway, embracing him in a big hug. He picked her up and swung her around, the dogs waiting patiently for their turn for hugs and kisses.

Layla felt teary suddenly, and a little empty. She wanted that. She needed that happiness. She'd never admitted it to herself before, but that—that was what she wanted, more than anything. It was more than living in this little town, although that was wonderful, or even Ducky, who had filled a hole in her heart she hadn't known existed. She needed someone. And, if she wasn't completely kidding herself . . . she had found him.

She stood up, leaving her seat, and wove her way through the crowd, but she couldn't see him. Was he still backstage? Had he left already? He couldn't have left. He would have stayed for the end, right? But maybe he was heading back to his apartment, getting ready to pack up, to leave and never come back. Maybe he wouldn't bother to say goodbye. She hadn't exactly been great to him. Instead she'd sent a mountain of mixed signals.

Finally, she spotted him, standing back against the wall by the kitchen, a plastic cup of beer in his hand, one foot kicked up against the wall. He'd taken off the wig, and the outfit looked less David Bowie and more Han Solo now. He seemed lost in his own thoughts, smiling a little, the corner of his eyes just a bit crinkled. His hair was a little messy, as if he'd run his hands through it nervously a few times.

Her pulse a drumbeat in her ears, she approached him. His smile widened when he saw her. "Layla!" he said.

She liked how he said her name, how it sounded in his mouth. She liked his smile, and his ears and that he had the smallest cowlick on the back on his head, no matter how short his hair was cut. She liked his warmth and his kindness and the way he treated every kid in the classroom with the utmost respect.

She loved him.

"Why are you looking at me like that?" he asked her.

Layla lifted a shoulder. "A little birdie told me that it's almost the end of the semester, and you're no longer my student teacher."

His studied her. "Are you trying to tell me something, Layla?"

She looked past him for a moment, and then into his eyes. "I guess I'm trying to say I'm sorry. I'm sorry that I've been weird, and I'm sorry that I've most definitely crossed lines. I'm sorry that

I'm so closed off and you had to deal with my issues. And I'm really sorry that I kissed you on the beanbags."

He crossed his arms over his chest, his eyes unreadable. "Well, what if I don't care?" he said, his words careful and deliberate. "I don't care about any of that?"

She looked up at him. "You don't? But I . . . I was supposed to be your . . . your mentor. I had power over you, and that's always inappropriate."

"Well, I have good news," he said. "That's over now."

She allowed herself a small, sharp note of triumph. "It almost is," she said. "And you know . . . your grandfather gave me some good advice."

Garrett's eyes sparkled. "What did he say?"

"He said I need to . . . let flowers in."

To her surprise, Garrett laughed. "He gave you that speech, huh?"

"You're familiar?"

"Oh, he's only been telling me the same thing since I was little."

Layla shrugged. "So? Have you figured it out yet?"

"Am I supposed to be your flower?" he asked teasingly.

"I was thinking more like . . . my boyfriend." Layla blushed as soon as she said it, but forced herself to look up at him, smiling. "I mean, I know you're probably moving back to the city," she said, "but I could go up there sometimes, or you could come down here—"

"I'm not planning on leaving," Garrett said. "I mean, if there's not any openings here, I'd have to take something else for a while—get my feet on the ground—but I'm not leaving my grand-dad. He's the only family I have." And he looked at her. "And, if I'm being completely honest, I don't want to leave you either."

Layla looked up at his, the corners of her mouth pulling up foolishly, her heart playing hopscotch in her chest. "So . . . you like me?"

He shook his head. "Was that ever a question?"

Layla laughed. "I put you through it, Garrett."

"You were just being a good teacher." He smoothed down a strand of hair that had escaped her ponytail, and then his hand found his way to her neck and stayed there.

She looked up at him, at his blue eyes flecked with brown, at his full lips, and his thick, gorgeous beard, and she wanted nothing more than to kiss him. Really kiss him. Not a lip brush. But something more. Something passionate. Something real.

She stood up on her tiptoes, reaching toward his mouth, when he jerked his head up. "Layla. Look!"

She turned her head.

And there he was.

Lucas.

Lucas, walking down the runway.

He was glowing.

He was dressed in a little tuxedo, like a small James Bond. His shoulders were back, his head was high, and he was smiling. A big, happy, proud smile. Like he was truly proud of who he was. Ducky walked beside him on a leash, looking equally proud to be accompanying the boy. He'd swapped his wings for a matching tuxedo. Together, the pair stole the show. Lucas was the youngest person to walk in the show—and the perfect adorable little kid to close it out.

Layla swelled with pride. "Woo-hoo!" she shouted, cupping her hands around her mouth. "Go, Lucas! Go, Ducky!"

Garrett joined her, cheering for them loudly, pumping his fist in the air. "You got this, Lucas! That's my guy!"

They pushed through the crowd until they were right next to the stage. And maybe it was the outfit that gave him the bravery. Maybe it was being cheered and recognized by everyone. Maybe it was Ducky, or that things had just been going better lately.

But he looked happy. Not tentatively happy, or happy for a fleeting moment, but truly, genuinely happy.

He looked . . . like himself.

Layla glanced to the left side of the stage, where his parents had prime seating. They were both glowing, and Lucas's father even stood up and whistled, beaming with pride.

Lucas finished his jaunt up and down the runway, but paused at the end to give Christine a happy thumbs up, which she returned, gleefully. And then, finally, Mayor Lopez took the stage.

"I think it's time for me to thank all of you. Tonight has been truly magical. It's no secret this town has had its fair share of hard times. But it's nights like tonight when our little town—and those around us—come together to support our children and the humane society—well, it all reminds me of why I've always loved this community so much in the first place." He paused, and reached his hand out to Christine, who was adjusting the phone, which was still live-streaming at the end of the runway.

"Christine Hsu," he said. "First and foremost I'd like to thank you. It's because of you that we were able to bring this fashion show to Two Falls. Tonight, we're going to help a lot of kids and save a lot of dogs. And I'm pleased to announce something pretty amazing: we have multiple people committed to saving dogs already this evening, and with your help, we're received over twenty-five thousand dollars in pledges to the Nebraska Humane Society—and over seventy-two thousand dollars for the school lunch program. Now, ladies and gentlemen, the evening isn't over yet! We're going to turn up the lights, and I'd like to invite all of you to bid on the clothing you've seen showcased this evening. And, of course, open your wallets and your homes—and feel free to make this evening even more special. So please, go on, be generous—and thank you, from the bottom of all our hearts, for showing us we matter."

The lights turned out on the far side of the room, illuminating a long row of tables with bidding papers, so the guests could bid on the outfits from the show.

"Now," Garrett whispered in her ear. "Do you think I can steal you away?"

She nodded and took his hand. He led her back from the crowd, which was slowly moving over to the tables, back to where she'd found him, a leather boot kicked up against the wall, and into the kitchen, which was dark, the only light coming from the glowing numbers on the microwave.

They stood together for a moment. Layla could feel his breath, hear his breathing. Her heartbeat was a steady drum in her ears.

"Layla," Garrett whispered. "Can I kiss you?"

She felt his hands on her waist, pulling her forward.

"Yes," she whispered. "You can."

He leaned down, slowly, and his lips touched hers. She leaned into the kiss, and her lips parted. She lifted her arms and pulled him closer, gently.

He pulled away, after a few moments, and ran his thumb over her jawline. "You're what I've always wanted."

She stood up on her tiptoes to kiss him again, her whole being flooded with the kind of happiness she'd never dreamed existed. "And you," she whispered, "are what I never knew I needed."

CHAPTER 43

Judith had a family.

She had a mom and a dad. She had a sweet neighbor named Mr. Rogers who looked in on her during the day.

She had a home.

Her dad didn't live with her mom, not yet, but they were talking about it. They loved each other a lot and spent a lot of time kissing. Judith kissed them a lot too. Sometimes when she kissed her mom on the face too much she would sputter and push her away, laughing.

Layla had walked Judith in the fashion show, and had driven to Omaha the next day to complete the adoption paperwork and officially welcome Judith into her home. Judith was thrilled. She'd known the moment she saw Layla that they were meant to be family. And she got a great dad, too, who liked to take her running. Only Judith didn't like running very much, so she usually lay down when she got tired, which was about three blocks from the house.

Judith even got a dog friend. His name was Ducky, and he was a tiny Yorkie who loved to play. But Judith had to be careful when playing with Ducky. He was very small and she didn't want to hurt him, so she usually pretended that Ducky was stronger and let him win all their fake fights. She also knew Ducky was very special and came to town a lot to work as a therapy dog for the school, which Judith was very impressed about.

Also, Judith knew a secret. It was a big secret. She knew it because secretly her dad, who Layla called Garrett, had been teaching her how to walk into the room holding a blue box with a funny texture that made her sneeze. She was getting better at it, and later, she had to do it for real, when Mom was in the living room. She was pretty excited about it.

A few months ago, she'd been totally alone—with no family, and no friends, and no mom and dad. And now, she had it all.

Her people were happy, and so Judith was happy too.

ACKNOWLEDGMENTS

For my agent, Melissa Edwards, for being a constant and unwavering supporter, even as my writing changed.

For my grandma, who will be gone by the time this book comes out, and always begged me to move back to Nebraska. You are the heart of this story.

For my own dog, Tinker, who is the sweetest, most wonderful dog in the entire world.

For my parents, who always supported me, no matter what and celebrate my successes more than anyone in the world.

For all the lovely social media dogs on the dog Discord—thank you for always being thoughtful, entertaining, and wonderful.

For Suzanne Young, who is my best friend and writing inspiration!

For my family, for always being supportive, and for all my nieces and nephews, just because.

—Amanda

Don't miss the humorous and heartwarming *Tatum Comes Home* featuring the real Tatum from @hi.this.is.tatum in a feel-good, fictional adventure about a charismatic canine's *Homeward Bound*–style journey . . .

An excerpt from Tatum's diary:

"Here's a few fings I learned on my vacation . . . beef jerkey is delightfoo, hikin is just walkin but for a long time, and if you get into someone's truck they don't know where you live also you have to tell them you're in the truck. Also I fink maybe I wasn't on vacation?"

The late-May air is filled with the rich scents of a Maine spring, and Tatum, a sweet, rust-colored rescue dog, is enjoying a trip to the hardware store with his dad when a heavy thunderstorm blows in. Frightened, Tatum scampers off to hide—and buries himself beneath a blanket on a nearby truck.

When Tatum wakes, hungry and confused, he's hours from home. The truck's kind owner promises to get him back to his family, but that'll be no easy feat. Tatum lost his collar during his travels, and with power out because of the storm, the local vet can't scan for a chip.

But Tatum, with his deep golden eyes and trusting gaze, has a knack for making friends—and for letting humans know *exactly* what's on his mind. While his mum and dad do everything they can to track him down, the people Tatum meets on his journey are just as eager to do their part to get him home. And in turn, Tatum has a way of nudging everyone he encounters to overcome hurdles, seek out second chances, and find—or make—the families they need.

TATUM TALKS

with MICA STONE

TATUM COMES HOME

A novel about one charismatic canine, inspired by the videos of real-life TikTok star @hi.this.is.tatum

Visit our website at
KensingtonBooks.com
to sign up for our newsletters, read
more from your favorite authors, see
books by series, view reading group
guides, and more!

Become a Part of Our
Between the Chapters Book Club
Community and Join the Conversation